MONSTROUS

MONSTROUS

JESSICA LEWIS

DELACORTE PRESS

Text copyright © 2023 by Jessica Lewis
Cover art copyright © 2023 by Kemi Mai

Visit us on the Web! GetUnderlined.com

Educators and librarians, for a variety of teaching tools,
visit us at RHTeachersLibrarians.com

Library of Congress Cataloging-in-Publication Data
Names: Lewis, Jessica, author.
Title: Monstrous / Jessica Lewis.
Description: First edition. | New York : Delacorte Press, [2023] |
Audience: Ages 14+. | Summary: When seventeen-year-old Latavia is
presented as a human sacrifice to an ancient beast, she is determined to do
whatever it takes to survive—even if that includes making a deal with the
monster and endangering her crush and family.
Identifiers: LCCN 2022041261 (print) | LCCN 2022041262 (ebook) |
ISBN 978-0-593-43481-9 (paperback) | ISBN 978-0-593-43483-3 (ebook)
Subjects: CYAC: Monsters—Fiction. | Human sacrifice—Fiction. |
Lesbians—Fiction. | Cities and towns—Fiction. | Horror stories. | Fantasy. |
LCGFT: Horror fiction. | Fantasy fiction. | Novels.
Classification: LCC PZ7.1.L518 Mo 2023 (print) |
LCC PZ7.1.L518 (ebook) | DDC [Fic]—dc23

The text of this book is set in typeset Berling LT Std.
Interior design by Jen Valero

Printed in the United States of America
10 9 8 7 6 5 4 3 2 1
First Edition

FOR GRANDMA, ALWAYS

1

Pastor Thomas drones on about Clementine May, the third closed-casket funeral in Sanctum, Alabama since I came down six weeks ago.

"She was a good woman," he says. Pastor Thomas is an old white man, with bulbous green eyes and a bad case of male-pattern baldness. His voice is cool and calm, and so quiet. He's nothing like Pastor Pride at my old church, with his booming voice and permanent sheen of sweat on his brow. Not that I ever went that much. "Clementine will be missed. Her unshakable character and selflessness are an inspiration. Congregation, take note of what kind of woman she was."

What the hell is he talking about? The little I know about Clementine is that she frequently fell asleep in front of the only grocery store in town and gave that old-lady candy to kids. Sweet, but I wouldn't call that "unshakable character." Everyone else must know what he means, though; they're nodding slowly, some murmuring prayers.

1

No one's crying. They're staring at Pastor Thomas with ashen faces and grim precision. I squirm in the uncomfortable pew, trying not to scratch at the lace at the end of my dress. Maybe something happened with Clementine before I arrived.

Jade nudges my arm. She points to a handwritten note on the obituary. *Poor Clementine. She was so nice.*

She offers me the pencil, and I write a note back. *Yeah but it's not exactly unusual for here.*

A flash of something crosses Jade's face—fear?—but it's quickly replaced by innocent confusion. The corners of Jade's mouth pinch downward as she scribbles on the paper.

What do you mean?

She can't be serious. It's the third funeral in six weeks! There's a whopping four hundred people in Sanctum, so three people dying is a significant population loss. I start to write again, but Allison nudges me.

"Avie, Jade," Allison whispers in my ear. "They're watching y'all."

Sure enough, I look up and straight into Auntie's death glare from the choir stand. Jade immediately crumples up the obituary and stares straight ahead. I do too, but slower. I know I'm lucky to be here, but Auntie is way too strict. We weren't even talking. But fine, while I'm here, I'll be good. Only two more weeks, and then I'm free.

Pastor Thomas talks about Clementine's life and the family in Chicago she left behind (strangely absent from the funeral). Finally, he motions for us to stand. I scramble to my feet, fighting the sleep tugging at my eyelids.

Pastor Thomas meets the eyes of everyone in the front row. "Remember, no one goes into Red Wood."

"Yes, Pastor," the people chant. Unease crawls up my arms like goose bumps. God, this place is so weird.

"It's time for the final prayer," Pastor Thomas says.

"May the Lord bless their sacrifice," a few hundred people say in unison, "and may the Lord protect us from the Serpent's fangs and lying tongue."

Pastor Thomas eyes the congregation, his face pale and serious. "Amen."

With that, it's over. Everyone starts talking in hushed murmurs, gathering their things. I stand and stretch, ignoring the glances my way. The air is thick and heavy, so heavy I can't stand it. I bump Jade's arm playfully. "What's next? I'm starving."

"Have some respect," Jade mumbles, her hands fiddling with her purse. "Can we at least get out of the church?"

I have to bite back an unkind reply. Jade's my cousin, a little over two years younger than me, but she definitely didn't inherit my sense of humor. I can't really blame her, though. Growing up in this weird-ass town'll suck the fun out of anyone.

"I'm gonna talk to Pastor Thomas," Allison says, flicking her blond hair out of her eyes. Her bangs are a little too long, so she's always moving them out of her face. "You don't have to wait for me."

"We will," I say quickly. Too quickly? No, Allison's smiling, the warm one that reaches her soft blue eyes.

"Thanks!" she says. "Won't take long, promise."

Jade and I wave, and she heads toward the pastor's

office on the second floor. On the way, an older woman approaches her and gives her a yellow plastic bag I recognize from John's grocery store. Allison nods graciously and tries to move away, but she's stopped by a middle-aged guy with a beer gut. He drops something into her palm, which Allison promptly stores in her pocket while she talks to him.

"She's popular," I say, almost to myself. This happened the last few times I came to church too. She's like a church celebrity.

"Jealous?" Jade says, smirking at me. I shoot her a poisonous look, but she just laughs and heads to the door.

We wander outside and sit on the porch steps. No one is milling around; the parking lot is half-empty already. It's like everyone is in a rush to get home. Even on non-funeral days, I hardly ever see anyone out shopping or hanging out in restaurants. I know it's a small town, but this can't be normal. I *know* it's not normal.

"I want to go for a run after this," I tell Jade, tapping my fingers on my knee.

Jade doesn't look up from her phone. "Mom'll kill you."

Yeah, I know. Auntie is strict about her rules: don't go into Red Wood, the thick miles-wide forest behind her house; no going outside after dark (that includes running); come straight home after funerals. Among a million other things. Before, when I'd visit Auntie and Jade on Thanksgiving and Christmas, I thought it was Auntie being a hard-ass. But now that I've been here for six weeks in a row, I'm starting to get nervous. I watch people pour out of the church, silent, grim. Population of four hundred, and at least three hundred packed into the single massive church in town. And not just for Clementine. The other two funerals were like this too. All three older people, not sick; here one day, dead the next. I tap my fingers on my thigh. I don't think Auntie is just being strict. I think something is wrong with Sanctum and they all know it.

I'm mulling over what the hell is wrong with this place when a woman and her kid approach us. I recognize her—Mrs. Brim, Deacon Brim's wife. She's a white woman with red hair, tall and gaunt. Her clothes are always a little too big. She smiles when she sees us. "Hey, girls. Waiting on the doctor?"

"No," I answer, because Jade hasn't looked up from her phone, "we're supposed to go straight home. Which sucks, but whatever."

Mrs. Brim laughs. "Dr. Roberts is a strict lady. Runs the choir stand with an iron fist!"

Yeah, I bet. Mrs. Brim moves a strand of hair out of her face, and I notice a bandage wrapped around her wrist. She's still wearing her sweater too, despite it being a hundred degrees out here. "What happened to your wrist?" I ask.

Mrs. Brim's smile wavers, but it's back in a second. "I had an accident at home. Delilah left her Legos in the kitchen, and bam! There I went."

I glance at the kid behind her, Delilah. She's crouched, hugging her knees. She draws a picture of two people in the dirt, one tall, one short. She draws Xs over their eyes.

"Ouch," Jade says, oblivious to the weird-as-hell kid. "Did Mom look at it for you? It seems kinda swollen."

Mrs. Brim starts to answer, but Deacon Brim appears on the front steps. He's a muscular man, with short brown hair and small, mean eyes. He ignores Jade and me and nods to Mrs. Brim. "We're leaving."

"Okay . . . Bye, girls! See you both on Sunday." She grins at me. "I'll talk to Dr. Roberts about letting you both loose every once in a while."

Jade and I wave to Mrs. Brim as she gathers Delilah, and they walk to a sleek black SUV. We don't speak until they've driven away.

"Do you think she's okay?" I say, watching the car disappear.

"I don't know," Jade says, frowning at the place where Mrs. Brim stood. "But I do know it's none of our business."

Her comment irritates me. It *is* our business. It's everyone's business if Mr. Brim is a wife beater. But I don't have any proof, just a hunch, and Mrs. Brim probably wouldn't tell me, an eighteen-year-old "outsider," anything. It's pointless; the church would probably protect him. Maybe she'd even protect him. I curl my fingers on my knee. Someone needs to hurt Mr. Brim's wrist. See how he likes it.

Allison emerges from the church, rejoining us. Thoughts of Mrs. Brim all but disappear. "Sorry I made y'all wait!"

"That's okay," I say, standing. "I was thinking we should go for a walk."

"You know Mom hates it when we're not home after funerals," Jade says, annoyance at the edge of her voice.

Jesus, someone tell this kid to lighten up. "It's a walk. It won't kill us, Goody Two-shoes."

Jade's brow furrows, and I know we're about to fight.

"Wait, wait," Allison says. She pushes in between me and Jade. "Let's go to the park. It's right by your house, so if you need to leave quick, it'll be fine." She smiles at me, and the bottom of my stomach does a tiny somersault. "Okay?"

As if I could say no. "Okay," I tell her. "Lead the way."

Allison leads me and Jade away from the church. She's still holding the yellow plastic bag from the old woman. I sneak a peek—looks like vegetables. That's nice; old ladies sharing their gardens with her. That's also normal. But as we pass unsmiling adults in a hurry to get home and a few listless, quiet kids staring at the ground, I'm reminded that Sanctum is anything but normal.

The whole town is like this. When I came down from Atlanta a month and a half ago, I didn't notice it right away. Too angry, I guess. But slowly, as we had funerals every two weeks, as the town glared at me, something felt wrong. I can't explain it. It's summer, but the whole town feels dreary, lifeless. Streets are empty, devoid of cars and people. Kids don't run in their yards and play. Dogs don't bark. It's like the town is holding its breath in case someone is listening.

"So," I say, loud to dispel the eerie quiet, "I was thinking about Sanctum."

"Thinking? You? Dangerous." Jade laughs, but also glances at Allison. Allison doesn't say anything.

"I was thinking . . ." I walk backward, my hands behind me. "Something feels kinda weird about this place. I mean, it's the third funeral in six weeks. Here one day, gone the next."

"People die of old age all the time," Jade says. She won't look at me, her gaze stubbornly on something behind me.

"Three in a row, all two weeks apart? All of them closed caskets?"

Jade and Allison don't say anything, looking everywhere but at me. The unease from before is back in full force. They know something, and they're not telling me.

"Well, what about that noise?" I ask. The night before someone dies, there's a rattling sound that's loud enough to carry through the whole town. Three times it's woken me up from a dead sleep. Three funerals.

"The wind gets up at night sometimes," Allison says. "It tears down the tree branches, and since you live right by Red Wood, it's probably loud."

Is she serious? She can't think I'd actually believe that excuse. But it looks like she does; her blue eyes finally meet mine, and there's an undercurrent of desperation in them. She wants me to believe her.

"There, see?" Jade says, kicking a rock at her feet. "Nothing to worry about. You're being paranoid, Avie."

I'm so frustrated, I could scream. "We're really ignoring this? Seriously?"

Allison looks at me, her eyebrows scrunched together. "Everything's fine, Avie. I promise."

I sigh, defeated. If they won't talk, no one will. If I want to know something, I'll have to figure it out myself.

"Okay, fine." I wipe my hands on the front of my itchy dress. "Don't tell me about the serial killer or whatever. At least he only takes old people."

Allison and Jade laugh nervously, but they don't deny what I said. Fucking yikes.

We walk in heavy silence until we reach the park. It's a pathetic collection of ancient swings, rusted metal slides, and rotten-wood playhouses. The only reason I come here at all is the gravel track looping the length of the park. Auntie won't let me run in town, so this is the only place to practice.

I start to wander to a swing and sit down, but I stop. Near the entrance is a massive stone slab with a ton of names on it. There's no marker or anything, so I thought it was a Civil War memorial and firmly ignored it. But today, I slow down and really look at it. It has names, like I thought, but the last few entries are newer. The last one is Clementine May.

"If the funerals are from old people dying of old age," I say, running my fingertips over Clementine's newly etched name, "then why is there a memorial for them?"

There's a thick, unbearable silence. I don't turn around to face Jade and Allison, a sick feeling in my gut. Something big is happening in this town. Something bad. I don't have any proof, but I don't need it; the silence of Jade and Allison tells me all I need to know.

"Avie, let's go home."

I turn around, and Jade has her thin arms crossed over her chest. Her expression is hard to read—anxious, confused, pleading.

"Mom'll kill us if we're not back by the time she gets home from the cemetery. Please."

I turn back to the memorial, struggling to sort out my thoughts. I'm unnerved because they're hiding something from me, clearly, but I'm not stupid. Maybe there's a reason why I'm not supposed to know what's going on in Sanctum. And so far, the victims have been sweet old ladies, so I guess I shouldn't be too worried about myself. I take a breath, in through the nose, out through the mouth. I'll play along for now. I just need to survive two more weeks, and then whoever's making old people disappear won't be my problem anymore. Though I'm a little worried about leaving Jade behind when I go to school. . . .

"Okay, we—"

"What're you kids doing?"

I know that voice. I turn around, my stomach sinking. Sheriff Kines strides toward us, hands on his belt. Dangerously close to his gun. He looks at me, his gray eyes like steel. "You know you're supposed to go straight home after the service."

I back up so I'm standing with Allison and Jade. Jade's practically trembling, and for good reason. Sheriff Kines is a huge man, not only wide, but tall too. He towers over us, looking down his long nose at us like we're bugs. He's got his police dog with him today, an unpleasant German shepherd that has bitten at least three people. The black-and-tan dog looks at me, nose twitching, ears pricked. I bet it'd bite me too if the sheriff ordered it to.

I give the sheriff my best smile. "We're taking a walk. We all grieve in our own ways."

10

"A smart mouth'll get you in trouble in this town," he says.

I keep smiling, but I can feel it turning into a grimace. No one can take a joke here.

"Sorry, Sheriff," Allison says, coming to rescue me. "We were just headed home. We'll definitely be in by dark."

Sheriff Kines nods stiffly. He looks at me one more time, his eyes narrowed. "Don't let newcomers get y'all in trouble."

"Oh, come on—"

"Yes, sir." Jade interrupts me, grabbing my arm and dragging me back toward Auntie's house. "Sorry again."

The sheriff stares as we leave the park. Then he leans down and says something into the radio on his uniform. My stomach fills with dread every step of the way home.

After a wordless journey home and a quick goodbye to Allison, I climb the steps to Auntie's guest room. It's a stale, tired beige, with that old-people flowered print lining the walls and a white comforter draping the bed. This was my grandmother's room before she passed away five years ago. We weren't close, but it's still a little weird to stay in a dead woman's bedroom. Jade won't come in here if she's alone.

I pace the room for a bit, my fingers tapping on my thigh. I want to go for a run, but Auntie would have an aneurysm. If I don't practice, though, my times will be terrible when I get to school. Coach Anders used to say I'm too easygoing and don't take track seriously. And I mean, he's kinda right. I run because it's fun and relaxing. The scholarship money to University of Georgia is just a bonus. A damn good bonus, but still.

I climb onto the bed and lie down, frowning at the popcorn ceiling. I put my feet to the sky, then roll to my side, then to my back. I'm bored. Maybe I can sneak out tonight after Auntie goes to bed. Then again, with all these dead people, should I risk it? My arms itch as I think about Clementine's closed casket. They were all closed, all three of them. Why haven't I ever seen a body?

I pull my phone from my pocket and scroll through the top few texts, hoping for distraction. Jade and Allison, of course, but I can talk to them anytime. Lindsay—no, she's still in France for the summer. Wish I was that lucky. Kendra—definitely not. I wince when I think about how we left things. My thumb grazes over Mom's name, and I get a pang so sharp, I have to sit up. Flutterings of panic touch my chest. I breathe in through the nose, out from the mouth to calm down, just like Coach taught me. I'm okay. I can survive a few more weeks, and then UGA athletes are scheduled to go to campus on August 2 for orientation. Auntie will drive me, Jade will complain the whole time because she gets carsick, and maybe Mom will meet us there and help me move in. Two more weeks, and everything will be fine.

I turn my phone over so I can't see the screen and close my eyes.

The sound of footsteps on the stairs makes my eyes pop open. Dinnertime, probably. I swing my aching legs off the bed and sit up as Auntie appears in the doorway of the guest room.

I grin at her, but she doesn't smile back. She's still wearing her floral church dress but looks severe and intimidating. She's so tall—at least a head taller than me, and I'm five foot eight—and her sharp brown eyes will cut anyone down if they're not careful.

"What's up, Auntie?"

"I heard you were in the park instead of at home." Her voice is lifeless, but her eyes are like fire.

I grit my teeth against my smile. "Just took a walk."

Auntie glares for a moment more, and then her expression softens. She comes to my side and sits on my bed. "What am I going to do with you, Latavia?"

I can feel my shoulders relaxing. Auntie is strict and disciplined (have to be to put yourself through medical school), but she's not so bad. And I owe her a lot, so I could be a better house guest. "You don't have to do anything. The sheriff chased us home, anyway."

"I don't have to tell you why that worries me."

Yeah, she doesn't. I sigh heavily. "Auntie, can't we go somewhere, do something? Anything. I'm bored to tears."

"You can have fun at UGA," she says, shaking her head. The motion makes the soft ceiling-fan lights catch on the pendant she always wears. It's like a locket, but the picture part is huge. I always wondered whose picture is in there. Maybe Jade's dad, who I've never seen or heard of. "Latavia, listen to me. I know it's tough, and you're having a hard time right now, but these rules are to protect you."

"From the serial killer?" I don't expect a real answer, but the flash of fear on Auntie's face surprises me.

"Don't speak about things you don't know."

"I would know if someone would tell me! I'm not stupid. Something's bad wrong with this town."

Auntie closes her eyes. "You only have two weeks here. Do what I say until then, okay? Everything will be fine."

Everything will be fine. That's what Allison said too. My skin crawls with apprehension and with it, anger. Auntie is hiding something, just like Allison and Jade. Why won't anyone tell me what the hell is happening here? But . . . Auntie also took me in when I had no place to go. She's the reason I don't have to be homeless for three months while I wait for school to start. I take a deep breath to calm myself. If she wants to keep some secrets, I'll let her. Two more weeks, and I'll be gone.

I open my mouth to tell her okay, I'll stay home and die of boredom, but something cuts me off. A sound. I pause, listening—a soft *chaka, chaka*. All the color drains from my aunt's face.

"No . . . ," she says. "No, it's too soon. There aren't any volunteers. It's too soon!"

The sound gets louder, until it's almost deafening. A rattling sound.

Something tells me we're about to have another funeral.

2

The next day, I check my messages outside of Telescoops.

One from Auntie: *where are you? I told you not to leave the house today.*

One from Jade: *Mom's pissed*

And one from Allison: *can you meet me for ice cream at one?*

So. Here I am.

I swear, it didn't used to be like this. I've visited Sanctum before, on holidays and a few winter breaks, and I've seen Allison hanging out with Jade. Back then, she was Jade's older friend and that was it. But I've been noticing the way she flicks her hair out of her face, the way she holds my gaze just a little too long, the way she gets a mischievous gleam in her blue eyes when she's teasing Jade. She's cute. She's nice. I like her.

But I can't try anything. If it were a normal summer, of course I'd be interested in meeting a cute girl from another town and going on dates and kissing in the warm moonlight. But this has been a summer from hell, and with something horrible going on in this weird-ass town, I'm really not in the mood for that. Well, that's what I tell myself. Clearly I'm a little in the mood, because I'm here. But whatever—quick ice cream, talk about the weird noise from last night, get out. No kissing. No thinking about kissing. Eyes on the prize, Latavia.

I text Allison and try to ignore the way my heart rate kicks up when she texts me back. *I'm about to be on break! Come in the back door. Katie won't care.*

Katie, Allison's manager, might not care, but I sure do. I wipe my hands on my jean shorts, suddenly nervous.

Still, I head to the back of the small shop. I don't want to bother Allison, but I do want to see her. Even if it's for a few minutes. Jesus, how pitiful. Lindsay would laugh her ass off if I told her this. If I could talk to her, that is.

When I round the corner, Allison's giant mutt with dirty white fur lifts her head off her paws. Shit. "Peach, stay over there," I tell her. Peach stands, tail wagging. "Don't do it. Do not—"

Peach barrels toward me, and I brace myself against the building. She licks me all over, whining, her butt wiggling so hard that I'm scared it'll fall off. I stand still, sighing. Jade and I found this beast a few days after I came down from Atlanta, trotting out of Red Wood behind Auntie's house. We tried to adopt her, but Auntie threw a fit, so Allison offered to take her. But man, this dog is wild. Allison hasn't had any luck training her; she's huge, over a hundred pounds, so it's mostly been Peach doing whatever she wants and us getting out of her way. Still, Allison persists. She says any dog who survives Red Wood is a dog to keep. Whatever that means.

Peach finally calms down, sitting next to my leg and panting. I pat her head wearily. "Thanks for ruining my clothes. Really appreciate that."

Peach looks up at me, her deep brown eyes bright. I scratch under her chin, smiling in spite of myself. Mom doesn't like animals, so Peach is the closest thing I've had to a pet.

"Okay, Peach, I'm going in. Got any tips for making me not look like an idiot in front of your owner?"

Peach gives my arm a lick. Dog version of support, I guess.

"Wish me luck." Peach lies down in the shade of the building, already yawning, and I wipe my arm on the bottom of my T-shirt and go to the back door. I consider knocking, but it's slightly ajar, so I push it open. I'm blasted by the air-conditioning as I walk in.

I don't see her at first. I'm in a long hallway, and I can glimpse the front, where customers sit. The store is adorable, I have to admit. It's space-themed, and there are planets and comets hand-painted on the walls. There's a cartoon drawing of the sun on an ice cream cone behind the counter. The shop is usually empty, but I'm surprised to see a good crowd. Delilah and Mrs. Brim (thankfully without her evil husband), a few more church members, Sheriff Kines. I even spy Pastor Thomas's shiny bald head. I guess all of Sanctum wants ice cream today.

"Avie, is that you?" Allison's voice calls. I follow it

around the corner, where she's manning the cash register. She's wearing a black apron stained with dried ice cream that accentuates her curves, and her hair is up in a messy bun. Silver studs in the shape of flowers dot her ears. Her face lights up when she sees me, and I try to push down the butterflies in my stomach.

"Katie, I'm gonna go on break!" Allison comes to me, untying her apron. She smiles and tucks a strand of hair behind her ear, and she's so cute, I'm gonna die. "Sorry I'm late. Did you wait long?"

I shake my head, not trusting my voice. This is bad. I haven't had a crush like this in forever.

"Oh good." Allison motions for me to follow her, and we walk down the long hallway to a tiny room with a fridge and a small wicker table. She places her apron on the table but doesn't sit down. "Ready for some ice cream? I'll treat you if you let me pick your flavor."

What is this, a date? Involuntary heat rises in my face. Allison looks at me, eyebrows raised invitingly.

"Uh, sure," I say, clearing my throat. "Don't pick something gross."

Allison flashes me a brilliant smile that makes my stomach flip.

"It's a new flavor; we haven't released it to the customers yet. I thought we could try it together." I watch Allison as she grabs a nondescript white tub from the freezer and spoons two scoops of light brown ice cream into plastic bowls. Maybe I'm reading too much into this. I'm probably just a test dummy for new ice cream.

Allison returns with the ice cream, and I take my bowl. "Thanks. What's the flavor?"

"It's a surprise!" Allison digs in, shuddering slightly. "Go ahead, try it."

I taste a little of the ice cream—coffee flavored. Nothing special, except there's a sort of sharp taste to it? I take another bite, trying to hold back a grimace. Why does it taste so sour?

"What do you think?" Allison's expression is anxious, so I give her a smile.

"It's horrible. But I'm not dumb enough to turn down free ice cream."

Allison laughs, and I do too. Some of the tension eases from my shoulders, and I lean my elbows on the table.

"So," I say, "why're you inviting me over for ice cream all of the sudden? Is it because I'm cute?"

Allison smiles down at the table, the tips of her ears turning pink. "Oh, yeah. Definitely."

My stomach is a lurching mess again, and I'm grinning like an idiot. I gotta get myself together. I didn't come here to flirt; I need answers.

Allison clears her throat, and the shy smile slips from her face. She meets my eyes and hers are serious, dark. Looks like she didn't ask me here to flirt either. "Avie. Are you . . . you know. Scared?"

I sit a little straighter in my chair. This is what I came for. I don't want to spook her into not telling me anything, so I need to go slow. I take another bite of my ice cream, trying to seem casual despite my thudding heartbeat. "I definitely don't like the idea of people suddenly dropping dead, but it's just old folks, right?"

"But there're no more volunteers," Allison says, circling her plastic spoon around the rim of her half-empty bowl.

My muscles tense, my grip tight around my plastic spoon. Auntie said something like this too. "Volunteers for what?"

Allison is silent for a while, her leg tapping, up and down, over and over. Finally, she says, "Avie, do you ever think of running away?"

"Uh, yeah. All the time. Why?" I hold back the question I really want to ask. *Should I run away?*

"Sorry, I just . . . I've lived my whole life here, and it's never been this bad."

"What exactly is 'this'?" When Allison doesn't answer, I think back to yesterday and what Auntie said in my room. "Do you mean the sound last night?"

Allison chews on her bottom lip, hesitating. I can practically see her deciding if she's going to lie to me. "If, theoretically, the sound was something other than the wind, I would say, theoretically, it's unusual to hear it two days in a row."

My breath is still in my chest. She's not looking at me, but this is it. She's trying to tell me something, something Auntie and Jade are too scared to.

"And, theoretically, of course," I say slowly, "are the volunteers connected to this sound?"

Allison's leg tap, tap, taps. "I . . . It's better if . . ." She looks like she's struggling for words. Then she looks right at me, her dark blue eyes boring into mine. "If I asked you to come to a party tonight with me, would you?"

It's my turn to struggle for words. Whatever's going on in this town is bad news, bad enough to have Allison scared. Bad enough to have everyone in town scared. I swallow the last of my melted ice cream, the sour taste clinging to my tongue.

"Yeah. I would."

A slow, relieved smile spreads over Allison's face. "Good. I'll see you at eight."

3

When I leave Telescoops, I run all the way home.

Auntie's house isn't that far. A little less than a mile. But I run like I'm at school, in a race, Kendra taunting me about getting second place. My feet pound on the pavement, my breath harsh and short in my ears. Adrenaline sneaks into my system, and I push myself, faster, faster, and before I know it, I'm at Auntie's front door.

I stand still, breathing harder than normal but not gasping. I hesitate, then turn around and run back to Telescoops to start over.

Usually, my mind would be blissfully blank, heart pumping and muscles straining to win, but today I'm thinking. I'm thinking about Allison, how nervous she was, how she tried to warn me about *something* but couldn't. Which is scary and makes me uneasy, don't get me wrong, but I keep getting distracted by the second part of our conversation. A party invite is kind of a date, isn't it? A scary, urgent, let's-get-out-of-town date, but it's a date, right? A party. I didn't know Allison was the partying type!.

I arrive at the ice cream shop again, grinning despite breathing hard. I jog in place and take deep breaths, in through the nose, out through the mouth. She's scared of something, but she's finally going to tell me what's going on in this town. Answers, and a date with a cute girl, here I come.

Jade interrupts my happy daydreaming with a text.

Since you're already dead, go to John's and get me some of that sour candy

I roll my eyes, still breathing hard. Auntie must be foaming at the mouth if Jade wants me to stay away longer. I sigh and start my journey to John's store.

The only good thing about staying in an extremely small town is that downtown has everything you need. Ice cream shop, Chinese restaurant, laundromat, and John's grocery store. What more could a couple hundred residents want? There's also a smattering of antiques stores and one high-priced boutique, but that's pretty much it. All the houses are outside of downtown, spread out in a circle until they bump against Red Wood. The exception is Allison's apartment, which is located above a permanently closed electronics repair store. The church is to the west of downtown, the only garage/gas station is in the east, and the cemetery is in the south. You can run a lap around the entire town in two hours (I would know because I've done it). Extremely small, extremely boring.

It would be quaint, nice even, if not for the eerie silence and the fact that no one is milling around, even at two in the afternoon.

I jog to John's, which is a general store that sells everything from pickled eggs to fertilizer. Sanctum is too small for a Walmart, so this is what they've got to work with. I hate coming here because the Sanctum residents always watch me like they're scared I'll steal something. That and, like everything else in this town, the store is creepy as hell. The front of the store has a hand-painted OPEN sign hanging in the window, but it's so faded from the sun, I can barely tell what it says. There are also thick bushes lining the front of the store, which would be normal, except for some unfathomable reason the bottoms have been trimmed almost two feet off the ground. You can see every gross, withered root and stem, plus the pathetically dry soil underneath. Why? It's like Sanctum takes everything that would be nice and twists it until it's something sinister.

As I approach the store, I pause at the rocking chair Clementine used to sit in. Someone has left a bouquet of flowers in the seat, along with an empty candy bowl. I get a twinge of sadness. She really seemed nice, and lots of people loved her. Does anyone care about finding out what happened to her? Or do they already know?

I shake my head and enter the store. John is at the front counter. He's a white man in his late fifties with mean brown eyes and short salt-and-pepper hair. He's got a patchy, disgusting beard too. John eyes me as I look around the store for Jade's stupid candy. John has always hated me for some reason, even when I visited Auntie on holidays. Since I moved in for the summer, he looks like he's stepped in shit every time he sees me. Jade so owes me for this.

I round the corner and almost run into Carter, who's grabbing a case of beer from the cooler. He's the town mechanic, and I always see him hanging around John's store. He's a white guy in his forties, with a mop of unkempt black hair and impressive dark bags under his eyes.

"Hey," he grunts. "Sorry 'bout that."

"Uh, no problem." I can see Jade's candy right behind him, but I need him to move so I can grab it.

"You the doctor's kid, aren't ya?" Carter says, not moving from the aisle.

"No, she's my—"

"That's the outsider," John calls from the counter. I shoot him a glare, but he can't see me over the shelves. Nosy asshole.

"Oh yeah," Carter says. He doesn't seem bothered by me being an "outsider," whatever that means. I've heard it a couple of times from Sanctum residents, and it doesn't feel any nicer the more I hear it. "You come for sulfur? Full moon's close."

Sulfur? What about the full moon? I wait for an explanation, but Carter is just looking at me expectantly.

"Um . . . no. Why do I need sulfur?"

"For pests," Carter says. "Ticks, mice . . . snakes."

Why the hell would I need that? I'm not hiking in Red Wood. And as far as I know, no one is. "Uh, I'm good, I think."

25

"Yeah, I'm sure the doc's got you anyway." Carter moves—finally—and points to the aisle next to the cooler. "If you want some, he's 'bout out. You can at least get some silver charms. They're for good luck. Protection."

What in the hell is this man talking about? I start to answer, but John yells at us again.

"Carter," John calls. "Get out of my store if all you're gonna do is run your mouth."

Carter rolls his eyes. He lifts his hand in a wave at me and lugs his beer out the front door. He doesn't stop to pay, which makes John curse under his breath.

O . . . kay. This town just gets weirder and weirder. Maybe Carter is drunk? Well, I'll take drunk ramblings over John. At least Carter is friendly. I grab Jade's candy, a tiny bag that fits into the palm of my hand, and try to shake off the weirdness. Pay and get out of this suspicious hellhole.

On the way to the counter, I pause to check out the aisle Carter pointed out. Sure enough, there's a huge, almost empty shelf that contains two lonely yellow boxes. I step closer and read the label: powdered sulfur. Huh. I didn't know you could even buy sulfur. What's it for? And why is John's store almost out of it?

"Are you gonna pay or what?" John grunts, making me jump. I clutch Jade's candy in my hand and head to the counter. I put the candy into his expectant palm, and he types something aggressively into his ancient till.

"Four seventy-eight," he says.

Bullshit! What candy costs five fucking dollars?! There's, like, ten pieces in here! I want to argue, but it looks like John wants me to. His eyes narrow, and one side of his lip is curled into a snarl.

"Sure," I say, gritting my teeth, and give him a five-dollar bill. I snatch the candy away from him before he can make up any more charges. "Keep the change."

I leave, foreboding mixing with rage. God, I can't wait to get out of here. I hope wherever this party is has better people than Sanctum. If another old white man glares at me, I'm gonna lose my mind.

I tuck Jade's candy safely into my pocket and stretch. Then I run home like I'm in a race. My mind blanks on everything except *run* and *win*. Adrenaline dumps into my system, and for a second, I'm breathing hard and my feet are pounding in time with my heart and I'm not thinking about anything. Not funerals or aggravating men or weird sounds or even Allison. For a second, I'm free.

4

I stare into the mirror of the guest bathroom, my freshly plucked eyebrows scrunched together. It's almost eight, and I'm ready to go to Allison's party. Lip gloss? Check. Legs? Shaved. Hair? Laid. I'm wearing a red tank top and jean shorts, and I'm borrowing Jade's golden hoops. My braids are getting fuzzy, but they're not so bad. They're pulled into a bun, and the loose hair at the top of my head is perfectly curly. I'm hella cute. Cute enough for Allison to want to kiss me. Maybe. Hopefully.

"Okay, Latavia," I say out loud. "Be cool."

"Giving yourself a pep talk?"

I turn, and Jade's standing in the doorway. She's wearing her pajamas, despite it being seven-thirty.

I grin at her and straighten. "Yep. How do I look?"

"Like you're gonna get killed by Mom."

"Lighten up." I hesitate, thinking of Auntie's explosion after I got back home. She was not happy with my ice cream meeting, and forbade me to leave the house for the

28

rest of the summer. And here I am, about to sneak out the same night she laid down the law. "Hey, Jade? Sorry for this. I know Auntie's gonna be pissed, but I'll tell her it's not your fault. And I'll be home before you know it."

Jade gives me a side-eye. "That's not gonna stop her from screaming at you when you get back."

"I know." I look back into the mirror, determined. "But this time it's worth it."

Jade laughs a little. "Okay, fine. I'll cover for you. When Mom gets back, I'll say you're asleep."

"Really?"

"Yeah." Jade smiles at me, a small half grin. "Can't stand in the way of my cousin and her date."

Warmth fills my face. I never told Jade how I feel about Allison, but maybe she figured it out. Or maybe Allison told her she likes me. She and Allison have been friends for forever, so it's possible. Would Jade tell me if Allison likes me back? I shake my head to dispel the frantic thoughts. This is definitely not being cool.

I meet Jade's eyes in the mirror to thank her, but some of my giddy excitement cools. This is a date, but it's also an information session on all things creepy as hell in this small town. Auntie's at the hospital, so Jade will be here by herself all night. Unease prickles my skin at the thought.

"What's wrong?" Jade asks.

"Do you want to come?"

"What? No, I do not want to see you making out with my friend. Ugh."

I let out a short laugh. So that's a yes to Jade knowing I like Allison, at least. "I'll give you a warning before I lay on my irresistible charm." Jade makes a gagging sound at the back of her throat, and I laugh harder. "Shut up, listen to me. I'm serious. Do you want to go with us? I don't want to leave you here by yourself."

I watch Jade's face closely. She's normally wearing a bored, slightly annoyed expression, but a flash of fear crosses her face at my words. She quickly goes back to normal, but I saw it. She's scared. She might know just as much as Allison.

"No, that's okay. I'll be a third wheel—"

"You're going," I interrupt her. "Get dressed."

"Avie—"

"Hurry! Don't make me late!"

Jade shoots me a quick, grateful glance, and I know I've made the right choice. "Fine, fine. When'd you get so bossy?"

I grin at her as the doorbell rings. "I've always been bossy. Now go let her in and tell her we're gonna be late because of you!"

Jade rolls her eyes and leaves the bathroom. I turn back to the mirror, my smile fading. I don't know what's going on in this weird town, but if I can keep myself and my little cousin alive, I'll be okay. Three more weeks, and I'll be gone . . . but what about Jade? Will she be safe here after I leave? I need to ask Auntie to stop taking late shifts at the hospital.

Footsteps thunder upstairs. Why's Jade so loud all of the sudden? Or is it Allison running up to meet me? I hear the bedroom door creak, and I hurriedly put another coat of lip gloss on.

"Almost ready—"

The words are choked out of my throat as I look into the mirror. Jade isn't standing behind me.

It's a man in all black.

I don't have time to scream. I barely have time to register this is John, from the grocery store, dressed in a jet-black robe. He grabs me, and hands are all over me, dragging me out of the bathroom. I try to hold on to the wall, and my nails bend backward and hands shove me forward and a scream finally bubbles out of my chest.

"Help! Help, help! Jade—"

Shit, where's Jade? Did he hurt her? I kick and scream, trying to get away, to my phone so I can call someone for help.

"Stop struggling," John growls. He shoves me forward, out of my room. I fall to my knees, but I'm up again, scanning Auntie's house wildly. A weapon, an escape route, anything—

A second man grabs me from behind.

He clamps his hand over my mouth as I scream again. "Get her legs, John. Hurry!"

Carter? That's Carter's voice. What the fuck is going on— Terror overrides my thoughts and I kick at John, nailing him in the eye. He swears and grabs my ankles, and I'm caught, like a struggling fly in a spiderweb. They hastily carry me downstairs.

I twist in their grip, my heart beating wildly, vomit climbing my throat. I can't let them take me out of here. I have to fight them off until Auntie comes home, or Allison—

They round the corner, and Jade is standing next to the couch, eyes wide and scared. A third man stands beside her. Sheriff Kines.

"Jade," I say, trembling, my voice muffled by the man's hand. "Help me, please."

"Sorry, newcomer," Sheriff Kines says as he puts a heavy hand on Jade's shoulder. He's smiling. His black-and-tan German shepherd sits by his feet. "No volunteers. We gotta make some."

Jade stands there, just stands there while I scream for help. She just stands there while they drag me out through my aunt's front door and into the night.

Fuck. Fuck, what do I do? Panic squeezes the breath from my lungs. I'm still screaming, but now I'm crying, begging. Men's hands are holding my arms so tight I can't move.

They drag me toward a car waiting in the driveway. Shit, if I get into the car, I'm dead, I'm seriously dead. I dig my heels into the gravel driveway, struggling against the men holding me.

"John, hold her tight—"

"Let—let go!"

I bite down on the man's hand. He yelps in pain, and for a second, his grip on me loosens. I wrench my left arm out of the other man's grip, and I'm running, blind, away from my aunt's and toward the forest behind the house. I barely feel the pain in my bare feet as I run, wheezing. I try to remember Coach's breathing technique, but panic burns in my legs, begging me to run as fast and far as I can.

Faster, faster, faster—

I don't know where I am. It's getting dark, and I'm running blindly into Red Wood. Rough ground tears into my feet, branches scrape my skin, but I keep going. Auntie said, whatever I do, don't go into the woods. Her words play over and over in my head as I run. I don't have a choice.

Voices yell behind me.

"Grab her!"

"Catch her! Catch her!"

They're not gonna catch me. I'm fast as fuck. Carter and John were huffing just holding me still, and I've never seen the sheriff get in a hurry a day in my life. Hope springs in my chest. I'll make it. I'll live, I'll make it—

A sharp, loud whistle sounds overhead. I flinch, confused. Who the hell is whistling? And why—

And then I hear it. Impossibly fast footsteps. Barking.

Sheriff Kines's police dog.

A scream rips out of my chest and the hope turns into blind terror. I can't outrun a dog! It's gonna catch me, it's gonna rip my throat out. I push myself to the limit, terror stalling the breath in my heaving chest.

"Help!" I scream to everyone, to anyone, to no one. Ragged panting gets louder and louder in my ears.

Faint artificial light peeks through the tree line. The road. If I can get to the highway, maybe—

Something heavy and hard hits my back, and I'm down on the forest floor, mud in my teeth.

The dog barks furiously at me, hot breath on my neck. I struggle, too scared to think, and shove it off my back. If

I can just get away from this dog, I'll live. I'll get away. I kick at the barking dog, heart in my throat. But it dodges my foot and clamps its teeth onto my left arm.

Pain rips through the shock and I scream, loud and ringing in my ears. My arm is burning, the dog is tearing into my skin, the pain is blinding. Fuck, fuck, this hurts! I tear at the dog's eyes, neck, anything I can find, but it won't fucking let me go. If I can just get its jaws open, I'll live. If I can just get away from this, I'll be okay. I grab at the forest floor blindly and snatch a sharp stick. I ram it into the dog's neck. It yelps, and for a second it lets go. I kick it in its bloody teeth, my own teeth gritted against my screams. I'm getting out. This dog isn't killing me.

But it's too late. I hear a harsh command and the dog backs away, and I look up into the blurry faces of three men.

They caught me.

"She's fast," Carter pants. He doubles over at the waist, wheezing. "Good thing you had the dog, Kines."

"Don't come near me!" My voice is choked by tears. My arm throbs with fire. The dog whines, looking up at one of the men.

"Fine," Sheriff Kines grunts. "But you're coming with us. Quit struggling."

"You'll have to kill me." It's a bluff, the biggest lie I've ever told, but everything in me is screaming that if I go with them, I'm the next closed-casket funeral in Sanctum.

Surprisingly, the men don't speak. They exchange uneasy glances with each other.

"What do we do?" Carter asks. He actually sounds . . . nervous? "She ain't gonna come along quietly."

"She will," Sheriff Kines argues, but his voice is weak. Almost scared.

I have no idea what's going on, but I can't focus on their argument. I blink tears out of my eyes so I can see. Carter is unarmed, as far as I can tell, but the sheriff has that gun and stupid dog, and John has a baseball bat dangling from one hand. He's also looking dead at me, his cold eyes boring into mine while the other two argue. Panicked thoughts run rapid fire through my brain. I'm not going with them. I can't. I can't outrun them, because the dog will catch me. But maybe not—it's panting harshly, lying on its side, the stick still jutting out of its neck. I stuff down the twinge of sympathy. I can't outrun the gun, but the highway is right there. I can see the lights from here.

Carter and the sheriff continue to argue. I take a deep breath, in through the nose, out through the mouth. I have to risk the gun. I'm dead if I stay here—I might as well try to get away or go down swinging.

I tense my muscles to run.

John moves suddenly, before I can take off, and tackles me. I yelp in surprise, crushed under his weight. I curse and scream while the dog barks and Carter and Sheriff Kines yell in alarm.

"John, what the hell are you doing—"

I'm scratching and screaming, but all at once, I'm scratching at air. Did they pull him off me? I search wildly for him and make eye contact with him for a split second.

35

He's glaring down at me, eyes cold and cruel, bat raised over his head.

He swings it down, and it lands with a sharp *crack*, just below my right knee.

For a single, horrible second, I'm too shocked to feel anything. But then pain, raw and deep and urgent blasts through my leg. I scream, but it's distant, broken, like it's not coming from me. My leg, he broke my leg—

"There," John grunts, tossing the bat to the ground. "Problem solved."

All the adrenaline rushes out of me at once. I lean over and throw up on someone's shoes, then slump against a tree, defeated. It's over. I'm not making it out of this. I'm a dead girl.

"John, you fucking idiot." Carter's voice is hushed with horror. "You know we can't hurt them! We're dead. Oh fuck, we're dead."

"Shut up," Sheriff Kines barks. "We'll have to carry her now, thanks to this asshole. Hurry up, we're already late."

I can't listen anymore. Pain and shock rob my brain of any coherent thought. Carter or John or whoever hooks their arms under mine. Someone grabs my legs, and the sharp pain pulls a small groan out of me. They carry me deeper into the woods, for what feels like forever. I close my eyes, crying quietly. I'm dead. I'm never going to UGA. I'll never get to work things out with Mom. I'll never see Auntie again. Or Allison. She's gonna go to my house to pick me up for the party and I'll be dead. Maybe it'll be quick. Maybe I won't suffer too bad. I try to say a prayer, but the words stick in my throat. The man upstairs can't get me out of this one.

At some point, I open my eyes and see an orange glow in the distance. A campfire? The light illuminates three more figures waiting in a clearing. . . . I'm doomed.

"What have you done?!"

I know that voice. Some of the life surges back into my body, and I blink sweat out of my eyes and focus ahead, at the people in the clearing. They're all wearing dark robes with the hoods up, but one has hers down, running to meet us, panic all over her face.

"A-Auntie?"

5

It's her, it's really her. Tears gather in my eyes, and I struggle from the men's grip. I kick the guy holding my legs, and he lets go, cursing. My right leg hits the ground, and hot pain lurches up my right side. I fall forward, but Auntie catches me.

"H-help me, Auntie, please—"

"Shh, shh, it's okay, baby." She holds me tight, so tight I'm having trouble breathing. "Where are you hurt?"

"M-my arm . . . my leg . . ." I'm sobbing, and the pain is so bad, I can't see. Auntie coaxes me to the ground and runs her hand over my right leg. I squeeze her arm, still crying. "It hurts, please help me—"

"Broken. Who hurt my niece?" Auntie's voice is strong, furious. I cling to her like she's a lifeline. I'm gonna make it. I'm going home.

"Take that up with John," Carter says, still breathing hard from carrying me. He glares at John, who looks away. "This ain't my first choice either."

"Look, she was gonna run," John says. He sounds bored, not even a little bit sorry. Some hatred leaks through the pain as I glare at him. "We don't have any more options. We got her here; that was the goal. If she hadn't taken off, we wouldn't have had to send the dog after her and break her leg."

"Whose goal?" Auntie's standing in front of me, shielding me with her body, and I've never loved her more. "I never agreed to this! She's so young, she's just a kid—"

"That's enough, Dr. Roberts."

Everyone goes quiet as another figure steps forward. My stomach roils when I recognize the gross watery eyes and bald head. Pastor Thomas. I scan the clearing frantically. Six people. Pastor Thomas. Auntie. John. Carter. Katie, Allison's manager. The sheriff. The whole fucking town, huh? I burn their faces into my memory. If I get out of this, I'll need to know who did this to me. Everyone's wearing black robes (even Auntie?) with silver trim on the sleeves, except Pastor Thomas; he's wearing a fancy white preacher's robe with gold on the sleeves and collar. Of course he'd be the ringleader.

Auntie backs up a few steps and puts a protective hand on top of my head. "This is wrong and you know it, Pastor. This is against the rules."

Pastor Thomas glances at me, and I can't stifle a shudder. "It is unfortunate that she's injured, but in the interest of an emergency, I'll allow it. John did well, as far as I'm concerned." John beams at Pastor Thomas, and I want to throw up.

39

"But she's a child! I didn't agree to this, Pastor." Auntie's voice trembles slightly.

Pastor Thomas doesn't look moved. In fact, he seems kind of bored. "I didn't ask you, because I decide who our sacrifice is. You broke the rules and brought a newcomer into my town without informing me first. If you want to be upset with someone, be upset with yourself."

"She didn't have anywhere else to go!" Auntie's voice is higher pitched now, a little desperate. My heart rate kicks up with the beginnings of terror. I've never heard Auntie sound anything but cool and confident and disapproving. "I know I didn't ask, but it was an emergency, and—"

Pastor Thomas waves his hand lazily to cut her off. "It's too late. Get her on the altar."

"I won't let you—"

"Yes, you will." For a second, Pastor Thomas doesn't look like a soft-spoken old man. His eyes flash with malice, and his body tenses, like he might attack Auntie. "You have two choices, Doctor. We have your niece, but if we want to save time, I can put you on that altar and have Jade's induction a few months early."

Altar? Jade's *what*? My head spins with pain and confusion. I have no idea what the hell this town is up to, or why my aunt is mixed up in this, but she's my aunt, my family. She'll protect me . . . right?

It's silent in the clearing. Auntie doesn't say anything for a long time, just staring at Pastor Thomas.

"Auntie?" My voice is soft, fragile.

Auntie turns to look at me, her expression full of regret, and I know I'm a dead girl.

40

"Excellent choice," Pastor Thomas says, and nods to the other hooded figures. "If you please, boys, I'd like to get started."

"No!" I try to scramble away, but Carter grabs me from behind and yanks me to my feet. He pulls me farther into the camp, my useless leg dragging behind me.

"Auntie!" I'm screaming. I can't stop. "Don't do this! Don't let them, please!"

"I'm so sorry, Latavia." Auntie's crying, but all I feel is stunned disbelief. I'm about to die. My aunt is gonna let these townies kill me. "I have no choice. There are no more volunteers. Please understand—"

Pastor Thomas puts his hand on my aunt's shoulder, and she clams up. "You've done well, Doctor. This is for the greater good."

The others nod and murmur to themselves. As if what he said makes sense. As if it's normal to kidnap people in the middle of the night and drag them into the woods.

Pure horror and understanding crash through the disbelief. These six people, including my aunt, are gonna murder me.

"It's time," Pastor Thomas says. "John, Carter, tie her to the altar, please."

I don't have much strength left, but I fight them every step of the way. I bite and scratch and tear into every inch of skin I can find, but they won't let me go. I can't get away. I'm exhausted by the time they get me to the altar, a stone slab just like the memorial in the park, but this one is horizontal. At least Carter and John have several cuts and bruises. I want them to feel pain long after I'm gone.

Carter forces my hands over my head and ties them to the top of the stone with a rope. John grabs my injured leg, forcing a scream of pain out of my raw throat. The cold stone presses into my back as I buck and kick, trying to get away one last time. But when John dodges a kick and ties my good leg down, I slump, spent.

"Finally," Carter mutters. He reaches into his back pocket and pulls out a knife. I have to swallow a whimper.

"What're you doing?" Auntie asks. She steps forward, something like concern on her face.

"I gotta cut her clothes off," Carter says.

"No." Auntie looks at me, but I look away, to the dark woods on my left. "No, she's been through enough."

"But the rules—"

"The rules say volunteers only too! And that we can't hurt them!" Auntie's voice trembles, but she's glaring at him with fire in her eyes. "The clothes stay on. She deserves that, at least."

Carter heaves a sigh. "You know what? Fine. We've broken all the other ones anyway. And I'm tired of messing with her. Lost a fucking tooth."

"If I get out of here, you'll lose a few more!" I yell. I'm proud to hear no tremble in my voice.

John and Carter move away, but Auntie steps closer until she's right beside me. If I wasn't about to die, I'd feel bad about how sad she looks. "I'm so sorry, Latavia. You can't know how sorry I am."

"Tell that to my mother."

Pain crosses Auntie's face. "Latavia, I know it's not right, and it's not fair, but this is the only thing I can think

42

of to do. You'll see when it gets here. If the barriers fail . . . I don't want to think about what would happen."

Barriers? *It?* What the hell is she talking about?

Auntie cups my face and strokes my cheek with her thumb. Her expression is a confusing mix of deep sadness and desperation. "I love you, Latavia. Okay? I'm so sorry."

I gather the last bit of strength I have and spit in her face. She jerks backward, shocked. I look dead in her eyes.

"Go to hell, Auntie."

Pastor Thomas clears his throat. "It's time, Doctor."

Auntie hesitates like she wants to say more, but just wipes her face with her sleeve and joins them, her head down. Pastor Thomas looks at me with his gross bulbous eyes and says, "We must thank this girl for her sacrifice. Thank her, congregation."

Everyone mutters something under their breath. The rope around my wrists bites into my skin.

"Katie, will you say the final prayer?" Pastor Thomas asks.

Katie looks like she's about to throw up. Join the club. "May the Lord bless her sacrifice," she says, her voice trembling, "and may the Lord protect us from the Serpent's fangs and lying tongue."

"Amen."

Pastor Thomas looks at me, his expression cool and heartless. "Goodbye, Latavia."

I swallow my fear, and it gives way to an icy feeling in my stomach. "You remember this, okay? You remember my face, my name. Because I'm coming back. You'll all pay for this, one way or another. I'll make sure of it."

Empty words, but I take savage pleasure in the fact

they look unnerved. Five white faces and, worst of all, my aunt's tormented brown one. I hope this bothers them. I hope they have nightmares for the rest of their miserable lives.

Pastor Thomas withdraws something from his coat. I breathe hard, my chest constricting. I can't go down like this. I can't show any fear—

Pastor Thomas swings the object up and down. A clanging sound, harsh and ugly, reverberates through the air. A bell?

Then, one by one, they leave the clearing. Auntie meets my eyes one more time, her expression tortured, before turning and disappearing into the trees. I stare after them, dumbfounded. They just . . . left? Why? Who's going to kill me, then?

I wait for a dumbstruck second, but then struggle against my restraints with all my might. I don't know what they're doing, but if I can get away while they're playing around, I'll be okay. I struggle and wrench at my restraints, but they're too tight. I move my right leg, and pain shoots up my knee into my stomach. I groan, vomit at the top of my throat.

I struggle for a few more minutes, but then I have to rest. My arm is killing me. My leg's on fire. I pant, rapid thoughts running through my brain. Where are they? Are they not gonna kill me? Shit, I bet some axe murderer is coming. Maybe Pastor Thomas is in debt to some psycho and he pays it off in bodies. Maybe it's something worse than that. Despite me wearing a tank top and shorts, sweat beads on my brow. I have to get out of here. I don't want to know what's coming.

Seconds tick by. Then minutes. Then more than a few minutes. I struggle against my restraints, then rest, then do it all over again. Over and over. The rope bites into my wrists, stinging, rubbing the skin raw. My body hurts all over, but I can't stop. I have to keep going. I have to escape.

But if I do get away . . . where do I go? The thought makes me pause, panting harshly in the wet summer air. I can't go home. I can't go back to Auntie's, not after this. Maybe I could convince UGA to let me come to campus early . . . but my leg. My track scholarship. Sharp pain hits my chest, and it's suddenly hard to breathe. I'm a goner either way. They've killed me no matter what. I have no future after this.

I lie still for a while, tears pooling in my eyes. Why would Auntie do this to me? How the hell is she involved in some secret cult that kills people? I don't get it. Auntie's a doctor. She's strict, but she cares for Jade. For me. We spent holidays together, joking about Jade's terrible driving and Mom's hatred of anything casserole. We're family. She loves me.

She let them tie me to this altar and walked away.

As I lie here, for at least an hour, the pain turns to hatred. She could have picked herself. She could have warned me about this weird shit—she was part of it! She was behind all these funerals all along, and she let me sit in my ignorance until it was time to get another sacrifice.

45

Me, someone no one would miss too much. Someone no one would look for. I want to start crying and never stop. No, I want to tear her throat out. Auntie knew I was doomed the moment she let me come here, and if I ever see her again, I'll make her wish she was dead.

I start struggling again, hatred and rage giving me power, and I let out a frustrated scream. If I can get this fucking rope loose on my right arm, I'll be fine. I'll be fine, and I can drag my broken leg to Auntie's front door and make her pay for this. I'm still struggling when a chill creeps up my spine. I pause, panting, and the hair on my arms tingles. Something isn't right.

I look to my right—just the low fire crackling. My left— just dark trees and underbrush. My gaze darts around the clearing, sharp anxiety filling my gut. Something changed. Something's different. . . . Wait. I hold my breath, listening.

The forest is dead quiet.

No bugs humming. No animals darting through the trees. No hooting owls. Silence.

Then I do hear something. A soft noise, like someone dragging cloth over a floor. I stare into the darkness, my chest heaving. Someone's coming.

The sound gets louder and louder. I squint—something's moving in there. Something big. A bear? Are there bears in Alabama?

Chaka, chaka.

The sound. The rattling.

Chaka, chaka.

My chest heaves as a dark shape comes into view.

Chaka, chaka.

It's not a bear.

A snake, an impossibly huge snake with jet-black scales, slithers into the clearing. It rears its head up, up, up, until it's taller than a two-story house. It flicks its tongue out, tasting the air, then turns its black eyes to me. It opens its mouth, revealing fangs longer than my arm.

It almost looks like it's smiling.

6

At first, I can't even scream. I just look up at the snake, with its huge fangs and black eyes and body that keeps coming and coming. Finally the tail shows up—there's a brownish sectioned-off growth at the end of it. When it moves, there's a soft *chaka* sound. A rattlesnake. The rattling sound came from its tail.

It leans closer to me. Its tongue darts out of its mouth and skims the hair on my arm.

Now I scream.

"No, no, no, no—" I jerk at my restraints, sobs interrupting my words. A snake. A giant fucking snake. Auntie wanted to feed me to a fucking monster. No, I can't do this, I can't go out like this—

"Humans are so *noisy*."

The screams freeze in my throat. It's talking. The monster is talking to me.

The snake moves its snout a little, its head pointed away from me. It flicks its tongue out, again and again.

"Don brings me less and less suitable humans. The last one was dead when I arrived. I give him a second chance, and he brings me the noisiest one yet! Insufferable."

It talks. The snake talks. Holy shit.

The snake looks at me again. Its black eyes glimmer in the firelight. "Now. Try to expire quietly, hmm?"

The snake opens its mouth again, and I groan weakly, yanking at the ropes around my wrists. This can't be happening. This can't be happening. A monster. These rednecks have been feeding old people to a monster. I'm gonna be sick.

"Please." Tears fall down my temples, into my hair. "Please don't kill me. Please, I'll do anything—"

The snake pauses, its mouth still open. "Why are you wearing clothing?"

"I . . . I . . ."

"What happened to your leg?" The snake nudges my right leg, and pain radiates through my whole body. I cry out like a wounded animal.

"Please, please stop! They broke it! They dragged me out of my house in the middle of the night and broke my leg, and now you're gonna eat me—"

The snake snaps its mouth closed. It straightens, rearing back so its head is level with the tops of the trees. "Something seems a bit strange now, doesn't it, human? I gave Don clear instructions. Willing humans, no clothes, no injuries."

Who the hell is Don? Wait—the word "volunteer" pops into my mind. "I'm not a volunteer," I say, the words tumbling out in a rush. "I'm not willing. I just moved here, and

49

I had no clue about this. They broke my leg so I couldn't run away."

The snake is quiet for a minute. It stares in the direction of the town. "So. Don has finally broken our deal." It opens its mouth wide, the fangs glinting in the firelight. "I didn't think he'd ever dare. Well, I suppose I must make good on my promise."

Don? Promise? I'm dizzy with confusion and nausea. I still can't get over the fact that they were feeding people to a *monster*. No wonder they were all closed-casket funerals! No wonder Auntie told me to stay out of Red Wood, though a lot of good that's doing me now. Wait, Auntie . . . She said something about volunteers and . . .

"W-wait."

The snake turns to me slowly. "What, human? I have more pressing matters than eating you, I'm afraid. That will have to wait."

"They—they were talking about some barriers or something."

The snake hisses, so loud I flinch. "No, it can't be. . . ."

I blink and the snake is gone. Trees and grass rustle furiously for a few seconds, and then silence. Probably going to see the barriers, whatever they are, for itself . . . which gives me time to get away.

I yank on my hands and good leg so hard, I hear my left wrist pop. I have to get out of here before the snake gets back. This is my one chance. My breathing is ragged with terror as I pull at the restraints. My left hand finally wriggles free, throbbing with pain from the ropes and dog bite, and my chest fills with hope. Three more, then I'll be free—

I whimper when furious rattling reverberates through the area. Back already? It's only been seconds—

The snake charges out of the woods, mouth open, tail rattling like mad. "Don! The arrogant wretch!" Its voice is a furious rumble, like thunder. "How dare he disrespect me! I'll kill him. I'll kill him, and I won't be quick."

The snake looks to me, its muscles tight and tail still shaking. "You, human child. What do you know about these barriers?"

I stay silent, panting, my left hand gripping my middle. I don't know a damn thing, except my aunt knew there was a giant snake in Red Wood and thought it would be fine to feed me to it.

"I know you hear me, child." The snake hisses. "Speak. What do you know about the barriers?"

My chest aches. Pain clouds my head, my vision, but I can't see a way out of this. Bitter rage surges into my chest at the thought of Auntie putting me through this. And Pastor Thomas. And the rest. My eyes narrow when I think of them, knowing I would be screaming until its fangs closed around my head. No. No, this isn't right, or fair. I didn't do anything wrong. I don't deserve this.

I'm not dying. I'm making it out of here.

I gather what little information I have. Volunteers. Barriers. Don, whoever he is. How'd this sacrifice thing get started? There are all kinds of rules and stipulations about the sacrifices. There has to be some kind of agreement—

a deal, like the snake said. Someone, probably this Don guy, had to make a deal with this monster to begin with.

Why can't I make one too?

I take a ragged breath. In through the nose, out through the mouth. This is my only option.

"You . . . you like to make deals, don't you?"

The snake coils its body around the altar, black scales rippling like an angry sea. "I do not have time to play, child."

"I know! I just—I think we can help each other out." I take a shaky breath. "I'll help you. I'll destroy the barriers for you. That's stopping you from meeting Don, right? So if I destroy them, you can go into town and talk to him."

The snake narrows its eyes. "And what would I owe you in return?"

"You could not eat me?"

"That would be a given. You cannot destroy the barriers for me if you are dead," the snake says. Am I imagining amusement in its tone? "You may ask for something else."

I pant, my brain struggling to keep up. I can have something else? I accidentally move my leg, and pain rockets up my right side. If I do live, my life is over. Ruined. I can't run with an injury like this. I can't live with Auntie again, not after what she did. I'll be homeless. And the idiots who tied me to this altar to die are the ones responsible. Fury engulfs me, choking out the pain, the fear, the hurt.

I told them I'd make them pay.

"I've got about six enemies I need taken care of. You can help me with that, right?"

The snake opens its mouth, and a laugh pours out. "Oh, I love interesting humans!" The snake closes its mouth and goes still, staring at something over my head. I look nervously behind me, but there's nothing but trees lining the dark clearing.

"If I make a deal with this one," it mutters, "it will need my strength."

"What do you—"

"Quiet," the snake snaps at me. I shut my mouth, because the last thing I want is to piss off a giant monster deciding if it'll eat me or not.

The snake lies down on its belly and circles the altar. It doesn't say anything, and I don't either, so the only sound is the crackle of the fire and its belly on the grass. I watch it make a few laps, anxiety spiking higher and higher. What is it doing? Why is it making a circle? The snake mumbles something, so quiet I can barely hear. Wait a minute—it's pacing. It's thinking.

Finally, after several minutes, it stops. It rises to its full height and looks down at me with black glittering eyes. "You will destroy the barriers for me. And in exchange, I will help you kill your enemies. These are the terms, correct?"

I nod wordlessly, fear choking my voice from my throat.

"And you will be satisfied, and we'll part ways after both agreements are fulfilled?"

I nod again, traitorous hope blooming in my chest. I'm gonna live. Oh God, I'm actually gonna live.

The snake slithers close to me, so close its face touches

my cheek. I don't move, terror and sweet hope freezing me to the spot.

"Well, young human," the snake breathes. Then it snaps its fangs around the restraints on my legs. "You have a deal."

7

I cling to the snake's scales, shivering with nausea and exhaustion. It broke the ropes, but they're still knotted tightly around my right wrist and ankles. My joints are numb and aching.

"Don't fall off, human," the snake calls. Its head is a few feet in front of me. It moves through the forest with liquid ease, faster than my stomach would like.

"Um . . . okay." Now that I'm off the sacrificial altar and riding on the back of a giant snake, I'm starting to think this was a bad idea. Actually, I know this is a bad idea. But what choice do I have? This monster would eat me in a second. The faces of Auntie and the five others who tried to feed me to it fill my vision, and I get a bitter taste in my mouth.

The snake slows as we reach a different clearing. I can't see shit in the dark, but there's a faint glow in the distance. Lights from the interstate? No, it's a light blue otherworldly glow.

"We're here." The snake coils its body so I'm sitting right under its head. It's so dark all I can make out is a giant shadow. "I must ask you a question, and then we will proceed accordingly."

My mouth feels like I've swallowed sandpaper, but I nod. "Okay. Go ahead."

"Are your enemies the ones who bring me food?"

I nod, rubbing at my sore wrists. "The ones who tried to sacrifice me, yeah."

"Hmm." The snake sighs heavily, like my choice in enemies has inconvenienced him. "Then yes, we will need to solidify our agreement in the cave."

I swallow the little spit I have left. "And that means?"

"I'll bite you," the snake says, like it's the most ordinary thing in the world, "and my venom will flow through your veins."

Oh. Yeah, that's just *wonderful*. I tug at the rope around my sore wrist. "Okay, wait. I have some questions too. This is going too fast."

"My apologies," the snake says. "We should become acquainted before we solidify our agreement. What do other humans call you?"

"Like my name?" I ask, and the snake nods. "It's Latavia."

"Then Latavia is what I'll call you as well. Do you have more inquiries before we start the ceremony?"

Sweat soaks my tank top, partly from the humid summer air, partly from the word "ceremony." I've had enough of that for one day. "Yeah, um . . ." I try to think of something to say, but all I can think about is that cold stone altar. I drum my fingers against my uninjured thigh.

"What's your name? If we work together, we should probably be on a first name basis."

"I have no name."

"Oh. Maybe I can give you one, then?"

The snake hisses, loud enough to make me jump. "How arrogant! A lesser creature does not name its superior. Does the hound name its master? Does the ant name the heel that crushes its head?"

"Okay! Damn." For a monster, it sure is touchy. "No name, got it. But are you a boy or a girl? Neither? Give me something."

"Hmph. Humans are obsessed with categories. But if it helps, you may think of me as male."

A boy snake. Got it. Despite myself, that little bit of information comforts me. He's a male monster, and he doesn't like names. I clutch that information like it's a lifeline. Maybe something will come up that I can use to get out of this.

"Come, we'll talk more in the cave." The snake starts moving again, jarring my leg. I grit my teeth so a whimper doesn't escape.

The snake moves closer to the blue glow, until it's almost as bright as the dimly lit moon. He slithers into a cave with a high ceiling, revealing that the glow is coming from blue crystals embedded in the walls. We go down, down, the crystals shining eerie light on the snake's scales, until we reach the bottom of the cave. A lake of dark water comes into view, wider than any pool I've ever seen.

The snake stops by the water's edge. "Here is where we'll seal our agreement."

Okay. Okay, cool. I'm going to be bitten by a giant snake next to a haunted cave lake. I take a few shuddering breaths, but I'm no calmer. I don't want to do this.

"What happens if I say I changed my mind?"

The snake is quiet for a second. Then he says, "I cannot force you into an agreement. But then I must eat you, so I can gain strength to break the barriers myself."

I close my eyes. It's this or die. I'm not dying. Not for Sanctum. Not for Auntie, not for the other five who betrayed me. Not for anyone. I grip the hem of my shirt with a tight fist.

"Okay. How does this work?"

"You will drink from the pool. Then I will bite you."

I do not want to drink nasty-ass cave water, but what choice do I have? "Let's go over the deal again, just to be sure. What exactly am I agreeing to?"

"You will destroy the barriers for me. I can sense their presence, but I do not know how many there are. In return, I will help you destroy the six enemies you mentioned. Tell me their names. I know them, but sometimes different humans enter my forest. I need to know which six you are targeting."

I nod slowly, dread coiling in my stomach. Can I really help murder six people, including my aunt? I can still back out. I can let him eat me and accept my bad luck of being sent to this weird town with a monster in its backyard. But how is that fair? Why do they get to get away with murdering people? There were so many names on that altar, maybe even hundreds. Why do I have to die so they can continue to live their rotten lives, laughing while their victims die screaming as a monster's teeth close around their necks? If I do this, I'll be doing the world a favor. I think fleetingly of Jade and Allison, but then Auntie, who let them tie me to that altar, knowing I would be swallowed whole. No. If they want this beast to be fed, they can feed it themselves.

"Pastor Thomas. John. Sheriff Kines. Carter. Katie." I hesitate, but only for a second. "Cora Roberts."

The snake looks down at me and nods. "Done. I will remember these names."

I look uneasily at the water behind me. "Do I have to do the water and the biting thing? I mean, I can just help you with the barriers. I want something out of this too."

"Unfortunately, I've determined that you need it." The snake nudges my leg, and I groan, gripping my thigh. "My venom will help with that. Along with other things."

"Whoa, whoa, what other things?" I grit my teeth against the throbbing pain. "I'm not agreeing to anything until I get all the information."

The snake opens its mouth and laughs. The cave amplifies the sound; it's so loud I have to cover my ears. "You are smarter than most humans. My venom will affect your reflexes, your strength, and your vision in darkness. It will also help heal your wounds faster."

Okay. Not my first choice to be turned into a super human by a snake, but at least my leg will be fixed. "Anything else?"

"Yes. You must be within a certain radius of me to continue to reap the benefits of my venom. If you stray too far, most of your abilities will return to normal."

So if I can get away from him somehow—

"Do not think of running." The snake snorts, as if he's actually laughing at me. "Don has tried many times to escape me, never successfully. I am very good at catching humans who try to run from our deals."

Sweat beads pop out against my hairline. This sounds so bad. Working with the snake might be worse than Sanctum. "I need some time to think about this. This is so much."

The snake is quiet for a moment. "Latavia, I neglected to tell you this before, but I am on a strict deadline. This discovery about the barriers could not have come at a worse time. Our agreement must be complete before the full moon."

Wait, full moon? Didn't Carter mention something about the full moon in John's store? I file that away in my get-out-of-this-without-dying mental folder. "What happens if we don't make it in time?"

The snake looks at me, his black eyes glittering in the low light. "You don't need to know the answer to that."

Shit, now he's being cagey. This full moon business sounds serious, and not like something I want any part of. I take a breath in through my nose and breathe out of my mouth. This deal sounds horrible, but I can't back out. I'm living and breathing for as long as I can. If that means I have to work with a giant snake to do it, so be it.

"Okay. Let's do it."

The snake surprises me by slithering into the pool, and water, weirdly warm, covers me up to my waist. Some of the pain eases in my leg. "Drink, Latavia. It doesn't have to be much, but it's essential to your healing."

I dip both hands into the water, resist gagging, and take a messy sip from my palms. The water is sweet, and it leaves a fizzy feeling on my tongue.

The snake climbs out of the pool again, curling around himself to face me. "Are you ready?" he asks. "Once I bite you, we cannot go back."

I swallow the remaining spit in my dry mouth. "I'm ready."

Without warning, the snake's head darts down, and before I can scream, a searing pain pierces my chest. Burning runs through my body, into my stomach, into my legs. I fall sideways, writhing in pain, but bump into something leathery and hard.

"It'll hurt for a little longer," the snake says, his voice soft and close. "Why not sleep for a while?"

I have no choice, because as the burning ramps up, darkness fills my vision.

8

There are hands all over me and a dog's barking in my ears and I'm running, and my legs break, worse and worse until they're splinters, until I'm running on nubs, until John smiles down at me and turns into a snake and the snake lunges at me—

I sit upright, the end of a scream dying in my throat. Fuck, a dream. A bad dream. I put a hand to my chest, trying to calm down. There's a . . . lump? I look down and my stomach sours. There's a golf-ball-sized bruise in the middle of my chest, with thin black tendrils radiating from it.

Only part of that was a dream.

"You are awake."

I look up, and the snake hovers over me. It's daytime, and now that we're out of the cave, I can see him much better. I wish I couldn't. His scales and eyes are jet black, and they glisten in the sunlight. His face is huge. It's as big as two of me put together, and longer too. I try to put some space between us, and my back hits something hard. I turn to look—it's his body. I glance around, horror choking out any sound. His body's curled around me, like a living nest, layers and layers of black scales stacked over each other.

The snake blinks slowly, the eyelid coming from the side. It's translucent, so I can still see his black eye staring at me. "You were screaming." His tongue darts out, right next to my ear. "Humans are so noisy."

I close my eyes and take a deep breath. In through the nose, out through the mouth. This is my new reality. I'm business partners with a giant snake. I can't freak out every time I see him. I open my eyes and give him a wobbly smile. "Don't you have that tail that makes noise?"

"My tail is different. It's a warning." The snake cocks his head to one side. "Why were you screaming? A warning as well?"

"No. I had a nightmare."

"Ah, I see. Does a dream trouble you that much?"

"No, I'm fine now." I rub my arms to dispel the leftover goose bumps.

The snake snorts. "I see that humans continue to have a bad habit of lying."

I roll my eyes, despite myself. "Whatever. I'm not lying."

"You are, as humans do." The snake straightens his head slightly, inclining his chin. "Monsters do not lie, but that's all your species can manage to do."

"You don't have a high opinion of us, huh?"

"No, I do not. But I will cooperate with you for the

sake of our agreement. It will be amusing, I'm sure." The snake opens his mouth and laughs. I shudder as his fangs glint in the weak sunlight.

"Anyway," I say, trying to get the fangs out of my mind, "what's the plan? What time is it?"

"What do you mean by 'time'?"

"Uh . . . I don't know, like, how much time has passed since I fell asleep?"

The snake twists his head from side to side, seemingly deep in thought. "Hmm . . . night has passed, and soon it will be night again." The snake looks at me, his mouth slightly open. "You understand now, don't you?"

Slight annoyance needles at my skin. I'm actually a little relieved by that, though; all I've been feeling for a while is terror and rage. "So you're gonna be completely unhelpful. Got it."

The snake stares at me for a heartbeat, opens his mouth wide, and laughs so loud birds in the trees around us fly into the sky. "This is wildly humorous, considering how helpless and inconvenient humans are. How funny."

Ah, the snake monster thinks I'm funny. Lucky me.

"But, enough playing." The snake coils around me further, until his head is at my eye level. "We must discuss our agreement."

Unease swirls in my stomach as I remember last night, but I push it down. "I have to destroy the barrier things, right? What are they? What do they look like?"

"They should be items. I do not know what kind of item, but you'll be able to tell when you get near one. My venom in your veins will react badly to it."

Cool, cool, not weirded out by that at all. "Okay . . . how do I destroy them?"

"Fire. Force. Anything you can think of."

I guess he wants me to use my imagination. "Okay, so I'll go into town, find the barriers, and break them. Before the next full moon." It sounds easy enough, but what exactly are the barriers? Auntie didn't give me much to go on. What if they're, like, statues? How the hell would I destroy that? Sweat beads on my brow. I really should have asked more questions before agreeing to this. Making deals with giant monsters while half-blind with pain and rage isn't a great idea.

"Yes," the snake says, cutting into my racing thoughts, "but after you break the first one, you must come to me." The snake stares into my eyes. "This is very important. Do you understand?"

"Yeah, I get it. But why?" I adjust my leg, and pain rockets up my thigh. Less than last night, but not by much. I groan and grip it tightly. "I thought this was supposed to be better? My leg's killing me."

"Yes, well, there appears to be a problem." The snake moves his body, exposing my legs. The rope burns and bite mark from the dog are gone, but my right knee is almost twice its original size, bulging and purple. I touch it—it's hot.

"Shit."

"The venom should be working by now. Something isn't right." The snake flicks his tongue out again. "Your body healed, but only partially. Your leg is hurt very badly."

I tug at my tank top, the neckline drenched in sweat.

"Okay, so I need a doctor probably. And the only doctor in town is my traitor of an aunt." Great. Wonderful. Perfect.

"Latavia, have you eaten any silver?"

"What?" I pause in my panicking to glare at the snake. "What do you think people eat?"

"This"—the snake nods at my leg—"looks like a reaction to silver. There must have been some on whatever struck you, and it entered your body through a cut in your skin."

Fucking John. He and the rest of them had silver sleeves on their robes. Hatred swirls in my stomach, so strong I almost can't keep it down.

The snake curls around me, supporting my back. "This is a problem. If you can't walk, how can you get to the barriers to destroy them?"

"I'll get there. I just gotta figure it out." I massage my temples, trying to ease a tension headache. Everything was supposed to be fixed by this giant monster biting me. Why can't I catch a break?

The snake is quiet for a moment. Then he heaves a sigh. "Latavia, I haven't made myself clear."

"What?"

The snake moves his head so he's right in front of me, a foot from my nose. "Humans have a remarkable ability to empathize with anything with a face. But you must remember: I am not a human." The snake inches closer as I try to swallow the lump in my throat. "I am protecting you because this is our agreement. The moment we fulfill our tasks, you will cease to be useful to me. Failing to understand this leads humans to trouble."

I don't say anything. The hairs on the back of my neck are standing straight up, and my breath is short and choppy. He's right; I forgot. He's a giant, talking, deal-making snake. A monster. I can't trust him.

The snake eases closer. My heart thunders against my ribs, but I stay still. He presses his snout to my forehead, his touch cool and gentle. His breath moves my hair.

"But for now, Latavia, you are useful to me. So we must take care of your injury so you will continue to be useful, yes?"

I nod, my mouth dry as a desert. I can't stop the tremble in my voice. "O-okay."

"Good." The snake rises away from me, and I let out a breath of relief. "I will take you back to the cave. The water has healing properties, though I fear this injury is too severe for—"

The snake stiffens. Slowly, painstakingly, he turns his head to the east.

"Uh . . ." I trail off when he's silent. "What's wrong?"

"There are humans in my forest." The snake opens his mouth, so wide it's like he's grinning. "Perfect. I was feeling hungry."

My stomach turns at the thought of him swallowing someone. That could have been me. "Do you really eat anyone who wanders in here? What if it's a kid?"

"Parents should teach their young not to play in dangerous areas." The snake uncoils himself from around me, his gaze focused on the trees to my right.

"But it's not their fault! They don't know any better."

"What is it Don used to say? Survival of the fittest."

67

The snake flicks his tongue out for a second. "I'm doing your species a favor."

"Hang on. I'm coming." I grab the part of his body closest to me and haul myself up. I let out a pained groan when my leg bumps his side.

The snake looks back at me, eyes narrowed. "You'll get in the way."

"Surely you can hunt with me on your back, being a big, bad monster and all." I don't tell him I don't want to be alone in the woods. Monster or not, he's sworn to protect me until we fulfill the contract. I don't want to be caught out here by myself. What if Pastor Thomas and his cult come back? My stomach churns when I think of seeing Auntie again. I'm not ready for that yet.

The snake snorts. "Fine. But hold on. And no noise."

The snake starts to move, and I cling to his scales like he's a life raft. He's moving slow, so slow I can barely hear the rattle of his tail.

"I will show you one of my secrets," the snake calls back to me.

"What secret—" I jump and have to choke back a scream. The snake is gone. Vanished. But wait a minute . . . I can still feel him under me, so he can't be completely gone. I stare down at where he was, squinting, and I can see a rough outline of his massive body. But he's shimmery and translucent, and if I stare too long at one place, my eyes lose him.

"Can you still see me, Latavia?"

"Barely. What'd you do?"

"You can see me because of my venom in your veins.

I will grow clearer to you as time goes on. However, humans and other animals cannot see or hear me. I am invisible." The snake laughs from far ahead. "It's a useful skill. You will have one too."

I hold my hand in front of my face. I can see it just fine. "I can become invisible too?"

"No. You will develop something else, something to help you survive. However, I don't know what that will be yet. We'll have to wait and see."

Huh. So I'll get a superpower soon? I hope it's something that allows me to get far away from this fiasco. "When will I—"

The snake cuts me off with a sharp hiss. Fine. Time to be quiet.

We travel for what feels like forever. I watch the thick trees and bushes pass by, trying not to think about my throbbing leg. I have to destroy the barriers by the next full moon, whenever that is. It was really dark last night, so I'm assuming we have some time. But maybe I can get out of this. I look down at the snake's clear body under me. What did he say about my leg reacting to silver?

The snake slows to a stop. I hold my breath, listening, but all I can hear is the wind in the trees. I let the breath go, breathing raggedly for a few seconds while I pluck up the courage to speak.

"What's wrong?"

"The humans," the snake says, pausing for a heartbeat, "are calling for you."

9

"Latavia! Avie, can you hear me?"

I peek over the edge of an embankment, my breath frozen in my lungs. The voices are getting closer, but I can't see them yet.

"Do you know them?" the snake asks. He's still invisible, his massive head shimmering beside me. I scrambled off his back as soon as I heard them calling.

I don't answer him. I know these voices. But I want to see them. I want to be sure.

Footsteps tramp closer. A dog barks. I sink my fingers into the grass, hopeful fire filling the hollow in my chest.

Peach runs into the clearing below the embankment, nose to the ground. Allison and Jade come after, still calling my name.

Tears pool in my eyes and run down my cheeks. They came. They didn't abandon me.

"Why are you crying?" The snake's voice is next to my ear.

"They . . . they're my friends. My cousin and my friend. They came to look for me."

The snake is silent. Jade bends at the waist, groaning, while Peach runs from tree to tree, happily sniffing them all.

"God, this sucks," Jade says. "We're never going to find her, are we?"

"That's not true." Allison moves her hair out of her face. It's a darker shade of blond than usual, sticky with sweat. "We have to go deeper into the woods. There should be a clearing, and then some sort of . . . big rock? I don't know, I've never seen it."

"Sounds like we're just lost." Jade kicks a stick at her feet. She's wearing a hiking backpack and shorts. Her T-shirt is drenched around the neckline. Allison's shirt is the same. "You said we'd find her, Ally."

"We will! Let me think." Allison massages her temples and paces in a tight circle.

"It is unfortunate that your friends have wandered into my woods," the snake says, his gaze locked on Jade and Allison. "They seem to care about you."

My heart stutters in my chest. "You—you're not gonna eat them, are you?"

"Humans know the rules. These two have broken them."

Panic chokes the air from my lungs. No, I can't lose them too— "Wait! I can't walk, but what if they take me to Sanctum so I can destroy the barriers? You need me in town as soon as possible to break them. I'm sure the full moon is close."

The snake is quiet for a few stressful seconds. Then

he says, "I don't like it, but I do need you to destroy the barriers. This is an emergency." He nods, seemingly satisfied. "In exchange for them delivering you to town, I'll forgive them for trespassing. But only this once. If they come again, I will eat them."

I look down at Jade and Allison, a confusing mix of relief, anxiety, and joy churning in my gut. I wipe my forehead with my arm. "Okay. Okay, thanks. It shouldn't take me long."

The snake gently nudges my cheek. I'm surprised when I don't flinch. "This is where I leave you. Heal your leg, Latavia. Destroy the first barrier, and then we will get started on our contract."

The snake moves a few feet away, then coils into a giant shimmery pile. "Don't worry," he says, his eyes trained on me. "I'm here. Call to them."

Don't worry, the snake monster says, I'm still watching your every move. I take a shuddering breath, my hands clammy and cold. Why am I so scared to talk to Jade and Allison? Though, I guess the last people I saw broke my leg and tied me to a stone altar.

I clear my throat. "He . . . . hey."

Peach's head snaps up immediately, but Jade and Allison are still arguing.

"Hey! I'm up here!" I call, louder this time.

Peach charges toward me, and Allison looks up. She meets my eyes, and her mouth drops open like a cartoon.

"Avie?"

Peach gets to me first, wagging her tail and licking

my face. Then Allison, crying and hugging my neck, and then Jade, kneeling next to me and asking if I'm okay. I can't say anything. Emotion chokes the words from my throat. They came back for me. They risked Red Wood for me, even though they're terrified of it. They didn't abandon me.

"Avie, look at me." Allison puts her hands on my cheeks, her face close to mine. My nose fills with the scent of strawberries and sweat. Allison's eyes are wet with tears, and she has the happiest smile I've ever seen. I want to kiss her so bad, it hurts. "Are you okay?"

All I can do is nod. Her thumb wipes away a tear, and warmth spreads from my face to my whole body.

"Don't cry. We're here. It's all okay."

"What happened to your leg?" Jade's brown eyes search my face anxiously.

The warmth is sucked out of me in an instant when I'm reminded of my injury, John's bat, the altar. "I think it's broken."

Jade curses when she looks down at my leg. She runs her hand over my knee, and I yelp as pain needles up my leg. "That hurts, stop!"

"Sorry, sorry! This looks so bad." She glances up at Allison, fear in her eyes. "We need to go to a hospital."

"No," I say, my mind on Auntie. "She'll be there."

Jade and Allison are quiet, looking everywhere except at me. A hollow feeling grows in my chest. I'm happy to see them, but a horrible thought worms its way into my brain. They came to look for me, but . . . why?

"You aren't—" My voice fails, and I have to clear my throat. I can't stop from shooting a nervous glance at the invisible snake. "You aren't gonna take me back to Pastor Thomas, are you?"

"Oh God, Avie, no!" Allison's eyes widen in horror. "We'd never do that!"

"This is a rescue mission," Jade says with a grin, and gives me a thumbs-up.

Some of the panic is replaced with relief. It doesn't feel good doubting my cousin or Allison, but with the night I've had, I can't be sure. But they're not completely off the hook. I replay last night, bitterly, and I'm feeling Carter's hands holding me down, hearing the crack of my broken leg. I squeeze Allison's hand, tighter than I should. "Thanks for rescuing me, but question for you both: Why'd you let this happen to me?"

Allison looks at me, her eyes still wet with tears. "I'm so sorry. I was in the truck, on my way to your house, and—"

"No." Anger leaps into me like lightning, and I let go of Allison's hand. All the earlier happiness is gone. "No, you knew something would happen, didn't you? That's why you were trying to get me out of town for the party. And *you*—" I round on Jade, the hollow feeling growing, eating me up inside. "You just stood there. Just stood there while they dragged me away."

"What was I supposed to do?" Jade whines. "I was scared! There were, like, a million of them—"

"Three." My voice is quiet, bitter. "John. Carter. Sheriff Kines."

74

Silence. I glare at Jade and Allison until they look away. The pit in my stomach is cold, yawning, creeping bigger and bigger as the silence grows.

"Let's . . ." Allison trails off, avoiding my eyes. "Let's talk about this on the way home, okay? It's not safe out here."

Oh, they have no idea.

"Okay," Jade says. "I'll crank up the truck. I'll find something we can stabilize your leg with in there." She stands, and Allison tosses her the keys to her old truck. Jade looks at me, like she's about to say something, but gives up and hurries away.

Allison and I don't speak for a while. I pick at the grass by my side, suddenly aware that the snake is watching this whole thing. I bet he's laughing his ass off. Or tail. Whatever.

"Avie . . ." Allison squeezes my hand gently. "I know you're upset, and I'm sorry. I'm so sorry I didn't make it in time."

"What do you mean 'didn't make it in time'?"

Allison shakes her head. A bead of sweat runs down her temple. "I was on my way. If I had just left ten minutes earlier . . ." Allison buries her face in her hands. "I didn't think they'd pick you. I didn't think Pastor Thomas was that cruel."

"Yeah. Well." Pastor Thomas's cold smile burns behind my eyes. "Trust me, he is."

Allison looks at me. Her expression is sad and almost desperate. "It shouldn't have been you. It should have been me."

Some of the anger melts away. I shake my head. "No, it shouldn't have been any of us. Why couldn't they sacrifice themselves? They're the ones who know about this mess."

Allison gives me a small, miserable smile. "Oh, they'd never give themselves up. You can count on that."

I start to answer, but freeze. Peach is sniffing around the snake—she's within biting distance. The snake watches Peach closely, his body tight. "Hey, Peach! Get away from there!"

Peach looks back at me, tail wagging. I call her a few more times before she bounds to me and licks my face again. Allison raises her eyebrows. "What's that about?"

"It's dangerous here," I say, a little too quickly. "I mean, we should stay close to each other."

A truck idles in the distance, and footsteps approach. Jade. Allison pets Peach's head, slowly. "Hey, Avie?"

"Yeah?"

"Did you . . ." Allison takes a shaky breath. "Did you see it?"

As Jade hollers for us and Peach takes off running to meet her, I look at the snake one more time. He opens his mouth in a grin.

"Yeah," I say, meeting her eyes. "I did."

10

Allison holds my left arm, her eyebrows scrunched with sympathy. "One step at a time, okay? You've got this."

I'm wheezing so much I can't answer her. We're at Allison's tiny apartment, but between me and paradise are fourteen steps on a steep incline, and a broken leg. We're on the eighth step and I'm sure death is coming.

"Let's rest," Allison suggests as I drag myself up the ninth. Jade is at the top, looking down at us with worry etched on her face.

"I can make it." I'm lying. I'm dying. Who the hell didn't put handrails on a dark, creepy staircase? I rub the top of my thigh, wincing. My knee stings like an angry hornets nest.

"Here, let me help." I'm surprised when Allison wraps her arm around my waist. Involuntary heat rises in my face, and I look to my toes. Fleetingly, I remember I'm still in the outfit I was going to wear to her party. I wish she'd seen me when I wasn't covered in sweat and dirt and dried cave water.

Allison coaches me up the last few steps, and Jade grins when we reach the top. "Knew you could do it! Come on, let's get in before someone sees us."

Jade opens the door to Allison's apartment. It's tiny; there's a small kitchen at the back, a big gray couch, a battered red armchair, a scratched-up coffee table, and a small TV. Her bedroom is at the very back, but the door's closed now. I've been here before, and I've always wondered why a seventeen-year-old has her own apartment. At first I was thinking old money, but her furniture doesn't match, and she has a bizarre assortment of decorations and trinkets around the house, including a corkboard covered in bracelets and a weird-looking chicken cookie jar. Her kitchen is barely used, covered instead by forgotten plastic bags and odd items. No pictures of her parents anywhere. I've always wanted to know what happened, but I've never had the courage to ask.

Allison doesn't let go of me until I'm collapsed on her worn couch. She hovers anxiously, shifting her weight from foot to foot. "Are you okay, Avie? Your knee looks bad."

"Fine." I grit my teeth, my knee pulsing with pain in time with my heartbeat. In through the nose, out through the mouth.

"Can I see it?" Jade asks.

I look up at her, grimacing. "Knock yourself out."

Jade kneels before me, frowning. My knee is huge, the size of a cantaloupe, and dark purple. She touches it, and I wince. Her fingertips are light, but even a little pressure is too much. She shakes her head. "Let me take a picture, and I'll ask one of Mom's doctor friends what they recommend. I don't think we'll be able to fix this by ourselves, though."

"Have some faith in us," Allison says as Jade takes several pictures of my knee with her phone. "We'll Google it. It'll be fine."

Ever the optimist. I can't keep a soft smile off my face. "Can we do first aid in a minute?" I ask. "I want to take a shower, if that's okay. I smell terrible."

"Oh, of course! You can borrow some of my clothes. And . . ." Allison trails off, frowning at the bathroom door. "You probably won't be able to stand up, though."

"We can use a chair," Jade suggests. She looks at me, nodding slightly. "I can help you, if you want."

I don't want, but I *really* don't want the girl I like to see me naked and struggling to get into her shower. I nod, and Jade helps me into the bathroom. I can put hardly any pressure on my right leg—I'm fucked. The snake is gonna eat me because I can't get to the barriers. I hope Allison finds a miracle in her Google search.

Jade closes the door, but she doesn't turn around.

"Well, come on," I say, easing down onto the toilet seat. "Let's get this over with."

"Avie." Jade's voice trembles, catching me off guard. "I'm sorry. I'm so sorry I didn't help you."

I rub right above my knee, looking at the floor. "Yeah, well, that was shitty of you."

"I know. I . . . I froze." Jade finally turns around. She's not crying, but her expression is tortured, like someone's twisting a knife in her side. "Sheriff Kines had a gun, and that dog. I still feel his hand on my shoulder. I was so scared. I was scared, and it made me a coward. You got hurt because of me."

For the second time today, I find myself softening. Jade and Allison aren't my enemies. They came looking for me, even though they knew better than to go into Red Wood. Auntie, and the rest of them, left me to die.

"Come here." Jade crosses the room, uncertain, but her eyes widen with surprise when I hug her. "Don't worry, little cousin," I say, holding her tight. "I'm not mad at you. Thanks for coming to get me."

Jade hugs me back. "Always. What's family for, right?"

"Exactly." Well, besides Auntie trying to sacrifice me to a monster snake, but I'll ignore that for now.

After a long, awkward shower, Jade helps me put on Allison's clothes and limp out of the bathroom. Allison brightens when we come out—she's got her laptop, a bottle of aspirin, and a bowl of water on the coffee table.

"Okay, so I googled some first aid stuff, and I think we need to keep it elevated and iced." She motions for me to sit next to her on the couch. "Here, come sit down."

I do, exhaustion begging me to close my eyes once I'm settled against the soft fabric, but I prop my leg on the coffee table instead. Allison presses an ice pack to my knee, her touch soft and gentle. She pauses, frowning down at me anxiously. "Avie, I'm sorry my clothes are so big on you. . . ."

"Shut up. I'm just glad I'm not gross anymore." I adjust the ice pack, wincing.

"Do you want something to eat?" Allison asks. "Or tea? I could make some. That would be nice."

"No." I take a deep breath. "I want to talk. About what happened."

Jade and Allison look at each other nervously. I need to know how much they know. I'm morbidly curious. How did these townies get stuck feeding a giant snake?

"Do you want to go first?" Jade asks.

"No." I meet both their eyes. "You've got a lot of explaining to do. You have to earn the right to hear what happened to me."

Allison sighs heavily. "Okay. Okay, hang on. I gotta get some stuff." She hurries to her room, rummages around for a few seconds, then comes back with a black notebook. She sits across from me and Jade and places the book on the table in front of her. It's old, worn leather, and the pages are yellowed with age. Allison looks at me and Jade, her expression grave.

"I'm not supposed to tell you this. I'm not supposed to tell anyone this. So you can't breathe a word to anyone else. Deal?"

Jade and I nod. I turn to Jade, my fingers curling into the hem of my borrowed shirt. "Wait, Jade, you were both acting shady as hell earlier. What do you know?"

"Honestly, not much." Jade glances at Allison nervously. "It's just part of living in Sanctum that once a year, in the summer, we have a big funeral and we can't ever go into Red Wood. But when you started asking questions, I kinda . . ." Jade trails off, her eyebrows pinched together. "I started noticing more. And Mom told me to make sure you followed all the church rules and to keep you out of Red Wood no matter what. I know why now, I guess."

I turn that info over in my mind. Auntie wanted to protect me through Jade? Yeah, right, since she tried to kill me. But if Jade was acting on fearful instinct, then that means Allison knows more. Otherwise, they wouldn't have known I was in Red Wood. They wouldn't have guessed I'd still be alive. I meet Allison's eyes. "And I'm assuming you know more than that."

"Yeah. A lot more."

"How?" Jade asks, frowning at Allison. "I had no idea any of this was going on until they kidnapped Avie."

I raise my eyebrows. Great question. Allison hesitates, but sighs. "Pastor Thomas called me into his office one day last year and told me everything." She waves the old book in her hand. "He gave me this and told me to keep it safe, and not tell anyone about what's inside. After everything they did to you, though, you deserve to know. But you can't tell anyone else, okay? Promise me."

I nod, and Jade says solemnly, "We promise."

Allison nods back and opens the notebook to the first page. "Okay, a lot of this is gonna sound unbelievable, but trust me. Way back in 1809, a guy named Donald Miller woke an ancient beast in Red Wood. He and a bunch of his friends attacked it, but that just made the beast angry. At least a hundred people died in its resulting wrath. Don felt responsible and made a deal with it—if Don could bring sacrifices whenever the monster asked, the carnage would stop."

So this is the famous Don. Sounds like a good deal for the snake, though—endless free food.

"So when we hear that rattling sound . . ." Jade trails off.

Allison nods. "That's the signal that the beast is hungry. And we must feed it, or else."

"Or else what?" I ask. *The snake was a little dodgy on that one.*

"Or else it'll come to collect what was owed to it—the entire town." Allison takes a shaky breath. "Death would be slow. Don said the monster hinted it would starve everyone. No one allowed into the town, no one allowed out. And then it would eat everyone while they were already weakened and suffering. Don called it 'end of days' in the notebook. Fire, screaming, and the sound of the beast laughing as it eats us all."

"Wait, laughing?" Jade leans closer, her eyebrows furrowed. "It can laugh?"

"It can talk too. That's how Don made the deal," Allison says.

"Okay, wait, wait. What are we dealing with here? What does it look like?" Jade asks.

Allison opens the book and flips to the back. She shows us drawings of the snake and a scale model of a person standing next to it. *Don was a good artist. Looks just like him.*

"It's a rattlesnake," Allison says. "A big one."

"We are so screwed," Jade says under her breath.

Allison makes a grim face but continues. "Anyway, Don made a complicated deal with the monster. Every time the snake calls, which is once a year, Don has to deliver a willing sacrifice. They can't wear clothes, and they can't be injured. And the rest of the town can't go into the woods unless it's on feeding days. Which is why I hoped you weren't dead, Avie. After all this time, Pastor Thomas broke the deal."

"I guess I understand what 'no volunteers' means now." I clench my hand into a fist.

"I don't understand why Pastor Thomas would do this." Worry creases Allison's brow, and she wraps a strand of her hair around her finger anxiously. "He's spent all this time keeping us safe. And now he does this horrible thing."

What? Is Allison okay? "Keeping Sanctum safe? He's sacrificed who knows how many people to a giant snake!"

"Yeah, but it was so the beast didn't kill everyone else," Allison argues.

I just stare at her. Is she seriously defending the guy who tried to kill me?

Jade massages her temples. "Pastor T aside, this is really bad, isn't it? That snake thing is pissed off because it got cheated out of eating Avie, so it's probably headed here now to kill us all."

"Not quite." Allison turns to the middle of the book, to a new drawing. "This is the result of decades of research, but the town is protected by four barriers."

I stiffen, my breath caught in my throat. So there's only four? Thank God there's not, like, a hundred. "What kind of barriers?"

"They're some kind of super repellant, I guess," Allison says. She frowns at the book. "They're made of a liquid the beast hates. Well, three of them are. The fourth is more like . . ." Allison hesitates and looks down at the book. "The fourth one is a little different."

"Where are the four barriers?" I ask Allison, trying to be casual. "We should probably try to protect them."

"I don't know," Allison says, shrugging. "The locations aren't in here."

Dammit. "What are the barriers? Like, what do they look like?"

Again, Allison shrugs. "No clue. I was wondering that too. Maybe there's another volume of Don's journal? Because I have a lot of questions."

Huh. So there might be more information somewhere else? Or maybe the six people at the ceremony know more than what's in Don's journal. Maybe I should ask them when I see them again.

"Wow, thanks, Don, for the help," Jade says, glaring at the notebook. "Who even is this guy? I want to punch him."

"Good luck, because he's dead," Allison says, laughing. "But I have a picture of him. Well, a picture of a painting. It's in Pastor Thomas's office." Allison pulls out her phone and shows us a painting. It's a white man in his twenties with blond hair and beady blue eyes. There's a deep scar on his right cheek, and he has an ornate gold ring with three red stones stacked on top of each other on his left ring finger. He's also wearing a Confederate uniform. Of course he is.

"Oh yeah, he looks like he'd doom us all," Jade says, her lip curling in disgust. "White guys screwing things up for the rest of us, as usual."

"Yeah, he was a pretty nasty man," Allison says. "Apparently, for the first fifty years or so, he used slaves as the sacrifices. The beast wanted 'volunteers,' but that's not how it's always worked. There's a section in the notebook where Don describes how he promised to free a slave's family if someone volunteered to get eaten. And even after slavery was banned, he kinda . . . kept doing that. And I guess the church kept up the practice after Don died; they'd offer money to homeless people's families, or convince terminally ill people to volunteer." Allison shudders. "There's some really horrible stuff in this book. I don't want y'all to see it."

Rage leaps into my chest, but I work hard to stuff it down. I'd like to launch into a rant about how living in the South is the worst and things haven't changed much, just evolved into a new breed of terror and oppression, but I need to focus. I need to know as much as possible about destroying the barriers so I'm not a giant snake snack. We can shit-talk Don later.

"Anyway, we're protected for now," Allison says. "But something's gone wrong. The beast only asked for a sacrifice once a year, up until this summer. Four in a month and a half is bad. Something's going on with the beast."

"Great," Jade says, staring up at the ceiling. "We've got a monster to kill, and it's apparently on the edge of something big. Cool. Love that for us."

I get a twinge of discomfort at the word "kill." Do they really think they can kill him? He's huge! His fangs are longer than my arm! No, I've gotta convince them to forget the "kill" route and embrace the "run-away-screaming" route. I can't let them get hurt, especially not to save this dumbass town.

"So," I say, my mind on the snake's grin, "have we considered getting the hell out of here?"

"Yeah, I'd love that," Jade says, but Allison shakes her head.

"Pastor Thomas says that a certain number of us have to be here in town, or the barriers won't work." Allison fidgets, picking at a strand of her hair. "I can't go. And I don't think your mom can either, Jade."

Jade sighs and slumps against the armchair. "Cool. We're stuck here to fight a big ole snake."

Allison and Jade might think they're stuck, but I bet I can convince them to leave. I just have to figure out a way to convince them that this town isn't worth their time. Or mercy.

Before I can say anything, though, Jade nods at me. "Avie, you ready to tell us what happened in the woods?"

I close my eyes and breathe for a few seconds. I'm obviously not gonna tell them I made a deal with the snake, but I can tell them a little. I open my eyes again, and Allison and Jade are watching me with concern.

"I don't . . . I don't want to talk about most of it."

"That's okay," Allison says quickly. "Take your time."

I smile at her, a little warmth creeping into my stomach.

"Thanks. I . . . There were six of them. Including Auntie." I can't keep the bitterness out of my voice. Jade looks down at her feet. "I tried to run away, but they sent Sheriff

87

Kines's dog after me, and it caught me. John broke my leg. They tied me to this altar thing and rang a bell. And then, after they left, I . . . I saw him."

"Was it like the drawing?" Allison asks.

"Yeah. He was huge. His head was so big. I kept screaming and screaming, and he eventually went away."

"How'd you get away?" Jade asks. Her whole body is tense.

"I, uh . . . The ropes were loose. So I pulled at them for a while and got free. And I wandered around the woods until you found me." I hold my breath, praying they won't ask for more.

Allison and Jade are silent for a few moments, frowning at their laps. Finally, Allison looks up. There's a quiet strength in her eyes, something like determination, something like rage.

"It's okay, Avie," she says, her voice soft. "They're never gonna hurt you again. I swear."

"Yeah." I agree, my mind on the snake and our deal.

"Okay." Jade jumps up from her position in the armchair, her brow furrowed. "We can't do anything about it tonight, and you need some rest for sure. I'll go home and get your stuff, Avie."

Hope springs into my chest. "Will you bring my phone?"

"I don't think you should use it," Allison says. "You don't want anyone to find out you're still alive."

Yeah, no kidding. "I know. I need it for something. I won't get on Twitter or anything."

Jade nods. "Okay, I'll bring it. Tomorrow we'll do some snake-killing strategizing."

I wave at Jade as she leaves, and slump against the couch. I watch Allison pick up the first aid items, chatting to me as she works. Do they really intend to kill the snake? No way. They won't survive. I take a deep breath through my nose. I'll convince them to skip town, and then I'll figure out how to get out of here too. Somehow. Maybe he'll be distracted by eating everyone in Sanctum and I can get the hell out of here.

Comforted, I close my eyes. In seconds, I'm asleep.

11

Hands. Hands all over me, dragging me out of bed, under my arms, holding down my leg. Panic, help me, someone— The snake appears, mouth open, fangs glittering. My leg shatters and I'm drowning in the cave pool and John's hateful smile leers at me as I drown—

"Avie?"

I gasp, my eyes opening. I'm staring at an unfamiliar ceiling . . . not the sky. My vision swims lazily. Where's the snake?

"Avie, are you okay?"

I'm still gasping, shivering. I touch my neck, expecting to feel the hands, but there's nothing but warm water. Water? No, sweat. The world shifts into focus, and Allison's face emerges. Allison's apartment. I'm sleeping on her couch.

I give her a weak smile. "H-hey. I'm all right."

"You're definitely not. You were screaming." Allison's eyebrows are scrunched with worry. She's usually in a full

90

face of makeup, but right now she's not wearing any. She has dark semicircles under her eyes that I've never noticed before. "You look sick, Avie. I bet you have a fever." She moves, too fast, her hand outstretched. I cringe from her, my shoulder pressing hard into the back of the couch. We look at each other for a second, both of us stunned at my reaction.

"S-sorry," I manage. My throat is hot and raw, my voice scratchy. "Sorry, I don't know why I did that."

"No, it's okay! I was just gonna check your temperature." She lowers her hand to her side. "I should have asked."

"No, you can. I'm fine." I nod at her and hold my breath.

Slowly, she reaches out and touches the back of her hand to my forehead. I'm relieved when I don't flinch. Allison grimaces and takes her hand away. "Yeah, you're burning up. I'll text Jade and ask her to bring over some more medicine." Allison pulls out her phone, and her thumbs fly over the screen. "I hope your knee isn't infected. We really would have to go to the hospital then."

"When's Jade coming?" My mind is on my phone. I think I left it on my bed, but who knows what Auntie did with it.

"She's on her way. She said she's bringing a change of clothes for you too. Mine don't exactly fit you." Allison laughs nervously, toying with her phone.

I roll my eyes. Allison is always saying dumb shit like this. She's a few sizes bigger than me, but who cares? I wish I had her body type. My ex-friend, Kendra, used to tease me that I was too thin and gangly. "They fit fine, stop."

Allison's quiet, so I lean back against the couch, my eyes closed. What's going on with me? Why am I so jumpy? I'm okay with a giant monster curling around me, but Allison can't touch my forehead? I rub my thigh uneasily, trying to massage some of the pain out of my knee. Something's weird. No, maybe something's changed. I've changed.

"Avie?"

I open my eyes again. Allison's looking down at her phone, but her expression is grave. "Yeah?"

"Did they . . ." Allison trails off, then meets my eyes. "What exactly did they do to you?"

Shivers race down my spine. I look away. "I don't want to talk about it."

"That's okay," Allison says quickly. "I just . . . You were screaming. You were saying, 'Please don't hurt me.'"

Shit. I slump against the couch and draw the borrowed blanket around me. How much can I tell her? Nothing about the snake. But I don't want to think about it. If I can get away from here, I won't have to think about it anymore.

Allison waits for me to say something, but I can't. I shake my head. Her expression softens and she has a kind of understanding in her eyes.

"Wait a second. Let me show you something." Allison goes to her room and returns with a heavy-looking shoebox. She puts it on the coffee table and opens the lid. There's a knife, the blade white instead of gray, the handle made of silver. She takes it out, holding it delicately. "This is a knife that's been in the church for years. It's made out of the tooth of a monster. Like the one in the woods."

Oh shit. I reach out to touch it, but inexplicable dread fills my chest, choking the air from my lungs. My knee throbs, and a headache throbs with it. I pull my hand back. Whatever that is, it's bad news. "Where'd you get it?"

"Pastor Thomas gave it to me. I've had it for almost five years now." Allison looks down at the knife, her expression faraway. "He said, one day, this would happen. That the monster would grow tired of the once-a-year sacrifice. He said this knife was one of our only defenses. Use in case of emergency." Allison holds up the knife to the light. "At first, no one told me about what was in the woods. It was just 'it's dangerous' and 'something is coming.' I was scared. I wanted to learn how to defend everyone against this monster in the woods, so I asked Pastor Thomas for help."

"And he gave you the knife after that?"

Allison nods. "Yeah. He said I could be the church's hero, but it was a big responsibility. I had to learn how to use the knife, so he made me take lessons from my mom. She wasn't the most forgiving teacher. We trained every day until she left. Every day, Avie, for four years. I wasn't very good at it. I mean, look at me, right? What can a fat kid do in a knife fight?" Allison's eyes glisten with unshed tears. "I wanted to quit, but it was too late. She reminded me that I'd asked for this, and since she'd started teaching me, failure wasn't an option. Mom made sure I figured it out, by any means necessary."

Hurt sneaks into my chest. That explains the lack of family pictures in Allison's apartment. Painfully, my mind wanders to my own mom, but I shut that thought down as soon as it arrives. "I'm sorry, Allison. You didn't deserve that."

Allison looks at me, her eyebrows scrunched with pain. "It's okay. It sucks, but I have to be a little grateful for the lessons. I'm not strong enough to be a hero, but I want to try. I don't want anyone, person or monster, to hurt you again."

Warm gratitude and a strange longing fill me from my head to my toes. She probably can't hurt the snake with a knife that small, but she said she would try, for me. My own aunt left me to die, but Allison is willing to take on a monster to protect me. I'm so overwhelmed with unfamiliar feelings, I can't speak for a second. I take her hand, intertwining my fingers with hers. "You don't have to be a hero," I say, squeezing her hand. "We can get out of this together. There'll be a way, I promise."

Allison smiles, but it doesn't reach her eyes. "I hope you're right."

Someone knocks on Allison's door, and we both flinch. She untangles our hands and jumps to her feet, putting a finger to her lips. "Who is it?"

"It's me," Jade's muffled voice calls. Relief replaces the tension in my shoulders. "Hurry up. I have a ton of junk."

Allison opens the door, and Jade eases into the room. Her arms are laden with tote bags, and she's clutching a black knee brace. Thank God.

"Sorry I'm late. You have a shit ton of stuff, Avie, I swear." Jade dumps the bags by the couch. "I got clothes, cold medicine, Mom's old knee brace, and your phone." I hold my hand out, excitement quickening my heart rate.

She puts it into my palm, and I grasp it tight. Only a little further to go now. "It took a lot to find this. Be grateful."

"Where was it?"

Jade hesitates. "In your suitcase. Mom . . . put all your stuff away."

My fist tightens around my phone. "So, what? She was just gonna pack everything up and throw it away? Just forget about me, like she didn't try to sacrifice me to a monster?"

There's a long, awkward silence, and the space between us feels like an ocean.

"Well," Jade finally says, not looking at me. "There's something else." She ducks out of Allison's apartment and returns with a cane. It's long and shiny silver. "I brought Nana's old cane. I figured you could try walking with this."

I take the cane and hold it in my hands. It's heavy, much heavier than I thought it'd be. Is this real silver? There's an intricate snake carved into the long part, the body wrapped around the cane in a loose braid, the head resting on the handle. Real silver or not, it's pretty cool. Nana had style.

"Wanna try it?" Allison asks.

"I guess. Hang on, let's see." I use it to support myself while I stand. It's a good length, strong.

Allison backs up a few steps and holds out her hands to me. "Come to me. You can do it."

I chew on my bottom lip. The swelling is down a little from yesterday and the pain has eased a bit, but should I try to walk so soon? "I don't know. . . ."

"I looked it up online, and most people are walking the

95

next day after knee surgery!" Allison wiggles her fingers, grinning.

"Yeah, but my knee was slammed with a baseball bat. Big difference." Still, I hold the cane in my right hand and lean heavily on my good leg, the bad one suspended above the floor. Sweat beads against my hairline. This is going to hurt.

"You have to put it in your left hand," Allison says. "I read that online too. It's to help with balance."

Seems counterproductive, but fine. I switch hands, but I don't feel any steadier. I feel a little sick.

"Slow," Jade says. "Take a little step. You've got this."

Yeah, sure. I touch my bare foot to the hardwood floor. No pain. I swallow, my throat dry, and put my weight on my hurt leg.

Pain, sharp and burning, rockets up my leg, but when I lean on the cane, the pain eases. If I can walk on it, that means it's not broken anymore, right? Thanks for a little help, snake venom. I take another tentative step, limping heavily, but moving. Allison reaches out her hand and I take it, hobbling toward her.

"You did it!" She's still smiling happily.

I try to smile back, but it's more of a grimace. "Hurt like hell."

"Yes, but if you don't use your leg, it'll get stiff, and then you won't be able to walk at all. One step is great!"

I roll my eyes. "Thanks, Doc."

Allison laughs. "You're welcome. Now we have to get some heat on it. I read it's good to alternate ice and heat."

I let Allison hurry to the kitchen and boil water,

listening to her hum a song. As the pain in my leg fades, warmth fills my chest. A few days ago, I would have loved to be here, holding Allison's hand, watching her smile at me. Her hands weren't as soft as I was expecting, but I like that. She's worked hard. But how can I sit here, enjoying her kindness, her touch, knowing I have a deal with the monster she's sworn to kill? What if she has to kill me? I tug at my loose shirt collar, warmth replaced with discomfort. What would I do if Allison tried to kill me? I can't die. Not for her, not for this town, not for the snake. Not for anyone.

I grip my phone in my hand. "I'm going to the bathroom," I tell Jade.

I have one last idea. Mom's from Sanctum; she and Auntie grew up here. She got out somehow. Maybe she can help us get out too. She's mad at me still, and we haven't spoken in six weeks, but I have to cave first. This is an emergency.

Time to call Mom.

12

I sit on the edge of Allison's tub, my heart in my throat. My grip is so tight on my phone that it's hurting my hand. I'm nervous.

Maybe I need to work up to it. I scroll through my messages first. I have one from Allison, from two nights ago: *almost there! :)*

I stare at the text, sorrow nestled deep in my chest. In some other lifetime, maybe Allison would have left her house twenty minutes earlier. Maybe we'd have gone to that party, and I'd have gotten a little drunk, and I'd have had the courage to kiss her. Maybe we would have sat in the bed of her truck and looked up at the stars and everything would have been perfect. But then again, in that universe, maybe they would have seen I was gone, and taken Jade instead.

I'm getting depressed. I close the texts and open a few apps, careful to avoid social media. I don't think Pastor Thomas has a Twitter account, but who knows. I Google "when is the next full moon?" July 25. Today's the eighteenth, so seven days away. Yikes, not a lot of time to break four barriers and kill six people.

I'm getting even more depressed, so I open my email, and my heart stutters in my chest. It's from UGA.

> Dear Latavia,
>
> We are so excited for you to join the Bulldog family! Remember, athlete orientation is **August 2**. Please fill out this form before **July 26** with details about your food and housing preference. We look forward to seeing you on the second!
>> Go, Dawgs!
>
>> Jenny Tribble
>> *Director of Athletics*

I close my eyes to try to hold back the tears. I don't even know how I would begin to explain what happened. *Hey, sorry, Jenny, I was almost sacrificed to a giant snake, and my leg is fucked now. Can you hold my scholarship money while I get it fixed?* I close the email without clicking on the link to the form.

I need to get this over with. I touch Mom's number and put the phone to my ear. I hold my breath, my heart throbbing painfully in my chest. It rings and rings. . . .

No answer.

"Oh, come on," I mutter. I know Mom heard her phone. Her ringtone is loud and obnoxious, and she never turns it off because of work. I call again, but there's no answer. I send her a text: *please pick up Mom*

Three dots pop up immediately. *I don't have anything to say to you.*

A few frustrated tears spill over and run down my cheeks. Still? It's been six weeks. *Mom, please, it's not about that. This is about the monster in Red Wood.*

I wait, but she doesn't text back. I call for a third time. This time, it goes straight to voicemail.

I stare at my phone in disbelief. She's really not going to answer me. She's really not going to help me. Wait . . . if she's from Sanctum, surely she knew about the snake, like Auntie? Maybe not the snake, but she knew about the funerals, the dead old people, the forest no one ever comes back from. She really let me go with Auntie, knowing something horrible was lurking in Red Wood.

The bubble of disbelief pops, and a loud sob rips out of my chest. For the second time, someone in my family has turned their back on me. Pain, so sharp it almost eclipses the pain in my leg, hits my chest, and I double over.

"Avie?" Allison's muffled voice calls from the other side of the door.

I don't answer. A tangle of emotions chokes me. Fury, pain, deep inescapable despair. I have no family to turn to, besides Jade. My future is ruined. I'm ruined. I stand up from the tub, using the cane for support. My skin crawls, my muscles twitch. My legs ache for a run. But I'll probably never run again.

I open the bathroom door. Allison and Jade are hovering nearby, anxiety on their faces.

"What happened?" Jade asks, her voice small.

"I have to go." My voice is tinny, robotic. I can't breathe. "I need some air."

"Avie—"

"I *said* I need some air." I push past Jade and stagger to the door, moving as fast as my throbbing leg will allow. They call after me, but I'm down the steps, outside, my body screaming to run but my right knee screaming for me to stop.

My mind is fuzzy static. Thousands of thoughts crash together at once. Mom won't answer her phone. I can't run from this. The snake will kill me if I don't help him, and the town will kill me if they find out I'm still alive.

I'm a dead girl if I don't do something.

But why am I trying to get out of the deal anyway? The six deserve what's coming to them. If they hadn't attacked me, destroyed my leg, my future, none of this would be happening.

This is their fault.

I suck in lungfuls of air, clarity finally lifting the fog. This is their fault. John. Carter. Sheriff Kines. Katie. Pastor Thomas.

Auntie.

Before I know what I'm doing, I'm hobbling to Auntie's house at the edge of the woods. My leg throbs with pain, but I keep pushing, teeth bared, cold fury driving me on.

By the time I reach her house, I'm panting, sweating. Thunder rolls in the distance. I grit my teeth so hard, my jaw aches.

Her car isn't in the driveway.

I stand there, seething, but the fury slowly leaks out of me, leaving nothing but cold. Her time is coming. I just have to show her I'm still here.

I go to the backyard, where I know the shed will be unlocked, and grab the can of red spray paint Jade and I used earlier in the summer to paint her bike. I shake the can as I return to the front of the house, and carefully spray the word "traitor" in red paint across the front door.

I step back and admire my work. The first *T* is lopsided and the paint drips down like a cheap Halloween prank. The more I look at it, the more my savage pleasure fades. This is ridiculous. Spray paint isn't gonna hurt her, make her really feel what she did to me. I'm being childish. Well, at least she'll have to get a new door.

I toss the can and hobble slowly down the steps, feeling low. Thunder rumbles a warning overhead, and thick, muggy air slaps my face. I need to get home before it rains. But where is home now? Not with the aunt who sold me out. Not in Atlanta, in the warm apartment me and Mom shared. Not even with Allison, not really. Not when she figures out what I've agreed to do.

I look to the woods, where they dragged me to an altar and left me to die. I take a step forward and stop. My leg throbs and my fist tightens around the handle of the cane. I'll go back, but not now. Soon.

I don't have anywhere else to go, so I limp to the park. Dark clouds hang low and heavy in the sky, and distant rumbles of thunder reverberate through the area. No one's out because it's about to storm; I'll sit on the swings for a while and mope, and then go back. If I'm lucky, Allison will come and get me. I look guiltily at my phone. Two texts from her, three from Jade. I don't read them; I can't. Not yet. I wander to the memorial so I can lean against something for a bit. My knee is killing me.

I stare at the memorial, eyes narrowed. Even though it's dark, I can read the names fine. The snake *did* say my vision would improve. I scan the names while I rest my knee, and freeze when I get to the end. In the bottom right corner, under a sea of names the town sacrificed, under Clementine's name, is mine. LATAVIA JOHNSON.

Slow rage builds in my chest. They have the nerve to put my name on this stone after dragging me out of the house in the middle of the night? They have the nerve to try and dignify what they did to me?

I take a rock from the ground and dig into the stone as hard as I can. Scratches mar my name until it's unreadable.

"I'm not dead," I yell to the silent park. Thunder growls overhead and rain spatters onto the stone, onto my skin. "I'm not dead! Do you hear me? I'm not dead!"

There's only silence in response to my screams. I'm panting, shivering, even though I'm burning up. I wipe rain from my face—no, this isn't rain. It's sweat. I take a shuddering breath, my heart rate going crazy. What the hell is wrong with me? I clutch my chest, a sour taste in my mouth. The snake's words pop into my head: "My venom in your veins will react badly to it."

The barrier.

I turn on my phone's flashlight, ignoring more texts from Allison and Jade, and shine it at the memorial. Just names and black stone. I lean over and run my hands along the base. Grass, dirt, cool stone . . . and something loose and hot.

I jerk my hand away, my heart pounding. It burned me, but just in one spot. I shine the flashlight at it. There's some sort of discolored stone sticking straight up, suspiciously in the shape of a handle. I grab it, my palm burning, and pull. Stone groans as I strain to tug it out of the ground. Finally, a ball attached to the stone handle pops out of the base of the memorial.

The ball is made of glass, with silver etching the sides and top. Bright orange liquid swirls inside it. It's the consistency of chocolate syrup, and it's giving off a radioactive glow.

"I found it." My voice is hushed with awe. I touch the glass with one finger, and pain shoots up my hand. I jerk back, hissing, and drop the object. It bounces on the soft grass and doesn't break. Well, the snake wasn't lying about knowing it when I see it. I poke it with the end of my cane. It rolls around, still glowing. I guess I'll have to smash it? But I can't let that orange stuff touch me. It'll probably melt my skin off.

I lean my shoulder against the memorial and raise the cane over my head. Here goes nothing. I bring the cane down with all my strength onto the glass.

Lightning snakes across the sky as the ball shatters underneath my cane. A pressure surges through the park, popping my ears and making my throat burn. The orange liquid oozes into the grass and evaporates before my eyes. No trace of it left. For a split second, it's quiet, deathly quiet, and then thunder crashes overhead, and rain pours down from the sky.

I grin at the shattered ball, warm rain soaking my head and shoulders, and pick up my cane.

Time to see the snake.

13

I stand at the edge of the forest, suddenly nervous. I have to tell the snake that I broke the first barrier, but what happens after I do? I don't know where the other three are. My right hand still aches from touching the glass, and my leg throbs with pain. Maybe I should go home.

Well, I would if I had one.

My grip tightens on the cane, and I step into Red Wood.

I don't bother to turn on my phone's flashlight. I can see every leaf on the trees, every sleeping squirrel and still owl. I step carefully, deliberately, over debris and roots. I won't have to go far. He'll come to me.

Sure enough, the sounds of the forest fade until there's oppressive, unearthly silence. I stop walking. One heartbeat, two. Then a shadow materializes before my eyes, stretching higher and higher until it reaches the top of the tree line. I smile up at the snake.

"Hey."

"Hello, Latavia." The snake lowers his head until he's level with my face. "You have done well."

I raise my eyebrows. "How'd you know I destroyed the barrier?"

"I felt it." The snake opens his mouth, revealing his fangs. "And I feel a bit stronger."

"Oh, well, good for you." I hesitate, shuffling my feet. "I found out some good info. There are four barriers in all. Well, three now."

"Ah, good work, Latavia. Three does not seem like an insurmountable challenge."

I nod, but I can't think of anything else to say. I'm trying really, really hard not to think about Mom and Auntie. At least a giant talking snake is a good distraction.

The snake moves, bringing his body closer to me. His head is still. "Is something wrong? You seem upset."

I look away, prickles of annoyance running down the back of my neck. Perceptive snake, isn't he? "No. Well, yeah, but it's personal. Nothing to do with barriers or anything."

The snake is silent for a moment. "Very well. If this doesn't affect our business, then I won't pry."

"Good." I shift my weight off my hurt leg, wincing. "What's in those things, anyway? It was, like, some sort of orange liquid. Burned the hell out of me when I touched it."

The snake closes his mouth. "I see."

"See what?" I ask, but he doesn't answer. "Uh, hello?"

"I'm listening," the snake says. He curls his body around me in a loose circle.

"So you're not gonna answer my question?"

"No."

I heave a sigh. Who knew giant snakes were so cagey?

"But now we must test a theory." The snake flicks his tongue out and curls tighter around me. "I think I'll be able to accompany you into the town now."

"You're gonna go like this? As huge as you are? You'll scare the shit out of everyone."

"I'll be invisible, of course." The snake unwinds himself and gently nudges my back with his nose. "Come, Latavia. Let's go."

I limp back the way I came, a little uneasy. Why does he want to come with me? I don't want to face the six alone, but I'm also not crazy about having this hulking giant follow my every move.

When we get to the tree line, he stops.

"What's wrong?" I ask, slowing.

He looks at the ground, rattling his tail slightly. "I should be able to do it, but there will be a price."

"What kind of price?"

No answer. Just more rattling. Is he . . . nervous? I get an unexpected surge of sympathy.

"Come on," I call. "Do it quick. Like ripping off a Band-Aid."

"I don't know what that is, but it sounds unpleasant." The snake looks at me for a split second, then disappears completely. I wait two seconds, five. He doesn't reappear.

"Well? How'd it go?"

No answer. I shift my weight, trying to ease the ominous throbbing in my leg. What happened? Did it kill him?

"I'm here," the snake calls, his voice much quieter than normal. "It's as I expected. I can now enter the town, but with the other three barriers still in place, I am significantly weakened."

"How bad is it?"

"Look down."

I do, and I burst out laughing. The snake is small, as long as my arm but no thicker than two of my thumbs.

He shakes his tiny rattle at me. "Enough of your ridicule. At least I'll be able to help you find the other barriers. Even in my weakened state, my senses are better than yours."

"Sure, tiny." I hold back another laugh and bend over, keeping my bad leg as straight as I can. I offer my hand to him. "Climb on. I'll have to carry you."

The snake hesitates, but climbs into my hand. His scales are smooth and cool against my skin. He slithers up my arm and circles around my shoulders, like the world's worst scarf. His head settles by my right ear.

"I don't like depending on a human," he says, his voice hissing in my ear.

"Well, I'm not too crazy about a snake on my shoulder, but here we are." I straighten, grunting with difficulty. "Let's go home. We can start searching for the other three tomorrow."

"Where is home?" The snake's tongue flits against my ear. I resist the urge to gag or rip him from my shoulders and run away screaming.

"My friend's house. I'm crashing on her couch. And look, you gotta be cool. I'm sure she hates snakes."

"I'll be invisible, don't worry. Only you will be able to hear and see me."

"Okay, good. And you can't hurt her. Or my cousin Jade. No eating my friends, or the deal's off."

"Fine, Latavia." The snake hisses, a hint of irritation in his tone. "I know they are useful to us."

Good. I suck in the heavy, humid air as I limp toward Allison's apartment. I'm starting to shiver from my wet clothes. The anger is gone, and that cold, hollow feeling is back. Six people, and this will all be over. And then maybe I can get my leg fixed.

The snake shifts on my shoulders, tasting the air. He climbs up my neck and around my bun, his head swiveling back and forth. "I haven't seen a human settlement in quite some time. Things have changed."

"Yeah. You'll die when you hear about the internet."

The snake says nothing, still glancing around. How long has he been in those woods? Two hundred years at least, but how long before that? An ancient beast, sleeping for years and years, only to return in the twenty-first century for revenge. It's almost like a fairy tale. A really dark one considering our deal, but still.

I'm almost at Allison's apartment when the snake lets out a sharp hiss in my ear. "Turn around, Latavia."

I freeze and look over my shoulder, heart hammering. At first I don't see anything, but then I catch a flash of red hair hiding behind a large oak tree. She peeks out at me, her eyes wide.

It's Delilah. Mrs. Brim's kid.

"Should I kill it?" the snake murmurs. His tail rattles next to my ear.

"No! She's a kid."

"We should move in silence if we mean to destroy the barriers. That means no witnesses."

I bite my bottom lip. What's a kid doing out in the aftermath of a thunderstorm anyway? And where's Mrs. Brim? Isn't all of Sanctum scared of leaving the house after dark? I can't let him kill a kid, so I need to think fast. An idea forms in my head. She's only six—this might work.

"Let me handle it. I have a plan," I tell the snake. When he doesn't answer, I limp to Delilah's side, smiling. She looks up at me with huge eyes. "Hi, Delilah. Do you remember me?"

"Yes," she says, her voice hushed. "You're dead."

Not what I was expecting, but I'll take it. "You're right. I'm a ghost."

"Oh wow," Delilah says, and I notice for the first time that she's in pink pajamas, and holding a stuffed rabbit in one arm. She and the rabbit are soaking wet. "I've never met a ghost before."

"Well, I had to come back. Wanna know why?" She nods, and I lean down to whisper into her ear. "I have to punish the bad people who killed me."

When I pull back, Delilah doesn't look scared, like I hoped. She's watching me with wonder, her eyes huge. "Are you punishing all bad guys? Or just the really bad ones who killed you?"

I hesitate. This isn't going well. I wanted to scare her

111

into telling no one she saw me, but I didn't expect this. Who does a six-year-old want to punish, anyway? I think of Mrs. Brim's hurt wrist, and my stomach sinks. I take Delilah's cold hands in mine, wishing I could help her. "I have to finish with mine first. If you're good and don't tell anyone you saw me, maybe I can help you."

Delilah smiles at me. "Okay, I won't tell anyone. Thanks, Latavia! I hope you get all the bad guys."

"Yeah, me too." I pat her head and straighten. "Now why don't you go home? It's not safe out here with all the bad guys running around."

"Okay," Delilah says happily. She waves at me and skips two houses down, and disappears into the back door of a brick house. I watch the house for a few seconds, but she doesn't come out again.

"Good job," the snake says. His tone is impressed. "You are quite good at manipulation."

"She's just a kid. It's not that hard." But I'm not thinking about whether or not Delilah will tell anyone. I'm thinking about her running out of the house in a rainstorm. I'm thinking about Mrs. Brim's sore wrist.

I'm thinking I wish Deacon Brim were one of the six on my list.

The snake and I don't speak again as I limp the rest of the way to Allison's apartment. I climb the steps, one after another, groaning as the effort strains my good leg. I raise my fist to knock on her door, but tightness grips my chest and freezes my hand.

"What's wrong?" the snake asks. He's curled around my frizzy bun like a scrunchie.

112

I swallow the lump in my throat. "Nothing. Now be quiet, we're here." I force my fist to rap on the door.

I only have to wait a few seconds. I hear footsteps, and then Allison jerks open the door. The snake suddenly stiffens, constricting around my bun like Allison surprised him. I guess her sudden appearance scared him. He's got a lot to get used to after his hermit-in-the-woods lifestyle.

I give Allison a wobbly smile, ignoring the snake in my hair.

"H-hey." I fidget awkwardly, finding it hard to look into her watery eyes. "Sorry I ran off like that. Not cool."

"It's okay. I was just worried!" Allison hesitates. "And God, you're soaking wet. Where'd you go? It's been, like, an hour."

Yeah, it takes time to destroy a barrier and convince a kid I'm a ghost. I smile at Allison, trying to put on my most convincing I'm-definitely-okay face. "I went to the park. Got some bad news, needed some time to clear my head. The cane works great, by the way."

"What bad news?" Allison asks tentatively.

I stare at her, smile frozen on my face. I really don't want to think about Mom. I just want to crash and forget about her, and Auntie, for one night.

Allison takes the hint. She steps back and motions me inside. "Never mind, come in. Do you wanna change clothes? You're probably freezing."

I step into the apartment and close the door behind me. Thank God for Allison's perceptiveness. Jade would have grilled me until I cracked. "Yeah, thanks."

Allison searches my face, uncertainty on hers. "Do

you want some tea or anything after you change? We can watch a movie, maybe?"

My heart does a pathetic flip at the thought of watching a movie in the dark with her, but I shake my head. I don't want the snake intruding on our definitely-not-a-date. "No, I'm exhausted. I'll take a shower and sleep, if that's okay."

"Yeah, sure." We stand in the middle of the room, silent, me firmly looking at my feet. "Avie? You sure you're okay?"

I take a deep breath and meet her eyes, trying not to think about the monster coiled in my hair. I give her my best smile. "I'm just fine."

14

Hands. Hands all over me, barking, a dog's panting and running at me, teeth white and bared, and I'm screaming, begging for help, and Auntie is just standing over me with dead eyes, and the snake hisses in my ear, and John raises his bat to break my leg, eyes glinting with hatred in the dark—

"Avie? Are you okay?"

I blink rapidly, my breathing short and hard. It's dark—where am I?

"Avie?" Allison's voice is close to my ear. I'm in Allison's apartment. It's dark. Middle of the night.

"You're screaming again, Latavia," the snake's voice murmurs. I blink and he comes into focus, his tiny body curled into a knot in the middle of my chest. Well, that's great to wake up to. From one nightmare to another.

"I'm okay." It takes me a few seconds to realize I'm talking to them both. I take a deep breath, trying to calm down. I deliberately look away from the snake and up at Allison instead. "Sorry. Did I wake you up?"

Allison shakes her head. I can see her face perfectly in the dark; hair flattened on one side, eyebrows pulled together with worry. "I was already awake. I heard you . . ."

"Screaming?" I laugh, but it's humorless. This sucks. Everything about this sucks. I'm so exhausted, and my throat is raw, and the snake just keeps looking at me. "Sorry, I'm fine," I tell her. "You can go back to sleep."

Allison hesitates for a long moment. "Actually, can I stay up with you for a while? It's almost five, so there's no point in going back to bed."

I blink in surprise, some of the frustration disappearing. "Oh, um, sure. Let me sit up—"

"No, don't move! You'll hurt your knee! Hang on." Allison hurries to her room and returns with a pillow. She places it on the floor next to me and lies down, her face turned up to the ceiling. Peach immediately pounces on Allison to lick her face, but after Allison laughs and tells her to go back to sleep, she returns to her dog bed beside the couch. I struggle to roll to my side, my knee throbbing ominously under the pink-and-purple blanket I'm borrowing. The snake topples from my chest to the couch, and he hisses irritably at me. He climbs to my shoulder instead.

The apartment is silent. Allison stares at the ceiling like she's lost in thought, her hands folded over her stomach. I watch her for a second, a funny feeling in my chest. Why does she want to stay with me? Is it because she feels sorry for me? My breathing is calmer now, almost back to normal, but the police dog's barks ring faintly in my ears. I pull the blanket to my chin. Pity or not, I'm glad she's here.

"Are you comfortable?" I ask.

She smiles up at me. "No."

I smile back, even though I know she can't see me. Thank you, snake venom. "You don't have to do this, Allison."

"I know, but I want to. I couldn't sleep, anyway." Allison clears her throat. "I thought we could talk until you got tired."

"About what?"

"Whatever you want."

Her head is right under my arm. On a whim, I reach out and move her bangs out of her eyes. "Let's talk about how you need a haircut."

She grins, a slight blush creeping into her cheeks. "I like my hair long!"

"Okay, but there are limits to this. You're about to achieve sheepdog status. You won't be able to see."

Allison laughs, a warm, light one. "I'll just wear it over one eye."

"Oh, I love it. Very edgy."

There's a small, pleasant lull in our conversation. Her bangs have already flopped back over her eyes. It takes everything in me not to move them again.

"Are you sleepy?" she asks.

I sigh. "Not even close."

"That's okay. Can I ask you something?"

"Sure. We've got nothing but time."

"What are you going to major in? When you go to UGA, I mean."

Sadness fills my chest. That dream is dead and gone. I'm pretty sure if the snake venom can't heal my knee, modern medicine isn't going to do the trick in a few weeks. And even if I could wait, if the stars aligned and UGA said, *Sure, take your time, we'll save all that money for you*, who would pay for my surgery? Who can I even trust enough to take me to a doctor? Not Auntie. Not Mom, that's for sure.

Allison is still waiting for my answer, so I try to push the depressing thoughts out of my mind. "I didn't have anything planned. I was just gonna wing it."

Allison's brow furrows. "Really?"

"Yeah. Everyone takes the same basics for a while. So I thought I'd have time to figure it out."

"Avie, that's nuts! What do you want to do? Like for a career?"

I wanted to run. I wanted to go to college and meet new people and go to parties and figure it out as I went. "It doesn't matter anyway. My knee is fucked." I close my eyes. "My scholarship is for track, and my grades aren't really good enough without it. I probably won't ever run again."

Allison is quiet, and I can't bear to look at the pity I know is on her face.

"Avie—"

"What about you?" I say quickly. "I know you still have a year left of high school, but what'll you major in when you go?"

Allison hesitates, but eventually says, "I wanted to major in chemistry."

"Wow, what a nerd," I tease. I open my eyes to find her grinning at the ceiling.

"I know, I know. But I thought it would be cool. I love science and math."

"Wow, mega nerd."

"We can't all be amazing runners with cool hair," Allison teases.

Allison thinks my hair is cool? I smile in the dark, glad she can't see me. "You and Jade are so much alike, you know? She's a huge nerd too." I laugh to myself, feeling a little sleepy now. "Did she tell you she wanted to be an accountant? What fifteen-year-old wants to do math for the rest of their life?"

"That would be a cool job," Allison says.

I roll my eyes, grinning. I don't think I've ever made above a C on a math test.

"I see why you two are friends." I yawn, sleepiness tugging at my eyelids. "You know, Auntie wants her to be a doctor. And Jade's definitely smart enough, but she hates blood, and her bedside manner sucks. But every Christmas it's 'Have you thought about med school?' or 'I can set you up with an internship.' Poor kid just sits there and takes it."

Allison is quiet for a second. Maybe she's sleepy too? "You and Jade are close."

I think about all the holidays, the fighting over my toys when we were little, the way she was so disinterested in me nervously coming out to her that she didn't even look

119

up from the game on her phone. She's too uptight, but she was my first friend and I'd kill for her. "Yeah. She's my dumb baby cousin, but she's pretty cool. Don't tell her I said that, though. She'll never let me live it down."

Allison laughs, and I do too, yawning at the end of it. "Are you tired?" she asks.

"A little." My thoughts wander to the nightmare, and I shudder. I can still picture Auntie standing there, silent, her eyes cold and emotionless. I'm not looking forward to seeing that again. "But we can talk some more."

"Okay. You pick."

I think back on our conversation. "I didn't ask you what you wanted to do with your chemistry degree. Are you going to be a professor?"

"I'm not smart enough for that," Allison says, laughing. "I thought I could go to community college first, and then I could transfer. And I'd be a high school teacher, because I don't like little kids."

I start to laugh at her kid-hating statement, but I pause. She said she "wanted" to be a chemistry teacher. Past tense. "Do you want to do something else now?"

"What?" Allison frowns. "No, that's what I wanted."

Wanted. Again. "Um . . . you keep saying you 'wanted' to be a teacher. But what about now?"

Allison gets very still. She stares at the ceiling for a second, shock and unease on her face. Then she clears her throat and says, "I decided I couldn't afford it. So I'll, uh, find a job around here."

Unease fills me too. Something tells me she's lying. But why would she lie about what she wants to go to school

120

for? Maybe she's embarrassed about it. Maybe I teased her too much. I frown down at her, my hand skimming her arm.

"Hey, don't worry about it," I say, my voice soft. "We'll get you some money. I'll rob a bank."

Allison laughs, a quiet, somber one. "Thanks. I appreciate it."

We sit in silence for a long time, and exhaustion pulls my eyelids closed. But it takes me a while to go to sleep, because I can't get the sound of Allison's quiet resignation out of my head.

Someone knocks on Allison's door.

I sit straight up, heart hammering, clutching my borrowed blanket to my chest. I'd been dozing, listening to Allison hum a song as she cleaned the kitchen, but now panic grips my heart, my lungs. My legs burn to run, even as my knee throbs fiercely.

"Who is it?" Allison calls, rounding the couch. Unlike me, she's not panicking. How is she not panicking? It could be any of the six—

"Jade Roberts, at your service," Jade's muffled voice answers through the door.

Oh. My heart rate slows and I take a quick, shallow breath. Allison frowns at me.

"You okay?"

"Yeah," I say quickly. "Let her in."

Allison looks like she wants to say more, but she goes to the door and opens it instead.

Jade waves to me as she walks in. She looks exhausted, her curly hair lazily pulled into a bun and sweat staining her shirt. "It's hot as hell. I hate walking here."

"Hello to you too," Allison says, a small smile on her lips. She closes and locks the door behind Jade, and my heart rate slows even more.

"Learn to drive, and you won't have to walk," I tease. Jade hates driving, even though Auntie's tried to teach her several times. I've been trying to convince her to let me teach her all summer, but so far, no luck.

Jade flips me off and collapses into Allison's armchair. "Let's talk about you. Did you have fun vandalizing my house last night?"

I grin at her. I honestly forgot, with Delilah, and the snake hanging out around my neck, but now I'm imagining Auntie's face twisted in horror. "How'd she like it?"

"What're y'all talking about?" Allison sits next to me on the couch, but not close enough to touch.

Jade glares at me. "Your friend spray-painted 'traitor' on my front door."

Allison frowns at me, and I can't help but laugh. "Look, I needed to blow off some steam. How'd she take it?"

"Well . . . it was kind of weird. She stared at it for a long time, and then she went to her room." Jade hesitates, not looking at me. "I think I heard her crying."

My smile slips and I reach for my neck, where the snake rests. His cool scales slide over my fingertips. That's not the reaction I wanted at all. I thought she'd be scared, or at least beg for forgiveness or something. But she cried?

In fear, maybe? I've never seen Auntie afraid of anything, except for Pastor Thomas.

"Anyway," Jade says after an uncomfortable silence, "I came to see what our snake plan is. Did you do any brainstorming last night?"

"I just went to sleep," I say, shrugging off my discomfort about Auntie's reaction. Jade doesn't need to know about the nightmares.

"I've been thinking. A little." Allison crosses her arms, frowning at the ceiling. "The monster rejected Avie as a sacrifice, right? But it didn't ask for another one. What's it planning on doing now?"

"And who will it eat instead?" Jade asks.

The snake laughs softly in my ear. "Curious, these humans."

Allison picks absently at a strand of her hair. "Maybe it'll target the guardians."

"Excuse me, the what?" I ask. "You didn't mention anything about 'guardians' before."

Allison flinches. "Shit, I didn't mean to say that. I'm really not supposed to be telling y'all this. . . ."

I frown at Allison. She's really resistant to telling us about this snake stuff. She showed us the notebook, but she only showed me the knife, not Jade, and now there's this. It's like it's physically painful for her to tell the truth. I guess if you guard a secret for so long, it's hard to give it up. "Too late now. Go on."

Allison sighs but continues. "Okay, so there are only a few people who know about the monster. Currently there are seven, including me. Pastor Thomas calls us the guardians because we help protect the town from the monster."

"Who are they? Besides you?" I already know the answer, but I want to hear it from her.

Allison looks away. "I'm not allowed to say."

"Are they the people who tried to kill me?" I press. "You owe me this much, at least."

Allison bites her bottom lip. I can practically see her resisting, then caving. "Okay, yeah, it's them. They're the only ones who know about the snake situation."

"This is crazy. Straight up madness." Jade massages her temples. "How the hell did my mom, of all people, get mixed up in this? She can't sleep if she doesn't brush her teeth before bed."

"It's based on family lines. Your grandma knew too." Allison points at my cane resting against the couch. "That cane has snakes all over it. I don't think that's a random design choice."

"Yeah, it is pretty cool," Jade admits. "I think it's made out of real silver."

I glance at the cane, and the snake stiffens around my neck. Why's he so nervous all of a sudden? He's seen the cane before. I take a closer look at it, frowning. There's been a lot of talk about silver lately. The barrier I broke had silver etched into the glass, and now the cane. Auntie and the other cult members had silver on their robes. And wait, didn't the snake say something about me eating silver? No, he said some silver must have entered my bloodstream through an open wound. Maybe the snake is nervous because silver is one of his weaknesses. A big one, if his reaction is to be believed. I try to keep my face a mask of cool, but I keep glancing at the cane out of the corner of my eye.

"Anyway," Allison continues, "when I turned sixteen, Mom dumped the entire truth on me, not just parts of it, and ran off to who knows where. And now I can't leave town until all this is over. Or until I have a kid to pass the legacy on to." Allison turns to Jade. "It's that way with you too. Dr. Roberts was probably getting ready to tell you. You turn sixteen in two months."

Jade meets my eyes, hers flat. "Happy birthday to me."

"So why weren't you there?" I ask Allison. "At the sacrifice, I mean."

Allison blinks at me, seemingly dumbfounded. "I . . . don't know. Pastor Thomas said I can't go to sacrifices. And I mean, I'm glad because it's horrible, but maybe if I'd been there, I could have stopped them. . . ."

"No, it's okay," I assure her. I'm glad she wasn't there, because then my list would have been seven instead of six. My stomach sours at the thought of having to hurt Allison in any way. "I was just curious."

"So, ignoring the bummer of inheriting the worst job in the world, what's our plan against our Giant Snake friend?" Jade asks. She leans back, her head hanging off the arm of the chair. "Any miraculous ideas?"

"We still have the barriers," Allison says. "That should keep it out of town, at least until we can think of something better. And maybe if we make an announcement about how dangerous things are, no one will go into the woods."

"No one with any sense goes to the woods anyway," Jade says. "Except, you know, Fools One, Two, and Three." She points at me, Allison, and herself.

"I didn't want to go," I argue. "I was dragged there."

"Good point. But eventually we gotta go back and kill the snake, Avie." Jade heaves a sigh. "Either we go to it or it comes to us."

The snake wraps himself around my neck, tighter than before. I clear my throat, uncomfortable. "Yeah. I guess so."

"I'll have to talk to the rest of the guardians," Allison says, still fiddling with her hair. "But it can wait for a bit. I'll see Katie at work tomorrow. I have to open."

Interesting. If Katie is Allison's first choice to talk to, Katie might know something useful. She should be our first stop for information too.

"Let's think about something else for now." Allison grabs the remote from the coffee table and turns the TV on. "Let's hang out, forget about the monster. I think *Love It or List It* is on?"

"Sure," I say, struggling to my feet. "Be right back. Bathroom." I grab the cane on the way and hobble into the bathroom.

As soon as I shut the door, the snake crawls down my arm and perches himself on the sink. His black eyes glitter in the harsh light. "So you humans are threatening to kill me?"

"Those humans are, yes."

The snake's tail shakes, so rapid it's a blur, and he bares his fangs at me. "It seems I should cut some flowers before they bloom."

126

"Calm down. They're just talking about it. And I'm not helping them. We have a deal, remember?"

The snake glares up at me. "Yes, we do. And if you break it, you'll be on the receiving end of my wrath."

"Real threatening from something the size of a stick." Despite my rebuttal, anxiety crawls up my neck. I don't think an ancient monster knows how to bluff. Whatever he says, he means. And I have no intention of letting him or anyone else kill me. I survived certain death once. I'm not throwing that miracle away.

I take a deep breath, trying to stuff down the fear. "Anyway, did you hear what Allison said about Katie?"

"Yes," the snake says. "It appears we have someone to meet tonight."

"Yeah. So until then, be chill. Do not kill my friends or the deal's off."

The snake hisses at me, but says nothing more. He crawls back up my arm and settles around my neck. Okay, time to act normal. Don't think about confronting Katie, the first of the six. The first I'll see in person since they tried to kill me.

I flush the toilet and run my hands under the tap. My burn still stings, but it's healing faster than it has any right to. Wish I could say the same for my knee. I grab my cane and exit the bathroom, all smiles.

"I'm ready! Can we order pizza?"

15

"I think I'm going to bed," I say, trying to disguise the desperation in my voice. I'm supposed to see Katie at Telescoops, but I forgot they close at ten. If she's closing, she'll only be there until ten-thirty, max. If I miss her, I'll have to go to her house . . . and I have no clue where she lives. I need Allison to go to bed *now*.

"Already?" Allison looks up from her phone, frowning. "It's nine-thirty."

"Yeah, I know, but I don't really feel too good." Not a lie. I've felt like shit all day, even though it was fun arguing with Jade and Allison about what redesigned house looks better. I've been running a low-grade fever for hours.

"I'm kinda worried about you, Avie," she says. "I really think we should go to the hospital."

"I can't. Not while she's there."

Allison's expression softens. "I'm so sorry this happened to you. I know—well, not exactly, but I can relate to having someone you trust betray you. We can talk about it, if you want."

I would love to talk to Allison about Auntie, but not right now. Right now, I need to go meet Katie. "Maybe some other time. Hey, why don't we both go to bed? It was a hard day."

Allison blinks at me for a few seconds. "Actually, yeah. I'm kinda tired."

I try not to collapse with relief. "We can talk tomorrow, promise."

Allison nods. "Sure, anytime. Let me get my sleeping pills, and I'll be out of your hair." Allison goes to the kitchen and rummages through a drawer.

Sleeping pills? "Do you take melatonin?"

"No," Allison says, laughing. She holds up a translucent orange bottle. "Prescription. Melatonin stopped keeping the nightmares away a while back."

I don't know what to say. I hate that she has nightmares, but what's worse is that I don't know what they're from. Being drafted into a snake-hunting cult? The pressure and fear from keeping Sanctum safe? Or maybe whatever happened with her mother. She only told me a little, but it sounds bad. I want to say something to comfort her, but I don't even know how to help myself. I have nightmares every time I close my eyes now.

I watch Allison pop two pills into her mouth and down some tea. She places her mug in the sink. "Man, I'm really tired all of the sudden. I'll see you in the morning, Avie. Come wake me up if you feel bad, okay?"

"Okay," I say, and Allison goes to her room, yawning. She closes the door behind her with a soft click.

"Hmm," the snake says.

"What?"

"Nothing," he says after a moment. "Just observing. Is it time to leave now?"

"Not yet." That was part one. Now I have to steal Allison's keys to Telescoops.

I wait ten agonizing minutes before getting off the couch. Her keys are in her room. I know because after her shifts, at least before all this happened, she kicks off her shoes and collapses onto her bed for a few minutes. She throws her keys onto her desk. I creep to her room, leaning heavily against the wall. God, I hope those sleeping pills are fast-acting.

I ease open her door, moving a millimeter per minute. I hold my breath—Allison's breathing is deep and even. The lights are out, but thanks to the snake venom, I can see her perfectly. She's curled on her side, eyes closed. She has a pink plush sheep in her arms. God, she's so cute.

"Focus," the snake breathes into my ear.

Okay. Keys. I look at her desk, but I don't see them. I slip into the room, my heart racing. This feels so bad. I should not be in her room while she's sleeping. I feel like a burglar. The worst burglar in the world because I can't find what I'm looking for—

A glint of metal catches my attention on the floor, covered by a crumpled purple shirt. I move the shirt, and bingo—keys. Car keys, house keys, and Telescoops keys all on one very noisy ring. I pick up the keys by a koala key chain carefully, slowly. I straighten, my knee groaning in pain, and limp toward the door. Almost, almost—

"Avie?"

I freeze, halfway out of Allison's room. I look over my shoulder, too scared to breathe. But Allison's eyes are still closed, and she's still curled into a ball. She pulls the sheep closer and mumbles something else under her breath.

She's talking in her sleep.

I leave the room, weak with relief. I close her door and practically melt against the couch.

"Well done," the snake says. "Though I don't know why you were so afraid. I would have killed her if she'd awakened."

"Yeah, that doesn't make me feel better." I take a few deep breaths and straighten, holding Allison's keys up where the snake can see them. "Ready to talk to Katie about those barriers?"

"Of course." The snake migrates from my neck up to my bun.

I leave Allison's apartment, still shivering with adrenaline. But also, I'm filled with warmth because Allison thinks of me while she dreams. I hope I'm in a good dream and not a nightmare.

I limp toward downtown, regretting my decision with every step.

It's raining, a light, annoying mist that's just enough to

leave a gross, muggy sheen on my skin. My hair's gonna be a mess tomorrow. These are no conditions to interrogate someone in.

"Is your leg hurting?" the snake asks. He's hiding from the rain in my shirt, his head on my shoulder and his body looped loosely down my back. "You've slowed your pace considerably."

"Yeah, well, it doesn't feel great." I wince when I step on a piece of gravel and pain shoots up my leg.

"I don't know why the healing didn't work. It did for Don." The snake pauses while I huff and puff up the hill to get to Telescoops. "I need to see him, eventually. I have something special in store for him."

I bite my lip but say nothing. I forgot the snake is bad with time; he has no idea Don would be over two hundred years old at this point. He's gonna be so pissed when he finds out Don's dead. Hopefully not at me.

"That reminds me," the snake says. "Your friend. Not the sleeping one but the curious one."

"Jade? What about her?"

"Who is she to you?" The snake flicks his tongue out, one dark eye looking into mine. "You smell frighteningly alike."

"Oh, she's my cousin." I pause, turning his words over in my head. "Are you saying you can't tell us apart?"

"I didn't say that," the snake says, but there's a defensive edge to his voice. "I can see that you are different in height and build. But the scents are very similar. I was curious as to why, but I see it is because you share blood."

I don't say anything, considering his words. I guess I never thought about what a snake's sense of smell is like, but it makes sense two family members would smell alike to him. Can I use this to my advantage somehow? I turn over a few scenarios in my mind, but short of sacrificing Jade to save myself—which is not happening—I can't think of a way that this will help. I file it away in my mental survive-this folder anyway. Just in case.

Finally, Telescoops comes into view, and I slow, catching my breath. The snake pokes his head out of my shirt, flicking his tongue out over and over. "I don't sense a barrier nearby."

"No," I say, my eyes on a car with a license plate that says KTBUG. "But I'm sure someone knows where it is."

I go to the back door, where I met Allison for ice cream what feels like years ago, and slip the stolen key into the lock. The door eases open without a sound. Faint music and the sharp smell of cleaning solution hit me—Katie's still closing. Thank God we made it. And since there's only one car out front, we're sure to be alone.

The snake pokes his head farther out of my shirt, his tongue flicking in and out. I press my finger to my lips, and he settles around my neck, his head resting on my throat. I walk in time with the song Katie's listening to, the noise of my cane disguised by the heavy beat. I peek into the kitchen; Katie's cleaning the counter with a rag, her back to me, bobbing her head up and down. I can't stop a grin from creeping onto my face. Perfect.

I enter the kitchen, leaning on my cane, and wait.

"Let me see ya get low, you scared, you scared," Katie sings, aggressively scrubbing melted ice cream. "Drop it down to the floor, you—" She turns, just a little, then whirls around to face me and screams. The rag drops from her fingers.

My grin grows wider. "Scared?"

All the color leaves Katie's face. She backs away from me, her hands trembling. "You . . . you're supposed to be dead."

I shrug, laughing. "Well, I decided to come back. I said I would, remember?"

Katie retreats until her back's pressed into the metal counter. "You—you're not real. You're not real, you're a hallucination—"

I step closer, leaning heavily on the cane. "Do you want to find out?"

Katie lets out a pathetic whimper, and I can barely stop a laugh from escaping my lips. My insides twist and roll with savage pleasure. Is she a fraction of how scared I was? I hope she pisses herself.

The snake nudges my neck. "You can play with her once our business is finished," he breathes.

Fine. I limp to the counter opposite Katie and press pause on her phone. The room abruptly fills with silence. "Okay, Katie. I need some information, and you're gonna tell me everything I need to know. If I'm satisfied, then you won't suffer. Sound good?"

Katie glances from me to the phone. She eases farther away from me, toward the sink. I narrow my eyes; anything could be hiding in the sudsy water.

"Katie, don't make this hard on yourself. Did you think I came here alone?" I pull the snake from my shoulders. His scales are black now, fully visible. He hisses irritably, but it's drowned out by Katie's scream of terror. I give her my brightest smile. "My friend and I have decided this town needs some cleaning house. And you're gonna help."

The snake wraps around my wrist, then climbs down my body to the ground. He slithers toward Katie, and she whimpers again, shaking her head over and over.

"Please, please don't! I'll tell you whatever you need to know, just get that thing away from me!"

The snake keeps going, creeping closer and closer. I shrug at her. "Better start talking, then. Doesn't look like he wants to stop."

"I'm so sorry we chose you," Katie babbles, pressing herself against the counter to get away from the snake. "There was—there was no one else! There were no volunteers!"

"I don't care about that. Tell me about the barriers."

Katie blinks at me. "What? Why?"

The snake shakes his tail, slow, threatening. Katie shrieks and climbs on top of the counter.

"Sorry! Sorry, I—I don't know anything. The Abercrombies know about that stuff, I don't."

Allison's last name is Abercrombie. But she said she doesn't know where the barriers are. . . .

"Humans are liars," the snake says, hissing at her.

Katie opens and closes her mouth helplessly. "I swear I don't know anything! I just made the ice cream! But there's a book, a book they gave me to keep safe. It's really old, so maybe that has what you want?"

"Where?"

Katie points behind me. "In the office, in the safe. The code is three-two-one-one. You can have all the money in there too, if you want."

I roll my eyes. I'm not interested in money. I'm interested in how to destroy this godforsaken town from the inside out.

"Snake, can you handle this?"

The snake looks back at me and huffs. "I'm insulted by your insinuation. Go, check to see if this human lies like the rest."

I guess the snake thinks he's the boss here. I limp to the office and flip on the light. There are two desks pushed together in the corner, covered in a mess of paper and receipts. The safe rests on the ground . . . where I'll have to kneel to open it.

"Fuck," I mutter, rubbing my knee. It's swollen under the brace and throbbing dully. This is gonna hurt like hell.

Slowly, I bend my good knee, keeping the hurt one straight. So far, so good. Easy, easy . . . I lower myself as much as possible, then fall the rest of the way. A jolt of pain races up my leg, but not too bad. Thank God. I punch in the code, and the safe springs open. Money, a few keys, and an old leather-bound book, identical to the one at Allison's. Bingo.

I put the book on the table and drag myself upright with the cane and the desk. My knee bends, just a little, and hot pain surges through my body. I let out a small scream and grip the table, tears stinging my eyes.

"Latavia?" the snake calls. "Are you all right?"

I take a shaky breath before answering. "Fine. I got the book."

I grab the cane and the book, fighting tears. My knee throbs, each heartbeat sending stabs of pain up and down my leg. My whole right side is on fire. I grit my teeth and grasp the handle of my cane in a tight fist. I take quick, jagged breaths, but then slower ones to calm myself down. In through the nose, out through the mouth. Don't let her see how bad it hurts. How bad they hurt me.

When I round the corner, I'm all smiles.

The snake and Katie are right where I left them. Katie has her knees pulled up to her chest, her eyes big and terrified. She looks like an overgrown kid. The snake moves lazily beneath her feet, trapping her on the counter.

"Thank you for your cooperation, Katie." I hold up the book, smiling. "I'm glad you weren't lying."

The snake looks back at me, his head alert. "What does it say?"

"Haven't read it yet."

"Hmph." The snake looks up at Katie, extending his body up the cabinets under the counter. "Is this all you have for us?"

Katie nods frantically. "I swear, everything I know is in there. I just started this, man. I wasn't even supposed to be at the ceremony. My mom was sick and they needed me for some reason, I don't know." Katie runs a hand through her hair anxiously. She looks at me, really looks me in the eye. I'm surprised to see remorse in hers. "I'm so sorry, Latavia. I really am. I didn't want to do it, I swear I didn't. But Pastor Thomas told me I had to, or else."

Some of the rage cools. Katie's only a little older than me. Maybe two months from now, Auntie would have made Jade attend the rituals too. This whole town is fucked, and sounds like Pastor Thomas is at the core. I shift from foot to foot, uncomfortable. This was a lot more fun when I thought Katie was a cruel redneck who had it out for me.

"Is this all you have to say?" the snake asks. He looks bored, his small head resting on the copper handle of a cabinet.

"Y-yeah. I'm sorry." Katie looks at me, tears in her eyes. "Please, will you let me go? I won't tell anyone, I swear."

Even if she did, who would believe her? I bet I could convince her I was a ghost. It worked for Delilah. I sigh, my resolve crumbling. She's kind of a victim, like me. And it's not like she held me down like the men did. Wrong place, wrong time. I run my thumbnail over my cane, un-sure. Can I really let her go? I have to, don't I? It's the right thing to do.

"Katie, I guess—"

The snake moves, impossibly fast, and clamps his jaws around Katie's ankle. She shrieks, a shrill, anguished sound, and leaps off the counter. When her feet hit the ground, she collapses to her knees, then falls to her side. Her face turns white, then blue, and she claws at her neck,

138

her eyes wide and bloodshot, staring right into mine. Within seconds, she's still.

Within seconds, she's dead.

The snake coils calmly around Katie's head. He looks at me, his tail shaking slowly, lazily.

"Five more to go."

16

I stare at Katie's body, a strange buzzing in my ears. The snake cocks his head to one side and speaks, but I can't hear him. Katie's lifeless eyes stare up at me, wide and pained. She's looking right at me. The buzzing grows louder, louder. I was about to let her go.

I watched someone die before my eyes.

The snake nudges my ankle and, abruptly, the buzzing stops. I step back, stumbling into the counter. "What have you done?"

The snake looks up at me, blinking slowly. "I killed one of the people who attacked you. As per our agreement."

"But she—she was—she didn't mean—" Suddenly the room is too bright, the walls too close. "I need some air. It's hot in here. I need to go outside."

"You are panicking." It's a statement. His tone is bemused, like he's seen something funny but is holding back a laugh. "Don't tell me her speech moved you."

I look at Katie's body, at the thin line of foam at the edge of her mouth. "She said she didn't want to be there."

"And yet, she was." The snake crawls up my bad leg, moving slowly so he won't hurt me. The stubble on my legs rises as his scales pass over my skin. "Pleading for one's life is a human behavior. All humans beg in the end. Even her." The snake reaches my thigh and looks up at me, his black eyes glinting in the harsh light. "Even you."

My tongue is too big for my mouth. I try not to flinch as the snake climbs my body until he's on my shoulders again.

"Fear not, Latavia," the snake coos in my ear, his voice soft. "You are far more useful to me than her. As long as we have our agreement, you are safe."

I finally swallow the lump in my throat. "And what about after the deal is over?"

"Well." The snake loops his body around my arm, his head resting on my shoulder. "We must take things one day at a time, hmm?"

I grip my cane, my chest tight. I'm fucked. I am really fucked.

But I can't let him see me falter. In through the nose, out through the mouth. I nod and pick up the book. "Fine. Let me take pictures of this and we can go."

"Pictures?" The snake cocks his head to one side. "Can you not read?"

"I can read, I just don't like reading in front of a dead body." I take out my phone and snap pictures of every

141

page. I don't want Allison accidentally discovering a dead woman's book I shouldn't have. I have to work hard to steady my hands. The snake watches me, blinking slowly.

"Human language evolves so quickly," he says. "I can't understand these symbols. The last time I saw human language, it was different."

I pause. So he can't read? I file that away in my emergency live-through-this plan. I finish taking pictures and close the book. Katie is dead; it's too late to change that now. But I need to make sure they're slow about connecting me to this. The full moon is still six days away. I can't get caught yet. But then again . . . I glance at the snake out of the corner of my eye. He's dozing, his eyes closed in contentment. Can I really trust him? What happens when I stop being "useful"? Well, I guess I know. And I'm not going down to the snake. Not after this.

I put the book back into the safe, careful to arrange it exactly how I found it, and take one more look at Katie's body. Her lifeless eyes seem to follow me all the way to the door.

When we get outside, the snake raises his head. "Finished, Latavia?"

"Yeah." I close the back door and lock it again with my stolen keys. Like we were never here.

"Good." The snake slithers down my leg to the ground. "I have to leave you for a while."

I work hard to keep the relief off my face. I need a minute to cope. And plan how I'm getting out of this mess. "Where are you going?"

"I have to eat." The snake slides over my shoe. "Whatever

I eat in this small form will not satisfy me. I will gather strength for a moonrise and then return."

"Okay." I watch the snake slither away from me, toward Red Wood. "I'll keep looking for the barriers."

"I know," the snake says, amusement in his voice. He moves behind Telescoops and disappears from sight.

I walk back to Allison's in a daze. Katie is dead, and I will be too if I don't figure something out. My stomach rolls as I remember her empty eyes following me around the room. I was gonna let her go. I was, but the snake isn't interested in compromises. Or changes to the plan. I gave him six names, and those people are doomed whether I want that anymore or not. I think fleetingly of Auntie. I close my eyes, a headache pounding across my forehead, and try not to think about anything at all.

I open the picture app on my phone, holding my breath.

Allison is still fast asleep; I can hear her soft snoring from the couch. Still, it was agony to move slow and re-place the keys I'd stolen back on her desk. I also borrowed more of her clothes, and put the wet ones in the washing machine near the kitchen. I hope I can wash them after she goes to work. I hope she doesn't remember what pajamas she left me in tonight.

Now that I'm safely snuggled into the couch, I might as well read what the book Katie gave me says. It wasn't nearly as long as Allison's; there were maybe thirty hand-written pages, and then the rest were blank. I read the first page, but it's all confusing numbers and nonsensical notes. Someone doodled a cat in one corner of the page. The next five pages are like that too, but then the sixth page is a diary entry.

April 2, 2015

> *I'm the new bookkeeper. I wish they'd picked anyone else. Mom and Grandma Margaret go to the rituals, though, so this is the least I can do.*

Katie's handwriting, maybe? It's the classic pretty script I never learned how to do in middle school. I doubt an old man from the 1800s would write like this.

> *Mom says I have to do my part. I hate this. But I guess every town has its dirty laundry. Crime, drugs, and occasionally giant snakes.*

I feel a sad twinge in my gut. Katie was funny. Maybe we could have been friends. Maybe, if she hadn't tried to sacrifice me to said giant snake.

The next few entries are just Katie complaining about her bookkeeping job. She records every sacrifice's name, their age, any family, and pays for the person's name on the memorial. In 2017, Pastor Thomas wanted to get rid of the memorial to save the town money, but Katie and, surprisingly, Carter, pitched a fit and it stayed. This was a whole thing. A whole underground network of sacrifices, secrets, and year after year of murder.

I scroll to the last two pages. Katie's handwriting is

messier here, like she's in a hurry. In all caps in what looks like a letter, she's written *BURN AFTER READING*.

Bingo.

> *What the hell is happening in this town? Three sacrifices in six weeks?! And Mom said they killed Clementine because she struggled, and the monster is pissed about that. Pastor Thomas isn't saying anything. He just keeps saying everything will work out. How?! He's not doing anything. He's not protecting us.*

Huh. So Katie was getting scared, and looks like she trusted someone else was too, considering she wrote this note to someone. Trouble in Pastor Thomas's cult? I keep reading, my eyebrows raised.

> *I know we've been dosing the sacrifices right before they leave for the woods, but I think it's time to up the dosage. I don't know how much it takes to kill it, but this isn't moving fast enough. Pastor Thomas doesn't have to know. But if we can kill the monster quickly, we won't give it a chance to kill us all. This is an emergency, and Pastor Thomas and John aren't doing shit to help us. What do you think?*

The letter ends abruptly. What the hell—dosing sacrifices? With what? I swipe to the next picture, but this is the last one. I scroll back to the beginning and stare at

the numbers beside the sacrifices' names. *78–100 mg slv.*
Wait a minute. Sacrifice number seventy-eight. A hundred mg—milligrams? And "slv" . . . Could it be silver?

My head spins with new information. This all but confirms my suspicions about silver—it's gotta be toxic to him. They've been poisoning the snake, according to the date of the first entry, for almost eighty years. Katie said she was upping the dosage on sacrifices, but I never even saw any silver. Was it because I was a last-minute replacement? Wait—

My hand flies to my mouth as things click into place. The snake asking me if I'd eaten silver. My leg not healing. Slowly, my hand shaking, I Google what silver tastes like.

*Silver is a soft metal that has a brilliant, white luster. . . .
Silver has a sweet and sour taste.*

The ice cream Allison had me try had a strange, sour taste.

I close my eyes and turn my phone off.

I was the next sacrifice, and Allison made sure I ate silver.

17

I pet Peach's head and listen to Allison make tea.

It's early, too early for us to be awake, but I didn't sleep and Allison has work soon. My hands curl into Peach's soft fur. How much did Allison know? She says she was trying to help me escape, but she fed me that ice cream anyway. Were she and Katie working together?

"Sorry I woke you up," Allison calls from the kitchen. "Do you want something to eat before I go?"

"No, I'm okay." I meet Peach's eyes. She licks my chin and whines, placing her giant head over my heart. The knot in the middle of my chest aches. "Hey, can I ask you something?"

"Sure!" Allison comes to my side, holding two steaming mugs. She places one with a fox decal in front of me, but I don't move to grab it. I don't know what she's put in it.

"So . . ." I trail off as Allison straightens her uniform. "Do you remember the ice cream you gave me? Before all this happened?"

147

Allison nods, her eyes bright. "Coffee flavor, Katie said. She made it herself. Why?"

Katie made it, huh? I search Allison's face for lies, but she's looking at me curiously, waiting for me to elaborate.

"Well, I was wondering if you could bring some back for me. After work."

Allison surprises me by scrunching her nose. "You liked that? It was kind of awful. It had a weird, like, sour taste to it."

I study Allison's face, but she seems genuine. She ate it too, knowing she couldn't possibly be a sacrifice. So maybe Katie didn't tell her. But then who was the *BURN AFTER READING* note for?

"Sorry for making you try it," Allison continues. She flicks her bangs out of her eyes. "Katie makes me pay for the ice cream I eat, but she told me I could have the one in the freezer for free because it was a prototype. Sorry I'm so cheap."

Allison laughs, and all the fear and distrust melt away. She couldn't have known. She never saw the message Katie wrote.

"But I'll bring you some, if you want," Allison says, standing to go. "You can have the whole tub, because I sure as hell don't want it."

I watch her grab her keys, anxiety quickening my heart rate when I realize she'll be the first one to see Katie's body. I don't want her to see what I saw. I don't want her to see what I've done.

"Wait," I say, before I can really think about it. "Don't go."

Allison blinks at me for a second, like I've shocked her.

Then her expression softens. "You haven't been sleeping well."

I clear my throat, my stomach fluttering and nervous. "No, not really."

"I figured. Here, hold on."

I watch Allison drag her armchair next to the couch and grab her phone from her pocket. She puts it to her ear, and after a few distant rings, she says, "Katie, I'm not feeling well. I'm staying home today. Sorry!" She gives me a grin after she hangs up. "I don't mind staying home. Hate that job anyway."

I try to smile back, but all I can think is that Katie will never get that message.

Allison sits down and pats the couch. "Come on, lie down. It's okay."

Heat climbs my neck—is she going to sit with me again? "Allison, you don't have to. I'm okay."

Allison raises one eyebrow, an easygoing grin on her face. "Yeah, right. You've barely slept since you got back. It might be easier for you to sleep if someone's with you."

I lie down, but a miserable jitteriness swirls in my belly. I hate making Allison stay home for me, but I also don't want to be alone. I reach for my neck, but the snake's scales aren't there. I close my burning eyes.

We don't speak for several minutes. I'm aware of Allison's presence beside me, her breathing, the soft tap of her nails on her phone. Close enough to touch me, if she wanted. If I wanted. My eyes pop open, my breathing a bit shallow. There's no way I'm going to sleep.

"Can't sleep still?" Allison asks.

I take a shaky breath. "Yeah. Sorry."

"Can I check your temperature?" I nod, happy she remembered to ask me before reaching over and scaring me. Her hand touches my forehead, cool and gentle. I still flinch, but only a little. I look up at her as she pulls her hand away. She's frowning. "Avie, you're still warm. Do you think your knee is infected?"

No, it's not my knee. It's because I ate silver and the snake's venom is freaking out. Just my luck. "I feel okay. I'm just tired."

Allison is quiet for a minute. Then, "Do you have flash-backs?"

I glance at her out of the corner of my eye. She's not looking at me; she's staring at the wall, one hand strok-ing Peach's back absently. Her expression is faraway, like she's thinking. Thinking about something other than my knee.

"I have nightmares."

Allison sighs, a small, defeated sound. "It's not fair. It's not fair what they've done."

She's quiet, petting Peach, but I keep waiting for more. It sounds like she's leaving something out. She doesn't speak for several minutes, so I ask, "What did they do to you?"

Allison meets my eyes, hers watery and sad, and I'm struck with the feeling I have no idea what this town has done to protect their secret. I'm not the only victim here.

There's a noise from downstairs—footsteps? Jade?

"Abercrombie, you still here?" a male voice calls.

Not Jade.

Allison and I stare at each other in silent terror for half a second, and then we're moving. Me grabbing my cane, Allison swearing softly and helping me stagger into her room.

"My stuff," I hiss, pointing at my bag, clothes, and the extra coffee mug. Allison groans and lugs my duffel bag into her room, and shoves the rest of my stuff under the blanket I was using on the couch.

"Abercrombie?"

"In a minute! I'm getting dressed!" Allison stares into my eyes, her expression serious, her face pale. "Not a word, Avie. Promise."

I nod, my heart hammering my ribs, and Allison closes the door in my face.

I immediately limp to the door. It's slightly ajar, a tiny sliver of her living room showing. I lean against the wall and hold my breath as she opens the front door.

Peach barks as two men shuffle into Allison's apartment. The breath I was holding leaves my lungs in an angry hiss.

John and Carter.

"Can't you shut that damn mutt up?" John yells over Peach's barking.

"Shh, shh," Allison says, petting Peach's head. Peach quiets, but doesn't take her eyes off the two men.

My hands won't stop shaking. Two of them are here, right here, and of course the snake isn't anywhere to be seen. Figures.

"What do you want? I have to go to work." Allison's trying to sound annoyed, but even I can hear the tremble in her voice. She's scared.

My grip tightens around the cane.

"Good we caught you, then," Carter grunts. "You ain't going to work for a while. Katie's dead."

Allison's face twists with shock and horror. Good thing she can't see *my* face. This is better than her finding the body, but not by much.

"How?" she finally manages. "I talked to her yesterday—"

"Snakebite," John says.

A heavy silence fills the apartment. Allison, Carter, and John stare at each other, horror on their faces. They'd feel even worse if they knew I made it happen.

"This is bad," Allison whispers. She's so pale, I'm scared she'll pass out.

"Yeah, no shit," Carter spits. "We got a real problem on our hands. The barriers ain't working no more. It's here. In the town."

"We don't know that for sure," John argues. "Could be a regular snake that got her."

"Yeah, and I fell off the turnip truck yesterday," Carter growls. "You think it's a coincidence we break the rules and then one of us comes up dead?"

John doesn't answer, anger and anxiety twisting his ugly features.

Carter scrubs his face with his hands. "We were so close. So fucking close, and everything had to fall apart right before the full moon."

The full moon again. What exactly is happening then? I know the snake won't tell me, but I have to ask Allison after the men leave.

"Now is not the time to doubt," John tells Carter. "It's always harder at the end. God rewards the patient and the faithful."

"Yeah, with dropping dead," Carter mutters. John shoots him a glare that is so poisonous, I'm scared Carter really will drop dead.

"*Anyway,*" Allison says, picking at her hair and twirling a strand around her finger anxiously. "Assuming it is the monster, what can we do to protect everyone?" Her hands are trembling. I want to hold them, to tell her she'll be safe from the snake because she's not on the list. "A stricter curfew?"

"We'll have to do the silver charms too," John says. His voice is soft and full of dread.

"You really think a few silver coins and necklaces are gonna stop it?" Carter's voice is high-pitched, scared. "No, we need to start taking serious measures. We need to talk to each other, team up against this thing."

Team up? Aren't they already the guardians or whatever? But Allison and John seem troubled, dark expressions on their faces.

"Pastor Thomas said that's not a good idea," Allison says slowly, not really looking at Carter.

"Pastor Thomas says a lot of things," Carter growls. "Don't y'all think it's strange? We can't talk to nobody about this, keeping secrets in old notebooks like we're in cowboy days or somethin'? And now we have a real threat; the monster is in town, and Pastor Thomas hasn't said a word. Twiddling his thumbs in his stupid office."

Oh, so this is what Katie's note meant. Based on how Carter's acting, I bet her note was for him. I study Carter's face, which is inching closer to beet red by the second. I wonder if Pastor Thomas knows his iron grip around his cult members is loosening.

And Carter has a notebook too? Do all the guardians have one? Now, that's interesting.

"Hey, now." John's voice carries a slight warning. "You better think about what you say about our Pastor."

"Right," Allison says, her voice strong and steady. Determined. "Pastor Thomas is protecting us. He wouldn't have rules in place if they didn't protect us."

How can Allison still trust that slimy guy? After knowing what he did to me? The hairs on my arms prickle with unease. I didn't know that this is how Allison feels. I didn't realize that Pastor Thomas had his hooks so deep into her.

Carter looks like he shares my sentiment. He looks mad enough to punch a hole in a wall. "Are y'all actually stupid? We're in the shit here. We fucked up with the Black kid. The monster saw right through us."

All my charitable feelings toward Carter dry up in an instant. Oh, so I'm just "the Black kid"? He can't even say my name? I bet he'll say it when I crush his teeth beneath my shoe. I bet he'll say it when I make him beg for his life.

"That's your fault. I told y'all not to pick her," Allison says, glaring at them. "I told you, and look what happened."

My breath freezes in my chest. They continue to talk, but I can't hear them too well. Allison told them not to pick me? But then that means she knew. She knew they wanted to pick me, and she didn't say anything about it. We ate ice cream together earlier that day, and she didn't say a word.

"We need to have a meeting with the others," John says.

"Tonight?" Allison asks.

"Now," Carter says, his voice grim. "I'm not about to mess around and get killed. We'll give you a ride to the church."

"I'll meet you there," Allison says. Then, in response to their raised eyebrows, she says, "I have to change clothes. I'm thinking Telescoops will be closed for a while."

"Fine, but don't take too long. We're solving this today," Carter says.

John and Carter nod at her and leave the apartment. Allison shuts the door after them, but waits a full minute before coming to me.

She's smiling. She has the nerve to be smiling.

"That was close," she says, breathing a sigh of relief. She opens her door wide, and I limp out of her room, my knuckles straining around the cane. "We forgot your pillow. Thank God they didn't notice."

"So," I say, my voice even, "you knew about them planning to kill me."

Allison's smile slips from her face in an instant. "Avie, I tried to tell them no, but—"

"But?" I'm waiting, fury coursing through me so strong I feel like I'm about to snap this cane in half. When she

155

hesitates, I keep going, my voice growing louder and stronger. "But you thought it was fine, since I was new, since no one would look for me, huh? You thought it'd be okay to get rid of me?"

"No!" Allison looks like she's close to tears. Cold anger stirs in my chest. "No, Avie, I begged them not to do it. And they said they wouldn't, but they went behind my back and did it anyway."

"You knew I was in the running, though, didn't you? Why didn't you say anything?" Hot tears prick my eyes, but I fight them back. "You sat there and ate ice cream with me, and you didn't say a goddamn thing."

Allison looks stricken, like I've slapped her. "Avie, please listen. Pastor Thomas told me that if I told anyone, something bad would happen—"

"Like what?"

Allison hesitates, looking away for a split second. "I— That doesn't matter. I just wanted to keep everyone safe."

"So you're saying you don't even know what would have happened if you'd told me?" Some of the anger is replaced by stunned disbelief. Oh my God, who *is* this guy?

"I just knew it would be bad," Allison says, her voice wobbling. "I thought if I told you, I'd make things worse. I couldn't risk that, Avie, please understand."

"Allison." I rub my face, holding back a scream. I hate that she believes in that slimy bastard so much. I hate that Pastor Thomas has somehow warped his cult members' brains so horribly that they'll do anything to defend his stupid orders. I hate that the girl I like is caught in the web of the man who tried to murder me. "Why the hell would you believe that telling me that there's a huge-ass snake in Red Wood would make some random bad thing happen? Who's gonna know you told me?"

Allison stares at me for a moment, like she's stunned into silence. "I . . . Pastor Thomas said—"

"Pastor Thomas is a murderer! He's killed God knows how many people before this summer, and he tried to kill me! Why are you trusting anything he has to say?"

Allison doesn't say anything. She's staring at me with wide eyes, like I told her the sky is green.

I can't do this. Rage and hurt and confusion swirl in my head, giving me a pounding headache. For the first time since coming to Sanctum, I need to be away from her. "Just go, Allison. You have a traitor meeting, right?"

"Avie," she says, her voice weak. "I'm sorry—"

I fold my arms, glaring at her. "I said go."

Allison's bottom lip wobbles, and some of the rage splinters. She wipes her eyes with a tentative swipe. "I didn't mean for you to get hurt. You have to know that." Allison grabs her phone and keys and goes to the door. She doesn't look back at me. "Sorry I'm such a rotten hero, Avie."

Allison leaves the apartment and closes the door with a soft click.

I grab the remote and hurl it at the wall, and savor the crunch of broken plastic. It leaves a huge black mark on the wall. I forgot about the super strength.

Peach whines and licks my hand. I'm breathing hard,

seething. My hand opens and closes into a fist, over and over. I need to get out of here. I can't stay here one more minute.

"Come on, Peach," I mutter, grabbing my phone. "We're going to see the snake."

18

It's a lot harder to creep around in broad daylight.

By the time I reach the edge of Red Wood, most of the anger has turned into adrenaline from dodging people and limping from shadow to shadow. Thank God it's early morning and most people are still waking up and not wandering outside.

I enter the forest and instantly feel calmer. It's quiet, with occasional birdsong, or rustling leaves from a squirrel. More importantly, it's away from everyone in Sanctum. The only human being allowed in Red Wood is me.

I walk for a while, waiting for the forest to go silent. I know he'll come to me. Peach darts ahead, sniffing trees, tail wagging, but she doesn't bark. I guess dogs know better.

"I won't let him eat you," I promise Peach. She looks at me, nose quivering, and runs to my side. I pet her head as the birds stop singing, the bugs silence their wings, and the soft *chaka* of the snake's tail grows louder.

Despite expecting him, I'm a little shocked when he appears, his giant head curling through the trees like water. He's huge again. He opens his mouth as he gets closer, showing a glimpse of his fangs.

"Latavia, hello." He rises above me, his giant body pooling into a coil. "Have you any more information about the barriers?"

"Oh, uh . . . no." I pet Peach's head, suddenly nervous. I don't want to tell him about the silver. I don't think he'll take it well that he's been slowly poisoned over eighty years. Besides, I can maybe use the weakness to get away if things go south. I'd very much like to not get eaten.

"Hmm. Then why are you here?"

I sigh, leaning on my cane. Might as well tell him the truth. "I got into a fight with my friend."

"Ah, I see. You've come for comfort." The snake coils around me and Peach in one motion, surrounding us with piles of his glimmering body. "I understand. Humans are very needy."

"Oh, come on." I can't stop myself from rolling my eyes. "I'll go home right now."

"Home, where your friend is?"

I stay quiet, glaring at his dumb, smug face. Who knew giant snakes were so annoying.

The snake twists himself into a tighter circle, snug but not too close. "Lie down and rest, Latavia. I too am tired. I just ate, and you are disturbing me."

I ease to the ground, still a little irritated at his words. But he's right; I'm not going back to Allison's. Not right now. I yelp as I hit the forest floor, my knee throbbing angrily under my borrowed pajama pants. Peach sits beside me and licks my chin.

"You're awful calm, aren't you?" I pat her head, and she pants her dog breath in my face. "Not scared of giant snakes?"

"I am familiar with this hound," the snake says. He curls his head toward Peach, who licks his nose.

"Whoa, what? I thought you'd, I don't know, eat dogs."

"Too small," the snake says. "Too much effort."

"What do you eat if dogs are too small? Besides you snacking on helpless kids who wander in here."

"Deer," the snake says. His tone is patient and faintly amused, like he's teaching a child how to read. "Humans aren't enough to sustain me. They are, as you said, snacks."

Touché. I thought he'd eat people full time, but eating deer makes more sense. I pat Peach's head, filing that tidbit of info away, just in case. "So how do you know Peach?"

"This hound lived in my woods for a time. I ate its masters."

"Jeez, do you have to eat everyone who wanders in here? Poor Peach."

"Humans are smart. They knew my forest was off-limits. Still, I felt sorry for this creature, who is too stupid to know any better. So I hunted for it, for a time."

"Very generous of you." Too generous. It's kinda weird for a giant snake to keep a pet. What'd he get out of it?

The snake sighs, his eyes half-closed. "It was nice, for a short while. But I was preparing for the full moon, so I sent it to be with humans, where it belongs. It's too soft to be a wild one again."

161

Peach cocks her head to one side, tail wagging. He's right about that. I'd like to see this huge lapdog be wild.

"Sleep, Latavia," the snake says, his voice quiet. "You are tired, and I need peace to finish digesting. We can resume this conversation when you awaken."

I lean against the snake's scales, exhaustion tugging at my bones. Maybe a little nap won't hurt. I stare up at the clear sky, listening to the faint sound of Peach's snuffling breaths and the snake's tiny movements. I can't hear him breathing, but I feel it, his scales moving gently against my neck. I close my eyes and match the movement, comforted by the heat of a dog and the nest of living monster coiled around me.

John breaks my legs, over and over, laughing, I'm screaming, Carter wraps his hands around my neck, sneering, "Black girl." I scream for help and Allison is there but she's watching, just watching—

I wake up, chest heaving, shivering. Peach is all in my face, whining, licking the sweat from my neck and forehead. The snake hovers behind her, his dark eyes on me.

"You're screaming again," he says.

I try to calm down, but I'm shaking too much. My stomach clenches and roils, my teeth chatter—what's happening to me? It was a dream. Only a dream. I'm okay. "I'm okay."

"You are not," the snake says. I yelp in surprise when he grabs the collar of my shirt and lifts me a few feet into the air. He sets me down gently beside a large oak tree. I

162

hang on to it, still panting. "If you must expel food from your body, do it here. Not on me, please."

"Fuck you," I say, but he's right. My stomach clenches, and I heave up yesterday's dinner. Peach whines and licks my ankles.

I wipe my mouth with one trembling hand, acid simmering on my tongue. The dreams are getting worse. And Allison was there. Allison's never been in them before.

"Latavia, can you look at me?"

I take a few quivering breaths, then turn to the snake. His face is close to mine, his black eyes blinking slowly.

"You are frightened."

It's a statement, not a question. I spit out some of the leftover bile in my mouth. "I said I'm fine. Just leave me alone. You don't know what it's like."

"This is true. I don't understand. Are you afraid of the humans remaining on our list?"

"No." Yes. Maybe. I take another shaky breath. Slowly, my shoulders relax a little. "It's not them. It's . . . I keep having these nightmares."

"What happens in your nightmares?"

"They break my leg." Every time. John always breaks my leg.

The snake nods. "I understand now. You are frightened of the pain."

I open my mouth to protest, but close it again. Maybe he's right. My knee throbs dully, always. I can't walk without this stupid cane. This is what some idiot townies did to me without any giant snakes or superpowers. This is what they're capable of.

163

"However, Latavia, you have nothing to worry about. Humans are cruel creatures who boast of intelligence, but have the mentality of terrified prey animals. They hurt their own because that's what prey do. Stampede their neighbor so they might live one more day. It's rather pathetic." The snake stretches to his full height, his head skimming the trees. Afternoon light catches his black scales, causing them to glimmer an iridescent color. He looks down at me, his fangs exposed. He's almost grinning. "Do not be afraid of humans, Latavia. Monsters don't have anything to fear."

I look up at the snake with his huge head and fangs, and despite myself, I feel a little bit better.

My phone buzzes in my pocket. I take it out—a text from Jade.

Come to the house. Mom's not here.

I glance at the snake and hold out my hand. "Are you ready to go back to town and look for the barriers?"

The snake huffs but touches his nose to my hand. In one fluid motion, he's back to his tiny snake form, curling up my arm and settling around my shoulders.

"Lead the way."

19

I come out of Red Wood in Auntie's backyard. It's almost nightfall, but not quite, so I move as quickly as possible to the back of the house. Peach settles by the back porch, yawning—she knows better than to come in. Auntie had a freak-out when we tried to bring her inside before. I hesitate when I reach the back door, my palms suddenly sweaty.

"Do not be afraid," the snake hisses in my ear. "I am with you."

Yeah, says the monster who threatened to eat me if I don't cooperate. I take a deep breath and knock on Auntie's back door.

I hear hurried footsteps, and I can't stop my body from tensing. I relax when Jade opens the door.

"Come in!" she says. "I ordered Chinese food."

I take a step inside, but can't move any farther. I meet Jade's eyes. "She's not coming back for a while, right?"

Jade's expression softens. "Right. All-night shift at the hospital." Jade steps back so I can come in. "It's okay. I wouldn't let her see you. Promise."

I reflexively touch my neck, where my fingertips meet the smooth scales of the snake. I take a deep breath and step into Auntie's house.

I lived here for six weeks, for many summers when Mom and I visited, for Thanksgivings and birthdays, but I feel like a stranger now. Auntie's collection of blue china is alien, the once familiar living room foreign and strange. Something is different from when I was here before the sacrifice. Dangerous.

Jade heads to the kitchen, and I limp after her, uncomfortable in the house I thought I loved. The kitchen is kind of a wreck; there are tons of unwashed dishes in the sink, and the table is piled high with junk and cardboard boxes. What is Auntie doing? She hates a messy house. Normally she would've had an aneurysm by now.

"I gotta heat this up since you took so long," Jade says. She pulls two Chinese takeout containers from a big paper bag.

"Takes a while to move around with my knee like this." I move some of the papers on the table. They're . . . tax documents? And bank statements. "What is all this, Jade?"

Jade freezes midserve. The lo mein noodles hang from the carton, swaying slightly. "Um. Nothing."

Yeah, right. "Come on, I'm not stupid. Auntie never leaves shit lying around."

Jade finally looks at me, guilt all over her face. "I don't really know. Mom's been so weird since . . . you know.

166

But I heard her talking to real estate agents. I think we're moving."

A number of emotions hit me all at once. She's just going to leave? She's going to let a monster eat me and then forget all about me? I'm so angry, I could break this cane in half. But . . . a part of me is relieved. If she can get Jade out of here, I can't be mad about that. Though, if the snake and I finish our business, Jade isn't going anywhere.

"Are you all right?" the snake whispers in my ear.

"You okay?" Jade asks, almost at the same time.

God, I must really look like shit. I need to get out of this kitchen, away from tax documents and lo mein and my soon-to-be-orphaned cousin. I clear my burning throat. "Um, can I . . . can I go up to my room for a second? I'll be right back."

"Okay," Jade says, her voice uncertain. "I'll wait to heat yours up."

I nod and leave the kitchen. It takes me a horribly long time to climb the stairs. When I get to the top, I just stand there, looking at my old door. I wanted to go in, sit on the bed, and calm down, but I don't think I can. I don't think I can be in the same place where the guardians of Sanctum grabbed me and sentenced me to death.

The guardians part makes me pause in my grief and slight panic. Auntie's a guardian too, so maybe she has one of those notebooks. The curiosity paves over more of the panic, and I can almost breathe normally. I take a breath, and instead of opening my door, I limp to the end of the hall. Her office door is ajar, which is weird. She never leaves it open. I touch the snake's scales nervously.

167

"Do you sense anyone in there?" I ask him.

The snake's smooth scales run over my fingertips. "It is only you, me, and the child in this house. You are safe."

I breathe out, relieved, and push open Auntie's door.

The office is a mess, like the kitchen. Documents flung everywhere, on the floor, stacked on bookshelves, scattered around on her desk. Her laptop is plugged in and still on, the glow illuminating the dark room. I flip on the light and go to the desk first.

A fireproof safe sits open under the desk . . . just like the one at Telescoops. They don't like variety among the guardians, huh? I don't have to bend over this time, though, because sitting on top of Jade's birth certificate and Social Security card is a worn, leather-bound book.

I pick it up, grimacing. I was kind of hoping I wouldn't find one. I flip it open to the first page.

> *The Monster in Red Wood takes the form of a serpent. It is intelligent, and can speak, if the person is allowed to speak with it. I shouldn't say "it." Through research, we have found that the creature is male.*

I frown at my aunt's careful, barely legible doctor scrawl. This isn't like Katie's journal at all. Hers was full of numbers, plus her complaints and doodles. This is almost like an academic paper.

> *The Monster has no name. He takes the form of a rattlesnake, though he is missing the characteristic*

diamond pattern on the scales. Coloring: black.
Eyes: black. Melanism? Unconfirmed. For
purposes of this study, he will be referred to as
Subject A.

I pause to Google "melanism," and frown at the results. It's the opposite of albinism, where animals are all
black instead of white. Weird. This *is* an academic journal. It figures that they'd give this one to Auntie; she's so
serious and methodical. I just don't get how someone so
smart would get mixed up in writing about the biology of
giant snakes. And murder cults. I shake my head and keep
reading.

WEAKNESSES

- *Silver. Drawbacks: has no effect unless ingested.*
  Pros: easily obtainable, and once ingested, it
  weakens the Monster's constitution and dulls
  the senses. Confirmed with Subject B.
- *Fire. Drawbacks: takes a long time to burn*
  through protective hide of Monster. Pros: can
  successfully kill a Monster if allowed to burn
  long enough. Partially confirmed with Subject B.
- *Monster Teeth and Claws. Drawbacks:*
  difficult to obtain. Pros: apparent venom is
  corrosive to a Monster's skin. Unconfirmed
  (rumored success with other Monsters).
- *Plasma. Drawbacks: difficult to obtain*
  ingredients. Pros: most effective tool against
  a Monster to date. Completely corrosive to

a Monster and will maim and kill within
minutes. Confirmed with Subject B.

- <u>*Notes:*</u> *Subject A is rumored to be fond of*
  spiced meats and popcorn. May be able to
  use these to bargain. Verbally confirmed by
  Donald Miller. Unconfirmed by anyone else.
  No preferences recorded for Subject B before its
  death.

I flip the page, but there's nothing else. A few pages
have been torn out, and the rest are blank. I stare at the
book in my hands, my heart rate erratic. What the hell
is "Subject B"? Another monster? And what is "Plasma"?
Would it have killed Auntie to add some damn details?

I sit in Auntie's computer chair to piece all of this together. First, silver is confirmed to hurt him, according
to this journal. So he *has* been poisoned for eighty years,
if Katie's journal is to be believed. I glance at my knee,
unease prickling my skin. Silver hurt me too. Or is it just
that it reacted with his venom? I don't know. There are
still too many holes to be sure. I need to be careful with
my cane. Now, this "Subject B." I flip through the book,
apprehension growing. Sounds like Sanctum found themselves another monster . . . and it sounds like they killed
it. If they can do it, so can I.

My heart rate kicks up, and I have to breathe deep to
calm it down. Silver is out because I'd like to see me try
and force my cane down the snake's throat and not lose
an arm. Fire is also out, because I doubt I could trap him
somewhere and set him on fire. But this Plasma thing is

really promising, if I knew how to make it. If I can get this, it'll be my secret weapon. He'll help me kill the rest of the six, and when he turns on me, I'll be ready. The snake said he'd kill me at the end of this deal.

Not if I can kill him first.

"Avie?" Jade calls from downstairs, making me jump. The snake moves around my neck, yawning.

"Are you calm now?" he asks. I close the book and place it back on Auntie's desk.

"Oh, you have no idea."

20

I come downstairs, and Jade's sitting in the armchair, two steaming plates of food on the coffee table.

"You okay?" she asks again. Her face is full of concern. "You were gone a while."

"I'm fine, don't worry," I assure her. All thoughts of Auntie's notebook and Plasma leave me as I inhale the delicious scent of Chinese food. "Is it shrimp lo mein?"

"Sorry, no." Jade passes me a plate and a plastic fork. "They were out of shrimp. Deal with chicken."

"Rude." I accept the food anyway, suddenly ravenous. Now that I think about it, I haven't eaten much of anything since I crawled out of Red Wood the first time. I twirl a massive amount of noodles onto my fork and shove them into my mouth.

"You act like you haven't eaten all day!" Jade laughs as I wolf down more noodles. Jade eats a few bites of her sesame chicken before continuing. "Though, I guess you haven't. I heard you got into a fight with Allison and you've been gone since."

I pause, the fork halfway to my mouth. I almost forgot, with the excitement of discovering a way to kill the snake and all, but now bitter memories surge through my mind. I put the plate on the coffee table. "Yeah, I did."

Jade searches my face, hers calm. "Do you want to talk about it?"

"No." But then I think about Allison's words, how she had the nerve to smile at me, knowing how much she'd lied to me, and I'm on fire. "Actually, yeah, I do. She knew I was an option for the sacrifice! She knew, and she didn't say anything to me!"

"You were going on a date with her that night, right?" Jade asks.

"Yeah, but she could have told me earlier that day. When we were getting ice cream."

"So you would have had *two* dates?" Jade wiggles her eyebrows, and some of the anger melts away as I laugh.

"Shut up, listen to me. I can't believe she'd do this. I was right there, sitting across from her, and she didn't say anything."

Jade nods. "Okay. I hear you. She made a terrible decision and you got hurt."

The snake moves lazily around my neck. More than just "hurt." I entered this crazy deal because she didn't warn me.

"You have a right to be mad about that. It sucks. But also try to see it from her point of view. How on earth

173

was she going to convince you there was a giant snake in the woods? What if you'd laughed and wouldn't agree to come with her to the party?"

"Then I guess we'd be in the same situation we're in now. Except I could trust her." Jade sighs, but I continue. "She said she thought if she told me, something bad would happen. Like, does she expect me to believe that?"

"I mean, yeah." Jade meets my eyes. "What Pastor Thomas says, Sanctum believes. That's how it's always been."

My rage stalls as Jade stares calmly into my eyes. "But . . . you really think she believed that?"

"Yeah. I do. And I think she was scared, but also trusted him not to go back on his word."

Now I'm feeling kinda rotten. I thought that was a flimsy excuse, but Allison really did seem dumbfounded, like this was the first time she ever thought to doubt the man. And the way she defended him against Carter was half sad, half horrifying. "So, what?" I can't keep the sullen whine from my voice. "You want me to apologize? For getting dragged into the woods and getting my knee fucked up?"

"No. But you can talk it out without yelling."

I mull over what she's saying. "I don't know, Jade. She's lied to me so much. I don't know if I can trust her."

I expect Jade to argue, but she nods solemnly. "I think that's fair. And I'm not saying you can't be mad, but maybe try talking to her about how you feel and not ignoring her all day." Jade pulls out her phone and shows me the screen. Nine texts from Allison, all asking (with increasing worry) if Jade has heard from me. "She cares about you, Avie; she just messed up. And don't think she isn't feeling guilty about it. She cried that whole night they took you, and the whole day we spent looking for you." Jade stares into my eyes, hers soft. "She was going to take you out of town, remember? Even though Pastor Thomas told her she couldn't leave."

I dig my nails into my forearms, but I can already feel myself weakening. If Allison really did think something bad, catastrophic, would happen if she even mentioned the snake, what did she think would happen if she left Sanctum? She was scared for me. She was willing to defy him to keep me safe. She was just ten minutes too late.

I meet Jade's eyes. "Fine. I'll talk to her."

Jade grins at me. "Good! Proud of you, cousin."

"Yeah, yeah."

The snake moves so he's next to my ear. "Good for you," he hisses. "Cooperation is very important for young humans, I've heard."

If he wasn't invisible and Jade wasn't watching, I'd hit him.

"Glad that's settled. She was driving me nuts today," Jade says. She eats a few more bites of chicken while I finish my noodles, my fortune cookie, and her fortune cookie while she's not looking. "Where'd you go all day, anyway?"

I fidget in my seat, my fingers tapping on my knee. Shit, I didn't prepare a lie for this. "I was at the edge of Red Wood."

175

Jade's eyebrows fly up to her hairline. "Are you serious?"

Yikes. That probably wasn't a good one. "I didn't go in. I sat at the edge. I figured everyone would be avoiding the woods, so it'd be safe."

Jade blinks at me. "You sat there all day?"

Nervous heat creeps up my neck. "Yeah."

Jade doesn't say anything for a while. I ate all my lo mein, so I look around the living room. It's still got that foreign weird feel. . . . Wait a minute. It finally clicks why things feel off—Auntie has taken down all the pictures of me. Baby pictures. Jade and me playing in the backyard. My high school graduation photo. Professional pictures of me, Mom, and the rest of our extended family. All gone.

Hurt, deep and yawning, jumps into my chest. I point to the empty wall, a wobbly smile on my face. "So she decided to pretend I never existed, huh?"

Jade's expression melts into one I've never seen before. Tortured, pained, full of pity. "I'm sure they're just packed up! For the move—"

"Don't be stupid, Jade." My tone is full of bitterness. "She packed them up because she couldn't look at me. Not after she put me on an altar for a snake to eat me."

Jade's face falls, and she puts down her Chinese food. "Can I ask you something?"

"Yeah," I say, but my muscles are already tight and my fist grips my unhurt knee.

"Mom isn't . . . doing so well. Tonight is the first night she's been out of the house since it happened, and that's only because she had an emergency at the hospital." Jade

176

takes a shuddering breath. "She packs, and then she'll sit around for hours, not saying anything. I hear her crying sometimes too. I'm scared she's, like, losing it."

I stuff down an annoying amount of concern. Why am I feeling sorry for her? This is her fault. This is her penance. "That isn't a question."

Jade picks at a spot of dried soy sauce on the armchair. "Do you think you can ever forgive her?"

"Jade. She tried to kill me."

"I know." Jade's head is down, so I can't see her face. "I just don't understand. I never thought she'd do anything like this. We're family. This isn't supposed to happen."

"Yeah, well, she threw family away when she decided it was okay to feed me to a giant snake." I'm itchy again. I'm hurt by the pictures being gone, and I'm mad at Jade for trying to make me feel sorry for Auntie. I'm furious at myself that I actually do. I take a deep breath and grab my cane. "I'm leaving. I'll see you later."

Jade stands too, her expression pained. "Sorry. I shouldn't have asked." She surprises me with a hug, her arms dangerously close to touching the snake. "I'm on your side on this one, Avie. Don't worry."

I want to believe her, but her question swirls uneasily in my head. Why does she want me to forgive Auntie? If Jade's really on my side, *she* shouldn't even feel sorry for her. I shouldn't either. I glance at the empty spots where my pictures once hung. I push down the pain and let icy numbness cover it. I can't feel sorry for her. She'll find that out soon enough.

Jade breaks our hug and smiles up at me. "Be careful on the way home. I kinda wish I could drive now."

"Wouldn't get in the car with you if you could!"

We laugh as she escorts me to the back door. She leans against the doorframe. "Don't worry about what I said. We can deal with Mom after we kill the snake. Too bad that Don guy's dead, huh? He could have given us some tips."

Shit. I haven't told the snake—

"What did she say?" The snake wraps himself around my throat, tight. "What did this human child say? Don is dead?"

"Avie?" Jade frowns at me. "What's wrong?"

I grip the snake's body in a tight fist, trying to control my ragged breathing. "I need to go. I gotta talk to Allison."

"Is it true?" The snake constricts tighter around my neck, pinning my fingers against my windpipe. "Is Don dead? Answer me."

"I can't breathe, you dipshit," I hiss.

"What?" Jade asks, her eyebrows scrunched in confusion.

"Nothing! I gotta go. I'll talk to Allison, promise." I grip my cane and limp out the back door. "Bye! See you later."

Jade hesitantly closes the door, and I stagger a few feet away, toward Red Wood. Peach follows us, stretching and yawning. The snake climbs from my shoulders as soon as we're out of earshot. When he's at my feet, he coils up, his tiny rattle quivering. "Explain to me what she meant. Right now."

"You could have killed me, you demon." I rub my neck, wincing at the sore spots. "Allison showed us a super old journal that belonged to Don. He drew some pictures of you and wrote some notes. But the dates . . . they were from 1809. I'm sorry, but people don't live that long. He'd be over two hundred years old."

"No. No, this can't be."

"When was the last time you talked to Don?"

The snake is quiet for a moment. "It was . . . years ago."

"Well, there you go."

The snake's tail trembles. He can't keep his head still; he actually looks upset. Poor guy. He's so awful with time, he probably doesn't realize Don died forever ago. Despite the snake being a ruthless monster, I find myself feeling sorry for him.

"Hey, sorry about this. I know you wanted to kill him, or talk to him, or whatever. I'm sorry you won't get your revenge."

The snake uncoils himself and lays his body flat on the ground. Peach licks the top of his head, which he ignores. "This is troubling news, Latavia. I cannot believe this. I refuse to believe this."

Is the snake . . . depressed? It's weird to think he has other emotions besides smart-ass and cryptic. "Maybe we can go check?" I offer. "So you can see?"

"How?"

"There's only one graveyard in Sanctum." I hold my hand out to him. "We might as well stop by on the way home."

The snake looks up at me, his eyes narrowed. "Yes. I want to check. I want to see with my own eyes." The snake climbs up my arm to my shoulders. His body is warm against my skin. "Let's find out if you humans are telling the truth."

21

Sanctum's graveyard is like the rest of Sanctum—creepy as hell. There's a mismanaged gatehouse right at the front, and then row after row of tombstones. There's no real order; some gravestones are new, with fresh flowers, and their neighbors are so old and cracked no one can read the names anymore.

I take a step into the graveyard, my knee burning. It's not a short distance from Jade's house to here. Now I'm wishing she could drive. Though it would be hard to explain why I'm wandering around a graveyard at ten p.m.

"Do you know where he's buried?" the snake murmurs in my ear.

"No clue," I whisper back. The graveyard is so quiet, it's unnerving. It's like the woods when the animals sense the snake coming. "We'll have to check them all."

The snake lets out a sharp hiss. He's really testy today.

Peach licks my sore knee. I pat her head absently,

glancing at the graves near the entrance. No Don. "Don't suppose you know where Don is, girl?"

"Stop playing with your pet," the snake hisses. "We must start our search. Do you have something to assist you in confirming his death?"

"Are you serious? You want me to dig him up?" The snake doesn't say anything, so I guess that's a yes. I limp to the gatehouse, my teeth gritted. "Unbelievable. I have better things to do than go grave digging with you. And my knee is messed up!"

"The knee is irrelevant," the snake says. "This is what you have hands for."

If I wasn't sure he'd bite me, I'd punch him in his smug little nose.

The gatehouse is unattended. The only thing protecting it is a rusty lock and chain on the door. A few good whacks with my cane break it, and the ancient door swings open. A lawn mower, a few plastic flowers—and a rusty shovel. Bingo. I grab it and head outside to start my search.

The snake doesn't speak as I wander along rows and rows of graves. Tyler McMann. Greta Yarbrough. Kim Ricks. No Don. "Donald Miller" if the books are to be believed. What a regular-ass name for a dude who doomed hundreds of people.

"Latavia, stop." The snake raises his head off my shoulder, his body tense. "I sense a barrier."

Oh? I glance around, a little nervous. The last one was a memorial, but all I can see are rows and rows of graves. "How do we find it?"

"I'm not sure," the snake says. He swivels his head back and forth, like he's confused. "It's very faint and . . . strange. It's possible that it's underground."

I don't say anything. The line silver *weakens the Monster's constitution and dulls the senses* runs through my brain. "Maybe they buried it with Don. Two birds with one stone?"

The snake doesn't reply, so I sigh and get back to work. I wipe sweat from my forehead. Curse Alabama's muggy summers. Why couldn't they have sacrificed me in October?

I'm skimming the graves, so I almost miss one of the fresh ones. Clementine May. That poor old lady; she struggled, like me, and they killed her for it. A twinge of pity surges in my chest, and I turn away, to the next grave. Right next to hers—

Latavia Johnson.

I stare at my grave, shock coursing through me. Then slow rage creeps into my veins, up my neck and into my face, burning, hot, livid. They had the nerve to make a grave for me? Knowing they murdered me? Knowing the snake would have swallowed me whole? The rage roars in my ears as I pick up the shovel and slam it into the gravestone. A crack appears in the stone, so I beat it until it's smashed into several pieces. I breathe raggedly, my arms sore, my hands stinging, savage pleasure coursing through me. I hope Sanctum sees this and gets good and scared. I'm not letting this go until they've paid for what they did to me.

"Are you done?" the snake asks after a few minutes of silence, broken only by my heavy breathing.

"Yeah." I look down at the grave, a bitter taste in my mouth. "I'm done."

"Good. While you were destroying that rock, I found it." The snake extends his head next to my face, like he's pointing. "The barrier is that way, and it's close. Hurry now."

Some of the adrenaline fades and it's replaced with a hollow feeling. This whole town needs to be burned to the ground. I limp in the direction the snake points, and I come to the edge of the graveyard, under a huge oak tree.

"Here?" I look around for a gravestone, but there's nothing. Just the tree, growing into the edge of the iron fence.

"Here." The snake hisses softly, his tiny tail rattling.

Unmarked grave for poor old Don? Though, I guess it's to hide the existence of the barrier. Too bad for them, I've got a living barrier detector on my shoulder. "Okay, I'll start digging. You keep a lookout."

Even with super strength, it's a lot harder to dig up a grave when you only have one good leg. I get ten minutes in and have to take a break, wheezing and light-headed. Whatever's in the barrier is affecting me now; I'm hot, sweating like last time. The skin on my arms burns.

"This will take too long," the snake says after I take my second break. "Latavia, have you asked the hound to help?"

"What?" Peach is lying down, taking a nap on top of one of the graves. She looks up and wags her tail. "What do you mean?"

The snake moves to wrap himself around my bun before answering. "I've been thinking about your ability. I can turn invisible, but you cannot. You must have something else."

Huh. He did mention something about this, a while ago. "Okay, but what does that have to do with Peach?"

"Do you remember speaking with the young human?" the snake asks. "You convinced her to go home. And with your friend, you asked her to go to sleep. She was not tired, but when you asked, she fell asleep."

"Whoa, whoa, wait a minute." My heart hammers with excitement. "Are you saying I can control people?"

"'Control' is not the right word. It's probably more of a suggestion," the snake says. "But you can test it on your hound. Animals should be more inclined to obey."

Well, worth a shot. "Peach, come here, girl."

Peach stands and trots to me, tail wagging. Did it work? Well, she came when I called even before this mess. I point to the grave.

"Help me dig."

She cocks her head to one side, panting happily.

"I don't think it's working, snake."

"Remember what I said. Suggestion."

I think back to my conversation with Allison. I think I said . . . *Why don't we both go to bed?* "Peach, why don't you help me dig up this grave?"

Peach stops panting and looks into my eyes. And, remarkably, she leaps at the grave and starts digging furiously.

"Good work, Latavia," the snake purrs. "This is a useful ability indeed."

I help Peach dig, in awe of my new ability. Strength, night vision, and now this? What else can I do? No, how far does this go? Will Peach do whatever I tell her to do? How complicated can my instructions—suggestions—be? I need to practice. I need to test what Peach and I can do.

With Peach's help, it doesn't take long before I hit something solid. "Let's stop now, okay, Peach?" I dig a few more shovelfuls of dirt, carefully, and expose a disgustingly brown and withered leg bone. I work hard not to throw up. "All right, here's Don. Presumably."

The snake hisses. "We'll attend to the body later. I need to see the barrier. Keep digging."

Roger that, snake boss. I keep digging, gagging as I unearth more bones and, finally, hit a sharp *tink* of glass. I move some earth around and expose a glass container identical to the one I smashed earlier.

But this one is already broken.

"What?" The snake climbs down my body with alarming speed and inspects the glass. There's no orange liquid, no silver, no nothing. It's empty.

"I thought you sensed a barrier?" I say, breathing hard from the work.

"I do sense one. It's close. It should be right here." The snake flicks his tongue out again and again. "The barrier's container was buried, so it must have shattered underground. If it's not exposed to open air, then it's still intact. But where did the blood go?"

Blood? What kind of blood is orange and radioactive?

"In the body?" The snake turns his head back and forth, like he's confused. "No, I don't feel anything there. But these roots . . ."

At the same time, the snake and I look up at the massive oak tree.

"You've got to be kidding me."

"It's in the tree." The snake climbs back up my leg and to my shoulders. His belly is cold and wet from the grass. "Clever. We'll have to destroy the tree."

"Well, we're gonna have to come back tomorrow. I don't have anything to chop it down with."

The snake sighs heavily. "The full moon is so close . . . but no matter. We will destroy it tomorrow."

That damn full moon again. I hope the next journal explains whatever is happening on the full moon, because this is driving me nuts.

I lean down to pick up the shovel. Freaking thing is in the tree. I hate that I wasted time digging up this grave. So can anything be a barrier now? What if we never find the other two?

"Is this truly Don, like you said?" the snake asks, pulling my attention to him. "Can you confirm who this body belongs to?"

I know I told the snake we could dig the body up and be sure, but I'm not a miracle worker. I don't know how the hell I'm supposed to identify a pile of bones. The body is an ugly deep brown, hardly discernable from the dirt around it. Tattered clothing clings to the bones, and . . . wait. I lean closer. On the left hand is a ring, a tarnished gold color with three rubies stacked on top of each other. I pull out my phone and scroll to the picture Allison sent me of Don. In the painting, an identical ring sits on Don's left hand.

"Well . . ." I show the snake my phone. "This is Don in the picture, right?"

The snake nods. "Yes, as I remember him."

"Then looks like that's Don in the ground too. See the ring? It's the same."

The snake is silent for several long moments. Then he turns his head away from my phone. "I see."

"Sorry, snake," I say, wincing as Peach pulls a dirty ancient bone from the ground. "At least we found Don. Not a wasted mission."

The snake is quiet for a long time. His head seems heavier on my shoulder. "No, it was not unsuccessful."

I touch the snake's scales gently. "Let's go home and make a game plan on how to destroy this tree."

He doesn't say anything, so I push as much dirt as I can back into the grave before turning to go home.

22

The snake is silent until I'm almost at Allison's apartment.

"Latavia, I need to leave you for a short time." He crawls down my head and back, and loops his tail around my left ankle.

"Need to eat?"

"Yes." The snake hesitates, his head resting on my shoe. "And to think."

Despite myself, I feel a twinge of sympathy. He's really taking Don's death hard. "Okay. Hey, listen, I'm sure Don lived a long time. And we can imagine he died a painful, horrible death, if that helps."

The snake doesn't answer me. He slithers off my shoe and disappears under a car. I wait for him for a few minutes, but he doesn't come back.

I kick at loose gravel as I continue to Allison's, feeling rotten. It bums me out that the snake is so sad. I didn't know he could even be sad. What kind of bond did he and Don have? Were they business partners, like us? Did Don come to visit him in the woods and fall asleep against his scales? I shouldn't even feel bad. He threatened to eat me, and I'm going to find some Plasma stuff to make sure that doesn't happen. But as I struggle up Allison's steep steps, I can't shake the feeling of pity in my gut. Maybe I'll get him some popcorn to help him feel better.

Thoughts of the snake all but disappear as I arrive in front of Allison's door. I'd almost rather go back to the woods. I don't know what to say. Now that we've found the second barrier, and we have to somehow chop a tree down, and the snake is all moody about Don dying, my argument with Allison seems stupid. I was upset, probably because John and Carter were a few inches away and I couldn't do anything. But she did lie to me . . . repeatedly. I don't want to, but we have to talk about it. I can't forgive her until we do.

I reach for the snake's scales, but all I feel is the too-warm skin of my neck. I lower my hand, take a deep breath, and knock on the door.

I have to wait a full agonizing minute before Allison opens the door. She's in her pajamas, her hair down. She's still wearing makeup.

I swallow the lump in my throat and attempt to smile. "Hey."

"Hey." Allison's voice is fragile, guarded. Waiting for me to say something.

I fidget a little, leaning heavily on my cane. My knee is swollen, throbbing under my borrowed pajama pants. There's a tense silence while I think of something to say.

"Allison, I—"

"I'm really sorry, Avie." Allison's caution breaks, and suddenly she's crying. "I've felt so awful all day. I should have stopped them, I know I should have, and if I could d-do it over, I would, but I can't and people are dying and I— I don't know what to do—"

"Whoa, hey, it's okay." I'm flooded with relief, even as I pat Allison's back and usher her to the couch. Thank God I didn't have to apologize first. I grab a few paper towels from the kitchen and offer them to her.

"S-sorry, this is really embarrassing," Allison sniffles as she accepts the paper towels. She blows her nose and tries to wipe her eyes, but the tears won't stop. "I had this whole thing planned. I ruined it."

"It's okay. I'm glad you don't get to lecture me now." She shoots me a dirty look and I laugh. Almost all the tension is gone; I just want to talk to her. "Hey, listen, sorry for yelling earlier. I was really upset."

Allison nods, sniffling. "I know. I know this has to be hard on you."

I start to disagree, to say I'm fine and this shithole will be toast soon anyway, but I sigh instead. "It is. It's been tough."

"Do you want to talk about it?" Allison's not crying anymore. Her face is blotchy and her eyes are red, but she's got the tears under control at least.

I take a breath to calm my nerves. "Yeah. I do."

"Okay," Allison says, wiping her face again. "I'm ready."

"I shouldn't have screamed at you. Not cool. But you lying to me isn't cool either." I pause again to steady my nerves. Allison is listening, her watery eyes fixed on me.

"I needed to know about the snake in the woods, Allison. Even if Pastor Thomas told you not to tell anyone. And I need to know what you know about the snake, and this horrible town. Because I want to trust you—" My voice hitches, and I clear my throat. "I want to trust you, but I feel like I can't. I can't until I know whose side you're on—mine, or Pastor Thomas's."

I stop, holding my breath, and Allison nods slowly.

"I'm sorry, Avie. I haven't been honest, and I feel so bad about that. I don't want you to think I'm not on your side, because I am. I'm trying. It's just . . ."

"Just?" I prompt gently.

Allison wipes her eyes one more time. She leans forward, her forearms on her knees, and for a second she seems a lot older than seventeen. "I've been thinking about what you said all day. I didn't even think to question what Pastor Thomas said. I just believed him."

A twinge of pain springs into my chest. My hunch was right. "Well, he is kind of persuasive. In, like, a gross way."

Allison laughs a little. "I've been going to that church my whole life. I was raised there. And this whole time, everyone's gone along with whatever Pastor Thomas said. Me too. But I . . . Things aren't adding up, Avie. You heard what Carter said, right? We're not allowed to talk about the monster with each other. We all have specific roles, and Pastor Thomas says this way we can do our parts without getting distracted, and everything will work perfectly. Like cogs in a machine." Allison picks at a strand of her hair, plucking it out and twirling it around her finger over and over. "But why can't we talk about it? Why aren't we working together to stop the monster? It doesn't make sense."

"It does," I say, thinking about Pastor Thomas's cold, bulbous eyes at the ceremony, "if you want to control a group of people."

Allison is quiet. She twists the strand of her hair around and around until it snaps. "I'm so sorry, Avie. I really didn't think he'd hurt you. He looked me in my eyes and promised, and then did it anyway. Even though he knew . . ." Allison trails off, then meets my eyes. Hers are serious. Scared. "You were right. I believed in Pastor Thomas because that's what I've always done, since I was a kid. But you don't know him, Avie. He's always taken care of Sanctum, of me. He always has everyone's best interest at heart, so that's why . . ." Allison trails off, a deeply troubled expression on her face.

I stare back, dread swirling in my gut. This isn't going to be easy. She's right; I don't know him. I don't know what he's done for her, or to her. I don't know what he's said to make her and John so fiercely loyal. If I push too hard, I might undo the little progress she's made on her own and make her go running back to him. I take a breath, and then gently take her hands.

"Allison, listen to me. I know he's been in your ear this whole time, but trust me, he does not have everyone's best interest at heart. At the very least, not mine. You have proof of that." Allison nods, her eyebrows still scrunched with worry, so I continue. "And lying to you about not sacrificing me is shady, right? As is not letting the guardians work together. We can agree on that, right?"

"Right." Allison sounds surer this time.

"So, for now, let's say that Pastor Thomas can't be trusted. But you can trust me, Allison. I promise that I'm doing everything I can to keep you and Jade safe." I keep my gaze steady, though I'm wincing internally. I'm promising her safety, but not the other guardians. I hope a half-truth is good enough.

Allison searches my face for a few seconds, but then the tension relaxes from her shoulders. "Okay." She's staring straight into my eyes, hers dark and determined and a little something I can't name. "I believe in you, Avie."

A strange softening fills my chest. I didn't know how much I needed to hear that until she said it. Jade and Allison are my allies, us against Pastor Thomas's cult. Relief crashes over me like a wave. "Thanks, Allison." I squeeze her hands in mine, careful to be gentle. "No more secrets, okay? Promise me."

She hesitates for half a second, but nods. "I promise."

I smile at her and she smiles back, and I think we've both forgiven each other.

"What's the first secret you're gonna tell me?" I ask teasingly.

Allison makes a big show of thinking, *hmm*-ing, and looking up at the ceiling. "I snore at night."

"I knew that already." I nudge her knee with my un-injured one. "I can hear you out here!"

Allison gasps, and her face turns a delicate shade of red before my eyes. "Oh my God, tell me you're joking."

I start laughing, so hard I can barely stop. Allison is so cute, cuter than anyone I've ever met in my life. And

I want to believe that she'll tell me everything from now on. I want to believe it can really be me and her against the world, and if I'm patient and understanding, I can convince her to let this wicked town rot from the inside out.

"Relax, I'm kidding. But thanks for being honest."

Allison gives me a soft, sad smile. "I'll be honest again. I'm scared of the monster and what it'll do. But all day, all I could think of was that you were mad at me. Isn't that terrible? I didn't think about the monster at all. Some hero I am, huh?"

"You're my hero," I say, grinning, and Allison rolls her eyes.

"God, you're the worst." Then she returns my smile and says, "Everything is kinda terrible, and I'm scared, but I'm glad you're safe. I'm glad you're here with me."

Warmth spreads from my neck to my face, and I want to hold her, to tell her she's going to be okay and I *know* that because I'll protect her. But what I end up doing is staring at her for too long, a goofy grin on my face.

Allison looks away first, smiling at her lap. "I do have something that might be interesting. It's about the monster."

I raise my eyebrows. Something new, or something I already know? "What is it?"

Allison lets go of my hand and picks up her phone. One hand is still holding mine, though, which sends pleasant goosebumps up my arms. I hope my palm isn't sweaty. She scrolls through her pictures. "After the meeting this morning, I went back to the church to talk to Pastor Thomas about the curfew idea, but he wasn't in his office. I saw a book on his desk that's kind of like the one he gave me with Don's notes in it. So I thought I'd better take some pictures." Allison grins at me. "Don't tell him, okay?"

Oh, perfect! Pastor Thomas's journal. Saves me the trip. I grin back. Thank you, Allison, for helping me out. "Deal. What'd it say?"

Allison shows me the picture. I scan it quickly—it's a list of fragmented thoughts.

> *The moon was full when we woke him*
> *Bigger than before, stronger*
> *Happening again?*
> *Revert to animal state? Sunrise?*
> *Can I run?*

Allison shrugs. "I don't know what it means exactly. What does 'revert to animal state' mean? It's already an animal."

I'm a lot less concerned about that than the top part of his ramblings. That damn full moon again. But this time, it seems that the full moon he's referencing is in the past? When Don woke him. I don't get it at all. "Can you send this to me?" Allison nods and sends me the picture. I study it on my own phone, like staring at my screen will magically give me answers.

"What's wrong?" Allison asks.

I tap my phone. "I've been hearing a lot about the full moon. He—" I barely stop myself before referencing the snake. "Carter, I mean, mentioned it earlier, when he was arguing with John. And here it is again. What's going on during the full moon?"

Allison looks at me, and for a second, fear crosses her face. I narrow my eyes. So she *does* know.

"Allison—"

"It's a rumor," she says, her words coming out in a rush. "A kind of . . . a scary one. But since Don woke the monster up on the full moon, everyone thinks that the deal will be over during a full moon too. I wouldn't worry about it; it's just something that the older guardians say. But it is kind of scary to think about. The full moon is only a few more days away. So if something big is happening, it's happening soon."

Huh. I search Allison's face to see if she's lying, but her fear and unease seem genuine. I stare at Pastor Thomas's list, my own dread prickling on my skin. I know something big is happening during the full moon, because the snake says our deal has to be done by then. But how did Pastor Thomas guess this as well?

And what's this about running? The snake told me Don tried to run away several times but the snake caught him. I narrow my eyes at the picture. Something's off about this, but I can't put my finger on it. . . .

All thoughts of detective work are sandblasted from my brain when Allison leans her head on my shoulder. "Thinking about the monster depresses me. Let's relax for a bit."

I nod, my head and heart pounding in tandem. Relax how?

"Wanna watch a movie?" she says.

My heart rate slows, but not by much. "Sure. You pick."

I watch Allison as she hurries around the room, picks a movie, pops popcorn, chats to me about how glad she is we can hang out a lot now. My pulse goes up at that one. Thank God the snake's not here. He'd never let me live this down.

Allison gets an ice pack for my knee and turns the lights off. She pulls a blanket over us, but it's not covering her legs. She hesitates, then moves closer so our arms are almost touching. I swear my heart stops for a few seconds before spluttering back to life.

"Is it okay if I'm this close?" Allison looks up at me, her face blue from the TV.

I can feel myself melting. All thoughts of the snake and tree and whatever's not Allison leave me. I take her hand again and lean my head on her shoulder.

"It's okay," I tell her, relaxed for the first time since I was dragged from Auntie's house. "But just for you."

Allison's breath catches beneath my ear. I smile to myself, warm and safe and comforted. We watch the movie in silence until my eyelids drag closed and I fall asleep.

23

John is slamming a bat into my legs until they fall off, I'm screaming for help, and the snake is around my neck, too tight, striking at him and I can't breathe, but suddenly John is Allison and someone is whimpering and someone is rubbing my back and someone is saying "Shh, shh" over and over.

Am I dreaming? The snake and John fade, but the pain in my knee doesn't. The hand on my back doesn't. I open my eyes, and Allison's coffee table and TV are hazy and swimming, like in the heat of a mirage. Am I still in a dream?

"Shh," Allison's voice says from somewhere above me. Someone's thumb circles my temple, soothing, gentle. "It's all right. I'm here."

I close my eyes again, exhaustion pulling me back into sleep. She's here. I'm safe.

I keep falling into and out of unconsciousness. I hear

running water and someone humming. A cool weight settles on my forehead, and I fall deeper asleep. When I can finally open my eyes again, Allison's apartment is clearer, but still pretty fuzzy. My eyes ache and burn. I feel like I have a hangover.

"You still alive?"

I'm wide awake now. I sit straight up, heart pounding. Who—I blink, and the room comes into focus. Jade's sitting in the armchair, her eyebrows raised.

I let go of the blanket I was clutching, but my hands are shaking. My heart pounds in my ears. "Don't scare me like that. What're you doing here?"

"Checking on you." Jade sits up in her chair. "Allison went to a guardian meeting, but you weren't awake. She asked me to come over and make sure you didn't croak."

"Oh." I glance around the room—daylight. How long have I been asleep? I was watching a movie with Allison. . . . I reach for my neck, but the snake's scales aren't there.

"Hey, Avie."

I look at Jade again, some of the fog in my mind clearing. I went to the cemetery with the snake, he left to mope, I watched a movie with Allison and fell asleep. I remember now. "Yeah?"

Jade's staring at me with an intense expression. Her eyes are narrowed and focused. "Are you sure you're okay?"

"Yeah. You know, lots of stuff going on."

Jade frowns. "I listened to you cry in your sleep for thirty minutes."

"Thanks for not waking me up, asshole."

Jade grimaces at me. "I wasn't sure if that would make it worse. I'm just saying, Allison told me you were having nightmares and you were flinching from her and stuff. I'm worried."

"Don't be. I'm okay." I sit up straight, exhaustion making my shoulders feel like they're a thousand pounds. Peach lifts her head from her dog bed, her tail thumping on the ground. "Where's Allison again?"

Jade looks like she doesn't want to let it go, but she answers me. "Went to talk to Pastor Thomas. He's talking about closing everything down for a while. Stores, restaurants, everything."

"What? Can he do that?"

"You know the church runs this town."

I'm liking Pastor Thomas less and less.

Jade gets up and stretches her arms to the ceiling. "Okay, gotta do my job now that you're awake."

"What job?"

"Allison told me you'd better be feeling better when she got back, or she was dragging you to a doc in a box." Jade grins at me. "So don't put up a fight."

I try to protest, but Jade makes me take some Tylenol and brings me an ice pack for my knee. She even brings me a thermometer.

"Jeez," I mumble around the thermometer in my mouth. "I thought you wanted to be an accountant. Did you change your mind to be a doctor like Auntie?"

"I'd rather die," Jade says, arranging the ice pack over my knee. She's careful not to touch my skin. "But I know

Allison will kill me if you're as bad as you were when she left."

I must have looked pretty horrible. The thermometer beeps, and Jade looks at it, frowning. "One hundred point one. That's not bad! You were way worse earlier."

I touch my forehead. Warm, but not burning. I don't know why it's so off and on like this. I felt fine in the woods yesterday. "I guess you can give a good report to Allison."

"Thank God." Jade sits back in her armchair, her legs stretched out. I watch her for a second, a strange feeling in my chest. Jade and Allison care about me, way more than I thought. Jade's my cousin, but we live five hours away from each other. I saw her less and less as we grew up. And Allison is technically Jade's friend, but she's already so kind to me. I knew I didn't know a lot about Allison, but I guess I don't know much about Jade either.

"Hey, can I ask you something?" Jade nods, and I continue. "How'd you and Allison get to be friends?"

Jade folds her hands over her stomach, frowning at the ceiling. "Church day care, maybe? We've been friends since forever. Actually, now that I think about it, she was always at our house when I was little. Mom and Allison's mom don't get along, though, so I didn't see her as much when we were out of elementary school. Haven't seen that lady since the day Allison turned sixteen. Guess we know why now."

"Do you know what happened with her mom?"

Jade shakes her head. "She won't say. But it wasn't good. Allison lived with us for a while, right after her mom left. She'd never talk about it, but I heard her crying all the time. She was really depressed too. Don't tell her I told you that."

My chest aches. Poor Allison. Sounds like she gets how it feels to be betrayed. "How'd she get this apartment if her mom's AWOL?"

"Pastor Thomas. He pays rent for it every month."

Pastor Thomas? Why would he give her this apartment? Maybe because she's a guardian . . . but I'm still wary. The more I learn about this guy, the more suspicious I get. He has his hands in everything. "Isn't that weird to you? Like, he's shady, right? I'm not just imagining it."

Jade's frown deepens. "Honestly, Avie, until you got here, I didn't realize how weird things were in Sanctum. But now it's all I'm noticing."

"Yeah?"

"Yeah. Like, it is weird that Pastor Thomas pays for her apartment. And it's weird that everyone in Sanctum has to go to church. All of us, the whole town. And we don't even talk about God that much. Every Sunday, it's about the creation story, and how the devil tempted Eve."

Can't imagine why that's what Pastor Thomas would focus on. I don't say anything, though, because Jade is on the verge of puzzling it out for herself.

"And Mom is wrapped up in this stupid guardian thing, which doesn't make any sense at all to me. She would never hurt anyone, but she sacrificed you, just because

Pastor Thomas told her to." Jade finally meets my eyes, hers wide with realization. "Avie, I think I'm in a cult."

I can't hold back a laugh. Nothing about this is funny, but it's a relief that Jade and Allison are starting to wake up. "Bingo. Glad you came to that conclusion on your own, cousin."

Jade shakes her head in disbelief. "You never think it'll happen to you, and then your cousin gets almost eaten by a snake and it all comes out. Jesus."

I have to try harder not to laugh. It's kind of funny, in a horrible, morbid way. "Now that you're no longer drinking the Kool-Aid, can you help me convince Allison that Pastor Thomas is the scum of the earth?"

"I'll try, but that won't be easy. He's kind of her mentor, you know? I know he helped her a lot when her mom left."

That's what I suspected. I'll have to keep chipping away at Allison's trust in him. Jade doesn't see him as someone to look up to, but Allison won't be as easy to convince. I'll just have to be patient. Normally I wouldn't even try this hard to convince someone to leave a toxic relationship. But I care about Allison, and she deserves better than hanging around that creep so he can manipulate her and the rest of the town. And, selfishly, I want to hold on to hope that all three of us can make it out of this horrible situation unscathed.

Jade sits up, determination on her face. "Anyway, Allison said she'll be back in a little while. The last part of my job is food. I'm gonna walk to China Wok before

Pastor Thomas shuts everything down. Shrimp lo mein again?"

I give her a finger gun and a wink. "You know it."

Jade laughs and rolls her eyes. "You're so lame. When I get back, we're talking about those nightmares."

No, we are not. But I grin at her anyway, and Jade leaves Allison's apartment with a wave.

After she's gone, I slouch against the couch. I pull out my phone and Google "how to kill a large tree."

I haven't forgotten—the snake and I need to destroy the second barrier tonight. I need to focus. Allison and Jade becoming ex-cult members is important, but barriers have a time limit, and I have no clue how I'm going to kill a tree that big.

Google tells me I'll need a chain saw for the tree. Yeah, right. I might as well scream to the whole town that I'm alive and trying to destroy the barriers. I scroll through the results, my head and knee throbbing faintly.

Oh, this is interesting. Google says we can also do a "controlled burn." I feel like that'll work better than a chain saw. Flashier, but I can leave before anyone notices it. Hmm.

Peach gets out of her dog bed and waddles to me. She snuffles her nose against my hand, and I pat her absently, Googling how to do a controlled fire. She whines and licks my sore knee.

"Ow! Stop that!" Peach pants up at me, with her silly dog grin. Actually . . . now would be a good time to practice my superpower on her. No one's around, and

China Wok has a horrible wait time. We'll be alone for a while. "Peach, why don't you lie down in your bed?"

Peach stares into my eyes, then gets up, goes to her bed, and flops down. She looks at me, but doesn't get up. I set a timer on my phone, watching her closely. At nine minutes, fifty-three seconds, Peach gets up and comes back to my side, tail wagging.

Ten minutes is the time limit for my suggestion, looks like. But with Allison, she went right to sleep and didn't wake up. . . . I need to try this out more, and not on a dog. A ripple of unease moves through me. Making Peach do something is one thing, but Allison? Using her as a guinea pig for my experiment, after all she's done for me? It's not right.

I rub Peach's ears with one hand. Maybe it's okay. If I can get through the full moon, with the six dead and the snake gone, I'll never use it on her again. And I won't make her do anything bad. Just a little test. A means to an end.

I hear footsteps on the staircase and put away my thoughts of practicing on anyone. I'll figure it out later. I'll eat, have a good day with Allison and Jade, and then tonight I'll sneak out and burn down that tree with the snake. One step closer to ending this whole thing for good.

The footsteps reach the top of the stairs, and I wait for Allison to open the door, but there's silence. Then a male voice says, "Abercrombie? You home?"

Terror leaps into me like lightning. It sounds like Carter's voice, albeit muffled by the door. I jump to my feet, and Peach stands too, whining. It's okay. It's okay. I'm alone with Peach, but he can't get in. He'll leave if I don't answer. I'm okay, it's okay—

"If not Allison," Carter says, pausing for a heartbeat, "then Latavia?"

24

I stare at the door in shock, my ears ringing. It can't . . . He can't have said my name. Everyone's supposed to think I'm dead.

"I'm assuming that's you. That's your name, right?" That's definitely Carter's gruff voice. He sounds frantic, a little panicked. "I knew it. I knew Abercrombie's been acting weird, and I saw a pillow on the couch. You made a deal with the monster to escape, didn't you?"

Sweat beads against my brow. I stumble backward, my chest tight, my heart hammering against my ribs. How— how does he know? How *can* he know?

"I'm real sorry," he babbles. He sounds closer now, like he moved closer to the door. "I'm so sorry for what we did. Forty years, and we never did anything like that. . . . You weren't supposed to get hurt. But oh God, if you're living, we're fucked. We're all fucked."

I can't breathe. I have to stay quiet, pretend I'm not

here, and he'll go away. He won't come in. He won't come in. I chant the phrase in my mind, sweat beginning to pool under my arms and at the backs of my knees.

"If it's really you, Latavia, meet me at the garage tonight after midnight," he says. "I know you probably don't trust me, but you can't trust that thing in the woods either. I ain't on the Pastor's side anymore. That ship has sailed. Meet me, bring Abercrombie if you want, but we need to come up with a real plan so we don't all wind up dead. I got something in my notebook I think'll help us. After midnight, okay?"

I don't say anything, my breath frozen in my lungs, and after a minute, the stairs creak and footsteps recede until there's silence in Allison's apartment.

I'm alone. It's okay; he didn't come in. I try to talk myself into calming down, but something's wrong with me. I still can't breathe right, and my heart's beating so fast, faster than when I'm pushing myself hard at the end of a race.

Peach whines and licks my hand. I'm having a heart attack. I can't breathe. I let out a whimper and stagger to the bathroom, but nothing's helping. It's so bright. I can't breathe.

I don't know why I'm so upset. Carter figured it out, but that doesn't change anything. I would have had to confront him anyway. In fact, it might be better now; I know he'll be in his garage tonight after midnight. But he could have come into the apartment, and the snake isn't here. Allison and Jade aren't here.

I close my eyes. My body aches to run, but I can't, and I want to breathe, but I can't. It's bright, too bright. I hobble into Allison's room, which is mercifully dark. I kinda feel better in here, away from the front door, so I let Peach follow me in and I close the door. I stand in the middle of the room, one hand over my thudding heart. It's okay. He didn't come in. The snake will be back soon. It's okay.

Slowly, my wheezing turns into harsh panting. God, what is wrong with me? I can't be sick—I can't go to the hospital if Auntie is there. I ease to the floor, fighting off Peach as she runs to lick my face. I forgot my cane, so I don't know how I'll get back up, but curling into a ball beside Allison's bed seems like a good idea right now. At least until I can breathe okay.

Peach eventually settles down and lays her head in my lap, and the longer I sit in the dark, surrounded by Allison's bunched-up clothes and Peach, the better I feel. My heart rate slows, and my eyes don't hurt as much anymore. But why did I freak out like that? I touch my chest, sudden nausea making my stomach churn. What the hell was that? I thought I was going to die. That was worse than when they were chasing me down in Red Wood.

I stiffen when I hear faint footsteps again. Peach lifts her head and trots to the bedroom door, staring at it intently. My heart rate climbs, faster and faster, as the footsteps get louder. There's a pause, and then the creak of the front door opening.

There's someone here. There's someone in the apartment, they're coming, they're—

"Avie?"

I blink, gasping for air. Allison's voice. She's back. Oh God, okay. I'm okay.

"Avie?" Allison calls again, concern in her voice. I should tell her I'm in here, but I'm still trying to get my breathing under control. Peach woofs softly, tail wagging, and a few seconds later, Allison peeks into her room.

I wave at her, smiling weakly. "H-hey."

Allison frowns, opening the door wider. I wince at the extra light. "Hey. You okay?"

Oh yeah, I'm huddled in a ball, in her room, in the dark. I swallow the lump in my throat and try to give her my best smile. I'm sure it looks miserable, though; I'm shaking. "Y-yeah. Sorry I'm in your room. I just felt kind of, um, overwhelmed for a second. But I'm better now, I think."

Allison stares at me for a second, then comes in. She's wearing a red T-shirt and white shorts, but also what looks like a handmade necklace fashioned out of shells. She puts her keys on her desk and kicks off her shoes. I'm relieved when she closes the door, shutting out the light of the living room.

"Can I sit next to you?" she asks.

I study her face for a second. Her expression is hard to read; a little concerned, a little something else. I swallow hard again and nod. "Um, yeah, that's okay."

She sits next to me, not too close, not too far away. Peach runs to bombard her with dog kisses, and she squeals, laughing and holding Peach at arm's length. I can't help smiling, and even though I'm still shaking, I feel a little better.

"Peach, let's leave her alone, okay?" I say.

Peach immediately stops and lies down at our feet, panting. Allison glances at me, a bemused grin on her face.

"That dog listens to you better than me. And I'm supposed to be the owner!"

I laugh a little. "Can't help that she likes me better." Normally I'd say more, joke with her for a while, but I don't feel like it. I kind of feel like throwing up.

Allison is quiet for a moment, but then says, "Are you feeling better? You were pretty sick when I left."

"I'm better," I assure her. "Fever-wise, anyway."

She nods, and there's another heavy silence between us. I should get up and go back to the couch and wait for Jade to bring Chinese food and just be normal . . . but I still have that sick feeling. My heart's still beating too fast. I'm still trembling.

"How'd the meeting go?" I ask to dispel the unbearable quiet. "First day on the job as a . . . what do you call it when you're spying for the enemy?"

"A mole?" Allison crinkles her nose, which creates a few adorable wrinkles over the bridge. "I don't like that. We can just say I'm a spy."

"No!" I laugh. "Cutest mole in Sanctum!"

"Oh God, *stop*." Allison laughs too, and some of that sick feeling fades. Maybe this is what I needed. Darkness, quiet, and teasing Allison. "I'm a lousy mole anyway. Nothing happened. Everyone was screaming at each other. Dr. Roberts refused to come, and she's usually the voice of reason, so it was madness. I had to listen to John and Carter argue about if they're going to do a funeral for Katie like normal or not. It was awful."

I feel a twinge of guilt when she mentions Katie. I hope they do have a funeral. For the first time, they actually have a body. "Did Pastor Thomas say anything?"

"No. He just sat there and watched. Carter got so mad, he left early, and Pastor Thomas said we should meet again after everyone calms down."

So that's why Carter came back before Allison. I can't stifle a nervous shudder at the thought of him being so close, and me alone. Just like what happened that night in Red Wood.

We're quiet again. All the tentative laughter from before is gone as I replay that night, feeling worse and worse.

"Did something happen while I was gone?" Allison's tone is gentle, and when I meet her eyes, her expression is soft and welcoming. For some reason, I kind of want to cry.

"I . . ." I take a breath, in through the nose, out through the mouth. I can't tell her what Carter said, but I can't lie and say I'm fine. Obviously, I'm not. "Someone came to the door."

Allison nods, frowning. "Do you know who?"

I shake my head. I hate that I have to lie to her, but that conversation would be really hard to explain. "They didn't say anything. But I knew it wasn't you or Jade because they didn't come in, and I . . ." I struggle for the words to describe what happened. I put a shaking hand to my neck, reaching for scales that aren't there. "I freaked out. Like, all at once I couldn't breathe or something. And

213

everything was so bright and I got shaky. . . . I'm in here because I thought sitting in the dark might help. It did, but I'm sorry for barging in without asking."

Allison nods again, her eyebrows furrowed in concern. "Sounds like you had a panic attack."

"Oh." Now that she says that . . . I guess that makes sense. My friend Lindsay used to have them before a big exam. "But I've never had one before. Why'd I have a panic attack now?"

"Well . . ." Allison hesitates for a second. "Avie, do you know about PTSD?"

I blink at her, confused. "Yeah? Why?"

"I think that's why you had a panic attack. I'm not an expert or anything, but I think you might have PTSD. From when they tried to sacrifice you."

I stare at her for a few seconds, my brain empty. PTSD . . . me? But, but I was fine. I am fine. I think I'm fine?

"Like I said, I don't know for sure," Allison hurries to continue, "but you've been having nightmares and flash-backs, and when I touch you without warning, you flinch. And you get really tense when you hear Jade on the steps. When they attacked you, I'm sure it was pretty traumatic."

Oh. Oh God, what she's saying makes sense. All the nightmares, the panic . . . I really might have PTSD. Sharp pain hits my chest, and I have to blink back angry tears.

"You okay?" Allison's voice pulls me out of my furious despair.

"Yeah . . . I guess I'm just shocked." I hold back a few more tears. I'm so mad, I want to hit something.

"It's okay. It gets better! We can look into therapy, and we can work through it together. Me and Jade'll help."

I take in Allison's sincere, determined expression. She said something happened to her too, right? Maybe she's already been through this. Maybe I'm not alone. "Do you have PTSD too?"

"Not exactly. I have nightmares sometimes, but not like yours. And I don't have any triggers. Not that I know of, anyway."

"But I don't have triggers either," I argue, my heart rate going up a little.

"Avie . . ." Allison's voice is unbearably gentle. "You do. If you get so scared you have a panic attack when someone comes up the staircase, that's a trigger."

I can't even say anything. Oh God, what have they done to me? They ruined my leg, my future, and now this? My own peace of mind? Tears gather in my eyes again, but they're not angry like before. Despair threatens to swallow me whole. Everything gets worse and worse.

Allison touches the back of my hand. "Is this okay?"

I nod, sniffling. She takes my hand, hers a little rough to the touch but holding mine in a tight, comforting squeeze.

"It's okay, Avie, I promise. It's not a life sentence. It gets better. And I'll help you, for as long as I can."

I meet Allison's eyes, mine full of unshed tears, and she makes a sympathetic face.

"Do you want a hug?"

I laugh a little. A hug, versus nightmares and panic attacks and suffering. But the hug is coming from Allison, who is sweet and soft and told me she'll help fix what Sanctum broke, and that might be just what I need.

"Yeah. Thanks, Allison."

Allison wraps her arms around me and holds me tight. I close my eyes and hug her back, a little dazzled by the smell of strawberries in her hair. And even though I'm confused and scared, Allison holding me close makes me feel like everything will be all right.

"I'm sorry this happened to you, Avie." Her voice is soft and right by my ear. But what's surprising is an undercurrent of fury in her tone. "I don't care if they hurt me, but what they did to you is so horrible. Unforgivable." She hugs me tighter, protectively, and I'm finding it hard to breathe again. "Don't worry, Avie. They won't get away with this. I'll make sure you and Jade get through the monster stuff, but they're not gonna hurt you and get away with it. I promise you that."

My breath catches in my chest, and Allison breaks our hug. She smiles, but there's a hint of dark promise in her eyes I've never seen before.

"Let's go back to the living room, okay? I'll make us some tea, and Jade'll be back with the food soon."

"Okay," I say, but I'm a little stunned. I didn't know Allison had a mean bone in her body. No, not mean—something quietly furious, something sharp and potentially dangerous. Something a lot like what I've been feeling lately.

Allison helps me up, and we leave her room, Peach at our heels, but all I can think about is that I may have had a small crush on Allison before, but I *really* like her now.

25

Peach and I stand at the edge of Red Wood, waiting for the snake.

It's late, almost midnight. I hung out with Jade and Allison all day, and Allison sat close to me as we watched *Chopped* and bet on who would win. I decided not to tell Jade about the potential PTSD, not yet. I don't know if I even still believe it. I'm confused and depressed and furious, and I can't do anything about any of those feelings. Plus, I have to tell the snake about Carter knowing I'm still alive and that he knows about our deal, which I'm not looking forward to. I already have a headache. I kind of want to sleep on Allison's couch for a hundred years.

But I can't mope around. We have a tree to burn and a Carter to meet and possibly murder, so I have to keep going.

I frown, glancing at my phone. It's been seven minutes; this isn't like him. Usually, he comes to me. I pet Peach's head, a little nervous.

"Wanna go in to find the snake?" I ask her. She wags her tail, so I guess that's a yes. I take a few steps into the woods, keeping an eye on the forest floor so I don't trip. The cicadas scream in my ears and an owl hoots overhead. He's definitely not close by.

At first, I wander around aimlessly, waiting for him to sense me and get all huffy about a person in his woods. But then I feel a kind of tug in my chest, pulling me deeper into the dense trees. I pass a familiar clearing—where Allison and Jade found me. I keep going, walking and walking and walking, until another clearing comes into view. A familiar blue glow shines near the back.

"Huh." I stop and fold my arms. Peach puts her nose to the ground and explores the clearing, tail wagging happily. How did I know where to go? It was like walking to Auntie's after church, or knowing where the bathroom is in the dark. I've only been to the cave once. It's like I came here on . . . instinct.

I shudder a little. I don't want to think about developing snake-sensing instincts.

"Come on, Peach." I walk to the mouth of the cave, but Peach whines and stops at the entrance. Bad sign. This is where white people in a horror movie would go straight into the cave and get killed, but I'm not stupid. Always listen to the dog.

"Hey, snake!" I yell. "Are you in there?"

I wait in tense silence until I hear the faint sound of his scales scraping against the rocks. It doesn't take long for his dark shadow to appear.

"Hello, Latavia," the snake says, poking his massive

head out of the cave. "I'm pleased to see you. Saves me the journey to your friend's home."

"Do you know what time it is?" I complain. "I gotta be home before sunrise because Allison wakes up hella early, and it's already past midnight. What were you doing?"

"I was swimming."

I wait for elaboration, but he doesn't say anything. "Okay. . . . Are you ready to destroy the tree?"

"Yes. I'm ready. Have you found a solution?"

"I was thinking, there's no way I can chop a tree down. Super strength or not. So I thought we could burn it."

"Yes, that will work," the snake says. "We have to be careful not to get too close."

Fire weakness potentially confirmed? But anyone would be hurt by fire, so that's not really helpful. "Yeah, of course." I hesitate. I should tell him about Carter now, but a part of me really doesn't want to.

"What's wrong?" the snake says after a heartbeat of silence. "You are upset."

"I'm not," I say automatically, but even I can hear the wobble in my voice.

The snake fully emerges from the cave and curls around me, his head close to mine. "You're not being honest, Latavia. Has someone injured you? Do you need comfort again?"

Oh jeez, how thoughtful of the giant snake monster. I shuffle my feet and take a breath to steady my nerves. "Carter came to Allison's apartment. He said he knows I'm still alive and that I made a deal with you."

"Ah." The snake closes his mouth and lowers his head

a bit, like he's thinking. "I see why you're upset now. This is an unfortunate development."

"Yeah." I take another breath, my chest uncomfortably tight.

"No," the snake says. He gets closer to me, so his snout is almost touching my cheek. "There is something else?"

I drum my fingers on my leg. I don't know why I'm even telling him; I doubt ancient, giant monsters even know what PTSD is. But I want to talk about it with someone, anyone, and Allison is asleep and Peach can't talk back. "When he came over, I panicked. Totally freaked out. I couldn't breathe and stuff. It was horrible."

To my surprise, the snake nods. "I understand. This is a manifestation of your fear. Like your screaming."

Whoa. I guess I need to give ancient, giant monsters more credit. "Yeah, pretty much. I don't know, I'm just feeling weird about it, I guess. I've never had a panic attack before."

The snake rests his chin on the top of my head, so gentle, it's shocking. "I am sympathetic, Latavia. Your pain is unfortunate. However, I'm sure you'll feel better once we get further into our deal. After all, humans cannot hurt you if they're dead."

"I don't think that's how PTSD works." But then again . . . I haven't dreamed about Katie since he killed her. Huh.

"I don't know what that is, but I assure you, you'll feel better." He lifts his head and uncurls himself, so his body's in a loose line. "First, we will meet this Carter and take

care of him. Before we end him, I'm sure he'll have fasci-
nating information for us."

"Yeah." I rub the top of my head, where the snake's
chin was.

"And then we will attend to burning the tree. One
step at a . . ." The snake trails off, his head tilted to one
side, suddenly alert. He turns and hisses. "Oh, how irri-
tating."

"What?"

"Humans. In my forest." Without warning, the snake
grabs my shirt collar and deposits me on his back. "I
will hurry, but I have to take care of this business first.
Hold on."

He doesn't give me a chance to say no. He rockets
out of the clearing. Peach barks in alarm and races after
us. "Jeez, give me some warning next time!" I yell. "Why
are you so sensitive about people coming into Red Wood
anyway?"

"It's about respect." The snake moves through the woods
with alarming speed. "Humans have the entire world; all
I ask is for one forest to hunt and sleep and eat in. And
they cannot even grant me that. Humans are greedy and
selfish, and even worse, arrogant. I have to be firm with a
species like this. They think they are above my rules, and
I have to remind them of their place."

I stay silent while the snake travels toward the edge
of Red Wood. Yikes. The snake is kind of scary when he
wants to be. I've gotten used to seeing him, hearing him
speak—I forgot about his monstrous side.

The snake slows. "We're here. Be silent."

I squint, and I can make out two people at the edge of the woods. "They're not even in the woods yet!"

"They are too close," the snake says. "But in the interest of fairness, I will wait until they step inside."

The snake eases closer, still out of sight. But I can hear them now, a man and a woman.

"Please," the woman begs. "I don't have any more money. I gave you all I have!"

"I know you have more!" the man yells.

A robbery? The woman starts crying, and my stomach clenches.

"Please, that's all. I don't have nothing else."

The man's eyebrows furrow, like he's evaluating her story. Then he grins at her, a nasty one that splits his face in two. "You've got something else I want." He pulls something out of his pocket. Metal glints in the moonlight.

"No!" the woman shrieks as he lunges at her, and she backs away from him . . . right into Red Wood.

The snake heaves a sigh. "Humans never learn. Stay here, Latavia. It won't take long."

"Wait!" I say, scrambling off his back. "That woman's being robbed. That guy basically forced her in here."

"So?" The snake sounds bored.

"Oh, you've done it now," the man says, taunting the woman. "You better come out before the monster gets you."

The woman trembles, hanging on to the trunk of a tree. She doesn't say anything—she's glancing around desperately, looking for a way out. My stomach rolls and I'm sweating, more than I should for an Alabama summer. This scene is too familiar. She's trying to get away, and the snake is about to kill her for nothing.

"Don't do it," I tell the snake. "Don't kill her, please."

"Please?" The snake lowers his head so he's eye level with me. "This human is in my forest. You want me to forgive this transgression?"

"It's not her fault!" I'm shaking. I want to say it's fury, rage that another man in this rotten town is trying to hurt someone, but I don't think it's solely rage making me tremble. "Okay, how about this? Kill the man instead, let the woman go. She wouldn't be in here if not for him, so it's his fault."

The snake is silent for a moment. "I believe you are projecting your experience onto these humans, Latavia. You wish someone had saved you."

My mouth dries up. I can't stop shaking. My knee aches, and my head hurts too. I'm hearing the men's shouts, the police dog's barking, the crack of my broken leg. This is just like earlier. I'm scared. But I stuff the fear down and reach for fury. It surges up and I stand tall.

"Yeah, maybe. But you can't treat every person the same. We're not chickens or cows. If someone has to die, at least let it be an asshole who would have hurt someone else."

The snake is quiet again. Then— "Fine. I do not see your point of view, but I will appease you this time, Latavia. Perhaps the female human will learn not to wander near my woods at night."

The snake changes into his small form and surges forward like lightning. A few seconds later, the man yelps in pain, collapses, convulses, and is dead. It happens in seconds. Just like what happened with Katie.

The woman's eyes are round. She peeks around the tree, confused. But the snake isn't done. He slithers back into the woods, and as soon as his entire body is within the forest, he swells to his full height and opens his mouth to reveal his fangs.

"Get out."

The woman screams, but doesn't move, her whole body shaking. She's in shock. I've stopped shaking, though. I glance at the dead man. I'm starting to feel better.

"Hey, leave her be," I tell the snake, limping to his side. The woman stares at me, her eyes so big I'm scared they'll pop out of her head. "You have no finesse, you know? She's in shock."

The snake's glaring at me like he wants to eat me. "You handle this, then." He shrinks and climbs up my leg to my shoulders. "Get the human out, immediately."

I give the woman my best smile. I really do feel better. My heart rate is almost back to normal. "Are you okay?"

"You . . ." The woman's voice is small and quiet. I recognize her now—Hannah Trevino, the daughter of the butcher. I used to see her hanging out at China Wok all the time. "You're dead."

"That's right." I smile at her. "I'm a ghost."

Hannah doesn't say anything; she's still stunned.

"Actually," I say, my chest swelling with confidence,

"I'm a vengeful spirit. This town murdered me, you know. The pastor, the sheriff, my own aunt. And I'm not going to tolerate any of this bullshit anymore." I nod to the dead robber.

Hannah follows my nod and stares at the dead man, then turns back to me. She looks into my eyes, hers wide and watery.

"You saved me."

I stand taller, secret pleasure coursing through me. "Well, yes."

"Thank you." The woman's voice is filled with wonder, like Delilah's was.

"Get her out." The snake hisses in my ear.

"Sorry, my snake friend is pissed off. You need to leave now." I point straight ahead. She walks on wobbly legs out of Red Wood, glancing back at me and the snake uncertainly. "Don't tell anyone you saw me," I say, but immediately change my mind. "Well, I guess you can. Make sure you say a ghost saved you."

I wave at her, still smiling. She looks back, but once she's a few steps away, she takes off running. I watch her leave, a strange mix of feelings in my gut. Slight embarrassment over her thanking me, pride over being able to convince the snake to spare her, happiness that she got away. And more than anything, relief. I was panicking, and watching another dreg of Sanctum get punished for hurting someone calmed me. The snake killed him, like he will Carter if something goes wrong. I'm okay. It's like he said: I don't have to be scared of the dead.

I glance at the dead man. He has a thin line of foam leaking from one side of his mouth, and he's staring at the sky with glassy eyes, like Katie. But unlike Katie, I don't feel sorry for him.

I feel kinda good.

26

It takes me almost an hour to hobble to Carter's garage.

I'm cursing his existence and his dumb idea to put his garage all the way on the other side of town. Doesn't he know some of us don't have cars? Some of us have to walk on a bum knee he helped destroy.

"Are you pleased with the outcome of your foray into altruism?" the snake asks.

I roll my eyes. "You don't have to be an asshole about it."

We left the man's body where he fell. Someone will probably find him tomorrow. But I haven't been able to shake the weird feeling of helping Hannah out. It's kind of scary. I didn't even flinch when he fell. Combined with the snake's words about PTSD earlier . . . yikes. But I really shouldn't feel bad; that man deserved the snake's fangs for what he did. I'm already doing the world a favor with the six, so what's one more scum of the earth taking a dirt nap?

"It was interesting," the snake says. "But do not become accustomed to relying on me for your games."

A prickle of discomfort races down my neck. It's not a game. I saw a woman in trouble, I saved her. That's it. I continue to walk in silence, Peach in step beside me. I need to stop thinking about it. It was a one-time thing. I need to focus on the original plan.

My heart rate kicks up as the garage comes into view. There's a yellow glow coming from inside; Carter's in there. He's in there, waiting for me, knowing I'm working with the snake, knowing I have a deal with him. He said his notebook might have something that'll help "us." I am curious about that, but the thought of meeting one of the six again, face to face and not through a door, sends tremors up and down my body. My breath gets short again, and I put a hand over my chest.

"Stop, Latavia," the snake murmurs in my ear. I stop walking, my legs feeling a bit like Jell-O. "You wait here. I will see where he is, so we have the advantage. I'll come back and we can strategize."

I nod, comforted by the plan. "Be careful. He's waiting on us, remember."

"I remember. I am simply unconcerned about that." The snake eases down my back to the ground. I shudder when his scales leave my skin. I've gotten used to him around my neck, but it's weird when he climbs down my body like I'm a tree.

I watch the snake disappear into the building, and then I hide behind one of the bulky gas pumps so no one can see me. I lean against it for support. Peach flops down at my feet, panting. She must be burning up, with all that fur. I tug at my shirt collar, and not just because of the heat. I'm nervous. Katie didn't put up a fight, but I don't think Carter will come easily. We can't surprise him; he knows we're coming. What if he's got one of the barriers and throws some of that orange stuff at us? That shit is radioactive. I don't know what the snake's made of, but I'm certain that'll melt my skin off. Rapid-fire worst-case scenarios flash in my brain. We shouldn't have split up. We shouldn't have come at all.

"Latavia."

I glance around the gas pump, surprised. The snake is still inside the building. I can see his tiny head poking out from under the garage door.

"Come. I have something you won't like."

"But what about Carter?" I whisper. The snake ignores me and disappears back into the building.

Well, this can't be good. I limp toward the building, my heart thumping hard against my ribs. I go to the front door of the attached garage and open it cautiously. It's dark, except for the soft glow of a light hidden from view. The snake leads me to an office at the back of the garage, dodging wrenches and patches of oil.

I peek inside, expecting Carter to be at his desk. I'm half-right. He's in the room, but he's not at his desk. He's flat on his back in the middle of the floor, eyes open and staring at the ceiling, dark bruises circling his neck.

He's dead.

I stare at the corpse for a moment, my brain short-circuiting. Carter is dead. Strangled, looks like. But the snake wouldn't strangle anyone—he'd just bite them. I limp closer; the bruises are in the shape of fingers.

I look at the snake. "You don't have hands."

"No," the snake says, coiling his body above Carter's head. "I do not."

I rub the bridge of my nose. "Okay, wait—someone got him before we did?"

"Yes, it appears so."

"But who? Why?"

The snake is quiet for a second. His tongue flicks in and out. "Perhaps someone did not want him to share his information with us."

Wait, wait—does that mean someone else knows about my deal with the snake? Or is this an unrelated thing and bad timing? "Can't you, like, smell who did it or something?"

"I am not a hound," the snake says, annoyance in his voice. "And even if you asked yours, it could not tell us."

I rub my temples. I have a headache. Who would want to kill Carter more than me? I don't get it. "It had to be one of the guardians," I say out loud. "The sheriff, or Pastor Thomas, or John—"

"Or your friend," the snake says quietly.

I stare at the snake, confusion and dread swirling in my gut. No. No way. Allison couldn't hurt anyone if you paid her. But I flash back to earlier today, her arms around me, the fury in her voice . . .

No. I shut that thought down. Carter is dead, and I don't want to meet whoever killed him. I can think about Allison later. "Let's look around and go."

I start searching Carter's office, trying to avoid his body. His eyes are staring straight up. What did he see before he died? I feel a twinge of revulsion. I wish he'd seen me and the snake, had really known what he'd done to me. But I'm a little relieved I didn't have to do it.

I open several desk drawers, but no notebook. He couldn't have made it easy for me, could he? Oh God, what if it's in his pocket and I have to touch his dead body? I'm shuddering with revulsion when I catch sight of a brown corner under a stack of papers. Thank goodness I don't have to touch a corpse. I pull it from under the papers and reveal a familiar, worn journal. I flip through it, but . . . the pages are blank.

"Did you find something of interest?" the snake asks.

"Uh, maybe," I say, distracted. I keep flipping, but it's blank page after blank page. Katie's and Auntie's notebooks were full of writing at the front, and then blank pages. Maybe this isn't it?

"Hmm," the snake says as I finally find a speck of writing in the last five pages. "Why are you so interested in these journals, Latavia? You also had one at the child's house."

I don't answer him at first, because the writing on the page says "recipes." Pound cake, lemon squares, strawberry tarts, and, at the very end of the book—

Plasma.

I have to be calm. The snake is around my neck, so if I let him, he'll feel my pulse, my excitement over finding a weapon to use against him. I take a slow breath to steady my nerves.

"It's a recipe book, for, like, human food," I tell the snake, careful not to look at him. "I want some of these.

231

Hang on." I take pictures of several pages to throw him off, but I'm aching to read the Plasma recipe. I glanced at the top line, and "two inches of hair" certainly doesn't sound like a regular dessert. I'll have to read it later, when he's not watching.

"I see," the snake says. His voice is neutral; I can't tell if he believes me. "We do not have time for food, however. Do you see anything else useful? Perhaps how to burn the tree?"

Oh yeah, the tree. We still have a ton of work to do tonight. I push down the excitement and find a cheap lighter on Carter's desk, and on the way out, I grab a can of gasoline. I leave the garage, the snake perched on my shoulders. Peach looks up at me when I get outside, tail wagging. I pat her head, my mind wandering back to Carter's still body.

"Hey," I say to the snake, trying to get Carter's dead eyes out of my mind, "was his body still warm?"

"Yes. It was."

I scratch behind Peach's ears uneasily. So he was just killed. There's a murderer out here, somewhere, and I don't know who's on his—or her—list. "Let's hurry up, snake. There's a murderer on the loose."

The snake laughs, long and loud. "Yes, Latavia. This town has at least three."

27

The snake and I arrive at Sanctum's cemetery, ready to burn down that tree.

I just want to get this over with. This has been a long night, and I need time to think. Who would kill Carter? For what? And will there be another murder? I don't really care if someone else is targeting the guardians. Less work I have to do. But I do care if Allison is on their list.

I do care if Allison has a list of her own.

I shake that thought from my mind as I limp to the back of the cemetery, my knee aching. It's swollen again, burning angrily under the brace. I need to go back to Allison's and cry into a pillow for a while. And take a shower. When I get to the tree, the pain in my knee amplifies and sweat beads on my brow. I groan, rubbing my knee. This is the worst.

"Are you all right?" the snake asks.

"Fine." I take a breath. In through the nose, out through

the mouth. "Let me toss the gas, and we can go home. My knee's killing me."

The snake doesn't say anything more, so I unscrew the cap off the gas can and toss the liquid at the tree. The trunk probably doesn't need much, but I make sure it's good and soaked. I lead a thin trail away from the tree, like they do in movies. Hopefully that works.

"Be careful when you light it," the snake says. "We must not get burned."

I look at the snake out of the corner of my eye. This is a strong case for confirming the fire weakness. I file that away in my get-away-without-being-eaten plan. "Okay. Let's get this over with—"

Peach, who had been diligently digging up Don's bones again, lifts her head and stares behind me. She lets out a soft growl and comes to my side.

I turn, slowly, and see two figures standing a short distance away. If I couldn't see in the dark, I wouldn't be able to see them at all, but I can make out two men as they step closer. Two men in police uniforms.

Shit.

"Do not panic, Latavia," the snake says next to my ear. "Remember what I said. Do not fear humans."

Easier said than done. As they get closer, I notice a dog slightly behind them. It barks, a deep threatening sound, and Peach barks back.

"What're you doing out here?"

I can't keep a slow smile from spreading on my face. I recognize that voice.

Sheriff Kines.

I don't say anything as they get closer. The other cop shines his flashlight in my face. I grin widely in the light, showing all my teeth.

"It's you." Sheriff Kines's voice is hushed with horror. "You . . . How . . ."

"Don't you know you shouldn't come to the graveyard at night?" I ask. I was scared before, but I'm not scared now. I was kind of looking forward to this one. I lean casually on my cane, nonchalant, unbothered. "You might see some ghosts."

The other cop drops his flashlight. The police dog growls and Peach snarls back. Sweat pools under my arms as I glance at Kines's dog, remembering its teeth in my arm. But I can't think about the police dog. Sheriff Kines is right here in front of me. I'm not interested in talking to him, like with Katie. Katie just stood there. The sheriff put his hands on me, dragged me into the night. This will be a fight. And when I win, I'll be at three out of six. Halfway there.

"Keep him distracted," the snake says in my ear. He slides down my back slowly, carefully. A surprise attack.

"Don't kill the wrong one," I murmur, but I don't know if he hears me.

"You're supposed to be dead," the second cop says, his voice trembling. He's only a few years older than me, poor guy. We really should let him go. "What's going on, Sheriff? What do we do?"

"Looks like he's been lying to you." I keep my tone

light as the snake slips down my leg to the grass. "Did you know there was a giant snake in Red Wood? That's why you have a big funeral every summer, you know. Sanctum sacrifices people to him. Including me."

The second cop looks at Sheriff Kines for reassurance, but the sheriff is glaring at me. "You killed Katie."

"No. The snake did." I shrug, grinning. "But I did help."

The police dog whines and backs up a few steps. It looks up at the sheriff, but he's staring at me.

"How'd you get off the altar?" Sheriff Kines asks. His voice is full of disgust. As if I'm the one who wronged him. As if this situation is my fault somehow.

"Turns out, the snake doesn't like it when people go back on their deals. And I don't like it when six town-ies try to kill me." I pause. I really should ask him about the full moon before the snake decides to bite him. "Real quick, Sheriff—do you know anything about some note-books? If you have yours on you, that'd be great."

Sheriff Kines glares at me. "You know too much."

Okay, no compromise, then. My muscles tense auto-matically for the fight. I nod at the other police officer. "You really should run. I don't want to hurt you."

He looks at the sheriff with a panicked expression. "Sheriff?"

"Stay strong, Roy," Sheriff Kines barks. "I'm done with this. We messed up the ceremony last time, but maybe if we do it right, this madness will stop."

Roy's expression hardens, and he reaches for his hip.

Wrong move.

The snake leaps, faster than my eye can follow, and

closes his fangs around Roy's arm. He screams, an anguished, animal sound, and then everyone is moving.

The police dog lurches forward, but Peach jumps in front of me, snarling, and the two dogs wrestle each other. The sheriff pulls out his gun, but I'm close, close enough to hit him, and I swing my cane and knock the gun from his hand. He swears and dives for it, but the snake hisses and snaps at him, curling around the gun. Roy is dead—lips blue and eyes staring, like Katie.

"How do you want to play this, Sheriff?" I'm leaning heavily on my good leg, the cane on the ground at my feet. I'm panting, feeling a little sick. Poor, dumb Roy. And dumb snake. Why the hell didn't he kill Sheriff Kines first? "You're not getting out of this alive."

The sheriff surprises me by returning my smile. "Looks like we'll see each other in hell." In one motion, the sheriff withdraws a baton from his belt and lunges at me. I stagger backward, but suddenly the sheriff changes direction and slams the club down on the snake.

"Charlie!" Sheriff Kines yells.

The police dog wrestles away from Peach and charges at me. Animal terror seizes me, and I'm back to that night, the dog barking in my ears, teeth sinking into my skin. I gasp, trying to force my heart to calm down. I can't panic right now— Fuck, the snake, the dog—

"Peach!" Peach is running, but she's so big and so slow, the police dog is on me before she can get here. It snaps at me, snarling, and out of the corner of my eye I see the sheriff grab his gun from the ground, and I can't breathe, I'm gonna lose this and it'll all be over—

The police dog leaps at me, teeth shining in the moon-light, and closes its jaws around my arm for the second time.

Pain shoots up my arm and I scream. The dog shakes my arm like a chew toy, but I'm stronger than when I was in the woods before. I'm not letting a fucking dog take me out. Not this time. Peach runs to me, but I point to the sheriff, teeth gritted against the pain, tears in my eyes. "Peach, the gun! Please grab the gun, won't you please?!"

And, miraculously, Allison's big dumb hound listens to me and tackles the sheriff.

The police dog lets go of my arm, confused, and I kick it as hard as I can in the ribs with my good leg. It yelps and cringes. "Fuck off, dog! I mean, it's time to stop attacking me, don't you think?"

The dog whines, belly to the ground, looking from me to Sheriff Kines, but doesn't move.

Sheriff Kines curses and shoves Peach off him. She's like a white Cujo, snarling, foam and blood dripping from her lips. He fumbles for his gun, but Peach snatches it and darts away. I grab my cane at the same time he grabs his baton. We make eye contact for a heartbeat, and then he raises his baton to hit the snake again.

I don't think before moving. I make it to my feet and ignore the screaming pain in my knee as I rush to stand in front of the snake and swing my cane with all my might at Sheriff Kines's head. The handle of the cane hits him in his temple, and he drops like a sack of potatoes.

He doesn't get back up.

I stand there, panting, my stomach aching and my

mouth dry. He's not getting up. Blood runs from his temple into his hairline. I watch his chest, but it's still. He's not breathing.

I killed him.

I lean over a grave and throw up.

Oh God. Oh my God, I forgot about the super strength. I killed someone. I wasn't thinking, I thought he was gonna kill the snake—

The snake.

I limp to him, my breathing ragged. The snake is on his back, not moving. Blood oozes from several points on his pale belly. Shit. "Snake? Hey, you okay?"

No answer. Fuck, don't be dead—

"Hey, snake, answer me. Are you still alive?"

I touch his belly with one finger, and he jerks, his tail rattling. He rights himself, his head wobbly, and snaps at my hand. I jerk it back just in time. "Well fuck you too! Are you okay?"

The snake blinks groggily up at me. "Latavia . . . ? What happened?"

"You almost got beaten to death."

The snake blinks again, his head swaying back and forth. "Oh. I forget how fragile this form is. What happened to the two humans?"

"You killed one." I look back at the still body of Sheriff Kines, and a shiver creeps down my spine. "And I killed the other."

The snake stares at the body for a moment, then up at me. He exposes his fangs in a grin.

"Well done."

I take a deep breath. The adrenaline is gone, and my hands are shaking. I killed him. I killed him with my cane. I had to, though, right? He would have killed the snake, and everything would have been ruined. And it's not like he was a good person. He terrorized this town with his gun and dog—

The dog. I look back at the police dog, who's lying down with its head on its paws. It looks at me, ears pricked. It listened to me, just like Peach. But not for long—I don't know how many of my ten minutes have passed already. "Hey, dog. Why don't you leave the cemetery? Keep walking for a while. That sounds nice, right?"

Slowly the police dog rises to its feet. It meets my eyes and then trots away, heading for the front gate.

"Latavia." The snake presses his head against my hand. He's still blinking groggily, and his voice is soft and strained. "Am I bleeding?"

"Yeah." Concern leaps into me all at once. He looks horrible. As horrible as a snake can look, I guess.

"You didn't touch my blood, did you?"

I pause, frowning. What a weird question. "No, why?"

"Good." The snake doesn't elaborate, but twists and rolls in the grass for a while. When all the blood from his belly is gone, he wraps himself around my wrist, resting his head against my arm wearily. "I have not felt such pain in a long time. I'm beginning to see why you want these humans dead, Latavia."

I can't help but laugh—as fucked up as it is to be

240

laughing at a joke a talking snake told, standing over the dead body of someone I killed. I take a deep breath. Hold it together, Latavia. One more thing, and I can go home.

"Hang on, snake." I take the lighter from my pocket. "Let's burn down that tree."

28

I'm halfway to Allison's house when I feel it.

Just like when I shattered the first barrier, there's a pop, like my ears on a plane, and the town is set in silence. The snake lifts his head from my wrist.

"It worked," he says. He sounds pleased. "I'm already feeling much better. You should be feeling better too, Latavia."

"I don't feel anything." Truthfully, I feel sick. All I can see is the sheriff's body, still, with a single trickle of blood leaking out of his crushed skull. My stomach clenches.

"Look at your arm."

I do, and I start. The wound from the police dog is gone, healed over like it never happened. I touch it; there are tiny bumps where its teeth sank into my skin, but there's no pain, no real scar.

"And now look at me." The snake climbs down my arm and drops to the ground. He winces a little at the impact, a quick jerk of his scales, but then crawls a short distance away. And then, before my eyes, he grows to half his height. He's now slightly taller than me, and his body is as thick as the tree we burned down.

"Whoa." That's all I can think of to say.

"I can see you are impressed." I don't miss the hint of pride in his voice. "Half of the barriers are destroyed, so I am at half strength. This is a good development indeed."

"Can you still be small, though? I'm not carrying you like that."

The snake chuckles and touches his nose to my hand. In a second, he's back to his small form, curled around my wrist again.

"Every barrier we destroy makes us stronger," the snake says, his tone happy and light. "One step closer to your revenge and my feast."

I don't say anything. Why are "we" getting stronger and not just him? And what was that weird question about his blood? He doesn't lie, but he doesn't tell me everything either. Carter was right. There's a lot I don't know, and a lot the snake isn't telling me.

By the time I'm climbing the steps to Allison's, I'm hit with a wave of exhaustion. I need to be extra quiet. I want to shower and collapse on the couch. My knee is angry and swollen, the snake is still tired, and I beat a man to death today. I need some rest. And probably some alcohol.

I take the extra key from my pocket and unlock the door. Every light is out and Allison's bedroom door is closed. Good.

"Let's make sure we're quiet, Peach," I tell the dog. I need to give her a bath to wash the blood from her fur, and I need to burn these clothes. I tiptoe to the couch and put the snake down on my pillow. "You rest for a bit. If you die, everything's ruined."

"Your concern is touching." The snake yawns, which is disturbingly cute, and coils up. "I will take your invitation of sleep."

I nod at him and ease to the bathroom, Peach right behind me. I turn on the light and almost scream at my reflection in the mirror—my face is splattered with a fine spray of the sheriff's blood. Thank God Allison is asleep. This would be hard to explain.

I spend the next hour showering, washing the blood out of my eyebrows, and giving Peach a bath. Her entire chest was covered in drool and blood, but despite her scrap with the police dog, she doesn't have any wounds. I'm so relieved, I'm light-headed. I'd feel even worse if Peach got hurt. When she's dry, and I have clothes on, I let her out of the bathroom. My knee is on fire; the fight made it swollen and sore. I know I pushed it too far when I ran to defend the snake. I wipe down the cane with tears in my eyes. I'm starting to feel less and less sorry for Sheriff Kines the more my knee throbs.

"Okay," I murmur to myself, hopping on my good leg. I can't hold back a few tears when I try to put pressure on my hurt one. It's too swollen for the brace. "Shit. Fuck, that hurts. Okay, I can do this." I limp out of the bathroom, my teeth gritted so hard my jaw aches, and round the corner to go to the kitchen.

Allison is sitting on the couch.

We stare at each other for one shocked second. Oh

dammit, I'm crying—I wipe my face hastily and give her a tentative smile.

"Hey. Sorry I woke you up."

"It's okay. I got up to pee and heard you in the shower." Allison's watching me closely, even in the dark. Sweat beads on my forehead. I hope to God I got all the blood off my face. "Avie?"

My rapid pulse throbs in my ears. "Y-yeah?"

Allison hesitates. "Why were you giving Peach a bath?"

Oh shit, here we go— "I was drinking some tea and she wanted some, and she knocked it out of my hand. She got all sticky."

Allison glances at my fox mug on the table. Thank God I drained it before I left. "Oh, well, you didn't have to do that. Your knee's hurt. She can be sticky for a few hours."

I exhale with relief. She believes me. "No, it was my fault. And I don't think tea is good for dogs." I hobble to her side and sit in between her and the snake, who's watching us lazily. I let out a small scream when my knee bends accidentally.

"Are you okay?" Worry creases Allison's brow as she stares at my knee. "Shit, Avie, it looks horrible. What did you do?"

Oh, just fought a dog and killed a man. Normal stuff. "I guess I bent it too much giving Peach a bath. Hurts like hell, to be honest."

"Wait a second." Allison jumps up and goes to the kitchen. I lean against the couch, eyes half-closed. I could fall asleep right now. I almost nod off, but Sheriff Kines's face pops into my mind and I jerk awake again. Allison

245

reappears with an ice pack, towel, and a bottle of water. "Stretch it out."

I put my foot on the coffee table. Allison wraps the ice pack in the dish towel and gently presses it to my knee. The ice cools some of the angry buzzing. I lean back, a little relieved.

"Thanks. It hurts so bad sometimes."

"It looks like it hurts," she says. She touches the ice pack tentatively. "Are you doing okay?"

"I guess." I don't really want to think about the PTSD. I have a bigger worry now, which is me being a murderer. "What about you? I know you've been stressed."

Allison blinks, like I've surprised her. Her shoulders sag. "Yeah, a little. Everything is a mess. Katie's dead, everyone is scared. . . ." Allison runs a hand through her hair. She twists it between her fingers anxiously, enough that a few golden strands float to the floor. "I need a drink."

"Me too. Pour us both one."

"Can't. Drank it all after Mom left. No one will sell me any more." Allison shrugs and gives a little laugh, but I'm not laughing. Allison has had it tough, hasn't she? With all this hero talk and her whole family up and leaving her. And I'm making everything harder on her. Her life will really suck once she finds out about Sheriff Kines, the second cop, and the barrier. And Carter, but that's not my fault.

I look at Allison, and I wish I could tell her everything. The shock has worn off, and I'm left with a deep uneasiness about what happened with Sheriff Kines. It was so easy to kill him. It was easy, and now I'm realizing—

I don't really feel sorry about it.

I reach for her hand. She lets me take it; hers is warm and soft. "Allison, can I ask you something?"

"Of course."

"Do you think good people can do bad things sometimes?"

Allison frowns at me. "Are you talking about your aunt?"

No, but that'll work, I guess. She'll give me an honest answer if she thinks we're talking about Auntie. "Yeah."

"Dr. Roberts did something unforgivable. She didn't have to choose you. It could have been me—"

"No," I say, interrupting her. "Not you. Why couldn't she have picked herself?" Pastor Thomas even gave her that option. It didn't have to be me.

Allison laughs. "I don't know anyone left in this town who would sacrifice themselves." She squeezes my hand gently. "But back to your question, I'm not sure. Dr. Roberts has really been there for me in the past, and up until a few days ago, I respected her a lot. I want to say your aunt cares about you . . . but I can't understand why she'd do something so awful to you."

I'm surprised by tears forming in my eyes. Thinking about Auntie—how she took me in when I had nowhere else to go, how she hugged me when I cried, how she let them tie me to that altar, knowing a snake's fangs would close over my head—is suddenly too painful. I don't want to think about her monstrous choice that Allison can't understand or forgive.

I don't want to think about my own monstrous choice.

"Let's forget it." I'm ashamed by the crack in my voice.

Allison turns to me, her expression soft and sympathetic. "Okay. When you're ready, Avie, I'm here to listen."

I nod, my throat burning with the effort not to let out a sob. The snake rests his head on my leg. Maybe I'm imagining it, but his black eyes seem sympathetic too.

"All right, bedtime for us." She pulls a blanket over me, fusses with the ice pack, and stands. I watch her, wishing for the first time, just a little, that I could call this whole thing off.

"Good night, Avie," she says, her voice a warm murmur.

"Good night," I mumble, my head on my chest. I don't remember Allison leaving, or me falling asleep, but I think Allison brushes my hair out of my face before the darkness envelopes me.

29

The next morning, while Allison pours us some cereal, I open my picture app to read about monster-killing Plasma.

Summer light steals through Allison's kitchen window, shining on the coffee table and my empty mug. I had a terrible night, once again. All these damn PTSD nightmares, and my knee is swollen and purple and ugly. I think I have a fever again. If I can't sleep, I might as well be productive.

The snake is wrapped loosely around my neck, snoozing. I move carefully so I won't wake him up, and flip through my pictures. I stop on the page for the Plasma. There's no intro or fanfare. Just a list of ingredients.

Two inches of human hair
Three fern leaves
Half a cup of powdered sulfur
Shavings of Silver

Bones/scales/part of any snake
Water
One cup of blood from a Monster

Underneath the list it says:

Combine ingredients in a pot. Simmer for 12 hours, or until mixture is bright orange. Store in airtight container ASAP; will evaporate quickly. Lethal if touches a Monster's skin. Must use different blood than the monster you want to kill. If you use their own blood, it's useless.

There's nothing else on the page. I glance at the snake around my neck. Bright orange, huh? So that's what's in the barriers—Plasma. But where the hell did Don or whoever find another monster to drain its blood to use in this? A cup is a *lot* of blood. I know the snake wouldn't lie there and let them take his.

There was the mysterious "Subject B" in Auntie's journal. I'm sure that was another monster, like the snake, but somehow a lot weaker and dumber than the snake if it got caught by Pastor Thomas's cult. I go back to my pictures of Auntie's journal, rereading the ominous experimentation details. *Fire . . . partially confirmed with Subject B.* What does "partially confirmed" mean? I read the list again, and my stomach sinks. Under Plasma, it says "confirmed with Subject B." They must have tortured that poor thing to death, first with fire, then with whatever concoction Plasma is.

But wait. Carter's recipe says the blood has to come

from some other monster for it to work, right? So if they only had Subject B, how did they make Plasma to kill it?

I fold my arms to think as Allison hums a song behind me. I feel like I'm missing something. The snake talked about blood at the graveyard. . . . He asked if I'd touched his blood, and was relieved when I said I hadn't. Wait. He also said *we* would get stronger from the barriers being destroyed, not only him. The barrier burned me when I touched it. Ingested silver affected my leg once he bit me. Everything that affects the snake, a monster, seems to affect me too.

My heart sinks with the realization. They must have gotten the blood from Don, because with the snake's venom coursing through his veins, he was probably considered a monster.

Just like me.

I close my eyes. Fuck, this keeps getting worse and worse. Though, it's not all bad—I have the recipe now. I can make Plasma myself. If the snake threatens me, I can kill him at any time. If I want to.

Instinctively, I touch the scales around my neck. The snake stirs at my fingertips, and rests his head on my shoulder.

"What's wrong, Latavia?" he says. His voice is quiet, sleepy. "Do you need comfort?"

"No," I say, turning off my phone. "No, everything's okay."

I hear a thundering of footsteps on Allison's stairs, and I sit straight up, heart hammering, breath squeezed out of my lungs. It's them. It could be—

"It's me, Avie, don't freak out," Jade's muffled voice calls.

Oh. Jade. I take a breath and settle back onto the couch as Jade opens the door. "What's the hurry? It's, like, six a.m."

"It's seven-thirty," Jade pants. "But listen. Have y'all seen the news?"

"Shit," Allison says from behind the couch. "I see it now."

"See what?" I'm trying my best to act innocent, though I'm pretty sure I know what they're talking about.

"Four murders last night. *Four.*" Jade's expression is a deep grimace. "And someone burned down the cemetery."

Oh shit, I didn't mean to burn the whole thing down. Good thing I told the police dog to run away. He sucks for biting me, but he doesn't deserve to burn to death.

"Things are getting pretty bad," I say, faking distress.

"This doesn't make sense. The snake's targeting the guardians, right?" Allison says. She comes from the kitchen and sits on the arm of the couch, frowning at her phone. "But only Sheriff Kines and Carter got killed. Who are the other two victims?"

"This website says one was an officer, and the other was a civilian found by Red Wood," Jade says, staring at her phone too. "Was there another guardian police officer?"

"No. That's the weird part. Why'd the monster kill him?"

Poor Roy. Wrong place, wrong time. I do actually feel bad about him. I told him to run, but he wouldn't listen. Once he tried to draw his gun, it was all over.

"And why the random guy?" Allison asks. She's staring at her phone like it might suddenly come to life and bite her. "Casey Stover? What does he have to do with the monster?"

"Maybe he was part of the church?" I suggest innocently.

"No way," Allison says. "He was super creepy. I heard he got kicked out of school for looking up girls' skirts."

I have to work hard to stop my lip from curling. What a pig. I'm glad the snake killed him.

"This really sucks, you know that?" Jade sighs and puts her head in her hands. "None of this makes sense. It's like the monster's just killing randomly. We've gotta start our snake-killing measures right now."

"But what can we do?" I ask. I know better than to mention Plasma while the snake is around my neck, but maybe while he's in the woods, I can bring it up.

"I don't know, but it's gotta be quick." I'm surprised to see pinpricks of tears in Jade's eyes. "Mom is a guardian too."

"Everything's gone to shit. Four in one night." Allison picks at her hair anxiously, and guilt eats at my chest. I wish she knew she and Jade will be safe. I wish she knew I'd never let anything happen to them. "I got a text— emergency meeting with John and Pastor Thomas at the church in a few. Jade, I want you to come with me. No one can get in touch with your mom."

"What's up with Auntie?" I ask.

Jade sighs, finally looking up from her phone. "She's been super paranoid. She refuses to leave the house. You really messed her up with that spray paint."

I stuff down the twinge of pity. I can't feel sorry for her. She should be tortured. But worry swirls in my gut. When I told the snake the names, I wasn't thinking about Jade and how this would affect her.

"Avie, we'll be back in a few hours," Allison says. Heat creeps up my neck as she watches me with concern. "I'll find some medicine while we're out, okay? Your fever is scaring me."

"I feel fine," I say, but my voice is weak.

"We'll take you to a doctor soon," Jade promises. "After we solve this, you know, serial-murder problem."

I wave to them both as they gather their things and leave Allison's apartment. I sit quietly until I hear their steps fade. Then the snake speaks.

"Latavia, take me to my forest. We need to talk."

"Bossy," I mutter, but I grab my cane and pull myself to my feet. Peach stands with me, panting. "But you're right. We have a lot to talk about."

30

When I reach the edge of the woods, the snake climbs down my leg and slithers ahead of me.

"Come, we will go to the pool," the snake says, growing in size as I walk deeper into Red Wood. "Your human friend is correct to worry about your injured limb and elevated body temperature. I need you to be able to move when the time comes to break the final two barriers."

"Thanks for your concern." I limp after him until he's his original massive size. Then he picks me up by my shirt and deposits me on his back.

"I'll move slowly," the snake says. I hang on to his smooth scales, frowning. His scales are still black, but they're a little duller than normal. It's almost like there's a layer of dust over him. I hope he's okay; Sheriff Kines beat the shit out of him with that club. If he was really hurt, I'm sure he wouldn't tell me. I'll have to watch him.

We get to the clearing in no time, and he heads straight into the cave. Peach stays out again, but this time I don't feel unnerved like before. I look up at the shimmering, wet walls and eerie blue crystals. It's kind of beautiful in the daytime. At night, it made me feel like I was getting sacrificed all over again.

The snake slithers into the pool. Warm water washes over my knee, and some of the soreness fades. I lean forward on the snake's back, soothed by the warm water.

"Do you think my knee'll ever get better?" I ask him.

The snake is quiet, swimming lazy laps around his pool. "I don't know, Latavia. I don't understand why my venom didn't heal you."

I press my cheek to his back, staring into the bottom of the clear water. Now probably isn't the best time to talk about silver poisoning. Especially if I can use said silver poisoning to my advantage.

I'm almost asleep when the snake speaks again. "Your human friends seem intent on killing me."

"They're gonna try," I say, my eyes closed. "But so far the only thing you're weak against is a billy club."

The snake snorts out a laugh. "Yes, this is true." He swims a few more laps before speaking again. "I can't help but think something isn't right."

I'm wide awake now. "What do you mean?"

"I mean that I've learned some alarming things over the past few moonrises."

"You mean about Don? People don't live that long, snake. He probably died of old age."

"No, I'm concerned about your fever." The snake stops swimming, so we're floating in the water like driftwood. "When you're here, or in the forest, your body temperature is normal. But when you're in your friend's home, your temperature elevates."

Heat fills my face as I think about Allison's gentle smile and the warmth of her hands. "That's not for the reason you think."

The snake opens his mouth and laughs. The cave echoes with the noise. "That is amusing, Latavia, but your attraction to your friend is not the issue. I also do not feel well there."

Hmm. My mind wanders to the knife Allison showed me and how nervous it made me feel. "She has a weapon. A knife made out of bone. It made me feel weird when she brought it out."

"Ah." Suddenly, all the snake's humor is gone. He crawls out of the pool and up the cave's incline. When we exit, I'm immediately hit with hot summer air. "I am afraid these humans have stumbled upon some information that will be dangerous for us, Latavia. We must move quickly now. Strike before the enemy has a chance to strike you."

There's the "us" again. I guess my theory about me counting as a monster is correct. "But we don't know where the other barriers are."

"Based on your conversations, it seems the so-called guardians have information. We will talk to one of them next time. If they are not deceased when we get there, of course."

"Yeah, we're running low on informants. Pastor Thomas, John, and Auntie are all that's left." I slide off the snake's back, careful to land on my uninjured leg.

"Who is this 'Auntie'?"

"Oh." I told him her real name. "Cora Roberts. She's my aunt. Part of my family."

The snake looks back at me with one shining eye. "Hmm."

"Hmm what?"

"I was thinking, that's all."

I nudge his giant body with my cane. "Well, think out loud! You're always so cagey."

The snake laughs, a loud, genuine one that echoes through the woods. "You are so curious. You remind me of my boy."

I freeze, cane stretched out in midair. "What did you say?"

The snake freezes too, and for the first time since I met him, he actually looks alarmed. "Nothing."

"Whoa, whoa, you're not walking that one back. Your boy? Like, your son? You have kids?" Oh God, how many monsters are in Red Wood? How many eggs can a snake lay? Wait, isn't he a boy snake?

The snake huffs, his breath kicking up grass and startling Peach. "I didn't mean to say anything. A slip of the tongue."

"Okay, but you did. Spill." The snake stays quiet, so I nudge him again. "Come on, snake, you gotta tell me! I saved your life."

The snake is silent, but I don't say anything either. We stare at each other for a long time. Finally, he blinks slowly and sighs. "I suppose I do owe you for that. Are you sure you want to trade in your favor for this?"

I hesitate, then nod. He's told me next to nothing, and

I can't walk out of here without knowing how many baby snakes I have to deal with.

"Very well. Sit. This may take a while." I do, resting my back against his scales, and he curls around me. He doesn't look at me; his gaze is far away, looking at something beyond the horizon. "The first thing you must know is that my species is not like humans. We do not need another to reproduce. The only thing we need is time, and blood from several hundred human beings."

Oh. The whole eating people thing makes sense now. "So you're eating people so you can make a baby snake?"

The snake chuckles. "He was not a snake. Truthfully, neither am I. My species comes from the Old Land, and we pick a form to manifest here."

"What's the Old Land?"

"A different world."

I wait for him to elaborate, but he's just watching me with one huge eye. Guess that's all I'm getting about that. "Okay, so what do you really look like?"

"You are not ready to know that, Latavia. This form you see me in now is a mercy for you."

Well, that's the most terrifying thing I've ever heard. I try to shake off the deep dread as my brain conjures up all sorts of horrors. "How many not-snakes do I have to worry about?"

The snake laughs again, softer, more thoughtful. "We can only have one child. Since my son has been born, I don't need to eat humans any longer. But I do now solely because of the human named Don."

I want to ask a million questions, but I stay quiet,

watching the snake carefully. He's still staring into the distance, resting his giant head on his own body.

"I did everything right. I ate my humans. I waited until it was time. I went back to the Old Land so my son would be born safely. But it wasn't enough." The snake's voice wavers, just a little. "My son was born ill. The others told me he would not last."

"Oh." I'm surprised by how stricken I feel. "I'm sorry, snake."

"It's okay. It is nature. Some children are born ill. It is nature." He repeats the last part like a mantra, like he's trying to soothe himself. "Despite his weak body and illness, he was still so curious. He wanted to see the human world. I took him here, because how could I say no? He loved these woods. He loved the autumn leaves, the smell of rain, the food some humans brought him. He was the first to talk to a human being. Do you know that it had never occurred to me to talk to humans before he tried?" The snake laughs, soft and distant. "I learned many things. My son taught me many things for his short fifty years. Unfortunately, I also learned the cruelty of human beings."

I hold my breath. This must be about Don.

"The humans came in a mob. They'd heard of a large monster and wanted to confront it. They'd heard of a much smaller monster, with precious blood and sharp teeth they could use for their weapons." The snake's tail thrashes against the ground, making me jump. "How arrogant! Our prey, turning its dull teeth on its predator. Our worthless food, attempting to steal my boy's life."

The snake takes a breath, then another, slower one. I

recognize the action; he's calming himself down. "I was away when they came for him. They must have planned on my absence, because I never would have allowed them to get close. My son was too friendly. He watched them approach and didn't even think of running. He wanted to talk with them. For his kindness, they hurt him. They stuck swords in his body, burned welts into his fragile skin. He managed to get away, but imagine my pain, my fury when I saw what they had done." The snake's voice trembles with rage, with fury, with heartbreaking sadness. "Why were they trying to steal him from me? He had so few years left. We had so little time left."

I can't form a single coherent thing to say. I never thought I'd feel sorry for a giant man-eating monster, but I'm close to tears. I wish I could go back in time and murder Don myself. Why the hell was he monster hunting anyway? The snake wasn't even eating people anymore. Sickening.

"I'm so sorry," I manage. I can't hide the tremble in my own voice. "I'm assuming you and Don didn't make up after this?"

"No, we did not." The snake's voice is venomous, bitter. "I killed everyone in my sight at first. Then I thought their deaths too painless, too merciful for what they'd done. I sought out those who smelled the same as the assailants and ate them while the attackers watched. I ate so many humans that night, their clothing sickened me for weeks. After a time, Don approached me. He shielded his kin and begged me for a deal to stop the rampage on his worthless human settlement. So I gave him the cruelest

261

one I could imagine; he was to give me a piece of his precious town whenever I asked, year after year until I'm satisfied. I added as many rules to the sacrifice as I could, because I hoped one day he would make a mistake and break our deal, and I could eat everyone he cared for while he watched. I waited over two hundred years for him to waver, but he did not. Until you."

Things are starting to make a lot more sense. Of course Don's journal made the snake sound like a horrible, unstoppable monster that had to be killed no matter what. But I don't remember Allison reading that all of this is Don's stupid fault. He played an awful game with the snake's son's life, and he won an incredibly terrible prize. A well-deserved one. "I don't blame you at all for what you did. I almost hate that we both made deals with you. I don't want to be associated with him."

The snake looks at me, his giant eye serious. "Don is a foul, murderous human who had to be reminded of his place. You and Don are both humans, but our connections are different. You and I are working toward a common goal. Don is being punished."

I'm quiet for a minute, considering that. Before this conversation, I thought the snake was distressed because he wanted to talk to Don and didn't know Don had died. But it sounds like the snake is just upset he couldn't torture Don for longer. Which is pretty impressive, honestly.

Another worrying thought enters my mind—Subject B. What if . . .

"What happened to your son?" I ask the snake, dread clawing my stomach to ribbons.

"He died," the snake says simply. "Nature took him, not Don's weapons. I'm certain his injuries shortened his life, but still, we had a few more peaceful years together."

"Did you bury him?" I'm thinking about how we dug up Don's bones, and how maybe the guardians of Sanctum aren't above a little grave digging too.

"No. We are born in the Old Land, and we must return there when it is our time. He is with the ones who came before him."

Okay, thank God. Whoever Subject B is, it isn't the snake's son, and for that I'm grateful. I think I'd raze Sanctum to the ground at this point. "That's a relief. I was thinking that Allison's knife came from him."

"Oh, no, do not worry. I would never let that happen. If I thought someone in that town had a piece of my son, I would have broken my deal and eaten every miserable human in there."

I don't say anything, because I believe him.

"I will have to see this knife," the snake says into the silence. "I am curious if it is actual bone. I doubt your friend has the bones of an adult, but it is possible to overpower a child who wandered away from their parent. Though difficult, it is possible for humans to kill us."

"Yeah, I bet," I say, thinking uneasily of the bone knife, the silver poisoning, and the Plasma. He doesn't know how hell-bent Sanctum is on getting out of this deal alive. Their monster hunt didn't go well two hundred years ago, but Don prepped his guardians well before he kicked the bucket. The snake doesn't know how dangerous people can be. I shake that thought off, because since I'm considered a monster now, Sanctum is exponentially more dangerous for me too. "Thanks for telling me about your son, snake."

"You're welcome. Hopefully your curiosity is satiated?"

"Almost." I laugh when he heaves a sigh. "Now that you know Don's dead, will you still eat the people of Sanctum?"

"Hmm. I'm not sure. I cannot get back what I lost. Perhaps two hundred years is punishment enough."

Maybe, but then I think of the snake, minding his own business and having his peace and his son threatened by Don's stupid meathead mob. I think of poor Subject B, tortured by fire and orange acid and then its body parts used for Allison's knife. I think of the pillars of Sanctum manipulating people, killing those who resisted, breaking bones so their victims couldn't escape. Revulsion and rage surge up so strong I want to puke.

"For what it's worth," I say, putting a hand against his scales, "I don't think you should forgive them. As long as you spare Allison and Jade, I don't care what you do. Swallow the lot of them whole until you feel better about what they did to you."

The snake looks at me, his dark eyes bright. "Thank you, Latavia. I'll take your opinion into consideration." Then he twists his body, grabs my shirt, and puts me on his back. "That's enough socializing for today. Your friends will soon wonder where you are."

I nod and call Peach, and we all head toward the entrance to Red Wood together. I stare down at the snake's dull scales, frowning. If I thought it was hard to make my own Plasma before, it's gonna be really hard now. I can't get soft; he's a monster. He told me he'd eat me after this is done, and I have to protect myself. I repeat that to myself as the daylight gets stronger as we come to the edge of Red Wood. But the image of the snake, curled around his dying son the same way he curls around me, sticks with me for a long time.

31

The whole way back to Allison's, I feel like someone's watching us.

I keep looking over my shoulder, but there's nothing there. There's no one in the streets, probably because they heard about the murders. Or smelled the smoke from the cemetery.

I get a tingle at the back of my neck again, for the fourth time, and I stop walking. I wait a few seconds, then whip around as fast as my bum knee will allow. I see it right away.

Sheriff Kines's dog.

The German shepherd whines and hides behind a mailbox.

"Oh, this is interesting," the snake says, climbing to the top of my head.

Apprehension lances through me. I don't want that dog anywhere near me. I still hear it barking in my nightmares. "Why is it following me?"

"Did you tell that hound to do something?"

I replay the fight in my head. "I think I told it to fuck off."

"Well," the snake says, laughing, "it's doing that. Try to call it to you."

I watch the dog, a little nervous. I killed Sheriff Kines right in front of him. Will he attack me? The dog is still cowering behind the mailbox, though, tail tucked between his legs. Pretty different from when he was biting me.

"Uh . . . here, boy. No, why don't you come here?"

The dog's ears stick up and he gets to his feet. Slowly, gingerly, he trots up to me. When he gets close enough to touch, Peach growls at him. He stops, glancing from me to her.

"It's okay, Peach." Peach stops growling and sits down, but she's still watching the dog closely. The police dog looks up at me, nose twitching. I reach out, hesitant, and the dog pushes his head into my palm, tail wagging.

"Interesting," the snake says. "Very interesting."

"What's going on? Why'd he come back? Is this because of my superpower?" I rub the dog's ears between my fingers. His fur is soft, and he's not so threatening without Sheriff Kines around. His tail thumps against the ground.

"Possibly. Your ability may affect animals more than humans. You told it to do something, and it came back for more orders."

Interesting indeed. I stop petting the dog, and he whines, nudging my good leg with his snout. Peach watches him with her ears back. Probably jealous. "Tell me more about this superpower. Will it get stronger as I use it?"

"No. But as it is, it's a very good one." The snake moves back to my shoulders. "Your ability helps you survive. Your knee is injured, so you developed the ability to talk our way out of dangerous situations. A very good ability."

I mull that over for a bit. The police dog tries to play with Peach, bowing and wagging his tail, but Peach turns her head and doesn't move.

"So what was Don's power?"

The snake is quiet for a moment. Then he says, "He could change his appearance. Many people in this town did not care for him after he incurred my wrath, so he changed his face to live among them. His ability was useful too."

A perfect power for the weasel that set all this in motion.

"So you're aware," the snake says, "your ability won't work on me. You and I are connected by my venom. It would be like trying to control yourself."

I try to let that horrifying image go. "Okay, so it's like we're . . . the same person?"

The snake chuckles in my ear. "No. We are related, like you and your aunt. We are family."

I climb Allison's steps, thinking hard. I sent the dog— "Charlie," I think Sheriff Kines called him—back to Red Wood. He trotted toward the forest without looking back, even though I'm pretty sure dogs don't know what a Red Wood is. This might work out.

But I'm also thinking about the snake. I expected to be repulsed by his "family" comment, but I'm weirdly okay with it. Which disturbs me. I don't like how I've been feeling lately. Not feeling guilty about killing Sheriff Kines is one thing, but thinking of myself as part of a giant snake's family is quite another. I need to sit down and have a heart-to-heart with myself.

I put my hand on Allison's door and freeze. It's unlocked.

I open the door, dread in my stomach. Allison and Jade look up from the couch. Allison seems concerned, but Jade's staring at me with narrowed eyes and laser focus.

"Where've you been, Avie?" Jade asks.

"Took Peach for a walk." I try to sound breezy and not guilty as I close the door behind me. Peach trots to Allison and licks her leg before flopping to her side on the floor.

"She looks pretty tired," Allison says, glancing at Peach. "Where'd you go?"

"Around." I limp to the armchair Jade usually sits in. I grit my teeth and try to keep in a scream as I fall into the chair. "Anyway, how'd the meeting go? What's the plan?"

Jade and Allison look at each other. Their faces are ashen and exhausted. Not good news, then.

"Pastor Thomas issued a mandatory curfew. All stores, businesses, restaurants close at four. No one leaves the house after twilight." Allison rakes a hand through her hair. "He also suggested everyone who can, take a vacation."

"Yeah, let the poor people get eaten by the snake," Jade mutters.

Ugh. I hate this guy even more with every passing second. "What else? Just a curfew?"

"He suggested doing patrols. Every night, from sundown to sunup, volunteers and the police will walk around the edge of the forest." Allison looks at me, and a flash of anxiety crosses her face. "But the guardians are in a separate group, since the snake is probably targeting us. I'm first. I have to go tonight."

"Seriously?" Hot anger surges into my bones. "They're making you go first? What assholes! As if John or Carter—err, well, Auntie or Pastor Thomas—can't go instead. I'm sick of them."

"I have the most experience with the knife," Allison says, but she sounds mildly nauseous. "It's the only way we know how to kill it. And I'll be wearing silver charms and stuff."

"I want to see the weapon," the snake hisses in my ear. "Ask her."

I'm a lot more concerned about Allison walking around Sanctum all night than a knife, but the snake will bug me if I don't ask. "Hey, can I see the knife again?"

Allison nods and goes to her room to get it. Jade glances at me, and unease swirls through my chest. Something's off about her expression. Her shoulders are tense. What exactly happened in that meeting?

Allison returns with the shoebox she showed me before. She lifts the lid, and the knife gleams in the light.

The snake recoils, his mouth open, tail shaking, fangs out. Well, I know how he feels about that.

"We'll take turns with the knife," Allison says, oblivious to the snake's sudden bad mood. "It'll be okay. Probably."

"Do you have to go by yourself?" I ask. I really am worried about her, but this is a good opportunity to get John and Pastor Thomas alone.

"Yeah . . ." Allison grips the shoebox tightly. "I wanted to do pairs, but there's only three of us now."

"Three? You, Auntie, Pastor Thomas, and John, right?"

Jade shakes her head. "Mom won't go, so I said I would. She still won't leave the house. And Pastor Thomas said he should be at the church, because that's where we'll check in during our shifts."

This is disgusting. This whole town is disgusting. They're sending Allison and my cousin, who is *fifteen*, to fight a giant snake. By themselves. Alone. I wish I had burned this whole town to the ground.

"I'll go with you. Both of you." I look them in the eye so they can tell I'm serious. I know they're safe from the snake; he's around my neck. But I don't know if they're safe from this weird-ass town in the middle of the night.

Allison smiles at me, gratitude in her eyes. "It's okay, Avie. Jade and I will go together both nights. We won't tell the others."

"Gotta stay safe from stranger danger. And giant snake danger." Jade holds up a peace sign, her expression blank.

"Anyway, it's fine. We'll be fine." Allison runs her hand through her hair again, but this time blond strands cling to her fingers. Her hands are shaking. "Does anyone want tea? I'm gonna make some tea."

271

We hang out for the rest of the day, until the sun sets and they have to leave. They both get up to go, but panic flutters in my chest. I'm thinking about that robber now. Who's to say there's not another one, lurking at the edge of the woods? And whoever killed Carter; they're still out there too. My chest is tight, like I'm about to have another panic attack.

"Hey, take Peach with you," I say. Peach lifts her head, tail wagging.

Jade snorts. "That dumb mutt wouldn't bite a biscuit."

I think about the number she did on Sheriff Kines. "I wouldn't count her out. Take her, for me."

Allison smiles at me. "Okay. But don't worry, Avie. We'll be fine."

Yeah, so she says. "Peach, come here," I say. Peach does, and I look her in the eye. "Make sure you protect them, okay? No matter what. Don't you think that's a good idea?"

Peach closes her mouth and stares into my eyes. She's got the message.

"Why'd you say it like that?" Jade asks, frowning at me.

I shrug and pat Peach's side. "Me and Peach have an understanding. You gotta talk nice to her."

Jade shakes her head. "All right, whatever. You ready?"

Allison nods. She looks at me, like she wants to say something, but she smiles instead. "See you later, Avie."

Something in her expression breaks my heart. She's saying it like this is the last time we'll talk. She really thinks she's going to be eaten.

"Be careful out there," I say as they descend the steps,

Peach in tow. "Text me every hour, okay? Come back if something happens."

"You got it, Mom," Jade says, smiling back at me. She and Allison wave, and disappear from sight. I close the door, dread in my stomach. I have about eight stressful hours to wait.

32

I limp around the room for thirty anxious minutes, waiting for their first text.

"You are nervous," the snake says. He's on the coffee table and not around my neck for once, moving slowly between the empty popcorn bowl and my mug of lukewarm tea. He was face-first in the bowl a few minutes ago, chomping happily at the leftover kernels. I guess that proves the weakness listed in Auntie's book. "Why? I am here with you, nowhere near the forest. They are safe."

"Yeah, but other people are out there." I glance at my phone again. "Remember the guy robbing Hannah?"

"Hmm. Yes, humans are dangerous. That knife will be trouble, Latavia."

I glance at him out of the corner of my eye. "Was it real bone?"

"Yes, it was." The snake circles the popcorn bowl, round and round. I'm suddenly reminded of the first day we met, when he paced around the altar. "This confirms why we are ill."

Actually, it doesn't. Why would another monster's bones make us feel bad? "I don't understand. Why do we feel sick around it?"

The snake continues to go round and round the popcorn bowl, silent. Finally, he says, "Would you not feel sick if someone was carrying around a human body part? Brazenly, in fact? Frankly, I am disgusted that the humans have murdered a young one and made weapons out of their lifeless body." The snake constricts suddenly, sending the popcorn bowl crashing to the floor. "If you and I did not have our agreement in place, I would do something about it."

Yikes. This conversation is heading into dangerous waters. This isn't Allison's fault; she doesn't know where the knife came from or how it was made. But, as I think about Subject B, my stomach roils with nausea. I hate to admit it, but I agree with the snake. That knife is cruel, even for Pastor Thomas and his cult.

"Let's get back on track. Will the knife be a problem when we corner the others?"

"I'm not sure." He's coiling around my coffee mug now, in a continuous circle. "We should be aware of it. Use stealth when we can."

I nod. No more head-on confrontations like with Sheriff Kines. Who knows what weapon John or Auntie has? And I can almost guarantee Pastor Thomas has some nasty surprise for us. "Let's strategize. Who are we going after tonight?"

"Why not your aunt?" the snake suggests. "She is at her den now, yes? Your friends are out, so they won't interfere."

Discomfort creeps up my neck. He's right. She's the logical choice, but . . . "Why not John or Pastor Thomas first? Pastor Thomas is at the church, allegedly, and John might have grown a spine and be on patrol tonight with Allison and Jade. We could catch them slipping."

The snake stares up at me with shining black eyes. "Are you sure this is strategy? Or is it weakness?"

"Strategy." I make sure my voice is confident. I don't want to see Auntie yet. I'm not folding; it's just better if we wait until the end for her. More dramatic. I nod to myself and stand up. I grab my cane and pick up the snake by the middle. He exposes his fangs and rattles his tail irritably. "Don't hiss at me! Come on, let's get to searching."

The snake sighs heavily. "If you're sure, lead the way."

The snake and I hide in Red Wood, just outside the church. Nothing so far. Earlier, I saw Jade and Allison, chatting and walking around with flashlights. It was kind of funny; they're looking for the snake, and he's around my neck, cozily wrapped in my shirt. But it's almost midnight now and I'm starting to get irritated. Where the hell are John and Pastor Thomas? I didn't really believe that they'd let Allison and Jade wander around by themselves, but I have the sinking feeling they're both at home, not a care in the world while teenagers look for their monster. And I don't know where either of them live.

"You're tense," the snake says.

"You'd be too if you were waiting for a guy to jump out at you." I adjust my shirt, nervously running my fingertips over his scales.

The snake makes a *hmm* sound, like he's thinking. "Do you mistrust humans that much?"

"Um yes? Didn't you see what happened to me? And to Hannah? And that kid we met? People suck, dude."

The snake considers this for a moment. "It's a shame that humans fear each other so much. No sense of co-operation."

"You're telling me you'd cooperate with other monsters?"

"I'm cooperating with you," the snake says. "A true test of my strength."

I roll my eyes. He's in a bad mood, I guess.

I turn to tell the snake we're moving, but he stiffens around my neck. His rattle starts, the sound deafening in one ear.

"What's wrong?"

"I hear something. Go that way." He points with his tail to my left.

I creep cautiously forward. Three steps, ten, twenty—then I hear it too.

"Hello? Latavia?"

That's not Jade's voice. It's not Allison's either.

"Do you know who's calling you?" the snake whispers.

"Uh, no." I can't place the voice, but it sounds vaguely familiar. . . . Wait, more importantly, why is someone other than Jade and Allison calling me? No one else should know I'm alive. Dread coils in my gut so strong I have to grip the cane extra tight. Maybe Carter told someone else before he died.

"Should I take care of it?" The snake's voice is grim. His muscles are tight against the skin of my neck.

"No! Relax. Let me see who it is first."

I limp closer to the voice, careful to stay away from the tree line. I take a few more steps, and I can see the person.

It's Mrs. Brim.

She's standing right at the edge of Red Wood, clutching her purse in tense knuckles. She's wearing sweatpants and a hoodie, as well as a thick necklace that gleams silver in the moonlight. And I can see from here that she has a black eye.

"Do you know this human?" the snake asks.

"Yeah." The panic from earlier eases and I put a hand to my chest. She has to be here because Delilah told her I wasn't dead. Guess my suggestions aren't long-lasting on people. But is it worth it to risk talking to her? I stare at her black eye and narrow my eyes. I touch the snake's scales. "Let me talk to her. You be quiet, okay? But don't turn invisible."

The snake doesn't answer, but he also doesn't gather that silvery sheen he has in Allison's house.

Okay. Here we go. In through the nose, out through the mouth. I steel myself and limp out of the woods, smiling. "Hey, Mrs. Brim."

Mrs. Brim gasps when she sees me. Her hands tremble

as she clasps them in front of her. "It's true. You're not dead."

"Well, I told Delilah I was a ghost." I shrug, still smiling. "You can choose what to believe."

Mrs. Brim's eyebrows knit together. "So you did see her. She told me she met a ghost, but she wouldn't give me any details. She drew a picture for you and wanted me to give it to you."

Mrs. Brim reaches into her purse and steps closer, but I put my hand out to stop her. "Don't come into the forest. If you do, I can't protect you."

She falters and stops walking. "O-okay. I'll give you the picture later."

I watch her fiddle with her purse, fascinated. Why is she here, chasing an alleged urban legend? What does she want?

"Latavia, I'm really sorry about what happened." Mrs. Brim's eyes fill with tears. "I had just talked to you at the church. I couldn't believe it."

"Yeah, well." My smile slips. "I couldn't either."

Mrs. Brim looks at me for a second, pity on her face. Then she takes a deep breath. "I don't know if you're still alive, or a ghost, or some sort of spirit. But I wanted to ask you for a favor."

A favor? The snake tenses around my neck. "Like what?"

"I know what you did for Hannah." Mrs. Brim takes a shaky breath. "I was wondering if you could help me too."

I raise my eyebrows, and the snake hisses softly in my ear. Not what I expected at all. So Hannah told her about me, not Delilah. And what I did for Hannah . . . "What do you mean?"

"I mean I . . ." Mrs. Brim wrings her hands. "I was hoping you could hide Delilah for a while."

"What?"

Mrs. Brim's eyes fill with unshed tears. "I'm sorry, I know it's a lot to ask for. But I was hoping she could disappear for a while, maybe in Red Wood? And everyone would think she's dead, so—"

"No." The snake climbs down my body and grows to his maximum height. Mrs. Brim covers her mouth, and even in the dark I can tell she's lost all the color in her face. "No humans in my woods. If you or anyone else steps foot in my forest, I won't hesitate to kill you."

"Relax," I tell the snake, patting his huge belly. He looks down at me with narrowed eyes. "Let me handle this, okay? You stay there." I leave the tree line so I can get a little closer to Mrs. Brim. She looks from me to the snake, her whole body trembling. "My associate doesn't like that plan. He's testy about his woods. But let me ask—why are we trying to fake Delilah's death?"

Mrs. Brim trembles. She's still looking at the snake. "I had no idea . . . the rumors were true. Oh my Lord, *that's* what's been killing the people who disappear?"

"Let's focus," I say gently. "I understand the shock, trust me, but I have something else to do tonight."

Mrs. Brim looks at me again. Her black eye is half-closed and swollen. "I've tried everything else. I don't know what to do." She takes a breath and rubs her face with her hands. "My husband, you know him, is . . . not a nice man. But I don't have any family here, and my friends from choir definitely wouldn't believe me. And I could take it, I know I'm not a good wife, I could take it, but I can't let him hurt Delilah."

Slow anger builds in my gut. "Are you saying Deacon Brim is hitting you?"

A few tears spill out of Mrs. Brim's eyes. "Yes," she whispers. "For a long time. But I can take it, like I said. But not Delilah. It was the first time, but he kicked her yesterday. She was crying because she wanted to go to Tele-scoops, but they were closed. She was really upset, and he kicked her. Like she was a dog."

The anger turns into fury. What kind of animal would do that to a kid? She's six years old.

Mrs. Brim continues, still crying, "I know him. Now that he's started, he won't stop. So I thought I could say she wandered into the woods, and he would think she was dead. And then, one night while he was sleeping, I could come get her and we could run away."

Not a terrible plan, but the snake's not gonna let Deli-lah hang out with him. "Let's brainstorm here. Is there anyone you can call to help you? The police?"

"I tried once before." Mrs. Brim rubs her right wrist uneasily. "It didn't work out for me."

Fuck this dumbass town. "Okay, how about family? You said they're all gone?"

Mrs. Brim nods. "I'm not allowed to have a phone or a computer, so I've lost touch. I knew it was stupid to give them up, but I loved him. I believed it would get better."

I massage my temples. This keeps getting worse and

worse. "Okay, let me think. There's gotta be something we can do." I fold my arms, frowning at the clear sky. No police, no family. I would say my spineless aunt would help—she helped me, once upon a time—but I don't trust her anymore. Mrs. Brim just needs an opportunity to get away, right? So if he left the house . . .

"Latavia?" I look back at Mrs. Brim, and she's watching me with the same wonder Delilah had. "I really appreciate you trying to help me. You're the first person I've ever told." Mrs. Brim starts laughing, but it's a little hysterical. "My last option is a teenager who may or may not be a ghost. I'm sorry, Latavia. I'm not thinking straight. I should go home."

"Wait!" I reach out to take her hand, but hesitate and put my arms back to my sides. "I think I can help."

"Latavia," the snake warns from the trees. "This is not related to our business."

I know. But I look at Mrs. Brim, who is so desperate to escape that she would try to make a deal with an alleged evil spirit. Not that different from me, lying on that altar, begging the snake not to eat me. Mrs. Brim and I are the same, except she has one tormentor and I have six. Well, just three now.

I look at my hands, the hands strong enough to kill Sheriff Kines in one well-timed blow.

If I have the power to help someone, why can't I use it?

"How about this. You bring him here, to me. I'll hold him for a few hours until you can get away."

The snake sighs from the trees, but I ignore him.

Mrs. Brim's brow furrows. "No, that's too dangerous. I don't want you to get hurt."

I point at the snake, who's still as big as a house and glaring at us. "I think we'll be okay."

Mrs. Brim looks from me to him. Then she meets my eyes, hers full of hope. "You'll do it? Really?"

"Really." Warmth courses through me. I shouldn't. I know I shouldn't, but what, I'm just supposed to walk away? I suspected something, way back before this whole thing started. And I did nothing. But now I can help, now that I have power at my fingertips and the entire town of Sanctum shaking. "Come back tomorrow night. Do you know about the patrols the guardians are doing? Ask for you and him to join, so he doesn't get suspicious. Then I'll hold him here, and you and Delilah can run."

Mrs. Brim's eyes fill with tears. "Thank you, Latavia. Thank you so much. And I can pay you! Anything you want, I'll give it to you."

I hadn't considered this. "Uh, how about an IOU? One day, I might need your help."

Mrs. Brim nods frantically. "Anything. I'm willing to do anything—except if it involves Delilah. But me, I'll do anything."

Mrs. Brim is a good mom. I get a stab of pain as I think about my own mother. I don't think she'd do this to protect me.

"Okay, deal," I say. "Tomorrow night. Midnight."

Mrs. Brim nods, crying hard now. "Thank you, Latavia. Thank you so much."

Warmth fills my body, the same warmth I felt when Hannah thanked me. The snake sighs heavily from the forest.

"Don't be late."

"I won't." Mrs. Brim pulls a piece of paper from her purse and places it in my hands. "Thank you again. Thank you so much."

She smiles at me one more time, then backs away. She waves, and I do too before she turns and leaves. I wait until she's out of sight before unfolding the paper.

It's a kid's drawing, done in messy crayon. It's a pretty poor rendition of me, wearing Allison's clothes and a big smile. Delilah's written THE GHOST in all capital letters at the top. But at the bottom she wrote: ANGEL. She's given me a pair of big black wings.

I smile and put the picture in my pocket. "Let's go, snake. We've got a busy night tomorrow."

33

"We need to talk."

I flinch in surprise. I'm back at Allison's, waiting for them to return. It's four a.m. now. I spent the rest of the night sneaking around, trying to find John or Pastor Thomas, but I just saw nervous random citizens of Sanctum. After a while, I didn't even see Allison and Jade. It was maddening. They started texting about coming home, so I gave up to get here before them. At least they're safe, which is a relief.

But the snake didn't say a word the whole time. He's probably mad at me about Mrs. Brim. Yeah, I volunteered his services without asking, but it'll be easy. Hold the dude down for a few hours, let them get away. Not a big deal.

"Uh, yes?"

"I have one question." The snake looks up at me from his position on the coffee table. "Did you offer to help the woman because you felt sorry for her situation? Or do you like feeling powerful with my venom running through your veins?"

I frown down at him, pinpricks of unease peppering my arms. "I want to help, that's all. I mean, I'm not crazy, right? He's a terrible man, and they need help."

"Hmm." The snake moves from the coffee table and coils into my lap. "I don't think you are being honest with yourself, Latavia. But I won't interfere. This is your game to play, if you want to play it."

What does that mean? I pull at the collar of my shirt, suddenly nervous. Does this mean he won't stop me? Or does it mean he won't help me at all?

My phone buzzes. I glance at it—a text from Jade.

I hate this job

Good work soldier, I text back. *Are you at home already?*

Yep. Allison's on her way to you soon, Jade says. *She's kinda stressed out fair warning.*

No kidding. She doesn't know she's safe. She doesn't know I'll do anything to protect her.

I grab my cane and swing my legs off the couch, catching the snake before he can fall. He hisses irritably and climbs to my neck.

"Sorry," I say, limping into the kitchen. "We'll finish this later. I gotta do something real quick."

"What are you doing?" the snake asks. He's dangling limply from my neck like a rope.

"Allison's coming back now. I'm gonna make her something."

"Very sweet," the snake says. He sounds kinda tired. Is he feeling okay? "I'm not sure how humans choose a mate,

286

but procuring a meal for your potential partner is a good start."

"Stop being gross." I put some water into her teapot and hunt for some tea bags. That girl loves tea, and we drank the last of it last night. I'll make her some more, but this time with more sugar. Hers is good, but not go-into-a-diabetic-coma good.

The snake doesn't answer me as I boil the tea bags, measure out an obscene amount of sugar, and mix it all together in a pitcher. Okay, now I can maybe make . . . a PB&J? No, just the tea. God, Allison needs some groceries. Her fridge is full of random snacks—a jar of pickles, a few bottles of water, one sad-looking container of yogurt. Nothing to make a four a.m. meal out of. Don't they pay you to hunt down giant snakes?

Though the way this snake is looking, that wouldn't be too hard. His scales are a little whiter than they were earlier. I touch the top of his limp head. "Hey, you all right? You look terrible."

"I'm fine." The snake loops himself more snugly around my neck.

"Don't you need to eat?" Now that I think about it, he didn't eat anything when we went to Red Wood earlier. The only thing he's had to eat in days was a few kernels of popcorn. And he said that anything he eats when he's in his small form doesn't count.

"I'm fine," he repeats. "I'm going to sleep now. Good night, Latavia."

Okay, conversation over. I concentrate on pouring tea into our usual mugs and bring them to the coffee table. I check my phone—it's four twenty-five. Did I make it too early? Maybe I should have waited. . . .

I hear the squeak on Allison's steps, and my heart beats faster. It's okay, it's probably Allison, but—

"Avie," Allison's voice calls. It's muffled and far away, like she's at the bottom of the stairs. "Don't worry, it's just me."

I breathe out, my heart rate calming. She knew I'd be nervous and warned me. Affection swirls up, and my cheeks get a little warmer. I didn't know I could like someone so much.

Allison opens the door a minute later. The neck of her camo T-shirt is soaked, and she looks exhausted. I get the urge to hug her.

"Avie?" she whispers, still at the door. Peach trots inside and comes to me, panting. I rub her soft ears, and her tail thumps against the arm of the couch. "Are you awake?"

"I'm awake." I pat the seat beside me. "Come sit down! I made something for you!"

Allison hesitates. "Oh, okay! Can I turn on the light?"

Shit, I forgot she can't see in the dark like me. "Yeah, sorry, go ahead."

Allison doesn't turn on the living room light; she tiptoes to the table beside the couch and turns on a lamp. The room fills with weak yellow glow. I grin at her, and she smiles back at me. There are deep, dark circles under her eyes.

"Sorry I'm so sweaty," she says, collapsing beside me

on the couch. Her shoulders sag with defeat. "I need a shower, but I'm exhausted."

"Take a shower tomorrow. It's four in the morning." I grab her mug and give it to her. "Made you some tea. Since you're out snake hunting and I'm just sitting at home."

Allison looks at me, right into my eyes, and for one wild second I think she's going to kiss me.

"Th . . . thank you." She takes the mug and takes a sip. She wrinkles her nose, smiling at me over the rim of her cup. "Avie, this is so sweet."

"Good! It's supposed to be!"

Allison laughs, and my whole body fills with warmth. I've got it bad. I gotta get myself together.

"Avie, thank you." Allison holds her mug in tight hands. She smiles at me again, but this time it's tired. "It's been a hard few days."

"I know." I ease closer, not so close that we're touching, but close enough that she can meet me in the middle if she wants.

Allison drinks more of her tea and sighs. "Everything's falling apart, Avie. I don't understand—the snake killed four people last night. And now nothing? I don't get it."

I resist the urge to touch the snake's scales. He's breathing evenly in my ear; still sleeping. "Maybe he's tired and needs a break."

Allison snorts out a laugh, covering her mouth right after. "I can just see it. 'Man, I need a vacation. Killing people is hard work.'"

"Where do snakes go on vacation? Disney World?"

Allison must be exhausted, because she's full-on laughing now. "Giant snake selfie in front of Cinderella's castle."

I imagine the snake wearing a tiny pair of Mickey Mouse ears, and I'm laughing too. "Do you think he'd like the teacup rides better, or roller coasters?"

"Oh, it'd love the parades. All-you-can-eat human buffet."

Allison's laughter dies in an instant, and she looks down into her mug. Her hands are shaking. "Avie, I'm going to die soon."

"You're not. I promise."

"You can't promise that." Allison twists her hair anxiously between her fingers. "It's been terrorizing Sanctum for two hundred years. Why do we think we can stop it?"

I start to answer, but I pause. Allison isn't just twisting her hair—she's plucking it out. Golden strands float to the floor like rain.

"Uh, Allison—"

"I'm so scared, Avie." She's not looking at me, but her eyes sparkle with tears. "And I'm so worried about Jade and you, and we can't predict what the monster is going to do and everyone's dying around me and I'm so tired but I can't sleep—"

I reach out and grab her hand. She starts, blinking at me in surprise. "Stop, Allison. You're hurting yourself."

Allison glances at the floor, and her face fills with horror. "Oh my God. I haven't done that in so long—" Suddenly she's quiet, her eyebrows scrunched together like she's on the edge of tears.

"It's okay," I say, making sure my voice is low and

reassuring. "You're stressed to hell, I know. But let's not tear our hair out, okay?"

"Okay." Her voice is fragile, like she's about to break. I want to hold her in my arms until she knows everything's okay.

"Good! First thing, don't worry about the snake. He's mad at the people who deprived him of his sacrifice. That's not you. Or Jade. You don't have anything to be scared of."

Allison still looks doubtful, but her breathing is better now. She sniffles, looking into my eyes. Hers are full of quiet desperation. "I don't think I can protect Sanctum, Avie. I'm one person, and I don't think I'm strong enough to do what I need to. Everyone is going to die because of me."

"Shh, shh, calm down." I ease closer and wipe a tear away with my thumb. "You don't have to protect this dumbass town, or kill a monster. You're not a hero. You're just a teenager who can't sleep."

Allison leans into my hand, staring into my eyes, and I swear this is the saddest expression I've ever seen on a person. Exhaustion, pain, torment, something I can't name. My stomach twists with guilt. I wish I could tell her everything so she could have a tiny bit of peace.

"Speaking of sleep, let's try it. You need some rest."

Allison shakes her head, pulling away. "I'm almost out of sleeping pills, and the pharmacist left town today, so I can't get a refill. I only have two more, and I should save them. I need to be ready right before the full moon. I mean, in case that rumor is true."

I look into Allison's exhausted blue eyes, and a shiver oozes down my back. I know exactly what to do.

"Okay, hang on." I lean over her, my heart stuttering as our arms brush, and turn off the lamp. The room is plunged into darkness.

"I don't think it'll help," Allison says, doubt in her voice.

"Shh, I've got a plan." I grab my pillow and place it in my lap. I pat it gently. "Here you go. Sleeping place right here."

"In your lap?" Allison's voice is strange . . . surprised, and excited maybe? I'm excited too, mostly from the idea of Allison sleeping so close to me. But I'm feeling guilty too. I don't like using this power on her . . . but it's for a good cause, right? She needs sleep, bad. And it's just this once.

"Yes. In my lap."

Allison hesitates, and I take a deep breath. Here we go.

I look Allison in the eye. "Let's try to sleep, okay? You can put your head in my lap. That sounds nice, right?"

Allison blinks at me for a second. I hold my breath. Then, slowly, she lies down and puts her head on my pillow.

"I am kinda tired," she murmurs, her eyes already half-closed. "But I haven't been able to sleep without my sleeping pills for a year. . . ."

"Shh," I say, smoothing her long hair behind her ear. It's soft and slightly damp from the humid Alabama summer. "Let's sleep. I'm here. I won't let anything happen to you."

Allison doesn't answer me. I bend over her slightly, so I can see her face. Eyes closed, breathing even. Fast asleep.

I lean back against the couch, grinning to myself in the dark. Allison is sleeping, when she was struggling so much before. I did this, with my power. The snake might doubt my motives with Mrs. Brim, but if I can use the power his venom gives me to help people who deserve it, I'll do it. Satisfied, I stroke Allison's hair until the room fills with morning light. Then I close my eyes and let contented sleep take me too.

34

Charlie is barking, fierce and loud, Auntie stares at me as I scream for help, for someone, anyone, John swings his bat down on my leg and it splinters like wood. I'm screaming, in pain and terror and rage. I'm crying, and the snake is wrapped around my neck, his scales cool and comforting, and someone is calling my name—

"Latavia."

Someone calls my name, but—

"Avie? Avie, wake up."

Something touches my face and I'm awake, gasping, harsh sunlight flooding my vision. Where am I? What—

"You were screaming again," the snake murmurs in my ear. His voice sounds exhausted.

"Avie?" Allison's face swims into focus, her eyebrows pulled together with concern. "Are you okay?"

I nod, but I can't breathe. Charlie's still barking in my ears, my knee throbs—my knee—

"You don't look so good. Can I check your temperature?"

I can barely process what she's asking, but I nod. I can't calm down. My breaths are quick and short, and everything hurts. My knee, my head, my bones—

Allison reaches for my cheek, and I flinch, even though her touch is so light and gentle. Her frown deepens. "Avie, you're burning up. Are you sure you're okay?"

I try to nod again, but nausea swims in my stomach, up my throat, onto my tongue. I shake my head and put my hand over my mouth. I'm about to throw up all over her.

"Okay." Allison nods to herself, her face determined. "Let's go to the bathroom for a minute."

Allison stands and holds out her hand. I take it, mine trembling violently, and she pulls me up off the couch. She asks me if she can touch my waist, and when I nod absently, she wraps her arm around it. Normally I'd be happily embarrassed, but my ears are ringing and my knee is throbbing and vomit climbs my throat at a rapid speed. She helps me into the bathroom, holding me close to her side. We stand in the middle, me unsteady and sweating. My mouth waters and my stomach cramps.

"We're here." Allison takes a shaky breath. "Do you want to sit down? Or do you think you're gonna throw—"

She doesn't get to finish, because I lean over and puke into her bathtub.

Allison gasps, and the snake hisses quietly in my ear. "This is becoming a pattern," he says.

If I wasn't vomiting up my intestines, I'd strangle him.

I lean my head on the edge of her tub. My mouth stings with acid and I'm on fire. Though I'm pretty sure half of that fire is embarrassment because oh my *God*, who throws up in their crush's bathtub? This is horrible. This is mortifying.

"Avie?" Allison shuffles her feet anxiously behind me. She has a tentative hand on my back. "You okay?"

"Y-yeah." I take a shaky breath. I do feel a little better after throwing up my guts. "Sorry for puking in your bathtub."

Allison laughs, relief in her voice. "Better than the carpet! Easy cleanup."

I wonder if this is what love feels like.

Allison helps me sit on the edge of the tub, but I'm still dizzy and nauseous. She watches me for an anxious second, then says, "Let's sit on the floor, okay? Actually, you should probably lie down."

The room is spinning lazily, so I nod. I barely feel her hands under my arms, or hear her gentle reassurance. All I know is that soon I'm lying on my side on the cold bathroom floor, a towel under my head, a pillow under my sore knee. Allison sits behind me and drapes a cool washcloth on my forehead.

"Sorry again," I mumble, my eyes closed. I'm cooling down . . . fever-wise. I'm still hot with embarrassment. I hear her running bathwater, rinsing my puke down the drain. Easy cleanup at least, like she said.

"It's okay," Allison says, her voice soft and soothing. "How are you feeling now?"

Embarrassed. Ashamed. And now despair—I'm getting worse, aren't I? First the dreams, now throwing up. I was shaking so bad, I couldn't walk without her help. I want to hide somewhere she can't see me. I want to curl into a ball and sleep for years.

When I don't answer, Allison adjusts the washcloth but doesn't touch my forehead. I can't see her face, but she's being so gentle I want to cry.

"Weird question: Do you want me to rub your back? That helps me sometimes when I'm feeling bad."

Yes. *Yes.* The snake makes a knowing grunt in my ear, but I clear my throat and ignore him. "Oh, um, sure. Yeah, thanks."

I flinch when Allison's hand touches the middle of my back, but I quickly relax. She rubs my back in slow circles, and her touch is so gentle, I want to fall asleep after a few seconds. The nausea creeps from my throat to my stomach, and exhaustion floods my bones. I'm so tired. I could sleep for a whole week.

"Do you feel better now?" Allison asks after a minute.

I blink tiredly at the tiled floor. "A little. Thanks, Allison."

"No problem." She rubs her knuckles next to my spine, and I don't know if I've ever been so happy and so miserable at once. After a few moments of silence, Allison speaks again. "Was it another nightmare?"

I close my eyes. "Yeah. A bad one."

"What happens in them?"

I take a shuddering breath, the dream mixed with reality replaying behind my eyes. "I'm running, and the police dog is barking and chasing me. And then John breaks my leg. He always breaks my leg."

I hear Allison suck in a sharp breath. I close my eyes tighter, full of a mixture of feelings. Humiliation, rage, deep, yawning sadness.

"The PTSD is getting worse, isn't it?" I sound defeated even to my own ears. "It's never going to get better."

"No, Avie, no." Allison stops rubbing my back, and when I open my eyes, she's leaning over me so she can see my face. Hers is full of anxiety and concern. "Don't say that. I know it sucks, but I promise it gets better."

"How?" Frustration threatens to overwhelm me. "I have these horrible dreams all the time, and now I'm throwing up. I can't sleep. Every time I close my eyes, I see them. And I feel what they did."

Allison makes a pained face. "Avie . . ."

"It's okay." I can't keep the bitterness out of my tone. "We can forget it."

Allison hesitates, then seems to make up her mind about something. She takes a deep breath. "I don't really like to talk about it, but I've been diagnosed with major depression and generalized anxiety disorder."

I frown up at her. Jade mentioned her being depressed, and I figured as much about the anxiety. I start to say something, but Allison hurries to continue.

"And at first it was just like this. Nonstop nightmares and intrusive thoughts and panic attacks. But I worked really hard, and it got better."

"Yeah?"

"Yeah. I went to therapy, and made a strict sleep schedule for myself, and I take my meds. Well, when I'm not running out, like now. But anyway, I'm saying it's not terrible forever. It takes time, and it sucks so much in the beginning, but I don't want you to feel hopeless."

I frown at the bottom of Allison's towel rack. Maybe she's right. Maybe I need to look into therapy after this is over. Maybe I need to finish my list and then see how I feel.

"I get being frustrated, though," Allison continues. She laughs, short and bitter. "I haven't pulled my hair out in years. It used to be so bad my mom made me shave my head because I couldn't stop. And I worked so, so hard, and last night I felt like I was back to square one."

"You're not, though." I roll over so I can see her fully. "You're right, you worked really hard. This is just really fucking stressful."

"Yeah. None of my coping mechanisms account for getting eaten by a giant snake."

We laugh, and I kind of feel better. Allison made it through. It sounds hard and painful, but she did it. And I think she'd help me make it too. "Hey, don't worry about your hair. I'll help you. Every time you try to pull a strand out, I'll stop you."

Allison looks at me, her blue eyes sparkling with something I can't place. "Thanks, Avie. You're always helping me, like last night."

Heat fills my face, and Allison's face gets a little pink too. "I'm glad! It might help you if you're close to someone, you know?"

"Yeah," Allison says, eyes locked with mine. "That makes sense. I feel really safe with you."

We grin at each other like idiots for a tiny, warm

moment. It's just now hitting me that I threw up in Allison's bathtub, but she helped me and soothed me and took care of me when she didn't have to. She said she feels safe with me, but I think . . . I think I feel safe with her too. I feel like that time when I went to the woods and the snake curled around me and I knew, at least for a little while, no one could hurt me.

Allison looks away first. She smiles down at her hands. "If you're feeling better, maybe we can move to the couch? You probably don't want to lie on the floor."

"Oh, yeah! Hang on, let me . . ." I struggle to sit up, and Allison helps me stand. She waits while I rinse the vomit from my mouth and brush my teeth, and we limp to the couch together. Allison fusses over me, covering me with the blanket and replacing the cool washcloth on my forehead. I settle into the couch, warm and exhausted and feeling safer than I have in a while.

"Oh God, it's already two o'clock! What do you want for lunch?" Allison calls from the kitchen.

"I'm fine," I say, my eyes closed. "I'm not hungry."

"You should eat something," Allison says, her voice disapproving. "Oh, you know what sounds good? Waffle House. Nothing better than breakfast after feeling sick!"

"That does sound good," I mumble, but I'm almost asleep. Allison doesn't say anything, and I'm warm but not too warm and maybe I could take a nap. . . .

Images flash in quick succession. John, the dog, the metal bat raised above his head—

I open my eyes, gasping. The snake moves around my neck, blinking slowly.

"It's okay, Latavia. You are safe." The snake tastes the air while my breathing returns to normal. "Though, your friend is away. She left to bring you food."

"Oh." I blink, rubbing my eyes. I don't know how long I've been asleep, but I feel a lot better. Still exhausted, but not so feverish anymore.

The snake moves in a lazy circle around my neck. He's quiet for a few minutes, and I almost fall asleep again before he speaks. "It seems I owe you an apology, Latavia."

I blink awake. This is definitely new. "What'd you do?"

The snake flicks his tongue out again. "When you stole the keys from your friend's room, I did not understand why you were so worried about her discovering you. I said I would have killed her, but you were not comforted by this. I see why now." The snake stops moving, his tiny face right in front of my nose. "When that human touches you, your heart calms and your panic does too. She is important to you."

I stare at him, uneasy. Why is he saying all of this? What does he want?

"If she is important to you, I will not threaten her life again. It is useful for you to be calm and happy for the remainder of our contract."

I smile at the snake, the anxiousness vanishing. "Thanks, snake. You're not so bad."

"Well," the snake says, settling around my neck. "I have a vested interest in keeping you alive. That's all."

I grin at the ceiling. Puking aside, this has been a pretty good morning. Allison slept in my lap, shared something personal with me, and rubbed my back. I mean, friends don't do that, right? I've certainly never rubbed Lindsay's back after she puked her guts up. At least, not in such a tender, comforting way. "Hey, snake, while you're in a good mood, help me out. Do you think Allison likes me?"

The snake sighs, deep and heavy. "Of course she likes you. Why would she help you if she didn't?"

"No, I mean like *likes* me. You know."

"I do not, and I am weary of this conversation already."

"Come on! Like, I'm getting a vibe. And Jade didn't say anything about us going on a date, you know? Like, she didn't make a big deal about it—"

"Good night, Latavia." The snake's voice is annoyed and frustrated, which makes me laugh. The snake isn't in the mood for relationship advice. Got it.

"Okay, okay. Good night."

He doesn't say anything, so I take a deep, calm breath and close my eyes. In minutes, I fall fast asleep.

35

"Charlie!" I call, wandering through Red Wood. "Come here, boy!"

"You should have told the hound to reside in a specific location," the snake says from around my neck.

"You could help, you know." The snake doesn't answer, so I roll my eyes and keep searching.

It's almost eleven p.m. Jade and Allison are on their second night of patrols, but I'm thinking about my appointment with Mrs. Brim at midnight. Since Peach isn't with me, I thought it might be good to have some backup.

After his speech, the snake was quiet and moody all day. He's sleeping a lot, and his scales are duller too. I think he's getting sick. Can snakes get sick? Should I take him to a veterinarian? Do vets see giant snakes?

I feel a buzz in my pocket and take out my phone. It's a text from Jade.

I wanna go home, she complains to the group chat between Jade, Allison, and me. *I hate it here.*

You still have like five hours, I text back. *Where are you now?*

After a minute, I receive a poorly lit selfie of Allison and Jade in front of China Wok.

Wish it was open, Allison texts. *I'm starving.*

If I see Don in these streets, we fightin, Jade texts.

I smile at my phone. I'm glad these two nerds are in better spirits. After I woke up again, Allison was back and I ate cold waffles and greasy bacon. She was okay at first, but when it was time for patrolling again, Allison seemed agitated and uneasy. She kept picking at her hair absently, and I had to tell her to stop several times. Jade didn't seem too much better; she told me she couldn't sleep because she was listening to Auntie cry. I can't wait for this to be over, for obvious reasons, but at least they'll finally be able to relax soon.

"Your hound is ahead," the snake says, startling me out of my thoughts.

Oh yeah, Charlie. I glance at my phone one more time before putting it back into my pocket. I'll text them after I'm done with Deacon Brim.

I find Charlie in a massive hole beneath a rotting tree. He pokes his head out, panting.

"Hey! Come here, buddy." I'm still a little wary about him; hard to forget his teeth sinking into my arm. But he comes out of the hole, butt wiggling as hard as Peach's, and jumps up to lick my hands. Maybe it was his owner who was bad. I rub his ears, and he leans against my good leg. "We've got a job to do. Oh man, you're so dirty. I should have brought a brush. And some dog food. I'm a terrible pet owner."

"No need to bring food," the snake says.

I look down at my feet, and my stomach turns. Dead birds, chunks bitten out of their chests, litter the base of the tree. Their feathers move slightly in the warm wind.

"Now, this one can be a wild one again," the snake says. He sounds impressed.

I ignore the carnage and lead Charlie to the meeting place with Mrs. Brim. She's not here yet, thank goodness. I check the time—eleven forty-five. Fifteen minutes to prepare.

"Okay, team," I say out loud. Charlie's ears stand up, but the snake doesn't react. "Here's the plan. I distract the guy, Snake, you get big and hold him down, and, Charlie, you're in the back in case things go south. Any questions?"

"Yes," the snake says. "What makes you think I'm involved in this?"

I stare at him, numb with shock. "What?"

"The woman asked *you* to help her. You agreed." The snake climbs down from my shoulders and curls up beside Charlie. "I agreed to nothing. This is your deal, not mine."

My mouth is dry. He's kidding. He has to be joking. "How am I supposed to hold a huge guy down for hours?"

"That is for you to figure out." The snake grows a little, spooking Charlie, and climbs a massive oak. He looks down at me, his eyes glinting in the moonlight. "I warned you about playing too much. I am working with you to kill

305

the six humans who attacked you. This situation is your business."

I can't believe this. I was counting on him to help me. How am I gonna stop a grown man from leaving? I can't even run if things get bad. My knee aches ominously, and I check my phone. Eleven fifty-two. Oh shit, she'll be here soon— "You know, you've had a real bad attitude lately. Not a team player at all."

The snake snorts but doesn't answer. I open my mouth to ask him to help me, please, but—

"Are you sure the group's this way?" a man's faint voice calls.

Shit.

"I'm sure," Mrs. Brim's voice says.

Shit, shit, shit—

"Good luck," the snake says. He almost sounds like he's laughing.

Okay. New plan. I touch Charlie's back, and he looks up at me. "Charlie, do you think you could protect me? If that man attacks me?"

Charlie stares into my eyes, just like Peach does. I think it worked.

Two people come into view. I can see them, but they can't see me yet. I take a deep breath. In through the nose, out through the mouth. Calm, be calm. Stay calm. I can do this. I'll forget about holding him down—I'll try to knock him out. Hopefully he'll stay out for a few hours. I lean on my cane and put on my best smile as Mr. and Mrs. Brim come into view.

"Hi," I say, waving. "Remember me?"

Mr. Brim stops walking, his eyes wide. "You're the dead girl."

"That's me!" I'm trying to sound cheerful, but my hands are trembling. I don't like these odds. Mrs. Brim is thin, and she's obviously been beaten by him several times. And he's huge! He looks like he lifts weights. I'm having flashbacks to John, Carter, and Sheriff Kines chasing me through the woods. I can't run this time. I drum my fingers on my good leg nervously.

"What's going on?" Mr. Brim turns to his wife, and Mrs. Brim cringes from him.

Her fear gives me a burst of courage. "Hey, we're talking. Stay focused, Deacon."

He glares at me. "I'm calling Pastor Thomas. You shouldn't be alive. You should be monster food."

Hmm. Seems like more people than the guardians know about the snake. The town isn't as innocent as I thought. My grip tightens around the cane. "Well, clearly I'm not. And I'm on a mission to punish the dregs of Sanctum. That includes you."

Mr. Brim glances at Mrs. Brim, who's backed a considerable distance away. "You bitch. You think that kid can save you? You're dead when we get home."

Okay, I've heard enough. I touch Charlie's back. "Charlie, honey, can you attack that man for me? Doesn't that sound nice?"

It must sound real nice, because Charlie takes off running like a bullet.

It's over in seconds. Charlie charges at Mr. Brim and grabs his arm, like he did mine. Mr. Brim screams and topples to the ground from Charlie's momentum. I hobble forward as fast as I can, trying to ignore his pained screaming, and step on his back with my good leg. I lean all my weight on Mr. Brim, trying to decide how I can knock him out without killing him, but he struggles, thrashing violently. I can't keep him still. Charlie can't keep him still.

This isn't going to work.

"Kayla!" Mr. Brim roars over the sound of Charlie's snarling. "I'll kill you! I'll kill you for this!"

"Go!" I tell Mrs. Brim, struggling to keep him from getting up. Blood runs from Charlie's teeth, but it's like Mr. Brim doesn't even feel it. He rips his arm from Charlie's mouth and swings his fist at the dog.

Mrs. Brim hesitates, her eyes wide with terror. "Wh-what happened to the snake?"

"Hurry! Go!"

Thankfully, she listens to me and bolts, her hair flying out behind her.

Mr. Brim won't stay still. He's too strong. I'm trying to hold him down, pressing with all my might on his back, but one of his flailing arms connects with my knee.

Pain, the worst pain I've ever felt, leaps into my body like lightning. I've been electrocuted. I'm dead, I'm dying—

I think I black out. I have to, because when I come to, Charlie is barking in my ear and Mr. Brim has his hands around my neck.

"I'll kill you," he spits into my face. His face is red and bulging and ugly. He looks like a monster. "I'll kill you, and then her."

I can't think. I can't breathe. I'm dying. My knee is on fire. I'm on fire. I have to do something—

Charlie bites into Mr. Brim's shoulder, and for a second his grip loosens on my neck. I ball my hands into fists. The snake's venom pulses through my body, my veins, my hands. I rear back and hit him as hard as I can in the face.

I hear a *crack*, and Mr. Brim howls in pain. I hit him again, and he rolls off me. I hit him again, and his teeth cut into my knuckles. One more time, and blood sprays in my face. I hit him, over and over, until my breathing is harsh in my ears and some of the blinding pain fades.

"Latavia."

I'm breathing so hard, I can't hear. Something's buzzing in my ears. My knee hurts. My knee—

"Latavia, stay calm." Someone's murmuring in my ear. Something licks my hand, whining.

I wheeze, my eyes squeezed closed. I have to listen to the voice. "I—I . . ."

"It's okay." I recognize the snake's voice now. I feel his familiar weight on my shoulders. "It's okay, you are safe."

"I . . . I thought you weren't going to help me."

"I was watching. When he hurt your injured leg, I decided to intervene. I was moments from striking, but there was no need. You handled this yourself."

I handled what myself? I'm scared to open my eyes. "What did I do?"

"You successfully completed your first contract." The snake touches my cheek gently. His scales are cool and comforting against my skin. "This man cannot hurt the woman anymore. You've done well."

Reluctantly, I open my eyes. My stomach groans and I'm shaking, though I know what I'm going to see.

Mr. Brim has his face toward the sky, but he's not seeing anything. His face and chest are drenched in his own blood, his jaw skewed and hanging. White bone peeks from the skin in places. He's not breathing. I close my eyes again. I killed him. Fuck, I killed him.

"Take a moment to recover," the snake croons in my ear. "I will assist you now. I know you're in pain."

I don't answer, and the snake leaves my shoulders. He grows, to half his normal size, and drags Mr. Brim's body to the trees. As soon as he passes into Red Wood, he grows huge, and he and Mr. Brim disappear.

I lie on my side, my eyes closed. Charlie lies beside me, licking blood from my knuckles. I didn't mean to kill him. I really didn't. But as soon as he hit my knee, I just . . . reacted. I breathe, shallow, quick breaths. I'm a murderer. First Sheriff Kines, now Mr. Brim. One is an accident, but two is a pattern.

But . . . as I lie there, eyes closed, pain in my knee easing from excruciating to borderline unbearable, some of the shock and shame fades. Yes, I killed him. But he was a horrible man, just like the rest. I was protecting Mrs. Brim and Delilah. I think of Mrs. Brim cringing from him, and Delilah asking me to punish all bad men. My

310

breathing becomes calmer, deeper. Strength crackles in my fists. I hear the snake approaching. My breathing is normal.

I open my eyes. I don't feel so bad about it anymore.

I feel powerful.

36

I clean blood from under my fingernails in Allison's sink.

We're back at the apartment. I asked about using the rest of the night to track John and Pastor Thomas, but the snake refused to allow it. I'm grateful for that because I don't feel so hot. I tried to shower, but my knee hurts too bad. It's swollen and more painful than it's been in days. I'm trying not to think too much about killing Mr. Brim, because if I do, I have to think about the fact that I'm not really bothered by it.

"Latavia," the snake says. "How are you feeling?"

I look at him in the mirror. He's back on my shoulders, looped comfortably around my neck. I look normal; all the blood is gone, and I've changed clothes. I threw the others into the dumpster behind Allison's house. I look normal, but something's changed in me. I can't see it, but I feel it.

"Snake, can I ask you something?"

"Yes, of course."

I stare at my reflection in the mirror. Fuzzy braids that need redoing. Even fuzzier bun. Thin face, dark skin. Brown eyes I've looked into all my life.

"Why don't I feel bad about killing Mr. Brim?"

The snake moves lazily around my neck. "Perhaps because you were defending yourself? Or defending that female human? You seemed quite amicable with her."

"No, that's not it." I felt the power in my fingertips, the ability to punish someone for what they did to me. He hurt me. He paid for it. I feel better, stronger. "Do you think I'm becoming a monster?"

The snake is quiet for a long time. Then he presses his face against my cheek. It's so gentle, I'm surprised.

"Being a monster feels good, doesn't it?"

I don't get a chance to reply. I hear Allison's key turn in the door, and then Peach's thunderous footsteps as she runs into the apartment.

"Keep it together for your friend," the snake says. He turns that shimmery color again—invisible.

"Avie?" Allison calls as Peach rockets into the bathroom. She whines and licks my hands, my arm, everything she can reach.

"Bathroom. Hang on, I'm coming out."

I look at myself one more time in the mirror. Keep it together, Latavia. Don't let her find out what you've done.

When I leave the bathroom, I'm smiling.

Allison smiles back. Her shirt's soaked again, and her hair's up in a high ponytail. She's exhausted; I can tell by her slumped shoulders and the dark circles under her eyes. But she still brightens when she sees me. A little bit of guilt sneaks into my chest. She wouldn't smile if she knew what I did.

"Hey! Another quiet night. Thank goodness." She steps toward the kitchen, but stops short. "Oh my God, Avie, your knee! What happened?"

I'm surprised to feel pinpricks of tears in my eyes. "I fell on it while you were gone."

"Oh God. Come here, come here."

I let her usher me to the couch and stretch out my leg. I yelp like a wounded animal when it stretches too far.

"I'm sorry! Let me get some ice."

I stare at the ceiling while she runs to the kitchen. Guilt eats me from the inside out. Allison is so kind to me, always, but she'd be horrified to learn what I did.

Allison spreads an ice pack on my knee. It hurts, but I hold in a groan so I won't worry her. She sits next to me on the couch, searching my face anxiously. "Are you okay? What happened?"

"I, uh, fell. But it's fine."

"It's not fine! I'm so worried about your knee. Do you think it's broken? Like a stress fracture, maybe?"

Who knows what's going on in there. I have no idea how silver and venom affect bones. "I'm sure I'll get an X-ray after this is over," I offer weakly.

Allison shakes her head. "God, this is such a mess. Everything's a mess."

I stay quiet. It is a mess—me especially. I can't sort through my tangle of feelings. Guilt, but it's from lying to Allison, not from killing two people. Pride, shame, power. I look at Allison, and for one second, I want to tell her every-thing. If she said it was okay, I think I'd be okay too. "Allison?"

"Yeah?"

"Do you think good people can do bad things? Some-times?"

Allison searches my face, frowning. "You asked me that before."

Yeah, I did. After I murdered someone the first time.

Allison clasps her hands in front of her. "This isn't ex-actly the same, but . . . My mom was a terrible person. I know it, Jade knows it, the whole town knows it. She tortured me. She called me useless, fat, told me I'd never make it. She said I would be better off as snake food."

Fury burns in my stomach. "Want me to kill her?"

Allison laughs. "No, it's okay. But what I'm trying to say is that even though she did all that horrible stuff to me, I still love her." Allison tucks a strand of hair behind her ear. "I know it's not right. But I do. I can't help it. I used to daydream that if I could kill the snake, she would come back. She'd finally be proud of me. But I know that's not a healthy way to think." Allison shakes her head, her expression resigned, heartbroken. "I know you probably still love your aunt, but she hurt you. It's okay to stay away from her. Even though it hurts. I know."

I struggle for words. Hurt aches in my chest for Alli-son. I want to hold her, to hug her until she forgets what her mom said. But also, dread creeps into my chest. I don't want to add to the hurt her mom caused. But I'd never hurt her . . . at least, not on purpose. I recall how I lost con-trol with Mr. Brim, and shudder. That's something I don't

315

want to think about anymore. This is about Allison, and bad moms, and if they can be forgiven. If I can be forgiven.

"My mom kicked me out."

Shock covers Allison's face. "Really?"

"Yeah." I take a painful breath. This is the first time I've talked about it. This is the first time I've allowed myself to think about it. "She kicked me out, and Auntie took me in. I thought Mom loved me. I thought, but . . ." I shrug, tears building in my eyes. "She doesn't, I guess. She wouldn't even answer my phone call after six weeks. Even after I said it was an emergency. Does she hate me that much?"

"I'm so sorry, Avie." Allison looks like she wants to hug me, but I lean back so she won't. I'll lose it if she does.

"And then Auntie took me in. She knew what happened, but she didn't care. She made me feel at home with her and Jade. And then, out of the blue, she tries to kill me." I'm almost crying. I can feel my tears about to spill over. "I'm not like you, Allison. I can't forgive her for what she did. I feel like I'm at my limit. Two people who I thought loved me abandoned me. One after another. I don't know if I can take much more."

"I'm here." Allison holds her hands out for me to take them, her eyebrows scrunched together. "I'm not going anywhere."

The pain and guilt and sorrow melt away, and I put my hands in hers. Allison is here. She'll forgive me, after all this is over. I just have to survive until the full moon, the end of the deal, and escape from the snake. It'll all be over soon, and I have someone waiting on me after all this is through.

"Why did your mom kick you out?" Allison asks. "If it's not too personal."

"Oh, uh . . ." I debate about lying, but it's time. It's time to say it out loud. "I went to a graduation party. Got totally wasted, and Mom picked me and my friend Kendra up. She was mad, but not mad enough to kick me out. Then she saw me kiss Kendra. It all went downhill after that."

Allison blinks at me slowly. "Kendra is . . . a girl?"

My heart rate kicks up, and my rib cage is suddenly too small for my lungs. I can do this. It's too late to back out now. I sit up straighter, trying to ignore the sweat pooling under the snake hiding in my shirt. "Yes. Kendra is a girl."

"Oh."

I wait for more, but Allison is quiet. She's not looking at me; her gaze is slightly above my head. Her cheeks are pink. Dread swirls in my stomach. Shit, this was a terrible idea. My mouth is dry, and I can't bear the silence any longer. "Is that a problem?"

"No!" Allison returns her gaze to mine. Her expression is hard to read. Sorrowful, but there's something else, just at the edge. . . . "I'm so sorry, Avie. You didn't deserve this from your mom."

I hesitate. A huge part of me wants to shut down, ignore it, stuff down the hurt like I've been doing for six weeks. But a small part of me wants to talk about it, to share the pain with someone else for a change. I take a shaky breath. "I was shocked. Like, really shocked."

Allison nods, her eyes focused and kind. I concentrate on the warmth of her hands.

"Mom has never said anything homophobic to me.

317

Never, in my whole life. I mean, I know she's real religious, but I don't know . . . I never thought to be afraid of her. I was already out to Jade and Auntie, and I thought she knew. I thought she wouldn't care. You know, when she told me to leave, I thought she was kidding. I laughed. I actually laughed."

My throat burns, and I blink rapidly to contain the tears trying to escape my eyes. The snake doesn't make it any easier; he presses his face gently against my cheek, like he's actually trying to comfort me. I'm about to lose it.

Allison's face softens in a way I've never seen, full of care and sadness and pain, and she lets go of my hands. She reaches for my face, and I cringe from her touch. "It's okay," she says, her voice kind and gentle. Her hand hovers in the air, close to my cheek but not touching me yet. Tentatively, I lean into her touch, and her warm hand meets my skin. She wipes away a few tears, staring up at me. "I'm so sorry you went through that, Avie. You didn't do anything wrong. Your mom doesn't deserve you."

I blink rapidly again, but I can't hold back the tears anymore. It hurts, more than I thought it would, to finally admit that Mom isn't coming back for me, and probably never will. But I'm also feeling a strange gratitude, a closeness I've never felt before. I smile at Allison, sniffling, and say, "Jeez, you're trying to make me cry, huh?"

Allison smiles back. "Never." She wipes my eyes again, and I find myself calming down, focusing on her gentle touch.

"Sorry," I say after a moment, pulling away to wipe my eyes on my shirt sleeve. "I haven't told anyone yet. I called Auntie, and she came and picked me up, no questions asked." That's another depressing relationship I don't want to think about, though.

"It's all right. I know it's painful. But I really mean what I said. It's not your job to make your mom be a decent person, you know?" Allison shakes her head, still smiling sadly. "I never got a chance to tell my mom, but I'm assuming it would be similar."

I frown at Allison, my heart rate kicking up a notch. "Tell her what?"

Allison stares at me, like a deer in headlights. "Oh. Oh, um . . ." She trails off, a number of emotions crossing her face. But then she settles on a mix of fear and determination. "Actually, I want to tell you something."

My heart rate goes even faster. "Okay. I'm listening."

"I, um, I'm actually interested in, uh . . ." Allison bites her bottom lip, then takes a deep breath. "I like girls too. Um, actually, I like . . . you."

Warm understanding fills my chest and expands my lungs. The snake hiss-laughs in my ear. "This answers your earlier question," he murmurs.

If I wasn't so happy, I'd hit him.

Allison searches my face anxiously. "Is—is that okay?"

"Of course it's okay! I like you too!"

Pure shock covers Allison's face. "Really?"

"Yes, really!" A laugh bubbles up in my chest, edging out the sorrow. "For, like, a while."

"Oh my God. I had no idea. I didn't think you'd say that."

I laugh for real this time. "Why do you look so shocked? I've been dropping hints for weeks!"

"Sorry, I'm overwhelmed!" Allison smiles too, matching my euphoric grin. "I'm not out to anyone except Jade. And then you came to Sanctum and I thought you were so cool and nice, and I thought maybe . . . but I was so nervous, like maybe I was picking up on the wrong vibe? I don't know what I'm doing. It's not like I've ever even kissed a girl before."

"Well," I say, feeling happier than I have in weeks, "we'll have to fix that, won't we?"

Suddenly the light mood changes. We're staring at each other, her pretty blue eyes big and round. My heart rate's going crazy. But then I remember the snake's around my neck, and I don't want to share this moment with anyone other than Allison.

I pull away. "I mean, not right now! We can take things slow."

Allison nods, but she seems a little disappointed. "Okay! But, um, I do want to say that I've liked you for a while, Avie. Like, a lot. If you haven't noticed."

I have to beat back more tears. A week ago, I would have done anything to hear those words from her mouth. And now everything's different and changing and there's a monster around my neck. And I might be a monster too.

After the full moon is over, after me and the snake aren't working together, after all six are dead and gone, it'll be okay. I'll be okay. I hold Allison's hands in mine.

"After all this is over, let's go see a movie."

Allison smiles up at me, and it's like being bathed in sunlight. I have to survive this now. For the first time since this started, I feel like I have a future. And now nothing is going to stand in my way of getting it.

37

The next day, after a night of talking and sweet cuddling that nearly sent me into cardiac arrest, Allison takes a shower. When I hear the water switch on, I pull out my phone, go to Safari, and Google "why is my snake's skin dull."

Tonight, we have to kill three people. John, Pastor Thomas, then Auntie. The location of the last two barriers is with them. It'll all be over tonight, and I can go back to being normal. I can go back to Allison, and it'll all be okay. But the snake looks like he's about to die on me, and I really need him to be able to back me up when we face the remaining three. He's been limp and lethargic all day, refusing to go to the woods to eat, refusing to even talk that much. I'm kinda worried he has internal bleeding from Sheriff Kines. Wouldn't that be something? Hero cop saves the town by beating the absolute shit out of a tiny monster. Almost poetic.

I touch the search bar, and results come up immediately.

The most common skin problem in snakes occurs
with shedding. Snakes are close to shedding when
they hide, refuse to eat, or the skin becomes dull
or translucent.

Oh! He's about to shed his skin. Totally normal for a snake, I guess. Even for an ancient monster one. I put away my phone, but then I pause. I'm getting that nagging feeling again. Something isn't right.

I pull my phone out again and look at my collection of notes I stole from the guardians. Katie's notes about the silver, Carter's Plasma recipe, Don's notebook. I frown at them, unable to ignore the feeling I'm missing something.

Then I remember—Allison sent me another picture of Pastor Thomas's ramblings. I go to her message and stare at the text. My heart stutters in my chest.

> *The moon was full when we woke him*
>   *Bigger than before, stronger*
>   *Happening again?*
>   *Revert to animal state? Sunrise?*
>   *Can I run?*

The clues click into place. The snake is going to shed his skin soon, most likely during the full moon. And whatever this "animal state" is creates a window of opportunity for them to run. Does that mean the snake won't be as intelligent as he is now? And instead, he'll just be a regular snake? I Google more about shedding, and the search results tell me that snakes are blind and irritable while shedding their skin. He'll be vulnerable for one precious night; for one night he won't be at full strength. He'll be blind, in pain, afraid.

And that's when we can kill him.

I touch the snake's scales reflexively. This is it. This is what I wanted to know the whole time, a way out. But as the snake sluggishly rests his head on my hand, doubt springs into my chest. He's a monster. He's eaten hundreds of people over hundreds of years. But he's also comforted me after nightmares. He joked with me. He gave me (albeit useless) dating advice. He let power flow through my veins so I don't ever have to be hurt again.

I stare down at the sleeping snake, a terrible feeling in my chest. Right now, today, I genuinely don't know if I have the guts to kill him.

The shower stops running, and I put my phone away. I need to calm down. I can think about what to do later, because I don't want Allison to see me upset. She'll notice, and ask me what's wrong, and lately I've been having a really hard time lying to her—

There's a noise from the outside stairwell. I freeze, fear shocking all thoughts of the snake from my brain. I wait for a heart-stopping second, and the steps creak again. Someone's outside, climbing the stairs.

Panic hits me all at once. It could be John, or Pastor Thomas, or a random robber, or someone like Mr. Brim—

"Latavia?" The snake's voice is quiet. If I didn't know better, I'd say his tone carried a hint of concern.

"I—I have to go." I scramble to my feet when the person knocks. I limp as fast as I can to Allison's room.

"Delivery!" a voice calls.

Oh, just a delivery guy. Allison probably ordered pizza or something. I try to convince my heart to calm down, but it doesn't. I pull Allison's bedroom door closed, my chest tight, my breath short.

"Be calm," the snake says in my ear. He curls himself more snugly around my neck. "If a human threatens you, I am here. Do not be afraid."

"Coming!" Allison calls. I hear her quick footsteps, her talking to the delivery guy, and the click of the front door closing. But I don't move. I can't move. I put my hand to my neck, and the snake curls soothing circles around my wrist.

"It's all right," the snake purrs. "You are safe."

My heart slows a little bit. He's right. What would a delivery guy want with me? A bit of the panic fades, and it's replaced with embarrassment. I'm still no better than I was before.

Allison knocks on her door tentatively. "Avie? You in here?"

In through the nose, out through the mouth. "Yeah."

"Can I come in?"

I nod before realizing she can't see me. "Oh, sorry, yeah."

She cracks her door and peeks inside. She's wearing a cute pink shirt with white flowers, jean shorts, and her hair is soaking wet. It falls in little ringlets around her face. "You okay?"

I try not to fidget. "Yeah. I heard the guy on the stairs."

"That's all right. He's gone now." Allison holds her hand

out to me, palm up, waiting for me to take it. She doesn't say anything, just gives me a warm smile. I hesitate. It's okay. Allison is here, and the snake is around my neck, and the guy's gone. I take a breath, then another, and limp toward her. I take her hand, and in an instant, the remaining panic disappears.

"Sorry," I say as she pulls me out of the dark room and into the kitchen light. "I heard the stairs, and I got really freaked out again—"

"You don't have to apologize. You can go in my room anytime." Allison squeezes my hand and smiles at me, and I swear my insides turn to mush. I lace our fingers together and grin at her.

"Thanks. What'd you order anyway?"

Wild excitement crosses Allison's face. "Dinner for us! I was completely out of food, so I thought, what the hell, let's get something crazy."

She pulls groceries from several white bags on the kitchen counter, still holding my right hand. There's popcorn and Oreos and . . . is that a birthday cake?

"It's snacks, mostly," Allison says. She's still grinning as she shows me a thick, raw steak. "But I got this too! I've never had steak before. Like, ever in my whole life. I'm so excited."

Frowning, I watch her pull out the piles of food. Something is a little off. She's smiling, huge and euphoric, but there's a hint of panic in her voice.

"What's the occasion?" I ask.

Allison pauses, looking at me shyly out of the corner

of her eye. "Well, I was kind of hoping . . . I was thinking this could be a date."

I stare at her for a few dumb seconds, my brain completely nonfunctional.

"Wow," the snake says, "your luck has been quite good lately."

His smart-ass comment kickstarts my brain again. "I—I mean, yeah, okay! Of course!"

"Oh, thank God! I thought you were gonna say no!" Allison's smile is radiant—it lights up her whole face. "I was thinking we can just, you know, spend time together today? And cook this steak together, because honestly I have no idea what I'm doing."

I hold up my free arm, pretending to flex my bicep. "Well, you've come to the right place. I'm practically a chef."

"Oh really?" Allison says, her eyes crinkling with laughter, and I think this may be the best day I've had in seven miserable weeks.

We spend the next thirty minutes cooking together, standing side by side at the stove. And she wasn't lying— Allison is a *terrible* cook. She put the steak on the stove with no seasoning, no salt and pepper even. No wonder she eats so much takeout! She also didn't buy anything to go with the steak, so we end up making popcorn and drinking too-sweet tea. But still, it's fun. It's fun being so close to her, knowing that she likes me and I like her too. And even though the snake is snoozing around my neck, it feels like it's just me and her, and nothing in the world can mess this up.

"Sorry I didn't get any sides," Allison says as we stand at the kitchen bar. I'm balancing on one leg, my bad knee propped up on a chair with a pillow on it. We could eat on the couch, but the kitchen is warm and smells great and Allison is standing right next to me.

"It's okay. Who doesn't like popcorn with New York strip?"

"I feel like you're making fun of me." Allison tries to give me a stern look, but her cheeks are pink and her eyes are soft and gentle, and, man, I wish I could kiss her right now. But maybe I could? Are we dating? I mean, this is a date. I usually talk for a while before making anything official. But we have been talking, right? For six weeks, we've been flirting, dancing around each other. I don't know. I'm a mess. I'm usually so much better about this stuff, but I've genuinely never liked anyone so much. I don't want to do anything to drive her away.

"Never, never," I say, instead of kissing her like I desperately want to. I take a small bite of my steak, but my stomach growls a warning. It's good, but I might throw up if I eat too much. I put down my fork. "What's next on this date?"

"Are you done eating?" Allison asks, frowning at my picked-over plate.

I shrug. "I haven't been able to eat much lately." I hesitate. Normally I'd stop here, but for the first time I want to say more. My hand goes to my neck, as if I need to borrow some of the snake's courage. He doesn't wake up, so I'm not sure it's working. "I think . . . I think it's from the, uh, PTSD. Maybe."

Allison nods, her expression turning sad. "It could be. I'm sorry, Avie."

"Don't be!" I smile against the hurt in my chest. "Come on, lighten up. It's a date!"

Allison smiles back. "Unfortunately, I don't have anything else planned."

I laugh, and some of the hurt disappears. "Movies it is. We already have popcorn."

"Are you ever gonna let this go?" She tosses some at me playfully, and I'm giggling, actually having fun for the first time since I left Mom's house and couldn't go back.

I wait for Allison to finish eating, and she dumps our plates into the sink.

"I'll help wash," I say, but Allison shakes her head.

"No, don't bother! It won't matter."

I frown at her. It won't matter? What does that mean? Allison has that slightly wild look again; she happily puts the dishes into the sink, the leftover food into the trash. She doesn't even try to save anything. Unease prickles my skin. Something's wrong.

"Allison?"

"Hmm?" She looks at me, eyes bright and happy.

I hesitate. Maybe now's not the time. "Nothing."

"Okay." She dries her hands on a kitchen towel. "I'm going to my room."

"Sure." To change clothes, maybe? We can watch a movie in our pajamas. Which reminds me, I'm *in* my pajamas and she looks great. I should have changed too. . . .

Allison walks to her door, but then stops. She stays still, frozen for so long, I almost ask her what's wrong.

Then she looks over her shoulder at me, just enough so I can see one blue eye. "Are you coming?"

All thoughts are sandblasted from my brain. Oh my God. Wow, is she . . . Okay. Okay, I can handle this. I can be chill about going to Allison's room, alone, just us. Get it together, Latavia.

I take a shaky, nervous breath. "Yeah, hang on—I'm gonna go to the bathroom first."

"Okay," she says, giving me a tiny, nervous smile, and disappears into her room. I limp to the bathroom as fast as my bum knee will allow, shut the door, and rip the snake from my neck. He grunts in surprise, and I hold him at eye level, glaring into his black eyes.

"If you follow me into her room, I'll kill you."

The snake laughs loudly, his tiny pink mouth wide open. His fangs are tucked away for once, so he looks toothless. "It's quite funny that you think I'd be interested in eavesdropping on two children."

"Excuse me, what—"

"I understand the implication, Latavia," he says, slithering down my arm and dropping into the sink. "I won't bother you and your new mate."

"We're not—that's not—"

"Have fun," the snake says, laughter in his voice. "Don't hurt your knee."

"I can't fucking stand you."

I don't have time to listen to the snake making fun of me. My heart beats raggedly against my ribs, and I kinda feel like I'm having a panic attack again. This isn't my first rodeo or anything, but Allison is different. This isn't a stupid homecoming party or a fling or even my last disastrous relationship. I like Allison. I like her a lot.

"Don't blow it," I tell my reflection in the mirror. I blink at myself. This is just like what happened before I was supposed to go to the party with Allison. Before everything went to shit. I nervously look over my shoulder, half expecting John to grab me, but there's nothing behind me but Allison's blue bathroom tile.

"Don't be nervous," the snake tells me. He crawls out of the sink and moves toward the towel rack. "You and your mate are very affectionate with each other. You'll be fine."

They shouldn't, but his words make me feel better. "Thanks, snake."

I wash my hands and splash water onto my face, and then I'm ready. Heart hammering, I leave the bathroom and enter Allison's bedroom.

She's sitting at the edge of her bed. The room is dark, but I can see her. Her hands are folded in her lap, and her shoulders are so tense, she's shivering a little. She looks just as nervous as I feel.

"Come sit down," she says. "Um, if you want to."

I sit, pretty far away from her. We stare at each other for a few nervous seconds. Normally Allison's bed is a mess of wadded-up sheets and blankets, but she's made it this time. Her comforter is neat and smooth, and she actually has pillows against the headrest. Her cute pink sheep is nowhere to be found.

"What'd your sheep do to get banished from the bed?" I joke, hoping she can't hear the anxious edge in my tone.

Allison gasps. "How do you even know about Lamby?"

"Lamby!" I can't hold in a giggle as Allison's face turns pink. "Oh my God, that's so cute!"

"Oh God, I'm mortified." So she says, but all the tension from her shoulders is gone and she's grinning. She nudges me playfully. "Are you gonna make fun of me the whole date?"

I laugh, relaxing more. "Of course! But don't worry, I'm having a pretty good time."

Allison's eyes shine with hope. "Really? You don't think this is lame?"

"Not at all." I lean back on my hands, smiling at her. "I like being with you."

Allison's cheeks turn bright red before my eyes, and I can feel myself melting. She's so cute. It should be illegal for anyone to be this cute.

"I like being with you too." Allison's voice is a happy whisper. "I just wish it could have happened sooner. We waited until it was almost too late."

My smile slips a little. Here's that ominous talk again. I sit up, looking straight at her. I can't keep ignoring it. I have to say something.

"Can I ask you something serious?"

"Yeah, of course!" Allison sits up straighter too.

"Are you . . . I mean, are you okay? You're not . . ." I trail off and take a deep breath for courage. "You're not planning on hurting yourself, are you?"

Allison stares at me, stunned into silence apparently. My heart rate increases and I hurry to continue.

"I'm worried. You keep saying stuff you wanted to do, past tense, and you bought all that food, but you didn't save any, and now you're saying it's too late. . . . I just want to make sure everything's okay."

Allison blinks a few times. "I . . . I'm sorry. I didn't mean to make you worry."

"But?" I prompt.

Allison doesn't say anything at first. She reaches anxiously for her hair, but I gently grab her hand to stop her. With my other one, I tuck her hair behind her ear.

"You can tell me anything." I'm nervous that I'm wrong, but I don't want to back off in case she really needs to talk. "It's okay. No more secrets, remember?"

Allison looks at me, blinking rapidly. She squeezes my hand and takes a shaky breath. "Truthfully . . . I have thought about it. In the past, though, not now. Back when I was pulling all my hair out, and Mom was hitting me, and I felt really alone . . . it was hard. It was hard to keep going."

My heart splinters into pieces. I knew it. I hold her hand tighter, trying to balance the heartbreak and creeping rage when I think of her mother hurting her. God, I wish I knew where that woman was. I'd have to add an extra person to my list.

Allison takes another shaky breath. "Now, I really don't want to die, I promise. But I can't . . ." Allison looks like she's struggling for words. "I can't help but think I will. The snake in Red Wood is going to kill me."

"It's okay," I tell her, easing closer. I want to wrap her in a hug and never let anyone hurt her ever again. "You're gonna make it through this. I promise."

"You can't promise that." Allison's voice is so sad, so defeated.

"I can promise. I am promising." I touch my thumb to her cheek, and she leans into my touch. "You're safe. If things get bad, we'll load Jade into your truck and let the snake eat everyone while we drive away. No big deal."

Allison laughs a little. "I can't leave, Avie."

"You can. 'What, Pastor Thomas? You want me to fight a giant snake with my bare hands? Sorry, I like to live.'"

Allison laughs harder, but her eyes are still sad. "It sucks. There are so many people who don't deserve to get eaten. I have to do something."

"Why you, though?" I rub my thumb over the back of her hand, careful to be gentle. "Why should you risk your life for this town? After all it's done to you?"

Allison struggles for words. She holds on to my hand, tight, her eyebrows scrunched together. She meets my eyes, and she looks like she wants to tell me something. But then she takes a deep breath, and smiles another sad smile. "I can't abandon everyone."

"Sure you can. Everyone abandoned me."

I wince as soon as the words leave my mouth. Way to make this about me. Great job, Latavia.

Allison squeezes my hand gently, a little relief in her expression. Maybe this is good; she probably wanted to change the subject. "Do you want to talk about it?"

"Oh. That's a shame. Snake, will you hold him down please?"

The snake slams his tail down on John's middle, pinning him to the ground. John screams and struggles, but the snake is too heavy. I walk to his side, disgust leaving a bitter taste on the back of my tongue.

"Let's start with the easy stuff. Do you have a journal? Like the rest?"

The way John's eyes widen tells me that he does. I don't want to touch him, so I nod at Peach. "Find that journal and bring it to me, please. That sounds nice doesn't it? Oh, and no need to be gentle with him."

Peach tackles John with enthusiasm, snuffling his pockets and tearing his clothes gleefully. John swears and struggles, trying to hold her back. He kicks at her, narrowly missing one ear.

"If you hurt my dog," I say, my voice liquid sweetness, "I'll make you wish you were dead."

John gets really still, his eyes wide with disbelief and terror, and Peach finally finds a worn leather journal in his left pocket. She bounds to me, tail wagging, and I pat her head as I wipe drool off the front of the book.

"So what's in yours?" I ask him, flipping the cover open. I scan the first page, eyebrows raised. The others had numbers, or Auntie's creepy scientific study, but this one is . . . a regular journal? The first date is 1984, but it's just ramblings of John's life. I flip through, my frown deepening as page after page is filled with boring details of running his grocery store, meeting his wife, having

343

children, divorcing his wife (good call, Kathy). "What is this? All the others at least had the decency to be useful."

John doesn't answer. He stares at me, cold hatred in his eyes. It scared me when this first started, but now I'm bored and annoyed that he's wasting my time.

Near the end, under an entry dated 2003, a phrase catches my interest. *Today, Pastor Thomas told me I am the chosen. And the chosen is privy to special information.*

Oh, finally! I scan the entry quickly.

> *Pastor Thomas told me the details of the creature in Red Wood. Its horrible fangs, the way it speaks with hatred. He said it's the living representation of the Devil. He said to defeat the Devil, sacrifices must be made.*

"What are you reading?" the snake asks, startling me.

"This guy's journal." I grin up at him. "Says you're the devil. Why didn't you tell me?"

The snake cocks his head to one side. "A devil? I'm unsure of what that is. I like the sound of the word, though."

I laugh, and John bares his teeth at me. "You mock me, little girl, but I know the truth. I know what he is! You're making deals with demons, and your soul is the only thing that'll perish!"

"Shut up, John." I go back to reading because I'm getting hot from the muggy summer air and I'm ready to end this once and for all.

> *I know sacrifices have to be made. So when he approached me and said we had no volunteers,*

I knew what I had to do. Pastor Thomas says
the Day of Reckoning is soon, a few more years
away, so we can't waver. I can't waver. It hurt,
giving up Sandy to the beast. But she only cried
a little. She understands her sacrifice will save
us all one day.

Sandy? That name sounds familiar, but I've already forgotten John's boring life. I flip backward, frowning, until I get to an entry near the front . . . Sandy, John's last-born daughter.

"You let Pastor Thomas take your daughter?" I can't hide the shock and disgust in my tone.

"It was for the greater good," John says, his voice subdued. "To keep the Devil from winning. God told Abraham to give up his son. I did the same."

I glance at the snake, who looks tired and bored, and then back at this book. It's so fucked up what Pastor Thomas has done to this town. The snake isn't a demon; he's just an animal, a big one with enough intelligence to outwit a pack of townies into feeding him. John would know that if he saw Auntie's journal, how they took apart a baby monster and tested weaknesses on it with no mercy until it died. He'd know that if he saw Don's own journal, where he described how his arrogance led him to ruin and forced him into the deal in the first place. But Pastor Thomas split them up, fed them individual lies, and controlled them to the point where John thought feeding his daughter to a giant snake was the right thing to do. It's so pitiful, I almost feel sorry for him. Almost.

In exchange for my loyalty, Pastor Thomas shared crucial information with me. He said he's thinking about barriers to keep the snake out. He shared their locations with me. I know I've done the right thing. Sandy's sacrifice wasn't in vain.

I turn the page, eager, and . . . the next pages are ripped out.

"Oh, come on!" I say out loud. There's a giant chunk missing, and all the rest of the pages are blank.

"Not good news?" the snake asks.

I glare down at John. "No. This one has decided to be difficult."

"I'll never tell you where they are." John's voice is full of fierce conviction. "I have to keep the monster out, for everyone's sake."

"Look, John, you're admirable, but don't you know he can already get in? He's weaker, sure, but you haven't saved anyone."

John's face pales at that, but he still shakes his head. "I won't tell you anything."

"You will." I look up at the snake. "Put some pressure on him. Not enough to kill him, though."

The snake's scales flex as he presses down on John's middle, squeezing a groan out of him. I toss the book to the side and bend down so John can see my face clearly. "I'm not messing around, John. Tell me where the other two barriers are."

He shakes his head wildly, his eyes white and rolling like a wild animal's.

"Okay. Suit yourself." I straighten and take a step back. I pick up my cane, raise it over my head, and slam it down onto John's right leg.

A sharp crack reverberates through the woods. John stares at me for a second, and then screams. I bring my cane down and lean on it, listening to him cry, watching him try to reach his leg. I try to feel something for him, like I did for Katie, like I did for the poor cop who was in the wrong place at the wrong time. But all I feel is a savage pleasure for making him feel the pain that I feel every day. The only bad thing is that his will be short-lived.

"John," I say once his screams have died into pathetic whimpers. "Where are the other barriers?" When he just keeps crying, I nudge his broken leg with my cane.

"At the church!" John screams. "One of them's at the church, in Pastor Thomas's office. It's—it's in a safe."

"Thought you'd never tell me." I grin at John. "What's the combination?"

John pants, his face bright red. "What?"

"The combination? For the safe?"

"It—it's not a combination. You have to have a key. Pastor Thomas has it, I don't know where."

"You guys really aren't making this easy for me, are you?" I sigh. "Where's the last one?"

John shakes his head. "I—I don't know. I only know about the one Pastor Thomas has. And—and he probably moved the others."

Yeah, that does sound like something the slimy bastard would do. John isn't gonna help me anymore; he looks like he might pass out with pain or fear. I sigh again, then look up at the snake. "Let him go."

The snake lifts his tail, and John gasps. He sits up, clutching his middle. "What're you gonna do with me?"

I shrug, smiling. "I'm not stopping you from running. Go ahead."

He blinks in disbelief. "I can . . . go?"

"Sure," I say. I know my grin is twisted and cold. I hope he's terrified. I hope he's pissing himself. "Good luck with your leg. Ice works pretty well."

He looks at me uncertainly. "Why are you doing this? You know if the barriers fall, the whole town is in trouble. That demon will kill us all."

"Sanctum tried to kill me." I'm still smiling. "What do I care?"

John snaps his mouth closed, a vein bulging on his forehead. He crawls away from us clumsily, his teeth gritted.

"What do you want to do?" the snake asks. I put my hand against his scales, searching one last time for softness, pity, mercy.

I don't find any.

"Kill him," I say, turning to leave. "Make him suffer. And after you're done, meet me at the church. We've got work to do."

39

I lean against the brick wall of the church, waiting for the snake. Peach is beside me, panting in the wet summer heat. I run my thumbnail over a crack in my phone and try to muster up any amount of remorse for what I've done.

When I think of Katie, guilt twists in my stomach like the snake coils in my hair. But I hear the crack of John's leg in my head, and I can't keep a grin off my face. The way he screamed, begged—it was everything I wanted.

This isn't good. I thought maybe what I felt after Mr. Brim was a fluke. But it's not—I really don't feel bad about John dying. In fact, I feel pretty good. I feel like he got what was coming to him. But does that make me a bad person? I think uneasily about my conversation with Allison. I asked her if good people can do bad things. But I should have asked her how she feels about bad people. Can bad people love their cousins and dogs and girlfriends, all the while killing people with a grin on their face?

And what's worse, now I have a decision to make. After

Pastor Thomas, after Auntie, the snake will have no use for me. And I'll have to kill him too. Dread prickles the back of my neck when I think about it. He's a monster, not human, so I shouldn't get sentimental. But he's helped me. We fought in the graveyard together. He comforted me after nightmares, joked with me about Allison, coiled around my neck and made me feel safe when I was staring down my attempted murderers. He made a deal with me instead of eating me.

Well, that's it, isn't it? We made a deal, and that's about to be over. I can't get sad about it. I have to prepare for what comes next.

Something touches my foot, and I look down. The snake climbs up my shoe and wraps himself around my ankle. His scales are even duller now. "Did I keep you long?"

"No. I was just thinking." I offer my hand to him, and he crawls up my arm to my shoulders. His slight weight is normal now, familiar. I touch his head and he slips through my fingers. "Did you do it?"

"Yes. Do you want details?"

I take a short breath. "No. Well, maybe later."

The snake is quiet for a while. Then, "Do you regret it?"

"Regret what?"

"Our deal. Taking revenge on those who wronged you. Killing them."

I close my eyes for a moment. "Too late for that, isn't it?"

I push away from the church's wall and head to the front so I can meet Pastor Thomas and end this for good.

The door is unlocked. It always is, because the church likes to boast about its open-door policy. I limp inside. My knee throbs, worse than usual, as I walk down the silent aisle. My head throbs too. Maybe this is wrong. Maybe this is a sign.

"Someone is here," the snake hisses in my ear. I stop walking, tense. He settles into my shirt, his tail vibrating against my back. "Two of them. Careful."

Peach barks, the sound filling the entire church, and rushes ahead. I start to call her back, but the two people come into shape as Peach jumps at their feet.

Jade and Allison.

"Oh, hey, guys." I try to smile through my unease. What are they doing here? It's gotta be one in the morning. I left Allison asleep. "What's up? I was on a walk."

Allison smiles back as we meet in the middle of the church, but Jade's watching me with narrowed eyes.

"It's a bit late for a walk," Jade says.

"Yeah, I know. With the curfew and all, I felt like no one would see me."

Jade and Allison don't say anything. Heat creeps up my neck, and the snake lets out a soft hiss. Something's wrong.

"Why'd you come here, Avie?" Allison's looking at me with her pretty blue eyes, and it's almost like she's begging me for something. Begging me to say the right thing.

I look from Jade to Allison, sweat making the grip on my cane slick. "I told you. I was taking a walk."

"You just stopped by? Because the church was open?" Allison's voice is tinged with hope.

"Ally." Jade's voice carries a warning.

"You were just stopping by because you knew we might

be here, right?" Allison moves closer, a pleading note in her voice. "Right, Avie?"

My head's pounding. The snake hisses in my ear. His tail beats against my back. Something's not right.

"I . . ."

Jade steps forward, her eyes narrowed and boring into mine.

"Or did you come here because John told you to?"

Silence permeates the room. I can't breathe—they know. They know, and this is a trap.

The snake moves down my back, but I slap my shoulder to stop him. Not yet. I can still talk myself out of this.

"What do you mean?" I'm smiling, laughing, trying to calm my desperate heartbeat. "It's like Allison said. I was on a walk and stopped by because the church is open. I was tired so I came to sit down, that's all."

"Yeah, you love going on your walks, don't you?" Jade's voice is calm, but has a dark edge to it. "You disappear all day sometimes, in the middle of a monster attack. And you've been real calm about all this, you know that? Always telling us we'll be okay. Is that because you know we'll be fine, because you know you're not gonna kill us?"

"I—"

"We went to that meeting, Avie, and Pastor Thomas said something wasn't right. There's no way the snake should have been able to come into town with the barrier things or whatever. And Carter was strangled, and last I checked, snakes don't have hands!" Jade's almost yelling at me. She's mad, but she's hurt too. Her voice is shaking.

"We all agreed that we'd go on patrol until midnight, then wait at the church. And if we see the snake, we tell it—and its accomplice—the third barrier is at the church. Nothing the first two days, when it's me and Allison. But in you walk on the third, and now John's not answering his phone."

My mouth is sandpaper. I try to think of what to say, but all I can see is Allison's eyes filling with tears.

"My keys weren't in the right place the morning after Katie died." Allison's voice wobbles, and what's left of my heart crumbles to pieces. "Why, Avie? Why did you do it?"

I take a deep breath and stand up taller. No more hiding. It's over. I owe them this much.

"Fine. You caught me. I killed them."

"Why?" Jade's voice drips with disgust. "Just because of the sacrifice?"

"*Just?*" Cold rage sweeps into my bones and pushes out the hurt, the sorrow, the regret. "They took everything from me! I can't sleep, my knee hurts all the time, I might have PTSD. I hear the sound of my bones breaking every night. It wasn't 'just' a sacrifice, Jade. They destroyed my life. They destroyed me."

Jade's eyebrows pull together, and for a second, she seems uncertain. But then she meets my eyes again, hers determined. "You can't murder everyone who makes you mad."

I hold my arms out, exasperated. "Well, I'm at four out of six, so I guess I can!"

"Six?" Allison's voice gives way to confusion.

"Katie. Sheriff Kines. John. Carter. Pastor Thomas." I meet Jade's eyes, regret filling me. "Auntie."

The color drains from Jade's face. "No. No, Avie, you can't—"

"She was there." My voice sounds hollow even to my ears. I can't bear to look at Allison.

Jade steps closer, panic in her face. "Avie, please, that's my mom!" Jade's too close, too loud. I feel the snake's fangs scrape against my skin.

"Back up, Jade."

"You haven't even seen her! You don't know how sorry she is—"

I grit my teeth. "I said back up! No, why don't you take a step back for me?"

Jade freezes, her expression confused. And then, slowly, deliberately, she takes a step back.

Allison's eyes are wide. "What just happened? Avie? What did you do?"

I take a deep breath. I'm in too deep. It's too late. "Listen. I have to find the third barrier. I have to finish what I started. I'm sorry."

"But if the monster gets stronger, it'll eat the whole town." Allison's voice is weak, and I almost waver. The snake's tail curls around my neck.

"I don't owe anything to this shithole." I point to the nearest pew and look Jade in the eye. "Jade, why don't you have a seat?"

Jade slowly lowers herself into the pew, her expression frozen in horror. I finally meet Allison's eyes. I hope mine look sorry.

"Allison, you too. It'll be nice to sit down, don't you think?"

She moves like molasses but sits next to Jade. Sharp pain fills my heart. I never wanted to use my power on her again.

"Can you please tell me where the third barrier is?" I ask, my voice weak and miserable. "I'm assuming it's been moved."

"It . . ." I can see Allison fighting it, but she caves. "It's with Dr. Roberts."

"Ally!" Jade whispers in horror.

"It's not her fault," I tell Jade. I reach into Allison's pocket and withdraw her truck's keys. "It's my fault. I'm sorry, guys. I really am."

"Avie, please," Allison says. She's struggling to move, her shoulders tight. Her face, the same one that smiled at me like the sun earlier, is stressed and pleading. "We can still fix this. We can still go back."

I want to believe her more than anything else in the world, but I'm not that naive. It's all over.

"Stay still, please." I turn to leave the church. Peach whines and looks back at Allison. I pet her head to reassure her. "You can stay and watch over them. It's okay." Happily, Peach settles beside Allison's pew, tail wagging.

I turn away from their horrified faces and leave the church to pay my aunt one last visit.

40

"We must hurry," the snake hisses in my ear. "It's bad that the humans have discovered us. They will be on their guard."

"People aren't so stupid after all, huh?" I limp to the back of the church, where Allison's truck waits. It's gonna be hell to drive with this knee, but I have to try. My order only lasted for ten minutes on Peach; even if I'm lucky and it lasts that long for people too, that's not enough time for me to hobble all the way to Auntie's without them catching up to me. I unlock Allison's truck, climb in, and say a prayer. This is going to hurt.

I press my injured leg onto the brake and scream. Pain shoots up my knee, hot, pounding. Still, I manage to crank the truck. It rumbles to life beneath me.

"Hold on," the snake says. He slides down my body to my knee, then wraps himself around it. He squeezes my knee and it hurts more, but only for a second. "This may not help much, but at least until we arrive at the next one's home. Can you make it?"

"Yeah." I take a deep breath, tears streaming down my cheeks, and press the gas. To Auntie's house we fucking go.

It doesn't take long. The entire town is deserted; there's not a single car on the road. All the houses I pass are dark. I guess everyone is heeding Pastor Thomas's warning.

I pull into Auntie's driveway. The lights are still on, even though it's almost two a.m. I close my eyes, just for a second. It's time. The others, the sheriff, Carter, even John, didn't mean anything. Not really. Auntie is the one I've wanted to see since the beginning. This whole thing is her fault.

"Come, Latavia." The snake releases my knee, causing a lightning bolt of pain to shoot up my leg. He climbs to my shoulders. "Do not be afraid. I'm with you."

I touch his scales, and my heart rate calms a bit. He's right. Let's get it over with.

It's agony to drag myself to Auntie's door. It still has the "traitor" I spray-painted on it. I grab the spare key under the ugly clay frog I made her one summer at Girl Scout camp. I'm surprised she didn't pack it up with my pictures.

When I open the door, she's waiting for me.

Auntie's sitting in her chair in the living room, hands folded in her lap. She's wearing a bathrobe, and her hair's wrapped in a silk cap. She has dark circles under her eyes that would rival Allison's. She looks up at me and flinches, and jumps to her feet. I tense, but she doesn't move. She's just looking at me, a hard-to-read expression on her exhausted face.

"Surprised?" I try to grin, like I did for the rest, but it feels more like a grimace.

Auntie shakes her head. "No. I knew you'd come."

The smile slips from my face. This isn't how it's supposed to go. She doesn't even seem scared.

"The barrier is here, Latavia," the snake hisses. "Ask her where it is."

"Auntie, I'll deal with you in a minute. First, I'm looking for the a barrier. You heard of it?"

Auntie nods. To my surprise, she reaches into her dress and shows me her pendant. The pendant she's been wearing as long as I've known her. "Here. You can have it."

I don't move. Confusion and fear and everything else swirls in my head. What's happening? She's just gonna give it to me?

"I'll get it," the snake says. He crawls down my leg, and I blink and his shimmery skin changes to his normal now-dull black. Auntie's eyes widen and she recoils, scrambling to stand in her chair. I get an unwelcome flashback to Katie.

"Give it to him. By the chain, please."

Auntie tosses the pendant to the ground. The snake hisses at her irritably, but grabs it by the chain and drags it to me. He returns to my shoulders, no longer invisible.

"Destroy it, and have your revenge," the snake says. "I'll be patient. Take your time."

I crush the pendant with the end of my cane. I have to do it several times, but on the fourth swing, a huge pop like before reverberates through the air and the snake shudders with delight.

"Only one left," he says. I don't miss the relief in his tone.

I don't say anything. It's my turn now, but everything feels wrong. I was supposed to be happy about this. I'm supposed to be laughing, euphoric like I was with John. But she's just standing in her armchair, waiting.

"What do you have to say, Auntie?"

Auntie still looks so sad. "I'm sorry, Latavia. I really am sorry."

Anger surges into me, and I'm relieved. Anger I can understand. "Sorry isn't good enough. Look at me! Look at my leg. I'll never run again. I was going to UGA for track, Auntie. My life is over." I'm mad, I can feel it rising, but tears are building in my eyes too. "Do you know how scared I was when a giant snake came out of the woods to eat me?"

Auntie doesn't say anything. She stands in the armchair and looks down at the broken pendant. The anger surges again, and I limp to her and yank her back to the ground.

"Look at me, Auntie. Look into my face and tell me I deserved to die."

Her eyes, usually so sharp and intense, are dull and full of tears. "I can't. I'm sorry, Latavia."

"How did this happen?" I'm supposed to be angry, supposed be to crushing her nose with my fist, shaking her, *something*, but instead I'm crying now. The anger is fading and being replaced by hurt—raw, deep hurt. First Mom, then her. She's worse than Mom, though; she held me in her arms while I cried, let me move in, let me eat dinner with her and treated me as a second daughter. We argued about curfews and late-night running and talking in church. We were family. She made me believe she loved me, and that's the cruelest thing anyone has ever done to me. "Just tell me why. Why did it have to be me? Why did you think it was okay to kill me?"

"I know you don't understand, Latavia, but I didn't want to kill you. Not even close."

I'm disgusted and horrified that a tiny bit of hope flutters in my chest. I squash that down as soon as it appears. "Don't try to weasel out of this, Auntie."

"No, I'm not trying to. Let me explain." Auntie takes a deep, shuddering breath. "You don't understand because you didn't grow up here, but the pastor's word is law. When my mother passed this secret on to me, I felt like I had no choice but to listen to the pastor before him, and now to Pastor Thomas. But I tried so hard to resist. I was so careful. I took the burden of the rituals so your mother could escape Sanctum and have a normal life. She never knew a thing about a monster in Red Wood. I worried when Tonya had you, because I thought Pastor Thomas would target you, but he didn't seem to care. And for a moment, I thought I'd won. And then, the year I turned forty, I found out I was pregnant."

I stare at Auntie, unsure of how to feel. She's never once mentioned Jade's dad, and now she's spilling her secrets in the moments before her death?

"I messed up. I thought I could have a normal life.

Marriage, family, everything. But I knew bringing Jade into this world would ruin her. I could have ended it. But I was so sad. I was lonely, in this horrible town, all by myself. So I had Jade, and I told myself I'd protect her no matter what I had to do. I made sure she never found out about the rituals. I raised her with the intention of having her transfer to your old high school after you left for college and live with your mother, so she'd miss her induction. Anything to get her out of Sanctum before she learned about the monster, and Pastor Thomas trapped her too. But then Tonya . . ." Anger flashes over her face. "After what she did to you, I couldn't trust her. And, God, all my plans fell apart then. I wanted to protect you and Jade. I never wanted either of you to know about that monster in Red Wood. But Pastor Thomas is cruel; he did this on purpose. He chose you on purpose, to punish me for even thinking of getting out of this with my family intact."

I feel like I'm on the edge of a panic attack. I thought Auntie hated me, thought it would be easy to get rid of me, but this . . . this isn't what I expected at all. This is all wrong.

"So why didn't you pick yourself?" My voice is weak, wobbly. I think I know the answer already, but I want to hear it.

"I wanted to offer myself, but I couldn't leave Jade alone, *and* you. Not in this horrible town. I didn't know what would happen the next time the beast demanded a sacrifice, and then all three of us would be dead. So I came up with a plan. It was reckless and stupid, but it was all I could think of at the moment."

"What do you—" Seconds after speaking, I realize what she means as I replay that night in my head. She let them tie me up, she didn't save me, but . . . "The clothes. You didn't let them take my clothes off."

Auntie nods, smiling a little now. "I hoped the monster would notice. It was stupid, reckless, but I hoped he would reject you, like he did Clementine, and you'd live."

And she was right. It worked. The first thing the snake noticed was that I was still wearing clothes. Oh my God.

Auntie seems to perk up in my silence. She looks exhausted, and much older than I've ever seen her, but more determined too. "You can kill me, Latavia. I know that's why you're here. I won't fight you. I know you probably promised that monster something to survive, and that's fine with me. I wanted you to. But before you do, we have to talk about what comes after." I watch in stunned disbelief as Auntie picks up a thick blue folder from the coffee table and places it in my hands. "I have all of Jade's documents in here. And I made out a will, and I left you the house."

I stare at her, my brain buzzing with useless static. "What?"

"You're eighteen. You can legally take care of Jade for me." Auntie nods to herself, her expression a little wild. "She might hate you, but you can lie and say the snake killed me. I know you love her, Latavia; all these people are dead, but Jade and Allison are still safe. So, please, just take care of her after I'm gone. Sell the house, get out of Sanctum, forget about this horrible town. And—" Auntie's voice hitches a little. "Please tell Jade I love her, okay? She's been so angry with me after what happened, so we haven't talked. I didn't tell her anything. I wish I'd told her everything sooner, but I wanted to protect her. I wanted to protect you both. Lot of good I did with that one." Auntie inhales deeply and takes two steps back. She stands tall, and she looks more like my aunt I've known all my life—strong, severe, confident. Resigned. "Okay, I'm ready."

I can't move. I can't think. This is all wrong. Everything is wrong. I came here to kill my aunt, to really make her suffer for what she did to me. But she tried to protect all of us, and Pastor Thomas ruined all of her attempts. She was a victim in this horrible game Pastor Thomas is playing, just like Katie, and the rest of the guardians. Just like me. And even at the end, her last plan worked. She made them leave my clothes on, and the snake noticed, and that set everything in motion.

There's a terrible heaviness in my chest. I should kill her. That's what I came to do. But all I can think about is making Jade, my precious baby cousin, an orphan. All I can think about is Auntie braiding my hair in the summertime, us eating Thanksgiving dinner at her table, the way she held me when Mom kicked me out and told me I could never come back.

The folder slips from my grasp and I back away.

"What are you doing?" the snake says, lifting his head from my shoulder.

"I . . ." I look at Auntie, who's watching me with pure shock on her face. "I can't do it."

"Wait." The snake descends from my shoulders and

363

coils up in front of my feet. Auntie backs away from him, but he ignores her. His black eyes are trained on me. "Are you saying you won't kill this human?"

I shrug helplessly. "I . . . You don't understand. I can't—"

"I do understand. I understand that this human tried to kill you, and your hatred brought you from the brink of death to return here." The snake's black eyes glitter in the harsh light. "What I do not understand is your hesitation."

I want to tear my hair out. I want to throw up. He's right, he always is, but this feels horrible. Wrong. "Why do you care anyway? Don't you see people as interchangeable? I killed Mr. Brim, so count him as number five and we can go."

The snake lets out a low hiss. "No, I will not allow this. Have you forgotten your pain? Have you forgotten your nightmares? Have you forgotten that you've given up your future, your happiness with your mate?"

I let out a groan. He's gonna fight me on this one. "Auntie, you should go upstairs."

Auntie's still watching me, stunned. "Latavia, are you sure? I did something unforgivable—"

"Just go."

She still hesitates, looking at the snake now. "But won't the monster hurt you? I'm ready, I have been since that night—"

"Auntie, *go*. Now, please."

The snake watches Auntie tentatively edge upstairs, his tail rattling. "Unbelievable. I cannot believe this."

"Snake, listen. She's family, okay? She tried to kill me, but—"

"You believe what she said? About her resisting the ringleader's efforts to control her?" The snake laughs darkly. "In my experience, humans will lie to save their skin. She's lying to you, Latavia."

Nausea swims in my gut. I shake my head, my eyes full of tears. "Even if she is, I can't do it. I'm sorry."

The snake seems exasperated; he keeps moving his head back and forth, shaking his rattle. "You're right, she is your family, but that means she's the most deserving of your fangs. Family should not betray each other. How many nights have you cried, screamed, begged for help that never came? How do you not feel rage burning in your bones at her? You have come far, but you are weakening at the crucial moment. I do not understand humans. All they do is lie, to each other, to themselves."

He's killing me. This is killing me. All I wanted to do was feel better. And I did, especially with John and Sheriff Kines, but this is torture. I feel like I'm being ripped in half. She put me on that altar, but she had no choice. She had no options. Just like me, when I stared into the snake's black eyes and swore I'd live, no matter what I had to do.

Before I can say anything, the snake suddenly stops moving. His tail stops rattling. "It's okay, Latavia. You are still young, still hurt. I'll take care of this for you." He moves toward the stairs.

Panic leaps into me, and before I know what I'm doing, I'm blocking his way. "No. You're not going up there. We're leaving, finding the last barrier, and going home."

The snake hisses at me, his tail vibrating furiously. "I will not allow for your softness. We are killing your family, and the final guardian, as per our agreement. If you disagree, you are a fool, Latavia. That human is only concerned with preserving her own miserable life. She will never care for you."

Some of the anger I felt for Auntie returns. He's pissing me off now. "Oh, so I'm the fool, huh? You think you're so much better than people, but look what they've done! They made barriers to keep you out, they made knives to kill you, and you needed me more than I needed you. You think you're so smart; then how come you didn't notice they've been poisoning you for eighty years?"

The snake's mouth snaps shut. "What did you say?"

I shouldn't have said anything, but I'm mad now. And relieved—mad I can understand. "You heard me! All those sacrifices Don fed you? Poisoned." I point at my knee. "Me too, turns out. That's why my knee is fucked. I ate silver before they tied me to that altar because they knew you would eat me."

The snake sways back and forth, his tail still shaking. "This . . . this is impossible."

"Look at my leg and believe it."

The snake starts to say something, but rapid footsteps thunder up Auntie's porch steps. Jade and Allison burst through the front door, panting.

"Avie, whatever you're thinking, don't do it," Jade wheezes, out of breath. Her face is covered with a sheen of sweat, and Allison's face is bright red. They must have run the whole way here. "I know you're upset, but—oh my fuck, is that a snake?"

The snake hisses in irritation. "I don't have time to play with children."

Allison stares at the snake with huge eyes. "It talks. Oh my God, this is the monster."

"Hey, we're in the middle of something," I tell them. "Stay over there, don't come closer."

"Yes, we have business to take care of." He looks back at the stairs, exposing his fangs.

"Snake, if you kill her, I'll beat you to death with my cane." It's an empty threat, because I don't know if I could hurt this frustrating reptile if someone paid me.

The snake looks back at me. His tail stops rattling. "So. You have made your choice. You have betrayed me."

I'm surprised by a surge of hurt. "Betrayed you? How? We're still gonna destroy the fourth barrier; I'm just not gonna kill my aunt. And I kept that secret to myself. No one knows except you and me. All the rest of them are dead."

The snake snorts. "You are stupid if you think I believe you."

"Oh, gotcha, I'm the stupid one. Don't think I don't know why your scales are gray and you're not eating. I'm not stupid, snake. I know more than you think. I've been looking for a way out of this from the beginning."

The snake gets really still for several long moments. Then he grows in size, bigger and bigger until his head scrapes the ceiling of my aunt's house. He gets right in my face, his scales milky white instead of the usual black.

"Listen to me, Latavia," he hisses, his voice low and

threatening. "If you refuse to honor your end of the deal, everything we've built is over. I will come for you, the way I'm coming for Don, and you will not live to see tomorrow's sunrise. And I'll take everyone in this house, in this town, down with you. You have a decision to make. I hope you're smart enough to make the right one."

I don't say anything, but I don't cower from him either. I can see the milky white of his scales creeping into his eyes. He wouldn't be trying to intimidate me if he wasn't scared of what I'll do.

The snake glares at me for a moment more, then turns and slithers toward the door. Allison and Jade flatten themselves along the wall as he passes. Soon he disappears into the night.

Auntie's house is completely silent. I look at Jade and Allison, suddenly conscious that they saw the whole fight between me and a giant snake. I lean on my cane, nervous laughter bubbling out of my chest. "Sorry you had to see that. Um . . . I guess we should talk?"

41

"Okay." Jade crosses her arms in front of her chest, watching me. "Explain."

I scratch the fox decal on my mug. We left Auntie at her house and drove to Allison's. I couldn't stay in that house. I don't know whether to hug Auntie or avoid her for the rest of my life. But now the alternative is to come clean to Jade and Allison, who have been on my side since the beginning. I guess I owe it to them.

"Take your time," Allison says, her voice gentle. She's sitting next to me on the couch, our thighs touching.

I take a deep breath. "I lied to you. At the sacrifice, I did see the snake, and he talked to me. I said I wasn't a volunteer, and he discovered the barriers were up. He was really mad. He wanted to see Don." I take another deep breath. "I told him I would help him destroy the barriers so he could get into town if he wouldn't eat me. I didn't want to die."

Tentatively Allison reaches for my hand, and I let her take it. I meet her eyes, and hers are so kind and sympathetic I want to melt. "It was an impossible choice, Avie. I understand."

"Okay, but you just had to break the barriers, right?" Jade asks. She's the opposite of Allison. Her gaze is cold and calculating.

I hesitate. Allison squeezes my hand reassuringly. "You don't get it, Jade. You weren't there. My life—it's ruined, okay? Do you really think they should have lived? After all the people they killed?"

"I don't think you and a giant snake need to take the law into your own hands, no." Jade's tone is ice.

"But the snake killed all of them, right? You didn't do anything, right, Avie?" Allison asks.

Now is probably not the best time to come clean about Sheriff Kines and Mr. Brim. I can omit that part. "Yes, he killed them. But he didn't kill Carter. We went to the garage, and Carter was already dead."

Allison and Jade frown at each other. "But if the snake didn't do it, who did?" Jade asks.

I watch Allison's face carefully, thinking of her quiet rage when she hugged me. "Do you think it was one of the guardians?"

"But who?" Allison says. Her eyes are wide and distressed, and there's no trace of a lie. Either she's a really good actress or she didn't kill him. I'm surprised by the twinge of disappointment in my chest.

"Maybe it's unrelated. He was a shithead, so I'm sure he had more enemies than me," I say. "But more importantly,

370

I found something in his office. Well, I found something with all of them."

I spend the next ten minutes explaining the journals, how the snake was being poisoned with silver for years, and my new superpowers. They listen closely, their eyes huge.

"Okay, so you're, like, superstrong now?" Jade asks. Some of the frostiness has faded and she's watching me with wonder. "Show me. I wanna see."

I roll my eyes. I pick up Allison's coffee table with one hand, careful not to spill our drinks. They stare at me in awe.

"Whoa," Allison says as I put the table back down. "Avie, that's . . . amazing. I had no idea."

"It's not that cool," I say. I haven't used the strength for anything except destroying Allison's remote and beating two men to death. I don't think "cool" is the right word.

"What about the other one?" Jade asks. "When you told us to sit down, and we couldn't move."

"The snake called it 'suggestion.' If I form an order as a suggestion, you have to do it."

"So that's why you were talking to Peach all weird," Jade says. "When you told her to protect us."

"That's how I went to sleep without my sleeping pills," Allison says, her voice quiet.

We don't say anything for a while. I scratch at my mug again, nervous. I should tell them about the snake shedding his skin. I *need* to tell them. I can't touch that knife, and if we don't kill him, he'll kill me. He told me. And the snake has never once lied to me.

"There's something else."

I tell them about the snake shedding his skin, the precious night of vulnerability, and the Plasma recipe.

"Oh shit," Jade says, her voice hushed. "We can actually kill it."

"Yeah." I take a sip of the too-sweet tea I made, a strange guilt swirling in my belly. It's me or him. He told me so. But I can't help feeling rotten. I wish I hadn't told them.

Allison scans the recipe I found. "Okay, I get the hair—gross—and the rest, but where the heck are we gonna get the actual blood of a monster?"

I point to myself. "Me. You can use my blood."

We're all quiet again. I think about the snake telling me monsters don't have anything to fear, and his concern about my touching his blood. He's been warning me, in subtle ways, the whole time.

"Okay," Allison says, standing up from the couch. She frowns down at me and Jade, her expression fiercer than I've ever seen. "Let's make some Plasma and kill that snake."

Allison, Jade, and I look down into a mixing bowl. It's full of melted silver jewelry from Allison's extensive collection, some weird plant Allison has in her bathroom, a generous portion of powdered sulfur, and water. Three ingredients left.

"Where are we getting the snake parts?" I ask. I really do not feel like snake hunting in the middle of the night.

I'm feeling a little sensitive about it. I think I'd have a hard time killing one right now.

"Gotcha." Jade goes to her bag and returns to the kitchen with a glass jar. Inside is a tiny, perfectly preserved snake skeleton.

"Do I even want to know where you got that?"

"Mind your business," Jade says, unscrewing the top.

"Isn't that from Dr. Roberts's office?" Allison asks, frowning.

"Yeah. Mom gave it to me the night after we found Avie. Just handed it to me without a word. I honestly thought she was losing it, but, well . . ." Jade trails off and dumps the skeleton into the concoction. The liquid hisses angrily as soon as the bones connect with it. Good sign . . . ? We watch the bones bob in the yellowish liquid, and something like fear raises the hair on my arm.

"All right, whose hair are we using?" Jade asks after a minute. "Not me, please. I'm begging."

"Can't use mine," I say. "Has to be human hair. And I'm not really clear on where I stand with that."

"I guess I can." Allison sighs.

"What about your hairbrush?" I suggest. "So you don't have to cut it."

Allison brightens. "Oh, great idea! Hang on." She runs to her room and returns with a hairbrush full of golden hair. She drops a clump of it into the bowl, where it floats in a disgusting mat.

"Hope this isn't like baking," Jade mutters. "Otherwise, we're screwed."

I laugh, but I'm nervous. One ingredient left.

"Are you sure you want to do this, Avie?" Allison puts her hand on my arm. "You don't have to. We can figure something out."

"No, it's okay." I pick up a kitchen knife and hold my breath. I try to touch the knife to my arm, but my right hand is shaking so bad I can't aim.

"Stop," Jade says. She takes the knife. "I'll do it. You look away."

I do *not* want my baby cousin cutting into me, but I nod. It won't be so bad, surely. I took a dog's teeth to my arm, a punch to my broken knee. This is nothing. Jade ties a shoestring around my left bicep. "It'll help with blood flow," she says.

"Oh, uh, okay." Despite my internal pep talk, I'm starting to get really hot. I pull at the neck of my shirt.

"Ready?" Jade asks.

I'm looking at Allison, who's holding my right hand. I don't feel so good. I'm sweaty and nervous and panting.

"Are you okay?" Allison asks. She squeezes my hand tighter.

"Y-yeah. Go ahead, Jade."

"On three," Jade says. Her voice sounds far away, even though she's standing right beside me.

My good knee is Jell-O. I'm burning up. My bad knee throbs angrily in my borrowed pajama pants.

"One," Jade says.

I don't feel good at all. I'm back in the woods, with John and Carter chasing me. I'm feeling that first crack of pain in my leg.

"Two."

I'm not okay. I'm shaking violently. The pain, it's coming, like my knee—

"Wait, Jade," Allison says. She looks at me, but her face is hazy and unfocused. "Hey, you okay? Talk to me."

"I'm okay," I say, but my words are slurred. And then I blink and sudden darkness shrouds my vision and I can't hear them anymore.

"Avie. Avie, hey. Can you hear me?"

I blink groggily. Where . . . where am I? Allison's ceiling swims slowly into focus. I'm freezing for some reason. I groan and hold my head. What happened to me?

"She's awake!" Allison leans into my field of view. Her hair falls around me like a blond halo. It's really pretty. "Hey, you okay?"

"Y-yeah." I try to sit up, but my head's killing me. "What happened?"

"You fainted," Jade says. I look to my left, and she's sitting in Allison's armchair. "We should have known, though. You were shaking so bad."

"Don't move too fast," Allison says, dabbing my forehead with a cool, damp washcloth. For a second, I consider marrying her. "You're burning up again. I'm sorry. . . ."

"Hey, it's not your fault." I hold my head in one hand and sit up. I'm exhausted, and so cold. I pull the blanket I've been using around my shoulders. "Sorry for passing out on you. We can try again."

"No need!" Jade gives me a thumbs-up. "I got your blood while you were out."

I frown at her, then look down at my arm. There's a thin scar running the length of my arm, but it's so faint, I can barely see it. "So you harvested a whole cup of blood while I was unconscious? I'm pretty sure that's illegal."

"That's what I said!" Allison says.

"Okay, but we got the blood, and you didn't feel it, and now that gross orange stuff is cooking. It worked out!"

I look over my shoulder toward the kitchen. Allison has a big green pot on the stove. It bubbles quietly.

"Oh wow. I hope it works." That's what I say, but I sort of hope it doesn't.

"Yeah, me too," Jade says. She leans back against the armchair. "Otherwise, our giant snake friend will have three extra meals."

Allison visibly shudders. I hold her hand. "Don't worry. I won't let him eat you. Promise."

Allison meets my eyes, hers searching my face. "Avie, what was it like? The snake, I mean. You were talking to it at Dr. Roberts's house like . . ." She trails off, her eyebrows knitted with worry.

"Like?"

"Like you were friends."

I look down at my free hand. I don't want to think about this, not when we have the secret weapon I helped make boiling away behind us. "It's not like that. He's kinda . . . I don't know how to describe him. He's really arrogant, and he thinks humans are beneath him. He doesn't lie, but he'll leave stuff out when it's convenient for him. Still, for a giant snake, he was pretty cool."

Jade's looking at me like I've suddenly turned into an

alien. "Avie, he's killed, like, five people in a few days. And the hundreds of others for years. You can't feel sorry for him."

"Yeah, I know," I say, but I can't look her in the eye.

"I'm going home," Jade says, standing from the chair. It's morning now, the first hint of blue light coming through the kitchen window. Exhaustion tugs at my shoulders, and even though I'm cold (probably from blood loss), when I touch my skin, it feels hot. That damn knife is the worst.

"Okay." I want to ask about Auntie, but I can't stomach it. I spared her, but that's it. That's all I can do.

Jade's looking dead at me, her eyebrows furrowed. "Avie, just tell me one thing."

"Yeah?"

"Would you do this all again? If you had to?"

I reach for my neck, but there's nothing there. I drop my hand to my lap. "Yeah. I think I would."

Jade's mouth presses into a line. "I can't believe you're not even sorry."

"Well, I am a little sorry about Katie. And the cop in the graveyard. But not for the others. They killed so many people—"

"That doesn't make it right. Now *you're* a murderer too."

"Hey, Avie didn't kill anyone," Allison says. She holds my hand tighter. "The snake was manipulating her. I don't think you or me would have done any better."

I stay quiet for a minute. My relationship with Allison and Jade hinges on a crucial lie. I want this to all go away, for us to go back to the way things were before this started. I want to watch HGTV and eat pizza and throw popcorn at Allison while she laughs. But I've changed. I can feel it in the venom coursing through me. I can see it when I look in the mirror, blood splattered on my face, my expression calm and disinterested in the men I killed. And it's not fair for Allison and Jade to be friends with a lie.

"Actually, I did kill someone."

Allison and Jade are still. I take a deep breath.

"I killed Sheriff Kines. He was about to kill the snake, so I jumped in front of him. I hit him with my cane, but I forgot how much stronger I am now. So, he died."

Allison looks at me, her expression desperate. "Avie, that can't be true."

"It's true. And I killed Mr. Brim. Long story, but I was supposed to hold him down for a few hours while Mrs. Brim skipped town with Delilah. But he wouldn't stop struggling. He hit my knee, and I snapped. It was like I wasn't in my body anymore."

I hold my hands in my lap. Just a little more.

"And the worst part is, I don't feel too bad about it. I do feel bad about Katie, I really do. Even now. But I don't feel bad I took out a few pieces of trash. The monster isn't just in the woods, you know. There are monsters everywhere."

Jade and Allison are quiet. Then Jade shakes her head. "I have to go home." She practically runs out of Allison's apartment without looking back at me.

I watch Jade leave, tears stinging my eyes. I expected this, but it hurts. It hurts so bad. My entire family has turned against me in one miserable summer. At least Jade is justified in leaving. Not everyone wants to hang out with monsters.

I look to Allison, resigned. "What about you? You can tell me to get out."

Allison hesitates, but then takes my hands. She stares into my eyes. "It's okay."

My heart stutters with hope. "Really?"

Allison nods. "You did what you had to do. I can't say what I'd do in your place. You were under pressure. You were in pain. It's okay."

"Do you think I'm a monster?" I whisper.

Allison slowly, and so gently, reaches for my face and brushes a tear from my cheek. Her hands are warm and familiar and safe. "You're not a monster, Avie. Not even close."

I look into Allison's eyes. I'm shaking now, trying hard not to cry. She's always been on my side. Even when I was angry with her, even though she risked everything to protect me, she still stood by me. I don't know if I can ever go home, not back to Auntie's. Jade has abandoned me.

I'm overcome with the feeling that I have to show her I care, that I liked her before and after my life got completely fucked by six townies and a giant snake.

I lean forward, just a little. The snake is nowhere to be seen; this moment is mine. Allison freezes, her shoulders tight.

"It's okay," I breathe. "Can we finish what we started last night?"

Allison searches my face. Her cheeks are turning red. "Are . . . are you sure?"

"I'm sure." I lean closer and she does too. My heart's pounding against my ribs. I'm so nervous, I'm hot and slightly nauseous. "Close your eyes."

Allison's eyes flutter closed. I close mine too, and press my lips to hers.

It's warm and sweet and I feel like melting. I pull her closer, brushing my hands through her hair. She kisses me back, and I can taste the sugar of the tea I made on her lips, and . . .

And something's wrong.

My lips are hot. Not the normal good hot, but unpleasant, burning—

I jerk away in surprise. Allison opens her eyes, but she doesn't look happy. Her eyes are filled with tears.

"I wanted to tell you," she says. "But I didn't know how."

"What?" I touch my lips. They're burning, actually burning like I've been scalded.

"You've been sick this whole time." Allison is sobbing now, huge tears rolling down her flushed cheeks. "You've had a fever, and it's my fault."

"Allison . . ." Fear and confusion are making my head hurt. "What do you mean?"

Allison wipes her eyes. "I didn't tell you what they did to me. He—I—" Allison takes a sniffling breath. "I'm the fourth barrier."

I stare at her, dumbfounded.

"When I turned sixteen, Pastor Thomas told me everything, about the snake, the barriers, the deal, everything. Back then, there were only three, and he thought if they were all inanimate objects, the snake would find them. So he asked me if I would volunteer to be a barrier. He said I had a special ability, that the snake wouldn't be able to sense me even if I was right under its nose. He said it was something only I could do."

"Allison—"

"I know. I know I shouldn't have done it, but at the time . . . I had to have something to live for, I guess. But I was stupid to believe him. It's kind of funny how awful he is, and I'm just now seeing it because of you. And now what he convinced me to do is hurting you. He always gets the last laugh, huh?" Allison shrugs, laughing, crying. "I didn't know you'd made a deal with the snake, but I get it now. That's why you've been so sick; you can't touch Plasma that's not made from your blood. And I'm full of it."

My ears are ringing. I can't understand. It's not true. "You're kidding, right? This is all a bad joke."

Allison shakes her head, still crying. "I wish. I really do, because if the Plasma we made fails, I have to do what Pastor Thomas asked me to last year."

No. "No, Allison, no—"

"The snake doesn't know I'm the fourth barrier, so if he eats me, he'll die."

I hold Allison's face in my hands, trembling. "Please don't say that. Allison, please tell me this is all a lie—"

"It's not." She holds my wrists in her hands, her blue eyes watery and red and brokenhearted. "I've always known I had to do this. I've always known one day during a full moon, I'd have to walk into Red Wood and never come back."

Grief, sharp and insistent, hits me. Allison is planning to die on me, sacrifice herself for this cursed town. And what's worse is that I can't stay with her anymore. We can't be together. I can't even kiss her without pain.

I don't have anything left.

"I'm so sorry, Avie." Allison is still crying. "I like you so much and I wanted to tell you, but I didn't know how. And now we c-can't—"

I stand up. I grab my cane and limp to the door. I barely hear her as she calls my name.

"Avie, please don't go." Allison's sobs break my heart. "Please. Today's my last day."

"Don't say that!" I snap at her, crying now too. "I'm going to figure this out, okay? I'm getting us out of this. Hang on."

I don't wait for her to call me back. I leave Allison's apartment, stumbling down the steep steps. I barely notice Peach running after me, whining. I didn't get a chance to see him, but I need to talk to Pastor Thomas. He's the kingpin in this whole mess. I tighten my grip on my cane. Either he tells me some way to fix this, or I'll make him.

I leave Allison's apartment and head to the church, my lips still burning from our kiss.

42

It takes me a while to get to the church.

Each painful step reminds me that I've lost it all in nine horrible days. I don't think I can ever see my aunt again. Jade can't stand the sight of me. And Allison . . .

No, it's not too late. I have to talk to the good pastor, and I'm finally going to get a straight answer.

When I get to the church, I reach for my neck, but nothing's there. I touch Peach's head for comfort instead, but it's not the same. Peach licks my arm, and we enter the church together. I limp down the aisle, up the steps, and stand right outside the pastor's office. The door is open, and there's a man sitting at Pastor Thomas's desk.

But it's not Pastor Thomas.

It's a young white man, somewhere in his twenties, with short blond hair. He's wearing Pastor Thomas's robes and his reading glasses. He looks up at me, and I'm shocked to recognize his face. Familiar beady blue eyes, huge scar on his right cheek. It's the man in the painting Allison showed us.

This is Don.

"Ah, I've been expecting you, Latavia." Don takes off his reading glasses and peers at me. "A few nights later than I thought, though."

"How?" I came for answers and, admittedly, this is a big one. "You're, like, . . . two hundred years old."

"Two hundred and thirty-two, to be exact."

My mind is whirring. Don is Pastor Thomas. But how? I saw the ring on the dead body . . . which, I guess, he could have given to someone else before they died. The clues click into place. The Confederate uniform in the painting, despite Don attacking the snake in 1809. I didn't recognize the voice on the phone with John. The snake saying he's coming after Don, present tense. Don's immortal, and he's been orchestrating this whole thing for two hundred years.

"You've been alive this whole time?"

"Yes. I can't die until our agreement has been fulfilled and the snake will mercifully end my immortal life." Don laughs, but it's humorless.

"But . . . I don't get it. Why did you look like an old man before?" He opens his mouth to answer, but I realize the answer seconds after I ask. "Oh shit, this is your super-power. The shape-shifting."

"The snake told you about my gift? I'm wounded. It was supposed to be a secret."

"And I can see your real face because your power won't work on me." I haven't seen him since that night of the sacrifice. Oh my God.

384

"Bingo. We're kin, you and I." Don gives me a hideous grin.

I shudder at the thought. "Don't . . . say that."

Don laughs again, deep and loud. "You'll get used to the idea. You have at least two hundred years."

I stay quiet, my mind working through the new information. I still have so many questions, but I need to find out about Allison, first and foremost. But if I open with that, I don't know if he'll tell me. I need to be careful here. "Can I ask you a few things?" I'm careful to keep my voice neutral.

"Of course. But I want to ask you something afterward."

I nod. Fair trade.

"I've been reading some journals. But I missed Sheriff Kines's. Kind of burned up on me."

I'm surprised when Don laughs. "Casualties happen. But don't worry, you didn't miss anything important. His detailed what would happen on the summer full moon two hundred years after the first awakening of the snake, give or take a few years."

Okay, so I missed the one I needed the most. Figures. I must look irritated, because Don laughs again.

"The journals are largely useless. I know everything about the monster in Red Wood, and I just gave the guardians pieces so they'd feel important. You give trust and you get trust back. Basic leadership. It doesn't work all the time, considering Carter, but it's worked pretty well for the others."

I raise my eyebrows in surprise. "You killed Carter?"

"A little bird told me Carter was unhappy with my rules. I planned to simply rein him in, but we had a disagreement. He demanded that I offer the snake another sacrifice to stop the killings. If not, he was going to lead a group into the woods and offer me. So he said." Don snorts out a laugh, cleaning dirt from his nails. "I don't tolerate insurrections in my little town. He knew that, and chose to die by my hands anyway."

Unease prickles my skin. Carter was strangled, and I'm pretty sure it takes a while to choke the life out of someone. This guy is dangerous. "That's what I don't get. Everyone in Sanctum is so obsessed with you. John was ready to die before telling me anything." Oh, wait, he did. He lied to me about the barrier and sent me into a trap, hoping Allison and Jade would subdue me. He was loyal to Don until his last breath. But *why*?

Don's face twists into an ugly grin. "I don't particularly care for Sanctum. This town is my prison. It can burn down for all I care. But people obey me because that's what I've trained them to do. If you tell a group of people that God sent a savior to protect them from a giant snake, they might not believe you. But the snake reinforced my power without knowing it. Every time someone wanders into Red Wood, they don't come back. Grandparents whisper to their grandchildren about a long-ago massacre that killed hundreds. Rumors spread about something horrible, something evil and deadly, lurking just beyond their eyesight. After that, it's easy. You don't know yet, but two hundred years is a very, very long time, Latavia. I can do anything I want, if I phrase my words carefully and keep the townspeople living in fear. I can control these stupid people and their stupid lives, rearrange them how I want, get them to track down sacrifices so I don't have to. Sanctum is mine; I built it, I've seen generations born and die, and I'm still here. If I want to abandon it for the monster to nourish himself, I can do that too. Sanctum belongs to me, and I can do what I see fit with it."

I'm too horrified to speak. Allison and Mrs. Brim and everyone believed in him, believed he was protecting them, and all the while . . . Tiny bursts of fear pulse through my body in time with my quickening heartbeat. I'm sort of feeling the way I felt when I first saw the snake come out of the woods.

"My turn," Don says when I'm silent. "What kind of deal did you make with him? What did you ask for?"

"Revenge." I meet his eyes. "Against the six people who tried to kill me."

"Including me, I assume." Don smiles, a small one that doesn't reach his eyes. "And in return you . . . ?"

"Destroy the barriers for him. So he can get into town and meet you."

Don nods to himself, steepling his hands. "I see. I didn't account for you in the plan, but I think everything will still work out."

"Which is?"

Don looks at me, his blue eyes sparkling. "I'm running."

Figures Don would be a coward. "He's not gonna let you go."

"Oh, he will. Two hundred years is a long time to think about an escape plan. I've laid the groundwork for my escape for years and years. Carefully. Meticulously. I created the guardians to make them feel like they're important, I researched the monster's weaknesses, I made the barriers. And the best barrier, Allison, will be eaten by the snake and he'll die. My hard work's paying off, finally. As soon as the sun sets, I'm a free two-hundred-year-old man."

My hand tightens around my cane. He's the most pathetic guy I've ever seen. "Let's talk about Allison for a second. Why her, of all people? Why not make a regular sacrifice drink the Plasma?"

"I thought about that, but my associate told me it would be too risky. He's got a similar issue in the Rocky Mountains. His is a crow, though. Seems a little more palatable than our snake."

"Get to the point, Don." I'm trying to sound tough, but I'm intrigued by this "associate" and his problem. But I gotta focus for now. Allison first.

Don scratches his chin for a second, like he's thinking. He's wearing a faint smile, like this is all some fun joke he finally gets to tell the punch line to. "Let me add some context for you, Latavia. The monster in Red Wood murdered my friends and family before my eyes, and then turned his fangs on me. He made me feed him, under strict rules, in hopes that I'd screw up and he'd get to eat me. But I survived. I persevered. For years, for generations, I survived under his rule. And with that survival came hatred."

I cross my arms. "You were going to murder his sick son, so forgive me if I don't feel sorry for you."

Don shoots me an annoyed glare, but keeps talking like I didn't speak. "I gathered information meticulously over the years. First the silver weakness, then the fact that monsters cannot touch each other's blood or fangs. This was a dead end, however—the monster we killed had small fangs, and I doubted anyone could get close enough to damage our snake's hide. I made the knife anyway, just in case. Then came the Plasma, which was promising, and then the best one of all—the night of vulnerability. The snake will shed his skin under the full moon, something that only happens once every two hundred years, and for a short night, he will be far weaker than he's ever been. My associate with the crow told me that when his molted, the intelligence leeched out of him. He became no better than a common bird, fearful and reactionary. My associate actually managed to strike several blows on the crow before it fled. So I knew I had to strike during this night, but the question was how."

I turn over that story in my head. That's what I figured out too, more or less. The snake will be a sitting duck. "But he's still a giant snake, Don. He isn't going to let you just walk up to him and stab him."

"I know that. So I devised a plan, using every weakness I knew about. First, the snake was carefully poisoned with silver for years. Not enough where he'd notice, but enough over time to weaken him significantly for this night. And another thing—did you know that monsters do not have a strong sense of smell? They can see well enough, but people who share a bloodline smell the same to him."

I nod despite myself. The snake mixed me and Jade up, way back before he killed Katie. He seemed almost embarrassed about it. "Okay, so . . . ?"

"So, my plan is to have a living sacrifice drink Plasma and approach him when he's in that reactionary state. He will snap at them, and even if he doesn't eat them, the Plasma will poison him and kill him once and for all. I thought first I would use John, or perhaps sweet Katie, but I am a cautious man, Latavia. What if he finds out I'm planning this, and kills the sacrifice by crushing them or by force? So I thought, Who does the snake hate the most in the world? In his weakened, pained state, who could he not resist swallowing in his jaws, crushing with his teeth, making sure they suffered?"

Slow horror creeps into my bones. "You."

Don gives me a hideous smile. "Bingo. Obviously, I'm not going to get myself killed. That meant I needed a family member to stand in my place, so he would confuse our scents and think he was eating me. However, I don't have any descendants. My wife and children are long dead and gone. Part of my punishment." Don pauses, like he's overcome with emotion. If he wasn't such a slimy bastard, I'd feel sorry for him.

"Okay? So what'd you do?"

"I didn't have a descendant, so . . ." Don looks at me, right into my eyes. "I made one."

Shock robs me of any thoughts, any words. No. No way. But the blond hair, the blue eyes—

"It was a lot harder than I thought it would be. I haven't dated since my wife passed on, and I find modern women insufferable. The more the world changes, the more I hate people. . . . Anyway, I ended up paying someone to help me out. I told her to raise the child until she was sixteen, and then she could leave.

"It was an interesting experiment. I thought the child might have superhuman capabilities, but she was an average baby and she's an average teenager now. Venom isn't passed on, it seems. And Rita, her mother, wasn't well suited for motherhood, but I paid her enough to grin and bear it. When she needed to let off some steam, I looked the other way, and that kept the peace until the child was sixteen. Overall, I think it worked out well. I would have preferred a boy, but Allison works just fine."

"Wait." My voice is weak, disgusted, heartbroken. "You're Allison's father? This whole time you . . ."

"Allison doesn't know. She also doesn't know I'm Don. She thinks I'm the dear old pastor who knows how to keep Sanctum safe." Don seems thoughtful for a second. "She is my fourth, but nothing like my three who have passed. She's always so quiet, so compliant. It's been interesting watching her grow from afar."

Slowly, the information he gave me sinks in. This disgusting man is Allison's dad. This horrible, murderous, manipulative man is her dad. It doesn't make sense. My brain almost refuses to accept it. "How could you do this? How can you have a baby and watch that horrible woman abuse her and not say anything?"

"Everything has its purpose," Don says, matter-of-fact. "Even Rita's abuse. Allison is compliant, but she's not stupid. If I had presented a happy child with this option to give her life for me—excuse me, for Sanctum—that child might have balked. I needed someone whose spirit was broken, who spent night after night praying for help that never came. I needed someone who cared for the town around her—the doctor who was a mentor to her, her best friend, the friendly church members who showered her with gifts—but felt she had nothing to live for. All I had to do was frame it so that she was a hero, and giving her life would save everyone in this town she adores. It did get rocky when her mother left, but overall I think it worked. Children are easy to manipulate if you get started early."

Pure horror chokes out every other emotion. He did this to her. He did all of this to Allison *on purpose*. Allison, who loves HGTV and snorts when she laughs and can't cook a steak to save her life. Allison, who held my face in her hands and said she'd never hurt me. Allison, who knew she was born to die and was going to let it happen to save someone who doesn't give a shit about her. The conversation we had in her room pops into my mind, how sad she looked when she said she thought she didn't want to live anymore. Sharp grief hits me so hard, tears spring into my eyes. "How . . . how can you do this?"

Don laughs, surprising me. "Latavia, come now. You know the answer to that." He leans forward over his desk, a wild, cruel grin on his face. "I'm a monster."

A wave of revulsion crashes over me, drowning out the horror and grief. And with it, hot fury. I can't stand the sight of him. He's using Allison, just so he can bolt as soon as he has the chance. Just so he can escape the punishment he *earned* for being a stupid bastard who hunts baby monsters. My hand squeezes my cane so tight, a crack splinters from the handle. I want to hit him until he bleeds. I want to kill him, more than John, more than Auntie.

But not yet. I can't react. He probably wants that, for me to leap at him so he can hurt me. He's a super human too. But apparently I'm immortal now, so I have all the time in the world.

"One more question, Don. Is there any way to reverse Allison's condition? So she's not a barrier anymore?"

Don raises his eyebrows. "No. Why should I? Well, it won't matter after tonight. I have faith in my chubby daughter. She'll go to the woods tonight like I trained her to do, the snake will eat her in a second, and then he'll lie down and die. Everything according to plan."

I grit my teeth, barely contained rage threatening to explode.

"And now," Don says, standing up from his desk. He turns his cold blue eyes to me. "I think you've given me everything I wanted."

A bead of sweat trickles down my back. "What does that mean?"

"It means you have also served your purpose." Don smiles at me, but it doesn't reach his eyes. "Truthfully, I knew you were alive and wreaking havoc on my guardians. But Allison is the only one who mattered, so I let you have your fun. She told me she likes you, you know that? When we were discussing who to sacrifice. And I thought if I killed you twice, she'd rebel against me. Have to keep your subjects calm and happy, right?"

The snake said the same thing to me about Allison. He said he wouldn't hurt her because she made me happy. The unease grows to full-blown dread. Allison and I were dealing with our own monsters, but we didn't know it.

"However, you've gotten a little too dangerous and you know a little too much for me to leave you alone." Don steps around his desk, casually cracking his knuckles.

Shit. Shit, he's gonna attack me. I back up, gripping my cane in a tight fist. "Wait, I have super strength too. This won't be like Carter."

"It'll certainly be more difficult." He keeps coming, his steps casual, slow. Like killing me is just a walk to John's grocery store. "But you're injured. And a child. I think I can manage."

Fuck. Fuck, what do I do—

I step back and stumble into Peach, who pants up at me innocently. Inspiration leaps into me like lightning. I don't want her to get hurt, but I can use her to bluff. Don is so meticulous, so careful. I have to rattle him. "You don't think I came prepared?" I point to Peach, who wags her tail at the approaching Don. "You didn't ask me what power I have."

Don stops, and weak hope flutters in my chest.

I keep talking, careful to sound unafraid. "I can make people do what I want them to do. But that's not all. When they are enacting my orders, they're as strong as I am. The snake said it's because your shithead cult broke my leg, so I have to substitute strength."

Don's eyes narrow, but he doesn't get any closer. "You're lying."

"You wanna find out?" I lean casually on my cane, smiling. "It'll be a super human and a super dog against you. And you know, Peach's teeth are pretty sharp."

Don looks like he's wavering, his pale face suddenly anxious. For one horrible moment he looks just like Allison, picking at her hair, eyebrows pinched with worry.

"Peach," I say, trying my best to sound breezy and not desperate, "let's show Don we mean business, hmm?"

In a second, Peach's lips lift over her teeth and she lets out a guttural snarl. She steps in front of me, the fur along her spine bristled, her body lowered to attack.

Don takes a fearful step back, and I know I've won.

"We'll take our leave now," I say, still grinning. "I would kill you right now, but I feel like the snake would be pissed off if I didn't let him get a shot at you."

"The snake won't live beyond today," Don says, his voice quiet. It sounds a lot less sure than it did a few minutes ago.

"Maybe, maybe not. But if he does live, he's coming for you. I am too. I told you—I made a deal to kill everyone who hurt me. You're not getting away from me."

"Sure," Don says. He has an ugly sneer on his face. "See you later, Latavia."

It takes everything in me not to run from the church, but when I'm outside, I take a deep breath. I made it. Somehow. Don is a problem, but not the one I need to focus on now. I lean against the church wall to think. I think about everything that's happened, everything I've learned in nine miserable days. I think about Allison's resigned face and how soft her hands were against my cheek, how warm the initial kiss was before everything fell apart. But I also think about the snake, betrayed by Don and about to be killed by my two best friends in the world.

I think about everything and decide what to do.

I push away from the wall, and Peach looks up at me, panting, tail wagging. I pat her head and turn away from the church and head to Red Wood.

43

I find the snake in his cave.

He's stretched out, his full length wrapped around the front half of the pool. His skin is bright white now. His scales move up and down sluggishly.

"You're early." Even his voice is slower than normal. "The process does not start until the sun leaves the horizon."

"I know." I step closer. Peach stayed at the cave entrance, but I picked up Charlie on the way. He sits next to me, his black nose twitching. "When were you gonna tell me I was immortal?"

The snake heaves a breath. Warm wind swirls around my head. "You are not immortal. You can still be killed, by force, by fire, by silver. You have simply ceased to age."

"That still seems like something I should have known."

The snake sighs again. "It was not relevant. I had planned on your revenge taking no more than a few

397

moonrises. Initially, I had something else planned for you at the end of our contract. But then I decided you should be freed."

Freed, huh? And not dead? I mull that over, rubbing Charlie's ears between my fingers. "Fair enough. Why didn't you tell me Don was still alive?"

"After you said he was dead, I became worried that it was true. If those humans had found a way to kill him, that would have been very bad for us, Latavia."

"Because we're monsters? All three of us?"

"Technically, yes. You and Don are monsters. But you are a weakened version of me. My extensions, if you will."

"So when you said I'd be freed, what did you mean? You'd let me go?"

"Yes. You would have lost your power of persuasion and your strength. You would begin to age again. But some residual of my power would have remained, so you would always be a little stronger than your human peers, a little slower to age, a little more persuasive. A gift, don't you think?"

Not a bad gift, if I'm honest. Things really might have worked out. "Next question. If I got far enough away from you, would I still be affected by the Plasma?"

"Unfortunately, yes. Once a monster, even a weakened one, you are always a monster. Your body has been permanently changed. I told you before we started our journey, Latavia. You cannot go back."

I close my eyes, defeated. It's all over. Allison made her

choice, and so did I. "Okay. Jade and Allison are on their way. Well, they will be. They made more Plasma. I told them about your weakness to silver, and your poisoning. They know you'll be weak until sunrise. They have a very good chance of killing you."

"Your information is incorrect. I will be finished shedding before sunrise; that was last time, when I was weaker. I am only vulnerable for half the night in my current condition."

"Does it take five hours to kill a weak snake?"

The snake doesn't answer at first. He turns to look at me, and my skin crawls—his eyes are bright white. He can't see me. "I will admit, Latavia, this is humiliating. Who would expect a farmer to be killed by his animals?"

"Well," I say, smiling, "we're a little smarter than the average cow."

The snake laughs, but it's weary. Resigned. Like Allison's was earlier. "Why are you here? Did you come to get a head start?"

"No. I received some bad news of my own."

"Oh?"

"Allison is the fourth barrier."

"Ah." The snake shakes his head wearily. "So this is why we weren't feeling well in your mate's home."

"He did it so you'd snap at her while you were shedding. Does she really smell like him to you?"

"Yes," the snake says. "I was initially alarmed, but then I thought he had simply reproduced multiple times, as humans do. I didn't want to tell you, in case you held a grudge against her. She is a child, and children should not be punished for the sins of their fathers."

I rub my face with my hands. I'm grateful that he was looking out for me, but this information would have been really nice to know a week ago. "Now that you know Allison is coming and not Don, can you just . . . not eat her?"

The snake sighs. "Once the sun goes down, I will temporarily lose myself. I will rely on my basic instincts while I'm shedding, which will cause me to lunge at anything that approaches me. Even though I know I shouldn't, if she attacks me, I will retaliate." The snake sighs again. "I have underestimated humans. Don is a cruel, clever man."

I have to hold in a scream of frustration. The snake is trapped in Don's stupid spiderweb, just like Don planned. "If I never hear his name again, it'll be too soon. He really fucked everything up for us."

The snake laughs, softly, sadly. "Latavia, I must apologize to you."

"About what?"

"I insinuated that I would kill you after our deal was over. But I have grown softhearted, like you. I have let a human deceive me. I have grown close to the food I'm supposed to eat. I called you a fool, Latavia, and for that I am sorry. The only fool is me."

I watch the snake's white scales move up and down sluggishly for a moment. Then I close the gap between me and the snake's head, leaving Charlie behind.

"Listen, snake. You won't survive their attack. We both know that. But if you're not interested in dying, I have an idea." I take a deep breath and stand right in front of his head, so he can feel my presence. I put my hand on his broad snout. "It didn't work out so well last time, but I was wondering . . . would you be interested in making another deal?"

44

The full moon is high in the sky when Peach's ears prick. She stands, tail wagging, and barks twice. I hold on to my cane and struggle to my feet. It's time.

Jade and Allison enter the clearing. As always, I can see them perfectly in the dark. Jade's wearing a look of pure torment, and Allison's been crying, her face red and puffy. Sorrow fills my chest as I focus on her face. Allison came, just like Don said she would.

I close my eyes for a second, so they can't see the pain on my face. Then I open them and smile.

"Hey, guys."

"What're you doing here?" Jade asks. She has something in her hand . . . a gun? I almost start laughing. It's a clear Super Soaker, bright orange Plasma sloshing inside. Allison has one too.

"I came to visit the snake. Thought he might be lonely."

Allison steps closer. Her red, splotchy face makes me

want to hug her to my chest and never let go. "Avie, tell me you're here to help us kill the snake."

I shake my head, my chest aching and full of regret. "I'm sorry, Allison. I can't kill him. I can't let you kill him either."

"Avie, come on." Jade's voice is a frustrated growl. "Why are you taking its side? It's a giant snake that eats people!"

"I know! But he's really not so bad. He really helped me out with the nightmares and stuff—"

"But we could have helped you!" Allison's eyes are full of frustrated tears. "You could have talked to us at any time."

"I know, that was just an example. He's not really a bad guy—"

"He's not a guy! He's a snake! A big one that eats people!" Jade yells at me. She rubs the heels of her palms in her eyes. "I don't know why I'm even arguing with you. I can't believe you were sitting on a secret this big the whole time."

"No, that's not fair! Allison hasn't told us the truth from the beginning." I round on her, a little bit of anger pushing past the sadness. "You promised me you'd tell me everything, and you just decided that you being a barrier wasn't relevant? What happened to 'no more secrets'?"

"Don't give me that." Allison's voice is low and reproachful, and for the first time since I met her, she seems really mad. "You were killing people for days and never said a word. Pretty sure your secret is worse."

403

I wince. "All right, I deserve that. But what about you not telling me you expected the snake to eat you? You were gonna die for this stupid-ass town and not say anything to me?"

Allison huffs, her face turning a delicate shade of red. "What else was I supposed to do! I didn't know we could make more Plasma or about the snake being weak tonight. It was that or—"

"Or living? Because I feel like staying alive is the logical choice here. Not sacrificing yourself because your cult leader told you to."

Allison opens her mouth to argue some more, but Jade clears her throat loudly. "Okay, enough. I know y'all are having your first couple fight, and it's cute, really. But we have a giant snake to kill, remember?"

"You're not killing him." I stand taller and glare at them both so they know I'm serious.

"Yes, I am." Allison's voice carries all the determination I feel.

Jade's eyebrows furrow as she glances from me to Allison. "So what now? We're gonna fight?"

"You're both gonna listen to me." I meet both of their eyes. "Now."

"Avie, please don't use that on us." Allison's determined expression fades into one of despair. Her eyes fill with tears. She's begging. I grit my teeth, my resolve crumbling. I promised myself I wouldn't use it on her anymore.

"I think you should—"

"Avie. Please don't. Please." Allison looks at me with those big blue eyes, and I can't do it.

404

"Okay, fine! I won't use it. But listen to me, okay? I'm trying to help you." I point to the cave, where the snake's working hard to wrestle out of his skin. "We were wrong. Yeah, it took ten hours for the snake to shed his skin the first time, when Don first met him. But he's bigger, stronger now. The snake said he'll be back to full strength five hours after sunset. And what time is it now?"

"Midnight." Allison's voice is a horrified whisper. "We only have, like, an hour."

"Yeah, and probably less than that since he knows you're coming. He's hurrying."

Fear fills Jade's face. "How are we going to kill it in such a short time?"

"You're not going to kill him." I rub my face in frustration. "Listen to me. I have a plan, and it's all going to work out, okay? No one has to die, if you'll just—"

"We can't waste any more time," Jade says to Allison. They nod at each other and raise their water guns. I sigh loudly.

"All right, fine. If you want to fight, we can." I touch Peach's head. "Peach, make sure you protect the snake, okay? But don't hurt them."

Peach looks into my eyes, then sprints for Jade.

Jade yelps in surprise when a hundred pounds of dog tackle her. I watch anxiously, but Peach doesn't hurt her. She lies on Jade's chest, panting in her face. Jade struggles, cursing, but she can't move.

I look to Allison. She's staring at me, her water gun slack in her hand. The bone knife glistens in the other. "Avie, let me go in the cave."

I shake my head. "I can't."

"Avie." Her voice is quieter, resigned. "I don't want to fight you. But I have to get into that cave. I have to save everyone."

"You're not a hero, Allison. You're just a teenager who can't sleep."

Allison smiles at me, a soft, tortured one.

Then she lifts the knife and rushes me.

I hold up the cane, and the knife slams into it. I meet Allison's eyes, hers focused and determined, and for the first time tonight, I'm afraid. She's really going to try to kill him. She's really not going to let me stop her.

"Let's talk about this," I say, pushing her backward. She doesn't stumble like I do. She's steady on her feet, the moonlight glinting off her knife. I think fleetingly of all the "training" Don and her mother made her do. I might be in real trouble. "I have one leg. Come on, give me a break."

Anxiety crosses her face, but only for a second. "I won't hurt you. I just have to get you out of the way so I can get in that cave."

"Sounds like you're gonna have to hurt me th—"

I don't get to finish. Allison rushes me again, and we're fighting, really fighting. She tries to grab my cane, but I knock the water gun out of her hand with a well-timed punch. Her hand recoils—did I hurt her? I didn't mean to—

Allison shoves me against the cave wall. I yelp in pain as the rocks dig into my back. Allison's determined expression changes to worry. "Avie, did I hurt you? Sorry!"

This is ridiculous. This is the most pathetic fight I've

ever been in. I need to end this quick. I take my cane and sweep Allison's legs from under her. She cries out in surprise, and I'm about to grab her wrists and tell her to stop struggling and let me take care of this, but then I see a horrifying sight.

Jade breaks free of Peach and runs into the cave, water gun at the ready.

"No! Jade, don't!" I try to run to the cave, but Allison grabs my good ankle and I'm face-first in the dirt. "Allison, stop, I have to stop her—"

Too late. Jade's scream tears through the clearing, along with guttural snarling.

"Jade?" Allison tries to get to her feet, but I tackle her.

"Don't go in!" I hold Allison down, using all my strength. "Charlie, let's not kill her, please! Bring her back out!"

"Who the hell is Charlie?" Allison yells, still trying to struggle from my grip.

We don't have to wait long. Charlie emerges from the cave, dragging Jade by the neck of her shirt. She's whimpering and holding her arm, but she's not dead. Thank God.

"That's Kines's police dog." Allison looks at me in disbelief. "How many dogs do you have?"

I almost want to laugh. I would, if I weren't holding Allison back from attacking the snake and getting herself eaten.

Allison slips from my grip and twists away. We stare at each other, panting. She glares at me. "Avie, this has gone too far."

I sneak a glance at Jade. She's lost her water gun, and

Peach is licking her arm. Charlie's at the mouth of the cave, growling. Allison is the only obstacle left. I'll have everything under control if I can just subdue her.

"Stay there, please." I'm panting too. I'm starting to feel not-so-good again, probably because of Don's Plasma running through Allison's veins. "The snake and I have a deal. You don't have to die. Neither does he."

"Does this deal protect Sanctum?" Frustrated tears build in Allison's eyes. "Is he gonna suddenly stop eating people? Are you gonna suddenly stop killing people who get in your way?"

"That doesn't matter! I don't give a shit about that town, Allison. I care about you, and Jade. And yeah, I care about the snake too. Just leave him alone, please."

Even as I say it, I know she's not listening. Allison's expression hardens and she runs at me again, her knife gleaming in the moonlight.

I can't bear to fight back and risk hurting her. I can't risk losing control like I did with Mr. Brim, and I also can't be another person to lay a hand on her. I use my cane to block the knife, over and over, but soon I'm backed up against the cave wall. She slashes down, and the tip of the knife shreds my borrowed tank top. It burns when it touches my skin. I grit my teeth and try to shove her away, but she's got me cornered, and when I duck, I lose balance. Suddenly, I'm on the ground, flat on my back, and Allison raises her foot to stomp on my knee.

I look up at her, wild terror gripping my whole body. *Defend yourself*, my muscles groan. I'm shaking violently, my mind on John bringing the bat down onto my leg, on the night I blacked out from the pain Mr. Brim caused me.

The pain is coming, my brain screams.

I can't take that pain again.

Kill her if you have to.

But I look up at Allison, the girl who held my hands and dabbed a damp washcloth against my burning skin and let me kiss her, and I beat back the animal fear. I can't lose control. I have to trust her. I have to trust that there's one human being in the world who won't hurt me.

Allison meets my eyes and puts her foot down on the ground.

"Oh, Avie," she whispers. She gets to her hands and knees beside me and pulls me into a hug. Her body trembles against mine. "I'm so sorry. I didn't mean to scare you. I'm sorry."

Allison rubs her knuckles against my back, so gentle, and the terror slowly leaks from my bones. My elevated heart rate slows as I lean into her and hug her back, and she kisses my temple. Thank God Allison is too soft for hero work. "It's okay. I'm okay. Can we stop fighting now? Please?"

Allison breaks our hug. Her blue eyes are full of tears and pain. "I don't know what to do."

I brush her tears away with my thumbs. "Let me handle it. I already have."

"But . . . but I was supposed to die here. Tonight." Allison wipes her eyes, sniffling. "I always thought it would be tonight."

I tuck a loose strand of hair behind her ear. I hear a sound, a faint one, and it's the best sound I've heard all summer. "I was never going to let that happen."

The sound gets louder, and I know Allison and Jade hear it too. They back away, their eyes huge and scared. I struggle to my feet. Charlie brings me my cane.

It's the sound of the snake climbing out of the cave.

I stand tall at the mouth of the cave. I watch his shadow grow ahead of me. Bigger than before indeed.

"Well done, Latavia," the snake says.

"A-Avie, you have to get away!" Allison says, her voice trembling. She backs away, her eyes wide with terror, but I don't move. Instead, I turn to the snake and smile up at him. He has a massive hood now, and he's so tall, his head is above the tallest tree in Red Wood.

"You're mixing your snakes," I say after looking him over. "Rattlesnakes don't have hoods. That's cobras."

The snake curls around me, laughing. His scales are black again, iridescent in the bright moonlight. "Maybe. But it is effective. Look at how scared these humans are."

"What . . . what's going on?" Jade asks, her voice shaking. "I thought it was going to kill you."

"I tried to tell you, we made another deal." I reach up, and the snake places his huge head in my palm. "I told you I'd take care of it. You guys don't listen."

"What did you do?" Allison's voice is small and horrified.

"What I had to." I take a few steps forward, and the snake moves to let me through. "I said I'd protect him from you two, and in exchange, he'll listen to me. No more indiscriminate killing. We'll only kill those who deserve it."

Allison looks up at the snake uncertainly. "So Sanctum is safe?"

"Don still owes me more humans from his little town," the snake says to Allison. "But in exchange for his life, I think I can forgive them. No more sacrifices."

Jade and Allison look at each other, stunned into silence.

"'Thank you, Avie,'" I say loudly, grinning. "'Thanks for solving a two-hundred-year-old problem in a week!'"

"God, you're insufferable." Jade looks at me, a tentative smile on her lips. "Thanks, Avie."

I smile back. "You're welcome."

"And Avie, listen . . ." Jade trails off, not looking at me. "I'm sorry about what I said. I mean, I still don't agree with killing people, and it's really messed up I'm in the minority about *murder*, but I don't hate you or anything. I get why you did it."

My heart soars with hope. "Really?"

"Really." Jade smiles at me. "Friends with a giant, murderous snake or not, you're still my cousin. You're still family."

I limp to her and hug her, so tight that she groans and complains. Allison watches us, grinning, and the snake laughs.

"Good for you, Latavia," he says as Jade struggles from my arms. I'm so happy, I could die. I didn't lose Jade, after everything. She's still on my side.

Allison looks at me then, and it's like I'm staring into

the sun. She's smiling, really beaming. "I can't believe it. I can't believe it's finally over."

"Yep. You and Lamby can sleep easy tonight!"

"Oh my God, Jade's right. You *are* insufferable." Allison's eyes are crinkled in delight, and for once she truly looks happy.

"I guess everything goes back to normal now?" Jade says. Allison nods, but I freeze, stunned by her words. Everything back to normal . . . I didn't think this far ahead. I was so focused on making sure everyone lived through tonight, I didn't think about what comes next.

"What about you?" Jade asks the snake, looking up at him nervously.

"I mean, I'm not crazy about a snake living in my house," Allison says, rubbing the back of her neck. "But I guess he's been here this whole time. . . ."

"Ugh, gross," Jade says, but she's watching the snake uneasily. "Maybe he can stay in the woods."

"Trust me, I do not want to live with you humans," the snake says to them. They both back away a little, nervousness all over their features.

I still don't say anything. A horrible feeling is welling up in my chest.

Jade frowns at me. "Avie? You okay?"

"I . . ." I glance at the snake behind me. "I don't think I can go back."

"Wait . . . ," Allison says slowly, her voice disbelieving. "What do you mean? You're leaving Sanctum?"

I bite my bottom lip. "I don't have anywhere else to go."

"You can live with me," Allison says. There's a desperate edge to her voice. "I don't mind, seriously—"

"And what of Don's poison, which runs through your veins?" the snake asks her, his voice measured and calm.

Allison looks from me to him, her expression growing more and more desperate by the second. "I—I can stay with Jade! And you can stay in my apartment."

And what, I'm just supposed to stay there all the time? Knowing I can never touch or hold or kiss Allison for the rest of my life?

I look up at the snake again. His black eyes, familiar now, are calm. "It is your decision, Latavia," he says.

I look at Allison and Jade and the snake, a terrible feeling in my chest. Allison is right in front of me, but if I go with her, I'll have to hide for the rest of my life. I'll be stuck in the town that destroyed me. I'll be close to my aunt, who I want to stay away from until I figure out if I can forgive her.

"Avie?" Jade's voice is small and scared. "What're you thinking?"

I'm thinking about Allison. I've never felt so close to someone before. Allison rubbed my back, kissed my forehead, laughed with me. We watched movies and made an awful steak together. Allison held my face in her hands and said she'd never hurt me. I touch my ripped tank top where her knife grazed me.

"We can work it out somehow," Allison says. "There has to be a way." She steps closer to me, her expression pleading. "Avie, please."

Am I supposed to be with her, getting sicker and sicker, until she accidentally kills me? Am I supposed to lie down and die, like Sanctum wanted me to? Am I supposed to watch her watch me waste away, looking into her tortured blue eyes knowing she couldn't save me?

"Let's go home." Allison holds her hand out to me, palm up, waiting for me to take it.

Way back when this started, when I was in the cave with the snake, I said I wasn't dying for anyone.

Not even Allison.

I take a step back.

Allison's stricken face almost kills me on the spot. "I'm sorry. I can't."

"Avie—"

"Goodbye." My voice sounds defeated and heartbroken to my own ears.

Allison takes a step forward, but the snake moves in front of me like lightning, his sea of scales blocking her. His face is inches from Allison's.

"She said," the snake says, his tone even, "goodbye."

I take in Allison's shocked face, Jade's tense shoulders, the snake's calm demeanor, and I know I've made the right choice.

"Peach, come here." Peach bounds to me, panting. I pet her one last time. "Make sure you're a good dog, okay? Protect Allison and Jade, please."

Peach licks my arm and then stands next to Allison. I try to work up the courage to look Allison in the eye.

"I'll take Charlie and leave Peach with you. She'll make sure you're okay."

"Avie, don't—"

"And, Jade," I say, talking over Allison before I lose my nerve. "Make sure you go become an accountant, okay? Don't let Auntie force you into being a doctor."

I look at Jade when she doesn't say anything. She's still holding her arm, tiny rivulets of blood falling to the ground. She stares at me, pain and confusion on her face. This is so painful. She forgave me, something I desperately wanted, and it's still not enough. Who's gonna defend her at Christmas when the adults try to bully her into med school? Who's gonna teach her how to drive? It's all over. I don't think I'll ever see my baby cousin again.

"Okay," Jade says slowly, her eyes locked with mine. "I get it. You just want some space from Sanctum, right? Maybe a few days and you'll come back."

"Jade . . ." I trail off. Denial is so much worse than I thought. "I don't think—"

"It's fine," Jade says, a stubborn edge to her voice. "You'll need some stuff for the road, won't you? I think Mom still has that tent. Stay right there and I'll be back."

Jade turns and sprints from the clearing. I try to call her back, but she disappears into the trees.

"You're not gonna wait for her to come back, are you?" Allison says after a few seconds.

"No, I'm not."

I finally meet Allison's eyes. Her expression makes me want to call everything off and stay with her until I get sick from Plasma exposure and die. "Move for a second, snake."

415

He does, and I close the gap between me and Allison. She looks up at me and I touch her face, one more time. "Allison, make sure you learn how to cook, okay? You can't just eat takeout forever."

Allison stares into my eyes, hers wide and stunned and hurt.

"And don't pull your hair out anymore, okay? Promise me. I . . . I won't be here to stop you, so make sure you're careful."

Allison closes her eyes. "You don't have to go. We can work something out."

"I do. I'm sorry."

Her hands grab my wrists so gentle, even now. Her eyes are still closed, and tears cling to the ends of her lashes. "Don't go, Avie. Please don't leave."

I take a shuddering breath, trying not to cry too. "And don't ever think you can sacrifice yourself for anyone again, okay? You're more than a pawn in Don's grand scheme. You don't deserve to die for anyone. Not even me."

Allison opens her eyes. She looks into mine and she forces a wobbly smile. "Okay. Maybe we can try long distance?"

I choke out a laugh. I think I love this sweet, wonderful nerd. I desperately want to tell her that, but this hurts enough already. That would be the cruelest thing I could do to us both.

I tip her head down and kiss her forehead, like she did for me that first time in her room, when I was still hopeful everything would be all right. Then I shake her hands from my wrists and turn away so she can't see the tears in my eyes.

"It won't be forever," I say, more to myself than her. "I promise."

Allison doesn't say anything, so I wipe my eyes and take a deep breath.

"Let's go," I say to the snake. He doesn't respond, but when I reach out to him, he shrinks in one fluid motion and climbs up my arm. When he's on my shoulders, I pat Charlie's head. "Time to go, boy."

Allison forces out one more heartbroken word. "Avie."

I don't answer. I take a deep breath and walk deeper into Red Wood. I don't look back until I'm sure I won't see her. Because if I met those pretty blue eyes again, all my resolve would crumble to dust.

"I'm sorry about your mate," the snake says after a while. He does actually sound sorry, I'll give him that. "I know you are hurt."

"It's okay." It's not, it's not even close to okay, but this is what I decided. It hurts more than anything, but I couldn't stay. I couldn't stomach the pain, the fevers, the nightmares. Don took everything from me in the end, even her. But maybe this is better for her. Allison came to the snake's cave, just like Don said she would. There's a part of her that still believes in him, in every hateful thing he's whispered into her ear for seventeen hateful years. There's a part of her that's not ready to let go of Sanctum, and I can't stand to be anywhere near it. Maybe it's good that she'll have time away from him, from me. Allison doesn't need to be around any more monsters.

"Perhaps there is a cure for her," the snake says. "The world is vast, and we have as much time as we need to search."

Wow, the snake's actually trying to be helpful? What a guy. Almost dying changed his perspective, I guess. I touch his scales. They're warm, and harder than before. He got stronger. So did I.

"Maybe we can torture the answer out of Don." The hatred for that horrible man dulls the pain a bit. I limp farther away from Allison and Jade and that shithole town, and every step I feel stronger.

"Hmm." The snake moves to my head, winding himself around my bun. "What are your intentions now, Latavia? Besides hunting down that spineless coward, Don."

"Well," I say, petting Charlie's head. The stolen police dog pants up at me, tail wagging. He still has Jade's blood in his teeth. "Answer a question for me. My power won't work on you, right?"

"Correct."

"But it will work on everyone else, right? Theoretically, I can use it for as long as I want, on anyone who gets in my way?"

The snake is quiet for a moment, and then he lets out a sharp laugh. "Your appetite is insatiable, I see."

I smile in the dark. I turned my back on the town, my family, Allison. But I have something that's almost better—the fear in men's eyes before I kill them, the screams of predators who know their time is up, the power

418

to take an entire town and crush it beneath my feet. I have the snake coiled around my neck, and the promise that no one will ever hurt me again.

"Let's go, snake," I say, limping my way out of Red Wood and Sanctum forever. "We have a lot of work to do."

ACKNOWLEDGMENTS

As always, I have to thank Grandma. We fuss and fight all the time, but you've been there for me every step of the way. I can never repay the debt I've accrued over the years, but I have a feeling you wouldn't allow it anyway. I know you're tired of hearing about giant snakes by now, but I'm so grateful you listened.

To my agent, Holly Root—fierce advocate, warrior, rockstar! You are an incredible person and I couldn't be happier to work with you on this book and many more. Similar thanks to my editor and her assistant, Krista and Lydia, and the entire Delacorte team for helping me put this book together.

Cheers to my best friend, Emily Chapman! You have carried me through so many struggles and worries, and you were one of the snake's first fans. Thank you for the snake memes, long-distance movies, and many, many hours of *Chopped*.

I also owe a huge thanks to Belinda Grant. Whip-smart editor, relentless cheerleader, all-around great human being full of love and light. I couldn't have written this book without you and your brilliance, and for that I am so thankful.

Shout out to Tas Mollah, my true friend who has stuck with me for years of endless chatter and late-night memes.

And to A. Z. Louise, Gigi Griffis, and Jay Audrey Alcott, the trio forming the mighty Scream Town, which has filled every day since its founding with nothing but laughter and delight. I'm so glad to know you, and I'm thankful for all the reptile TikToks, amazing book recommendations, and perfectly timed pet pictures.

Thanks to my many readers and friends: J. Elle, Meg Long, Marisa Urgo, Alexis Ames, Jen Klug, Elvin Bala, Ruby Barrett, Mary Roach, Chandra Fisher, Zoe Zander, Rain Ashton, Cas Fick, Marith Zoli, and Sher Lee. All of you helped get this book off the ground, and I'm so grateful for all the support given to me. My writing groups deserve to be thanked as well: the slackers, WiM, AltChat 3.0 and of course the famous Scream Town. I'm happy to know you, and thank you for everything you've done.

And, finally, thank you to young Jessica. You stayed, and that made this book possible. Thank you, always.

ABOUT THE AUTHOR

Jessica Lewis is a Black author and receptionist. She has a degree in English literature and animal science (obviously, the veterinarian plan did not work out). She lives with her way-funnier-than-her grandmother in Alabama. She is the author of *Bad Witch Burning* and *Monstrous*.

AUTHORJESSICALEWIS.COM